Copy1

CW01513045

The characters and events portrayed in this book are fictitious. Any similarity to real persons, living or dead, is coincidental and not intended by the author.

No part of this book may be reproduced, or stored in a retrieval system, or transmitted in any form or by any means, electronic, mechanical, photocopying, recording, or otherwise, without express written permission of the publisher.

ISBN-13: 9798797199182
ISBN-10: 1477123456

Cover design by: Franziska Stern
Library of Congress Control Number: 2018675309
Printed in the United States of America

The Uncrowned Queen

Lucy Steele

TABLE OF CONTENTS

Chapter One

Chapter Two

Chapter Three

Chapter Four

Chapter Five

Chapter Six

Chapter Seven

Chapter Eight

Chapter Nine

Chapter Ten

Chapter Eleven

Chapter Twelve

Chapter Thirteen

Chapter Fourteen

Chapter Fifteen

Chapter Sixteen

Chapter Seventeen

Chapter Eighteen

Chapter Nineteen

Chapter Twenty

Chapter Twenty-One

Chapter Twenty-Two

Chapter Twenty-Three

Chapter Twenty-Four

Chapter Twenty-Five

Chapter Twenty-Six

Chapter Twenty-Seven

Chapter Twenty-Eight

Chapter Twenty-Nine

Chapter Thirty

Chapter Thirty-One

Chapter Thirty-Two

Chapter Thirty-Three

Chapter Thirty-Four

Chapter Thirty-Five

Chapter Thirty-Six

Chapter Thirty-Seven

Chapter Thirty-Eight

Chapter Thirty-Nine

Chapter Forty

Chapter Forty-One

For my mom, who knew I would be an author
before I ever did

CHAPTER ONE

Kinna wondered how much trouble she'd be in if she shot an arrow at her sister. She wouldn't hit her; she would just let it skim close enough to startle her. The thought of her sister's shocked face was almost worth the tongue lashing she would likely receive from her mother and then lady's maid. Still, the idea was tempting.

She had spied Evelyn out of the corner of her eye, hovering in the doorway of the training room. The eldest princess rarely came here, uninterested in learning how to use any of the weapons that lined the wall or callusing her delicate hands. Picking up another arrow, Kinna pretended to not have seen her sister, and locked it into place before releasing it and hitting another perfect bullseye. She smiled to herself as she dropped her bow onto the rack. She was nothing if not consistent. "What are you doing here, Evelyn?" Kinna called from across the room, back still turned.

"Father wanted to see us," Evelyn said softly. "He is waiting in the throne room for us."

"I'll meet you there. I need to change," she said, grabbing her cloak off the bench and heading for the door.

"He said he wanted to see us now." She grimaced, bracing herself in the doorway as if she was prepared to stop Kinna if she didn't agree to come with her.

She just nodded in response and followed Evelyn down the hallway, keeping a few paces between them. Just close enough to keep her from turning around and checking on her, but far enough that she could spend an extra minute attempting to re-braid her hair.

She watched Evelyn walk in front of her, her head held high with golden hair swaying against her back. She looked every bit the princess, but Evelyn Elena Braunlin had been born a queen. It was written into her very being, from the set of her elegant jaw to her lithe dancer's body, she was regal. Most of her features came from the Braunlin line, including her creamy complexion and hair color. Her eyes were the only thing she had gotten from our mother, the soft brown eyes that when paired with her fair skin and honey colored hair, were beautiful.

The White Rose, that was their people lovingly called her, likened her to a pure and delicate flower. Every year on her birthday during the annual ball hosted in her honor the castle would be transformed into a garden with white roses adorning every available surface. Some were brought in at the behest of her mother, but many others were delivered by Ferryn's nobility and wealthiest citizens to honor their most lovely princess. Even the stores and restaurants in the capital would decorate, painting white roses onto the windows and city sidewalks.

Kinna on the other hand, had barely a drop of her father's lineage and a reputation for wildness. She had a dark complexion gifted from her mother, born in Vanna, the capital of the kingdom to the south. Her skin had always come in a variety of tan, deepened by her days spent training outdoors or walking along the shore at the beach. Her hair was a deep brown and curled wildly, which meant she mostly kept it braided back. But her eyes were undoubtedly from the Braunlin line. Her eyes, so grey that most thought they looked like molten silver, were a sharp contrast to the rest of her dark features.

They had come from her grandmother, Queen Idalia, who had often been called the silver wolf. She had the same eyes, but they had matched the queen's silvery blonde hair and icy personality. On Queen Idalia, they had been formidable, they were the eyes of a ruler. But Kinna was not a ruler, she was a storm, and her eyes were often the only indication of the wildness that lurked inside her, desperate to come out.

Many had speculated during her childhood that she could have inherited a drop of her grandmother's magic. Queen Idalia had been the last of their line to show any abilities, and even hers were weak, nothing like the power of the generations before her. Idalia's affinity had been water. In her prime, she had been able to control the tides of the ocean that curved along the capital and on the small stretch of beach by the castle, but only for short periods of time. Afterward she would be drained, having used all her energy to bend the ocean to her will. Even though Kinna had always loved the ocean and spent hours on its beach, she had never been able to control it the way her grandmother had. As she grew, most gave up hope that they would one day see a ruler possess that kind of magic again.

Magic had been steadily dying out in families for years and each person with an ability was weaker than the last. Most believed that it was because the gods had forgotten them, no longer caring what happened to those in this world, but Kinna wasn't as sure. She'd heard the stories about Eldridge, how they spent years rooting out those with magic and turning them into weapons. Kinna sometimes wondered if perhaps the gods were taking back the magic they had gifted to try to protect them and prevent anyone from being turned into a puppet. It didn't really matter though; the reality was still the same, magic was disappearing, and no one could do anything to stop it.

They had finally made their way to the throne room, and Evelyn was no doubt annoyed that Kinna's slow pace had caused them to take longer than necessary. Two guards stood on either side of the open door, swords hanging from their sides and eyes fixed forward. Their cobalt uniforms were perfectly pressed and even the gold stitched crescent moon over their chest seemed to shine.

Evelyn didn't bother to look in their direction before she strode through the door, holding her head just a bit higher than she had a moment before. Kinna caught the eye of one of the guards, a man only a few years older than her named Gavin. He was often her sparring partner in the training room and a welcome distraction when she needed it. He was handsome and well-built, but she had been drawn to his easy laugh and clever comebacks. The few hours they shared were always fun, a release for them both from their more serious lives. She gave him an overly flirtatious wink as she passed him that earned a snort in response. Maybe she'd go seek him out later, it had been a while since they snuck off to one of the many dimly lit alcoves that he often brought her to.

Evelyn had stopped a few feet away from the large oak table that had been placed in the middle of the room. Kinna stood a step behind her sister and quickly tossed the images of Gavin out of her mind to focus on what laid before her.

On top of the table sat a brightly colored map of the continent, along with several polished figurines representing companies of soldiers. The king sat with his hands resting on the edge of the table, head bowed slightly while he listened to General Resten go over the placement of troops along their northern border. Kinna could see a few silver hairs dotting her father's head as he bent over the table, the light streaming through the windows causing them to gleam brighter than his honey blonde hair.

Her mother was seated behind the two men on the raised dais, resting her chin on her bejeweled hand and staring out the large arched windows that made up the western side of the room. The thick velvet curtains had been tied back, allowing the sun to stream through, the marble flooring gleaming in its light. She stared out towards the ocean, trying very hard to ignore the conversation happening in front of her.

The only indication of her discomfort was the hand that she held clenched in a tight fist. Unease began to trickle down to Kinna's stomach. It wasn't often that something worried her mother, who was notorious for keeping her emotions under lock and key.

While her father now sported a few grey hairs and deepening creases around his bright eyes, her mother held on tightly to her youth, her iron grip refusing to relinquish anything to the passing of time. Like Kinna, the queen had dark curling hair that settled on

11

her chest in smooth waves, but unlike Kinna her eyes were a gleaming topaz.

Everything about her appearance was warm and inviting and purely feminine but underneath lay a cool and calculating mind. Kinna often wished she could emulate her mother's charming façade, wielding other peoples' assumptions about her against them. Evelyn had inherited that trait from their mother. Kinna however felt all her emotions deeply and without pause, causing her to be prone to rash behavior and general mischievousness.

Outside the floor to ceiling windows sat a small stretch of beach. Kinna studied her mother, noticing how she was expending all her energy on just staying still and quiet in her seat. It was unusual and Kinna's unease grew as she realized how deeply her mother was being affected by it. Noticing their arrival, the king lifted his head. "Thank you for coming, ladies," he said quietly, his smile not quite reaching his eyes. "General Resten has some concerning news to share with us."

The general nodded to the king before turning towards Kinna and Evelyn. His stormy blue eyes met theirs with hesitation and concern obvious on his face. Kinna noticed the deep lines that ran across his forehead and the corners of his mouth as his face fell into an involuntary frown. Being the general to Ferryn's armies and an advisor to the king was a job that weighed heavily on a person, even someone as capable as Davon Resten. Kinna had seen him age more rapidly over the past few years, the weight of his position was now seen in more than the grey that was sprinkled throughout his dark hair.

"There has been some unrest on the northern

border," he began. "We will be sending soldiers to monitor it, mainly stationed in Edgewood, but also in some smaller villages."

"What kind of unrest?" Kinna asked, stepping past her sister.

Their mother stood abruptly from her chair, her deep purple dress swishing around her as she moved. "Do they really need this information," she demanded, eyeing down the two most powerful men in Ferryn without an ounce of hesitation.

General Resten looked to the king for answers. "Lena," the king soothed. "They are not children any longer. Evelyn will one day rule in my stead, with Kinna standing behind her. It is important that we begin including them both in these discussions. Continue your report, General."

The general threw an apologetic glance at the queen but continued. "There have been reports of small groups coming into the villages at night to light homes and some wooded areas on fire. In Edgewood, a few of the fires set have ended in casualties," he told them. "There has been growing unrest in the area. We believe that a new group of rebels is gathering, possibly connected to the Rising, trying to take action in their own hands."

"How many companies are you sending?" Kinna asked eagerly.

"Likely three," he answered. "I'll be going to oversee things for a few weeks as well."

"I want to go," she volunteered.

"Out of the question," her mother interjected, her temper flaring over the one thing that was guaranteed to break her mask, the safety of her children. "There is no reason for you to be there."

"Please!" she begged. "I have been training more than usual. I wouldn't even be in any direct danger. I could just run patrols."

"Absolutely not," her mother repeated firmly.

"Father, please," she continued, passing her mother and going straight for her father's hand. "I can do this. You know how hard I train. General Resten can tell you firsthand, I am better than most of the guards we have here, especially with a bow."

The king glanced at his general. "It is true, unfortunately," Resten answered his unasked question. "She is an excellent shot; better than even you were at her age."

"You are not seriously considering this, Calvin," the queen interjected. "She is a child."

"I am not," Kinna shot back. "I am the same age you were when you married Father and came to Ferryn."

Her mother rounded on her, gripping her shoulders. Kinna could feel her mother's nails press firmly into her arms to further emphasize her point. "That is exactly how I know you are still just a child," she whispered, staring her down. Kinna had inherited her mother's stubbornness as well as her looks and this was not the first battle of wills they had waged.

"Your mother is right, Kinna," the king added gently, placing a hand on her mother's back. As usual he was trying to diffuse their argument before it escalated further. She released her and walked back to her chair to resume her vigil now that she knew she had won. "I know you want to go, but your place is here with us and your sister."

"Please, Father," she asked again. "I can do this. Let me go with them."

"I'm sorry, but the answer is no," he repeated.

"Kinna," Evelyn murmured, coming behind her to gently take her hand. It was the first words she had spoken since they arrived and as usual, she was taking their parents' side. Kinna wasn't surprised, Evelyn always took their side, but it still stung regardless, and she let herself be pulled back by her sister.

The general cleared his throat behind them. "Cal," he said, "I could actually use someone to coordinate guard shifts and training while I'm gone. I think Kinna would be excellent. She knows the men and the schedules we keep."

Her father looked at her expectantly, obviously pleased with the proposed compromise and hoping she would immediately accept. In reality, Kinna thought that sounded awful. Making guard schedules and running drills every day was more boring than just having her time to herself. It did give her an idea though. If her parents thought that this offer had appeased her, they may not suspect she could have other plans.

"Thank you, General." She nodded brightly, hoping she could sell her false enthusiasm. Her father's approving smile was indication that at least he had bought it.

"It's settled then," the king finished, satisfied. "You ladies are free to go."

Both women nodded and turned for the door, Kinna already three steps ahead of her sister as she strode out into the hallway. Her mind was already turning, thinking of ways she could use these new responsibilities to her advantage. She was so absorbed in her own thoughts that she didn't realize that her sister had caught up to her.

"They will never let you fight, Kinna," Evelyn whispered, despite being out of earshot of the nearest guard. "You should stop asking; it only upsets Mother."

Kinna halted. She regretted ever telling her sister that she dreamed of being a soldier and sharing the secret she had only dared whisper in her heart. That she wanted to do something important instead of filling her days with the silly tasks others assumed a princess should engage in.

Granted, she had been twelve when she told Evelyn that, and their relationship had been far different in their youth, but it was still a secret that she wished she had never shared at all. At the time, she had believed that one day Evelyn would take the throne and Kinna would stand beside her as a general. But even after Evelyn had rejected her idea, she had hoped that if she just trained hard enough or was given the chance to prove herself, she would be taken seriously one day.

"That's easy for you to say." She sighed. "You will be a queen, your name living on forever in the history books, just like Father and Grandmother. But what do I have?"

Her sister was quiet for a long moment before answering. "Freedom," she whispered. "You have the freedom to choose. To choose the life you want to have or the person you want to be. I have not had that for one single second of my life."

Kinna stood there, stunned at the revelation that perhaps her perfect sister, always acting as the queen she would one day be, was already growing weary of her crown. "I thought you wanted this," she mumbled.

"Of course, I did. I think I still do," she insisted. "But sometimes, I see you, getting to spend your day at the beach or with Ellio, and I wish that I could choose for myself. I wish I could choose this, instead of it being chosen for me."

She didn't know what to say to her sister's abrupt confession. It had been a long time since either of them had been so honest with each other. As they had grown up and more responsibility had been given to Evelyn, the two had begun to drift apart. Their lives had moved in different directions, and they had stopped trying to bridge the gap a long time ago.

"I'm sorry," she choked out. It seemed like the right thing to say in a situation like this, although she didn't really know why she was apologizing.

"You don't have anything to be sorry about," Evelyn said, grabbing her hand. "But it does feel nice to be able to say that out loud. To feel heard."

"I know how you feel," she murmured.

They stood there in the hallway for another moment until Evelyn sniffled and straightened herself, dropping Kinna's hand. "I'm going to be late for my lessons," she replied.

"I need to take a bath," Kinna responded. "I smell after training all morning."

Her sister smiled softly at her before turning to head down the hallway in the direction of the library, where her tutor would likely be waiting for her. Kinna on the other hand, had no plans for the afternoon, a common occurrence that often led her to the beach. First though, she really did need a bath and some lunch.

CHAPTER TWO

She pushed through her door, already ripping the braid out of her hair and heading for her bathing chamber when she heard a cough. She turned to find her best friend waiting on her bed. Ellio was leisurely stretched across it, his long arms and legs dangling off either side. He was still in his training clothes, a black shirt and matching black trousers that showed off his lean muscular body. His tanned fingers flipped through a book from one of the stacks on the floor, his every movement causing his sandy curls to bounce.

"Finally," he drawled, tossing the book down.

Kinna smiled to herself at finding him waiting for her in her room, something he'd been doing since they were children. In the weeks following his mother's death, he would creep into her room in the middle of the night, crawling into bed with her as if only she could keep his nightmares at bay.

Of course, back then it hadn't been improper or caused any gossip, but even now Ellio was still using his father's position to bully guards into letting him inside without her there. She found a small bit of satisfaction in that even with court ladies swooning over him, he still sought out her company first.

"Hope I didn't keep you waiting." She smirked. "What do you want?"

"I came to find you in the training room, but you were gone," he said. "One of the guards said your sister had shown up and you'd left with her."

"Father wanted to see us," she replied, sitting on the edge of the bed beside him and snatching the book from where he'd tossed it. "Something about a border skirmish up north."

"I wouldn't exactly call it a skirmish, Kin," he countered.

"A couple of fires set? Sounds a little juvenile." She shrugged, returning the book to its proper stack. She kept all her books in a meticulous order that made little sense to anyone but her. "I know there was a casualty, but it was probably accidental."

Ellio sat up slowly, his playful demeanor gone. "Is that what he told you?"

"Yes," she answered slowly, her head buzzing with a thousand questions. "What do you know, Ellio?"

He pushed off the bed to pace in front of the empty fireplace, rubbing his face nervously before answering her. "It's much more serious than they told you," he cautioned. "Are you sure you even want to hear this?"

She nodded quickly. Of course, her parents weren't telling the whole truth, her mother's reaction should have been the first indication that there was more to the story. She cursed herself for accepting their version so easily and allowing herself to be misled.

Ellio hesitated for a long moment before telling her. "They were setting fires but not just houses, to people too," he explained. "People have been disappearing and their bodies are being found days later, charred and unrecognizable. They started around the border, but we keep finding bodies closer and closer to the capital."

"That's why the general is traveling himself," she whispered to herself. "I should have known he wouldn't leave the capital unless it was something important."

"I think they are trying to send a message. I think they are coming here, to the capital."

"Why?"

"I'm guessing it's the same reason it always has been, who really has the right to Edgewood. Although this group has escalated things far beyond anything the Rising has done. We think they could be a more fanatical sect that has broken off from the other rebels and is trying to reclaim Edgewood. They may be working with Eldridge, but we don't have any proof."

The Rising was a rebel group that spent most of their time illegally smuggling people from Eldridge into Ferryn and fighting with the soldiers on the northern border over just about anything. There were a few groups of them that roamed the northern half of Ferryn, living like nomads. Some rumors claimed that they had magic wielders within their ranks, but Kinna thought that was unlikely. Eldridge had outlawed magic years ago, she couldn't imagine anyone with even the smallest gift getting close to the kingdom for fear of being discovered.

However, Ellio could be right, she thought. There had been disputes over who the city belonged to for generations. Edgewood was nestled along the edge of the Glenwood with the ocean on their eastern edge, a location that made the city prosperous because of their access to timber and proximity to the ocean. It had also made them the target of a frequent power struggle between the two kingdoms.

After the last war between Eldrige and Ferryn towards the end of her grandmother's reign, the city had been brought solely under the control of Ferryn. Her grandmother had sailed with their navy to the northern city, using her abilities to turn the tide in their favor during one last stand off in the city's harbor.

Rumor had it, the citizens closest to the border had never forgiven them for the destruction that followed and blamed magic wielders for their loss. It had only been a few months after losing the city when the kingdom had outlawed the practice of magic in their lands. It was definitely a viable theory at the very least.

"It's possible," she agreed. "So, what is your father's plan?"

"I know what you're thinking, Kin, but do not try to get involved in this," he warned.

"I'm not," she lied, changing the subject quickly. "Actually, I came up here to take a bath. Want to meet me in the kitchens for some lunch?"

He knew she was lying. She would never drop something like this so easily, but he figured she was trying to appease him now so she could try to persuade him to help in whatever she was plotting later. "I'll meet you in half an hour," he agreed.

———

Kinna sank down lower into the tub, savoring the last of the hot water on her already sore muscles. She had been mulling over what to do about the threat brewing to the north. The gods had finally given her an opportunity to leave her home in the pretty castle by the sea and she was going to take it. It didn't matter that her parents forbade it or that her best friend was already suspicious of her, she would not let this chance slip through her fingers.

Kinna rolled debates around in her head, trying to predict and counter every argument. She quickly realized that while her parents were a dead end, the general was another story. Perhaps she could convince him that she would be valuable to have with him. He had trained her himself, and there was barely a guard she couldn't beat in a fight. Not to mention that her education had given her more insight into the politics and strategy needed for a mission like this. He had never underestimated her skill, why should he start now?

She got out of the tub quickly, wrapping a towel tightly around herself and walked to her closet. The spring weather was still cool, so she opted for a pair of dark, thick knit leggings and a loose white linen shirt. Her golden ring laid on her desk, the large aquamarine stone shining as if it had been freshly polished. It had been a gift from her mother on her tenth birthday and she'd worn it every day for the past nine years. She slid it on her left pointer finger before stopping in front of the mirror to run a comb through her damp hair, hoping to not damage the curls that were already forming.

After a thin layer of her favorite amber scented oil had been applied to them, they were silken and shining in the sunlight that streamed through her window. There were not many things Kinna loved about her appearance, but her long, dark curls were her favorite, and often the only thing she put any real effort into. Satisfied by her reflection, she made her way down to the kitchens hoping that Ellio had not eaten all the pastries while he waited on her to arrive.

The kitchens were hot and bustling, people

running in every direction to clean up after lunch while simultaneously preparing for dinner. A massive wooden table spanned the length of the room, worn from years of use and covered in nicks from stray knives. Ellio sat at one end with the head cook, Maude, an ancient looking woman who had lived in the castle for years. She had been here since her grandmother's reign and was renowned for her skill in the kitchen. Some even whispered that she had a drop of magic that made all her food so delicious.

Kinna highly doubted that; abilities usually came in the form of an element, not cooking skills, but she did have to admit, she had never tasted anything as wonderful as her desserts. Kinna adored anything with sugar in it and could burst into a fit of rage if anyone threatened her sweets. Ellio had earned himself quite a few bruises over the years trying to steal something from her plate.

Despite her deep wrinkles and short stature, Maude still ran the kitchens with the same ferocity of a woman half her age, moving so fast she was almost a blur. Ellio and Kinna had spent many afternoons at this table, watching Maude cook and sneaking bites of whatever dessert she had made. While she feigned annoyance at their presence in her kitchen, she had never turned them away when they had come, no matter how long they stayed.

Kinna wound through the kitchen staff and made her way to them, kissing Maude's cheek swiftly while grabbing a slice of fresh bread off the tray in front of them. "Hello, Maude," she chirped.

Maude batted her away smiling. "Hello, Princess." She smiled.

"Is there any butter?" she asked, taking a seat opposite them.

"You know there is," she answered, sliding it across the table to her. "I saved you a few blueberry scones, too."

"Did Ellio try to eat them all again?"

"Of course."

"I'm right here you know?" Ellio interjected. "And I would have saved her some."

Kinna gave Maude a disbelieving stare. "I doubt it," she muttered, taking a scone.

"What trouble are the two of you going to get into today?" Maude asked them.

"None," they answered in unison.

She snorted and got up from the table. "I'll send over some roasted chicken," she said.

"You are truly an angel," Ellio declared.

She waved off his compliment and left to oversee two young women who were undoubtedly stirring something incorrectly. She must have dismissed one of them to find their promised lunch because the younger of the two disappeared only to return with a whole roasted chicken. She sat it down carefully between them, looking up at Ellio through her lashes and giving him a timid smile, staring at him for longer than necessary.

"Thank you for bringing this over," Kinna interrupted.

Her thanks broke the girl's doe-eyed stare and she flashed Kinna a quick curtsy before darting back to her post. She rolled her eyes at her retreating figure and tore a piece of chicken for her plate. "So, are you going north with the general?" she asked, trying to sound casual.

"Yes," he admitted. "I'll be leading one of the companies."

"When do you leave?"

"In five days."

Five days. Kinna wasn't sure if that would be long enough to convince General Resten to allow her to travel with them. She had expected a few weeks to be able to win him over; this was going to ruin all her plans. "So soon?" she asked.

"Everyone is worried that things will escalate further if the situation isn't handled soon."

"I guess you'll be busy preparing for the next few days."

He grinned smugly. "Don't worry, I'll still have time to kick your ass every morning in the training room."

She snorted at his slight, tossing a pinch of bread at him that he easily dodged. She knew he was trying to change the subject, still unwilling to tell her any more than he already had. So, she let it drop. Besides, if anyone thought she wasn't content with her assigned duties, they may try to keep a closer eye on her. "I think I'm going to go down to the beach this afternoon. Do you want to come?" she asked.

"I can't. I have to go to a council meeting soon, but I'll meet you in the morning for a run," he offered.

"Have fun." She smirked. She knew how much he hated those meetings, but as the general's son, he was often sent in his stead. Lately it seemed that Ellio was the only one attending these meetings. She couldn't recall the last one General Resten had personally attended.

He rolled his eyes at her as he got up. "I'll see you

tomorrow," he called.

Kinna said a quick good-bye to Maude, taking the last blueberry scone, and headed for her room. Council meetings were notoriously long, which meant that it could be hours before Ellio was able to leave, maybe she would try to find the general later while he was otherwise occupied.

She grabbed a blanket and the book she was currently reading to take with her before sliding off her jewelry. She nodded to the guards stationed in the hallway, Macklin and Eron. They had been guards for the Royal Family since she was a child and were often assigned to her hallway. "I'm going to the beach. If anyone comes to find me, tell them I'm in the library." She winked at them.

Eron, the older of the two, shook his head. Macklin just laughed; he was always more willing to go along with her schemes. "Yes, Your Highness." He smiled.

She strode down the hallway, heading for the gardens on the eastern side of the castle. The spring season had started a new flurry of activity here and the gardens would soon be overflowing with flowers and courtiers spending lazy afternoons in the shade.

They, like much of the castle, stood overlooking the ocean and even in the dead of summer, you could always feel an ocean breeze here. She walked through the hedges working her way towards the far side of the garden, already able to feel the cool ocean air. The hedges opened to a large, tiled patio that would soon be filled with furniture and a set of stairs that led down to a small stretch of private beach.

While the gardens would eventually be busy with

activity, the beach would remain empty. Most courtiers wouldn't risk their fine clothes against the sand and seawater, which made it an ideal place for Kinna to spend her afternoon. She slipped off her shoes, leaving them on the last step, before sinking down into the sand. The sand was warm around her feet as she leisurely walked down the beach. She threw her blanket down, using the book as a weight to keep it from blowing away, and went to stand at the edge of the water. Rolling her pants up, she braced herself for the cold water and walked into the surf, wading in as far as she could.

She had spent countless days on this beach, regardless of the weather or time of year. It was a place that she could escape to, a place where she could relax. It once had been somewhere she shared with her sister and Ellio, but as they got older, they joined her here less and less. During the sweltering summers they had taken refuge on the beach, frolicking in the surf and leaving covered in sand. It used to bother her, being here alone, but now she was grateful for the quiet.

She stood in the water until her feet were engulfed by the sand and she could no longer feel her toes in the icy water. Retreating to the shore, she shook out her blanket and laid back, careful to keep her freshly washed hair out of the sand. She had barely made it through a few pages of her book before she found herself nodding off. Normally she devoured books, easily reading one or two in a day if she was left alone, but the sun was warm on her skin and the rhythm of the crashing waves soothed her like a lullaby. In moments she was asleep, her book resting open on her chest.

The rain woke her, pulling her from a murky

nightmare that was already slipping away. Dark clouds had rolled in while she slept, obscuring the setting sun and promising more than just rain. Her clothes were already damp, and sand was dried and crusted on her feet. She needed to get back inside before the storm broke and she was drenched. Quickly grabbing the blanket and her book, she jogged back towards the stairs as a harsh wind whipped at her, almost forgetting to take her shoes from the bottom step.

All the lanterns had already been lit as she walked through the hallway towards her rooms. She had been on the beach longer than she had planned. Normally she would have gone back to the training room, maybe even had a chance to speak with General Resten, if she hadn't fallen asleep. The missed opportunity annoyed her. Macklin and Eron were still stationed in the hallway; she nodded to them as she opened her door.

"How was the library?" Eron asked, eyeing her wet clothes suspiciously.

"Wet," she replied, closing the door and cutting off Macklin's laugh.

Her bedroom was warm, the fire having been stoked, candles lit, and a tray of food left on the small dining table that sat in front of the doors that led to her small balcony. Kerin, her lady's maid, must have come while she was away. A dry set of clothes, a flowy lilac dress and stockings, were also draped across the edge of her bed. Kerin had likely asked the guards about her whereabouts and the guards, being the gossips that they are, told her she was at the beach.

Normally she would be annoyed that they had disobeyed her command and told someone, even Kerin, where she was, but at this moment she was just grateful for the dry clothes and toasty room.

Kinna sat the tray carefully down in front of the fireplace, forgoing the table, and settled onto an over-sized cushion to eat. Even with dry clothes on she was cold after falling asleep in the rain and the fire was too tempting to ignore. While she ate, she spied a book on the continent's geography, *The Geographical and Economical Lands of Ferryn*, on one of the overflowing shelves beside her desk. It was something one of her tutors had given her while they learned about the politics of land holdings. It had been horribly boring to learn about at the time, but now it might offer some insight into the conflict in Edgewood.

Dropping her empty tray on the table, she grabbed the book and went back to her spot in front of the fire. She laid it down on the floor in front of her, opening the worn leather cover and skimmed through the first few pages looking for something that could be helpful. She found a section of maps that marked roads, rivers and a collection of towns that were sprinkled from the capital city of Strafford to Edgewood where the general and his company would be staying.

Lines sliced their way through the continent, inter-secting in seemingly random areas. One line even ran through the capital, splitting the city down the middle. The key listed them as ley lines, but it was a term Kinna was unfamiliar with. It wasn't a grand discovery, but it couldn't hurt to have a copy of it if she was travel-ing through the area. She quickly grabbed a pen and a square of paper and began copying the map as best as she could, hoping to maintain some shred of accuracy.

It was late by the time she had finished her ren-dition and her eyes were tired from glancing back and forth in the dim light as she drew. She dropped the book on her desk to continue reading tomorrow and laid the map carefully on top of it, careful not to smudge the still drying ink. The map would have to be stuffed back inside the book in the morning before anyone could spot it and question why she would need it. Blowing out the few remaining candles, she flopped into her bed, nestling down beneath her thick quilt, already dreading the early morning run she had agreed to.

CHAPTER THREE

She waited on the bottom step, arms wrapped around herself, trying to stay warm in the frigid morning air while she waited on Ellio. Kinna hated being cold and she rubbed at her arms furiously in an attempt to get the goosebumps that peppered her skin to fade away. The sun had already started to rise, and it was unusual that he was late, but the council meeting could have lasted into the night and kept him trapped with them. Finally, she heard footsteps against the stairs and his voice called out. "Get up, Kin! We don't have time to sleep on the stairs."

"In case you hadn't noticed, you are the one that is late, not me," she argued, reluctantly standing up.

Ellio had already slipped past her, his bare feet stomping through the sand and kicking up small grains as he went. Kinna was left to catch up to him, grumbling insults under her breath. He turned to mock a bow as she joined him. "Many apologies, Your Highness."

She rolled her eyes at him. She hated that title and insisted no one call her that. Of course, that gave Ellio the ammunition to use it as an insult instead, which he often did.

They walked to the water's edge and stood shoulder to shoulder, facing south looking out over the few miles of beach while they stretched. They had long since grown tired of racing and instead had begun trading turns to set the pace for the run. The rules were simple, whoever sets the pace can run at any speed for any length of time. If you fall behind by more than 5 paces or can't keep up, you lose. Today was Ellio's turn, which likely meant more sprinting than Kinna would like.

"It's my turn." He smiled.

"I'm aware."

"I hope you're ready. I need to let out some energy after sitting at the council meeting all night."

"Are we going to stand here talking or are we going to run?"

She knew that comment would set him off and his smug smile turned feral as he huffed a laugh. "You'll regret that," he whispered. He threw an elbow to knock her off balance and then took off running full speed, already putting her behind.

"Cheater," she yelled and raced off after him.

The first few moments were always the most blissful to Kinna. Her heart pounded in her chest and a wide smile stretched across her face as they sprinted towards the sunrise. Wisps of her hair that had come loose flowed out behind her as she fell into step beside Ellio and for a few seconds she swore they weren't running at all. Sometimes it felt as if her feet weren't actually touching the ground but instead flying over the wet sand that glistened in the morning light. It was pure freedom, and she would never grow tired of this feeling.

By the time they came to a stop, they both were gasping for air and unable to talk. Kinna walked further from the water to the driest parts of the sand and sat down. Ellio followed behind her, throwing himself down on the sand with a dramatic grunt, sending grains flying around them.

"How was the council meeting," she asked once she had her breathing under control.

"Awful. We were there for hours while they all argued over how many companies we should send or if we should go at all."

"I thought your father had already decided."

"He has. He sent me so he didn't have to listen to them try to persuade him. He outranks them all so his decision is final, but they think I will somehow be able to convince him otherwise."

"They must think highly of you if they believe you would change the general's mind."

"Perhaps. I think they just don't know him well enough to understand there is no changing his mind once he has made his decision."

Kinna frowned at his response. That was not the encouraging sentiment she needed to hear if she was going to convince General Resten that she should go to Edgewood. At least he had agreed that she was as skilled as any of his soldiers, perhaps if given the choice, he would have allowed her to go. "Let's go find some breakfast," she offered.

"I bet Maude has some muffins waiting on us," he suggested.

Kinna stood, her legs still shaky from a long run, and held out a hand to help Ellio. He took her hand and she pulled him up while sand rained down from clothes. He was covered in it, with every inch of his exposed skin encrusted in sand and sweat. She reached up and gently dusted sand off his neck and face. The sand and his short stubble scraped lightly against her fingertips. She stopped abruptly as soon as their eyes met. His eyes

LUCY STEELE

were the color of the deepest parts of the ocean that they visited each day and that she loved so much, but they were staring at her with a quiet intensity she had not seen before. A sort of confusion and longing swirled in them that made her actions feel too intimate.

"Thanks," he said, shaking out his clothes and breaking the spell.

"Maude will kick us out if you get sand all over her kitchen," she explained quickly.

They made their way through the gardens without a word but stopped when they heard a familiar laugh. Gemma rounded the corner, trailed by her two lady's maids, and dressed in a silky lavender dress that bordered on inappropriate for a morning walk. The dress clung to her figure, accentuating her curves and tiny waist. A white fur wrap was slung across her shoulders, obscuring her chest.

The attempt to convince others that she intended to be outdoors was half-hearted at best. Her auburn hair was braided tightly against her head and silver pins dotted with tiny white butterflies had been woven throughout her hair. It was obvious she had been waiting here, hoping to be seen. She barely glanced at Kinna before turning her attention to Ellio, her eyes roving over him, no doubt because his shirt clung so closely to his muscular chest.

"Ellio!" she squealed. Before he could stop her, she threw herself at him and wrapped her arms around his neck, her head laid gently on his shoulder. The possessive way she held him made Kinna's blood boil. "Oh, it has been far too long since I have seen you."

"Out for a morning walk, Gemma?" he gasped, untangling himself from her tight grip around his neck.

"It's such a lovely morning." She smiled, smoothing her dress around her hips. "I just couldn't stay trapped inside any longer."

"Well, we would hate to keep you standing with idle conversation," he agreed, edging around her. "Kinna and I are needed inside but do enjoy your walk."

She frowned at their retreating figures, obviously upset by their too quick encounter. "Perhaps we will run into each other again soon," she called.

"Of course," he answered, dragging Kinna along by her elbow. "She's a nightmare," he whispered to Kinna as soon as they were out of earshot, dropping her arm.

Kinna thought so too. She had never liked Gemma, and the feeling was mutual. Even as children they had never gotten along, likely because she was always trying to insert herself into whatever Kinna, Ellio, and Evelyn were doing at the time. Unfortunately, as the daughter of the Lord of Edgewood she spent much of her time at the castle, and now that she was of marrying age, she used the castle as her own personal hunting grounds and Ellio was her most prized target. "You know she thinks she's going to marry you," Kinna whispered back.

"She can think whatever she wants. That is not happening."

"You don't think your father would have you marry someone to form an alliance?"

"I know he would, but lucky for me he hates Lord Duran, so Gemma wouldn't be much of an alliance. Marrying you would give him the strongest alliance he could hope for."

Kinna froze at his words, her heart hammering in

her chest. Ellio didn't think of her that way, did he? She glanced up at his face; it gave no indication that he was seriously considering marriage to anyone, especially her. But she couldn't help the picture that began forming in the back of her mind.

She would never be forced to marry some stuffy prince that she had never met and would complicate her life. Everything could stay simple. Ellio understood her better than anyone, accepted her for exactly who she was and never cared that she wasn't the poised princess others wanted her to be. There would be a lifetime of morning runs and training sessions, something that she knew would one day disappear if she married.

She had to admit, she could imagine a life with Ellio Resten. "You could do worse than to marry into the Royal Family, I guess," she teased, testing his response. "Prince Ellio."

"Trust me, I couldn't care less about a title," he answered gruffly, pushing open the kitchen door. Her heart sank a fraction at his response. She was being silly, Ellio was her best friend, of course he didn't think of her in a romantic way.

They were greeted by a rush of hot air, silverware clanging against dishes, and Maude shouting commands from her post in front of a giant iron stove. She glanced at them and nodded towards the center of the table. "Muffins are there," she said.

Ellio blew her a kiss. "Maude, it's like you can read my mind sometimes," he mused.

She snorted at him and rolled her eyes. "Only because you came into my kitchen demanding muffins before the sun had even risen."

"So that's why you were late to the beach this

morning," Kinna interjected.

"I would never dare demand anything from our most honorable Head Chef," he said in mock outrage, taking a muffin in each hand. "And a gentleman is never late."

"Good thing you aren't a gentleman then," Maude muttered, turning back to the stove.

Kinna chuckled at the slight and grabbed one of the muffins in Ellio's hand, sliding onto the bench beside him. "Are you training this morning?" she asked.

"No. My father is sending me back to the council. They have called one last meeting to discuss logistics." He sighed. "I'll be there for at least a few hours to listen to them argue."

"Well, I will be there all morning, reveling in the empty training room that I will have all to myself," she said cheerily, grabbing a second muffin before swinging her legs over the bench.

"Brat," he muttered.

Kinna smiled and ruffled his still damp curls as she made her way to the door. "Enjoy your meeting," she called, not waiting to hear his response.

Just as she had hoped, the training room was completely empty. The morning session had already ended, and most guards were likely squished into the few tables in the common room outside their barracks, inhaling whatever breakfast Maude had sent over. She occasionally joined them there for meals, enjoying the loud, boisterous company that the group provided. She had always been jealous of the family that the guards created; the constant flurry of activity had drawn her to them in a way that her sewing lessons never could. Part of why she had dreamed of being a soldier stemmed from the time she had spent around them, witnessing the bond they formed together and longing for the same camaraderie.

Still, she enjoyed having the space to herself. This was where she spent most of her time and a place where she felt at home. As a girl, Kinna had begged Ellio to bring her along to one of his lessons and she had been eight when she first tried to convince Resten to let her train with him. He had said no at first, agreeing with Kinna's mother that this was no place for a princess. A week later Kinna had started a fight with another lord's son, breaking his nose in the process before Ellio could break it up. Afterwards the general managed to convince her parents that this would help, he explained that it would help her channel her energy into something more productive and keep her temper in check. Her father had agreed despite her mother continuing to protest.

Ellio had offered to be her partner, knowing none of the other boys their age would truly spar with her. He had always been Kinna's closest friend, always training together and finding ways to escape their tutors. As the son of General Resten, he was one of the only people that had grown up in the castle like Kinna and her sister had.

She crossed the room, reaching for a polished bow and a quiver of arrows and headed for the row of targets. Setting the arrows down at her feet, Kinna tugged at the bow string with her fingers, making sure it was taunt before grabbing an arrow and nocking it into place. She tested her bow, enjoying the familiar stretch in her right arm as she pulled her arrow back, positioning her hand by her face and held it for a few seconds. Inspecting a bow before use, especially one in the training room that everyone used, was one of the first things Resten had taught her.

The bow was the first weapon she had been allowed to train with, mostly because it was the hardest for her to injure herself with. She still remembered the first few months, when she had barely been strong enough to pull the small bowstring back, let alone take the time to aim and release her arrow. But she got stronger, and her aim better, and she gradually began to outshoot every arm guard in the castle. While she had eventually been trained in multiple weapons, from knives to long swords, the bow was still her favorite.

Planting her feet, she took a deep breath and raised her bow, keeping her eyes locked on the tiny black bullseye of her target. In the silence of the training room, she pulled her arrow back, letting everything around her disappear except the target in front of her and released. The arrow struck and she stalked forward to inspect her shot. It had hit the bullseye, but landed just a hair to the left, not within the tiny grey dot the center. Annoyed, she ripped the arrow from the target but paused when she heard a muffled laugh.

She turned to find General Resten standing in the doorway shaking his head at her. "Only you would be disappointed by a bullseye." He chuckled, making his way towards her.

"It landed to the left," she explained, pointing at the small nick in the wood.

"As your arrows normally do. You should anticipate your own tendencies in the same way you anticipate the wind."

She nodded, accepting the same advice he'd given

her a thousand times. "You aren't wearing your arm guard," he chided.

"It affects my shot," she muttered.

"It prevents bruising on your arms." He held up her left arm, a small red whelp was already forming from the string slapping her arm.

"You know I don't care about that."

"You do not, but the queen certainly does."

"I'll wear long sleeves and she will never know. Promise."

He sighed, Kinna had always refused her arm guard. It was a pointless battle to fight. Even when he did convince her to put it on, she would tear it off the second he was out of sight. "Fortunately, that is not why I am here," he said. "I came to ask for your help with coordinating guard shifts. I was hoping to have a few weeks planned out before I left for Edgewood."

Kinna knew this was her chance, her one shot to convince him to reconsider and take her with him, but she had to be careful. She had to out-maneuver him. "I can make the shift plans," she began. "Which captain will be overseeing them in your absence?"

"I believe Gavin will," he answered. "He will also be in charge of seeing to your family's personal guard detail."

"He must be very pleased that you chose him," she hedged.

"I trust him," he said. "He's a good soldier and has a sharp mind. I wouldn't leave your family's care to someone who wasn't up to the task."

Kinna hid her smile. He had done exactly what she had hoped. His admission of trust in Gavin gave her an opportunity to make the argument that she was not needed here and could travel with the company. He couldn't argue without contradicting himself or admitting things were not as they seemed. "So, if Gavin has the castle and my family in capable hands, there is really no reason that I could not go with you and Ellio, is there?" she asked. "Especially if the guard shifts are already planned before our departure."

General Resten glanced at her, realization of her little exploit clear on his face, and huffed a laugh. "You would make for an excellent strategist, Kinna." He sighed.

"Then take me with you," she pleaded, gripping his arm. "I know this is more serious than you told us. Let me go. Let me do something besides sit in this damned castle. Please!"

He rubbed his face, the very same gesture Ellio had made just yesterday as she tried to pull information out of him. "He could never deny you anything, could he?" he whispered to her, patting her hand that still gripped his forearm.

"Please don't be upset with Ellio," she asked quietly, releasing his arm. "I made him tell me."

"Surprisingly enough, I believe you could force information out of anyone you wanted."

She couldn't help smiling at his half compliment. They waited in silence, Kinna not wanting to push him any further while he mulled over what to do. Finally, he broke the silence.

"Kinna, as much as I think you would be an asset to our company, it is not my decision to make. Your father, *my king*, wishes you to be here," he explained. "I will not disobey my king's orders or lose the trust of my friend."

Her heart sank and the last of her hope vanished from her heart. She tried to hide the disappointment on her face, but the general saw it. He, like his son, could read every emotion on her face. "I am sorry, Kinna," he said, squeezing her shoulder. "Truly I am."

She nodded, not trusting her voice to speak. He gave her one last apologetic look before heading for the door, leaving her in the training room. Without the general's presence or any hope of getting to leave the castle, she felt more alone than ever in the empty room.

CHAPTER FOUR

General Resten

There was a sharp knock at his door that interrupted his writing. He sunk his pen back in the ink jar and moved to stand from his chair, knees protesting slightly at the sudden movement. "Come in," he called as his son walked into his study.

He studied him for a moment, his sandy hair was still damp, his cheeks slightly flushed and frowned. "I was expecting your report from last night's Council Meeting this morning," he scolded lightly, returning to his seat.

Ellio ducked his head slightly. "I'm sorry," he said. "I lost track of time."

"Yes, you always seem to lose track of time when you are with her," he agreed. "You also seem to forget what the phrase classified information means."

He winced at his father's words. "I know I wasn't supposed to tell her," he began, "but she was acting as if nothing serious was happening and I could tell she was planning something. She needed to understand that this wasn't something she could be involved in. I didn't know how else to stop her."

He had to give the boy credit, he had a talent for reading people and Ellio had spent his entire life studying

Kinna Braunlin. "I don't doubt for a moment that she was trying to scheme her way into leaving the castle with us and likely still is." He sighed, Ellio relaxing as his tone softened. "She managed to snare me in one of her schemes just this morning."

"She has a way of doing that." Ellio smiled softly.

He saw his son's smile at the memory of her. He knew that even if her safety hadn't been in jeopardy, Ellio would have told Kinna anything she wanted to know. He had never been able to deny her anything, not since he had first brought her to the training room, all tangled curls and a firestorm of energy. His son had demanded she be allowed to train with him. The resolve had been so clear in his child's eyes that he had caught a glimpse of the man forming within and it had made him proud.

The pair had gone from rowdy children to a talented albeit deadly duo. He had seen such potential in them from a young age that he had personally overseen the majority of their training throughout their life. They had surpassed nearly all of his guards, their competitive natures driving them to be the very best. They were exactly the type of leadership Ferryn would need very soon.

The general shook the old memory from his mind and focused back on the present. "So, how did you fare in the Council Meeting?" he asked, allowing Ellio to begin his report of the previous night's events.

CHAPTER FIVE

She left the training room after quickly shelving her bow and quiver, not bothering to practice with any of the knives or swords she'd been eyeing earlier, and began to walk aimlessly around the castle, not wanting to go back to her room yet. She avoided the gardens, afraid to run into Gemma for a second time today. Instead, she made her way to the stables, situated outside the castle's exterior walls. She had loved coming to feed the horses when she was a child, but rarely made the walk to see them anymore.

The stables were empty, but the horses closed into their stalls popped their heads out as she walked inside, likely hoping she was carrying treats for them. She found Ellio's horse, Ash, a white and grey spotted stallion that stood three hands taller than most other mounts. Ellio had raised him from a colt and took him out to ride every day, no matter the weather.

"Hello, handsome," she cooed, reaching out to stroke his velvet cheek. He nosed her hands searching for an apple, huffing into her empty hands. "Sorry, I didn't bring any treats with me."

She searched for the feed bucket and grabbed a heaping handful to take back to Ash, hoping he would accept it in place of the sugary treat. She held her hands out flat to him and he took it happily, his tail swishing back and forth while he ate. She stayed a bit longer, petting Ash and sneaking him a few more handfuls of feed before heading back to the castle, her heart feeling just a little bit lighter.

Kinna walked back through the front courtyard of the castle to find five supply wagons being loaded by guards in anticipation of the general's departure. They seemed to have even wrangled some of the younger children that lived in the castle to arrange things inside the wagons. She noticed Parker, the son of the stable hand, shifting bags of grain in the wagon closest to her.

He noticed Kinna and gave her a big, toothy smile, followed by a short bow. "Hello, Your Highness." He grinned.

"Parker, you know you can call me Kinna," she chided. "And there is no need to bow."

"Yes, Your Highness." He blushed. "I mean Kinna."

She smiled at his properness. Most of the children in the castle had no issue calling her by her name, but Parker had always referred to her as Your Highness just like his father, no matter how many times she corrected either of them. "What do they have you doing today?" she asked.

"They needed help loading the wagons," he explained proudly. "They want them stocked and ready by tomorrow morning so General Resten can inspect them before they leave."

"Well, it looks like you've got this under control. I will leave you to your post," she said, saluting him. "Thank you for your service."

He giggled and saluted her back. "It is my honor," he told her with mock seriousness.

Waving goodbye to him, she headed for her room.

She almost couldn't believe her luck. Parker unknow-
ingly had just handed her the perfect escape. If she
could sneak into a supply wagon tomorrow night, after
they had been inspected, she would be able to leave with
company unnoticed. Once they were out of the city,
they wouldn't be able to send her back, even sending a
smaller group to escort her wouldn't be as safe as letting her stay among the dozens of guards riding with
the general. They would simply have to let her stay until
they returned to the capital.

Her head was spinning as a plan formed and
pieces fell into place. Slowing her steps, she tried to look
casual while walking back to her room even though
all she wanted to do was scream with excitement. She
would have to be smart while she prepared, drawing no
suspicion, especially from Kerin who would notice anything missing from her rooms.

Standing in front of her closet, she debated what
she should bring. She had already taken two pairs of
wool leggings, something she usually wore during winter, down from the basket Kerin had stored them in.
In the back of one of her drawers she found some old
socks and tucked them in the bag as well. She added two
tunics before her eyes drifted over a worn cobalt knit
sweater. She had stolen it from Ellio years ago after he
had hit a growth spurt and outgrew it. Kinna shoved
it towards the bottom of her bag, not able to leave it
behind.

Her bow sat in the corner by her door. She would
have to leave it since moving it now would only bring
up questions, but she still packed her arm guard and a
quiver of arrows. Before leaving, she also grabbed the
makeshift map from the book she'd hidden it in, care-

fully folded it and added it to her bag.

She heard her door creak open, thankful once again for squeaky hinges, and quickly tossed the bag into the corner of her closet. Kerin was making her way noisily towards the table with a tray of food in hand. The savory smell of whatever Kerin had brought up was heavenly and she quickly realized she hadn't eaten anything since the muffin she had swiped from Ellio this morning. She crossed the room, lifting a lid off one of the bowls and smiling as her stomach rumbled loudly. Maude had made chicken and potato pies, one of her favorites. Her smile vanished though when Kerin grabbed her arm and gave her a look that could curdle milk.

"Why do you insist on making these horrid marks on your arms?" She glared, her grey eyes holding her stare. Kerin could be intimidating when she wanted to be. She stood a head taller than Kinna and her signature tight bun made her look even more severe.

Kinna gulped. She should have known to cover her arms better around Kerin. Despite being old enough to be her grandmother, Kerin was as sharp eyed as ever, never missing a single thing, which was probably why she had been assigned as Kinna's lady's maid when she was only four. Even as a child her parents had seen her wildness and paired her with the only person that would not back down from the challenge that she was.

"I forgot my arm guard," she mumbled, sitting down and preparing for the lecture that was coming.

"You must think me a great fool if you think I am going to believe that lousy excuse," she told her tersely, sitting down across from her and sliding her a pie. "Keep that arm covered around Her Majesty for the next few days or I will sew that arm guard to you," she added when Kinna didn't respond.

"I'll be careful," she said, cutting open her steaming pie.

Kerin's expression softened. "Eat," she ordered. "I know you haven't had anything since breakfast."

Kinna rolled her eyes, but a small smile returned to her face. Bossy as she was, Kerin loved her, she knew that. Kerin had no children of her own and had been a widow long before Kinna was born. She had come to work in the castle after her husband passed and found her own family here, among the other ladies in the castle and with Kinna.

They ate in a comfortable silence which they did almost every night, except on Sunday when she and her sister dined with their parents. It had started as a way for Kerin to teach Kinna her table manners and quickly began a routine. Some nights they discussed Kinna's studies or what books they were currently reading, other nights they just sat in the quiet, enjoying each other's company. Once Kerin had said goodnight and taken their empty dishes down to the kitchen, Kinna was alone and able to continue her planning.

———

Kinna had been hiding in the training room all afternoon sparring with anyone who wandered in and even recruiting a few passing guards to keep herself busy. Before that, she had spent her morning in the kitchen with Maude making her favorite dessert, cinnamon crumble cake. Her fingers were still slightly sticky from handling the cinnamon sugar mix, some of it stuck beneath her nails.

Once a week her father insisted their family dine together, just the four of them, but that wasn't why she was avoiding returning to her room. She actually enjoyed their weekly dinners, listening to her father tell them the same stories from his youth, their mother laughing as they grew more fantastical every week. No, she was hiding from Kerin, who had informed her last night that she had ordered a new dress for her, and she must wear it tonight. She sighed and rolled over on her stomach. The mat she had been laying on for the last hour had started to get uncomfortable which was her cue to get up and go back to her rooms before Kerin sent one of the guards to come find her, or worse, came looking for her herself.

Kerin was waiting for her when she opened the door to her room, already shouting for her to get in the bath so she could start on her hair. Kinna spent extra time detangling her hair and scraping the sugar from underneath her nails before Kerin dragged her from the bathtub, fussing over her hair. Kerin's nimble fingers began twisting her hair into small braids, crossing them behind her head and forming a crown across her brow. She left half of her hair down and added extra oil to form perfect curls that hung down her back.

Kinna dusted her cheeks with a hint of blush as Kerin shuffled towards her closet. She reappeared with a gown of the deepest emerald green, the material swishing quietly as she carried it across the room. Kerin helped her step into it and began on the seemingly endless line of buttons that ran up the back, each dotted with a single pearl. Kinna watched herself in the mirror, surprised by how much she loved the dress. The skirt clung to her like water, hugging her curves and puddling at her feet. The bodice was tightly fitted but not uncomfortable, tucking in at her waist while the neckline hovered just over her breasts, forming a small vee in the center. Two small straps circled her biceps, the fabric dotted with the same tiny pearls that lined the back of the gown. Kinna looked almost regal as she stood with her chin held high and thought perhaps she should let Kerin dress her more often.

"Bow your head towards me," Kerin directed, breaking the trance she had fallen into.

She obeyed and Kerin tucked thin golden pins with various sized pearls on the heads into her braided crown. Adding a gold chain with a single teardrop pearl the size of a coin around her bare throat she announced she was perfect. Kinna slid on her matching golden shoes and moved to her dresser to tap her perfume onto either side of the neck, giving herself one last glance in the mirror.

"Thank you, Kerin." She grinned, kissing her cheek. "You really outdid yourself."

Kerin gave her a disbelieving stare but patted her arm. "I never thought I would hear you thank me for buying another gown, but I certainly won't forget it. Now go and remember who you are."

Kinna smiled at Kerin's trademark goodbye and waved as she left for dinner. She had heard her say those four words over and over, often in warning when Kinna was about to do something mischievous. Other times, like today, they were used to bolster Kinna's confidence, a subtle reminder of who she was and everything she was capable of.

Macklin's low whistle sounded as she emerged from her room and earned him an elbow in the ribs from Eron. She only laughed as she twirled past them down the hallway. She had been admiring the skirt's material, running her fingers across the soft, delicate texture when she collided with someone. Her flimsy shoes slipped against the ground, and she felt herself losing her balance.

Strong hands wrapped around her arms, stopping her from falling backwards onto the stone floor. Kinna looked up and found Ellio staring intently down at her. The blue of his eyes barely visible around his enlarged pupils as they ran over her body, lingering around her waist then her chest.

"Thanks for catching me," she said, his attention snapping back up to her face.

His hands relaxed as he realized he was still holding her, his hands brushing down her arms as he let her go. "You are so beautiful," he murmured, not hearing what she had said.

Kinna immediately stopped toying with the ring of her finger. She stood frozen, heat sparking low in her stomach and spreading through her body. She had no idea how to respond. Ellio didn't say things like that to her, ever. He didn't think of her like that, he had made that perfectly clear. Her silence seemed to bring him back to reality and he quickly stepped back, putting a more appropriate distance between them.

He cleared his throat. "Are you going to dinner?"

"Yes," she breathed even though he already knew the answer.

"Well, enjoy your dinner. Send my best to your parents," he added, stepping around her and continuing quickly down the hallway.

Kinna was left feeling unsteady. Her skin was too hot and sensitive against her dress. A long moment passed before she was able to get her feet to move in the right direction again.

CHAPTER SIX

Evelyn and her parents were already seated in the small family dining room attached to her parent's suite when she arrived. The ornate wooden table was set with bright, white dishes topped with cobalt-colored napkins embroidered with a dozen tiny golden crescent moons, a nod to the sigil of her family. Fat candles sat burning on the table, casting a glow on the faces of her family and making the jewels hanging from her mother's neck glisten.

The queen was dressed in a deep crimson gown with a high neck that left only her collarbones exposed. A garnet necklace with three large stones sat at the base of her throat. Her dark hair shining in the candlelight was pulled up in a simple knot at the base of her neck, letting her necklace be the center of attention.

Where her mother was dressed in something dark and sensual, Evelyn was her opposite. Her gown was the purest shade of sky blue it bordered on being white. The gauzy long sleeves were dotted with small white and silver beaded flowers that mimicked the larger ones on the hem of the skirt. Her honey blonde hair was softly curled and held back by a beaded white velvet headband, highlighting her perfect cheekbones and slender neck.

The king had forgone his usual practical attire in

favor of a charcoal gray jacket with golden buttons over-top a white linen shirt with a crimson pocket square to match her mother. He smiled at Kinna as she joined them at the table, standing to pull her chair out for her to sit.

"You look lovely, my dear," he said, planting a kiss on her head as she sat.

"Thank you," she said.

"That is a lovely color on you," her mother agreed. "You should let Kerin dress you more often."

She smirked at her mother. "For once I agree with you. It is a beautiful dress," she said, brushing her hands over the skirt. "I almost fell trying to get here though. Not very practical."

Her father tried to hide his laughter but was un-successful. Her mother was giving him an exasperated look when Maude arrived with four bowls of a creamy soup to start off their meal.

"You really do look beautiful," Evelyn whispered while they were served. "Kerin will have to tell my Su-zannah where she found that dress."

Kinna knew that Kerin would sooner cut off her own hand than share her secret tailor that made all her clothes. It was her most well-guarded secret. "You know she will never tell," she snorted. "She'll take that to the grave."

Evelyn sighed. "I know, but a girl can dream."

As the night continued, their father fell into his favorite pastime of storytelling. By the end of the night, he has chosen one of Kinna and Evelyn's favorite stor-ies, the first time he met their mother. Between bites of roasted beef, potatoes, and sugar glazed carrots he began the familiar tale.

"I was twenty-three you know when your grand-mother announced I was going to get married and that my future bride would be arriving in just two weeks," he told them with a conspirator's grin. "For the next two weeks I was quizzed on everything about Cidora and the capital city of Vanna. From politics to geography to culture, all in preparation to meet Princess Lena, the flower of Vanna. A great beauty cherished and loved by her people."

The queen shook her head, hand covering her mouth so she wouldn't laugh as he continued. "Finally, she arrived," the king whispered reverently. "She was dressed in all white, absolutely glowing when she emerged from her carriage into the summer sun. I thought she was the most beautiful woman I had ever seen. Truly, she looked closer to a goddess than a mortal."

"What did you say to her when you saw her?" Kinna whispered just as she had the first time he told the story, prompting him to continue.

"I bowed before her and introduced myself," he continued. "Then I offered her my arm and asked if I could give her a tour of my home."

"And what did she say?" Evelyn murmured, playing her part in the story that had been told repeatedly for years. Kinna noticed the usual smile her sister wore during this story was absent, her heart not in the charade. Her attention was quickly diverted though as the king grinned and continued.

Glancing at his wife who was now covering her ears in anticipation of the next part to the story, he leaned over the table, the tension growing. "She said no," he whispered. "And then just walked past me."

The women gasped theatrically before everyone fell into a chorus of laughter. Lena placed her hand in Calvin's as they laughed over their less than romantic first encounter, the king pressed a kiss on her knuckles. "That is not *exactly* how I remember it," she teased.

"No," he argued. "That is exactly how it happened."

Kinna was still smiling when Maude motioned for her. It was finally time for dessert, and she had insisted that she bring up the cake they had made this morning and serve it herself. Carefully walking the square cake back into the room, she set it on the edge of the table and began slicing through it, serving her father an extra-large piece, much to his delight.

The sun had fully set when they finished their meal and Kinna kissed her parents goodnight, ready to peel off the dress that was now pressing tightly against her full stomach. Before she could turn towards her room, Evelyn's hand slipped around her arm.

"Will you take a walk with me?" she asked shyly.

It was an odd request, but for her sister to ask anything of her was unusual. After their conversation outside the throne room, Kinna had softened a little towards her. She realized she hadn't been entirely fair to Evelyn and her mind had been dredging up memories of their childhood, when they had been each other's closest confidants. She could admit to herself that she missed that.

"Of course," she agreed and allowed Evelyn to lead her through the halls and towards the garden.

One of Evelyn's stoic guards tailed them as they made their way outside, staying far enough back that their conversation would be a private one. The night air was chilly, and Evelyn kept Kinna tucked close as they walked towards the eastern edge that faced the Glenwood. Kinna knew where Evelyn was heading. Her favorite spot as a child had been sitting underneath the Crimson King Maple tree that stood on the furthest point of the gardens. It's never changing leaves hung like teardrops from the branches in varying shades of red, most a deep garnet. Evelyn had always been fascinated by the tree and would read any book she could find about the legends behind them.

The moon was just a sliver, the crescent shape still casting a hint of silver light from the clear night sky. Evelyn stood at the edge of the tree's shadow, her face hidden in the darkness as she stared up at its branches stretching out in every direction.

"I used to love coming here," she said softly, as if she could disturb the giant in front of her.

"It was always the first place we looked if we couldn't find you." Kinna smiled at the memory of a small blonde girl curled up between the roots with a book, oblivious to the world around her.

"I've been coming here a lot lately," she told her. "I feel like I can think more clearly when I'm here." Kinna understood that. She felt the same way when she held a bow in her hand. Her mind quieted and everything melted away during those few seconds that she stared down the target.

"I'm going to be engaged by the end of the year," Evelyn whispered without looking at her, her voice barely loud enough for Kinna to hear.

"What?" Kinna blurted out too loudly, the shock momentarily shorting out her brain. "To whom?"

Evelyn's carefully crafted mask of calm cracked.

Kinna could clearly read the hesitation but there was something else beneath it, sorrow clouded her eyes. Evelyn wasn't just unsure about a potential marriage, the thought of it made her miserable, even though she was desperately trying to hide it.

"Mother and Father were approached by two families, two potential matches. One is the second eldest prince in Zotia, Karyk Okoro. The other is Lord Astford of Carabelle's eldest son, Lennon," she explained. "I have until the winter solstice to make my choice."

Kinna vaguely remembered Lord and Lady Astford visiting the capital over the years, their two children always whispering quietly to each other but never engaging with her or Evelyn. Unfortunately, she knew even less about the four princes of Zotia. Ferryn shared miles of border with Eldridge to the north, Yarrose to the west, and her mother's kingdom, Cidora, to the south, but Zotia was the largest and southernmost kingdom on the continent. Only a sliver of Ferryn's border touched the vast kingdom. It was mostly desert, but a few cities still flourished in the heat. Their king had spent years building a vast army and naval fleet, designed to protect his kingdom and raise a generation of warriors. Kinna couldn't imagine her kind, soft spoken sister with one of the warrior princes. "Have you even met Prince Karyk?"

"No, his family sent advisors to propose the marriage to Father. However, he will be attending the summer solstice celebration so I assume I will meet him then."

"What about Lennon?"

"The Astford's were at last year's winter solstice. I spoke with him briefly, but he was shy, so the conversation didn't last very long."

Kinna's fingers tore through her hair, raining jeweled pins on the ground. The initial shock was beginning to wear off and be replaced with anger. "Gods, this is insane, Evie. There has to be a way to get you more time."

"No there isn't. I will make my decision before the year's end."

Kinna hesitated. "Is... that what you want?"

"Does that matter?" Evelyn asked. "I'm the heir. I'll have to get married and I'm years older than Mother was when she married Father."

"Of course, what you want should matter. Mother and Father would not force you to marry."

"They won't have to," Evelyn breathed. She had walked underneath the maple to run her hands over the smooth, papery white bark. "I will make my choice by the solstice."

Kinna was struck by the resignation in her sister's voice. Despite her feelings, she had already decided her fate, to choose her kingdom and her duty above all else, including her own happiness. A strange mix of admiration and pity swirled in her chest. The desire to comfort her sister took hold and Kinna found herself joining her at the base of the maple tree, weaving her arm around Evelyn's waist.

Despite being the taller of the two, she bent her head down to rest on her sister's shoulder. The two stood in the silent garden, comforted not by words but by each other's presence, until the cool night air forced them back inside.

CHAPTER SEVEN

Kinna had been unusually quiet the next morning, earning herself a few odd glances from Ellio as they finished their morning run. It had been her turn to set pace and she had spent almost an hour just keeping them at a light jog before they silently returned to the castle. She knew she was being conspicuous about her feelings when Maude took a seat beside her on the worn kitchen bench to ask her what had her head in such a tailspin.

Kinna had lied and blamed her monthly cycle for her mood and lack of appetite, knowing it would prevent Ellio from asking any further questions. Maude had seemed satisfied with her answer but had made her drink a steaming cup of peppermint tea before allowing her to leave the kitchens.

The training room was partially full, a dozen guards lingering at each station to be judged. General Resten had decided to open an additional captain position who would stay at the castle while the general and his companies traveled north. The guards in the training room were all competing for the position and currently going through a skills evaluation. Instead of staying to watch or practicing with her bow, Kinna decided to return to her rooms.

The book she'd been reading the day before still

laid on her unmade bed. Snatching it from atop the comforter she headed onto her balcony and dragged one of the cushioned wooden chairs past the potted plants and over to the edge of the metal railing. Sitting down, she slipped her legs through the gaps of the railing, letting her legs dangle, and opened her book, hoping she could get lost in another world for a few hours and stop thinking about her sister's disappointed face or the trouble stirring in the north that Evelyn was still ignorant to.

Her plan worked for a few hours until Kerin dragged her inside for dinner, insisting she eat since Maude had told her that apparently Kinna had skipped breakfast.

She blushed as Kerin caught her in a lie. "I knew it would stop Ellio from asking questions," she explained.

Kerin sighed. "Yes, it does normally render a man speechless. I will never understand how they can charge into battle with no hesitation, but a cycle will have them blushing and stuttering in the opposite direction."

Kinna chuckled as she began devouring her food, her empty stomach catching up to her. They ate in silence, Kerin sensing not to push her to explain what was bothering her or why she was hiding it from Maude or Ellio. Once they were finished, Kerin quickly stacked up their plates and disappeared into the hallway as she called out a goodnight.

Without any distractions, Kinna's thoughts turned back to her sister and before she could stop herself, she was closing her door behind her. She turned to Eron and Macklin, who were once again stationed in her hallway. "I'm going to see Evelyn," she said, hoping to sound casual.

They nodded as she headed for her sister's rooms, her footsteps echoing through the empty hallway. Evelyn's room was closer to the center of the castle situated at the beginning of the Royal hallway where parents' suite was. Kinna had at one time had the room right across from her sister but moved to a smaller room further away two years ago. Part of the reason had been to have more privacy, so her family could not track her comings and goings so easily, but she had also been drawn to the small balcony she now had. It was overflowing with so many plants that she had begged the gardeners to drag up to her room that it could now only accommodate two chairs. Despite the tight quarters, it was an escape she often sought in the summer months to avoid the crowds in the gardens.

She glanced out the windows as she walked, the sun had already gone down, just leaving the faintest purple hue on the horizon before it bled into the inky black of the night sky. The days were getting longer as summer approached and, despite the heat that would soon descend on the capital, she loved the long days of summer.

Kinna rounded the corner and was immediately greeted by two guards standing on either side of the hallway entrance who nodded to her as she passed them. Two more guards were stationed opposite Evelyn's room and four surrounded the entrance at the end of the hallway to her parent's room. She definitely didn't miss having so many guards always stationed outside her room. She reached Evelyn's door and knocked, waiting for her soft voice to answer before going inside.

"Yes," she called out.

Evelyn was seated at her desk, neat stacks of paper sitting on either side of her and writing quickly, not yet having looked up to see who she had admitted into her rooms. She finally finished writing and startled slightly when she saw Kinna smirking at her and standing in front of her door.

Slowly she scooted her chair back and stood, as if she was trying not to scare a wild animal. "Kinna," she said, in a questioning tone. "Is everything okay?"

"Of course," Kinna replied. "Can a girl not come visit her sister without something being wrong?"

"Of course you can," she agreed, still hesitant. "Would you like to sit? I can have Suzannah bring us some tea."

Kinna nodded and headed to the seating area across the room in front of the fireplace. Unlike Kinna's rooms, Evelyn had a formal sitting room and dining room that was separate from her bedroom and attached bathing room. Her rooms were decorated in soft pastels that felt purely feminine. Kinna chose a green velvet chair with golden claw feet that was situated closest to the fire. Evelyn joined her, sitting beside her in the matching chair.

Suzannah appeared with near silent steps and sat a lavender porcelain tea set on the small table between them. Unlike Kerin, Suzannah was much younger, only a few years older than Evelyn, with a soft, melodic voice and a kind face framed by copper colored hair. She tried to keep it pulled back, as did many of the lady's maids, but her silken hairs would slip out of her simple knot by the end of the day and float around her face. She watched her tuck strands behind both ears as she approached. Kinna gave her parents a mental compliment on choosing their lady's maids. Suzannah was a perfect companion for her sister.

She poured them both a cup and then added extra sugar to Kinna's tea, just as she preferred it. "Thank you." She smiled at her. "You always remember that."

"You are most welcome, Your Highness." She smiled at the compliment and turned to Evelyn. "Will you need anything else?"

"No, but thank you," she said, touching her arm softly.

Suzannah gave a short curtsy before leaving them. "I forget how much I like her," Kinna whispered, mostly to herself.

Evelyn smiled in the direction that Suzannah had left. "Yes," she agreed. "I love her so. I would be lost without her."

Kinna took a drink of her tea, feeling its warmth slide down her throat and settle into her chest. Evelyn sat stirring hers, staring intently at Kinna. "Please tell me why you have come," she asked. "I know you have a reason, and my imagination is running wild right now."

Kinna straightened in her seat. "Before I say anything, you must *promise* me that you will not share this with anyone," she whispered seriously.

Evelyn blanched. "I promise," she murmured.

"Father and General Resten did not tell us the whole truth about the unrest in Edgewood. It is much more serious than they let us believe." Evelyn's eyes widened but she did not interrupt. "Bodies have been found, burnt, out in the Glenwood, not in homes from Edgewood and the other villages," Kinna continued. "Each one has been found closer to the capital."

"Why?"

"I'm not sure. Ellio thinks that someone, maybe a new rebel sect, is trying to send a message."

"Is that why General Resten is travelling to them? So, they cannot get any closer to the capital?"

"I think so."

Evelyn leans back into her seat, closing her eyes and forgoing her usually perfect posture. It's obvious that she was frightened and Kinna wondered if she had made the right decision to tell her sister. "Are you okay?" Kinna asks quietly.

"Yes," she whispered; her eyes still closed. They sit in silence for a long minute before Evelyn opens her eyes. "Why did you decide to tell me?"

"I thought you should have the truth. You are going to be queen someday and if anyone deserves to know what is happening in Ferryn it is you."

Evelyn gives her a soft smile. "Thank you for telling me," she said. "I am not sure what I can do with this information, but you are right, I am glad to truly know what is happening, not just the watered-down version Father told us."

Kinna nodded in agreement. "I better get back to my room before Eron or Macklin come looking for me."

Before she could take a step towards the door, Evelyn grabbed her with surprising strength and pulled her into a tight hug. "Please don't do anything reckless, Kinna," she whispered into her hair.

Pulling away from her sister, Kinna gave her a reassuring smile. "I wouldn't dream of it, Evie," she replied, using the nickname she called her sister as children.

Her sister gave her a disbelieving smile and kissed her forehead. "Goodnight, Kinna," she said.

"Goodnight," she replied, a bit surprised by her sister's affection but pleased at the new direction their relationship had gone.

Instead of returning to her rooms as she had told her sister, Kinna walked quietly through the castle. Leaving her body on autopilot, she let her feet take her wherever they wanted as she thought through her plan for the next day. If she was going to make it out of the castle undetected, she needed to ensure that every detail was perfect. She made a mental list of things she needed to gather tomorrow and the best location for her to stow away inside one of the wagons.

She had just completed a full lap of the castle's exterior hallways when hands pulled her into a small alcove, and she grinned. A small bench sat against a window facing the garden and the lantern that hung beside it had been extinguished, remnants of smoke still hanging in the air. The hands slid around her waist and a familiar voice huffed a laugh. "I thought we had trained you better than this, Princess," Gavin whispered close to her ear. "It was far too easy to capture you."

Kinna's grin spread wider at the challenge in his words. She had known he was following her from the moment she left her sister's room, allowing him to tail her as she meandered around the castle had been a part of her game. Letting him hunt her allowed the excitement to build further and offered her a welcome distraction from her scheming.

Before Gavin could make another taunt, she had pulled a small blade from where she'd tucked in against the small of her back and spun around him, arms locking around his neck with her knife placed gently against it.

His gasp faded into a quiet laugh as she nipped his ear. "You were saying something about this being easy?" she teased, still not releasing him.

"I yield, Princess," he amended, hands raised.

She slowly lowered her blade watching his movements. Once the knife was clear of his neck, he turned on her, one hand slipping around her waist and the other moving to find the wall behind her. "I was disappointed when you didn't show up last night," he drawled, running his nose up the side of her neck, planting a single kiss just below her ear.

"I was busy," she breathed.

"And you're not now?" he asked.

A clear invitation and one she would accept. "I have some time."

That was all it took. Gavin tightened his grip around her waist, using his other to hoist her up to meet his face while she wrapped her legs around his waist. Their lips met and he pressed her against the wall, the stone cold against the small strip of exposed skin on her back. Her fingers slid up the back of his head, feeling the stubble of his short, military style cut and down his jaw. Pressed against him she could feel exactly why he'd sought her out, especially as his hands moved up the back of her shirt and across her stomach, a not-so-subtle reminder of where he was headed.

She didn't linger with him as she sometimes did, her lips swollen from his stubble and her body spent from the last hour. He'd offered to walk her back to her room, but she didn't need the questions it would bring from Eron and Macklin.

She didn't know why but her thoughts drifted to Ellio as she walked. He didn't know about her trysts with Gavin or if he did, he never spoke of it. It was one of the only secrets she kept from him. Gavin was always discreet, and she doubted he would ever jeopardize his career by telling anyone, but she could imagine Ellio telling her to be careful instead of teasing her, knowing what kind of trouble they both could be in if they were caught.

While she liked Gavin, she certainly didn't love him. It was almost a pity; he should be exactly the kind of person with whom Kinna could fall in love. All warm smiles and rugged handsomeness, lighthearted and fun, he should be exactly the kind of man Kinna could love, but she didn't. The voice in the back of her mind whispered that deep down she knew why.

CHAPTER EIGHT

Kinna woke before the sun despite her exhaustion. She had not been able to quiet her mind since she had woken in the middle of the night, her plans to leave the castle and her sister's plea for her safety had her thoughts bouncing from one topic to the next. She needed to burn some nervous energy off or she would start to draw too much attention to herself.

Dressing quickly, she headed down to the beach for a run while the rest of the castle was still asleep. A fine mist hung in the morning air as she dropped off the last stair and into the sand and she knew her hair would be uncontrollable after only a few minutes outside. The sun still hadn't risen but faint light was beginning to break over the horizon.

She walked to the water's edge and hissed when a freezing wave washed over her feet. Starting at a jog, she slowly picked up her pace, until she could only hear her feet slapping against the wet sand and her breath coming faster with each step. She charged ahead, driving out all thought except the feel of her burning muscles and ran towards the rising sun.

She slowed her pace as she saw the castle come back into view, the sun now fully risen and reflecting a brilliant orange off every window. A shadow standing on the stairs let out a long, clear whistle at her approach, catching her attention. *Ellio.* She would know that sound from anywhere, not to mention recognize his silhouette and stance almost immediately. She sped back up to meet him.

"You shouldn't be out here alone this early," he scolded.

"Good morning, Ellio," she chirped brightly, ignoring his disapproving stare. "How did you sleep?"

He ignored her and met her on the sand, squaring his shoulders in front of her, forcing her to look up at him like a petulant child. "You know there is an unidentified threat, one that I told you about against orders so you wouldn't try to do anything stupid," he continued. "Being out here alone puts you at extreme risk. Who would be able to help you if you were attacked miles down the beach? I cannot believe you would be this reckless."

"No one is going to attack me this close to the castle."

"They are burning people, Kinna," he argued, grabbing her arm firmly. "Do not come out here alone again. Send for me if you want to go for a run."

Anger flared through her, hot and quick, and she ripped her arm away from him with more force than necessary. "You do not give me orders Ellio Resten," she seethed. "Do not grab me again."

Hurt flashed across his face before a steely resolve set in. "If you will not take your safety seriously, I will not hesitate to go to the king," he threatened.

She was horrified. Who was this controlling man that had replaced her best friend? Why was he reacting this way? Did he learn something more that was causing him to panic?

It didn't matter, she decided, she just had to placate him long enough for her to sneak away with the general and his company. "Fine," she snapped. "I will bring a guard with me the next time I come to the beach, either Gavin or Macklin."

His jaw twitched at the names as if he'd known where she'd been last night. As if she chose his name purposefully to wound him. Well, maybe she had. Gavin certainly wouldn't be responding this way over a simple run on the beach.

"I just want you safe, Kinna," he whispered and motioned to the stairs. A clear dismissal that this discussion was over. His eyes were downcast, but Kinna saw the hurt gleaming in them.

She took the stairs quickly, leaving him behind to catch up to her. She knew she had hurt him with her decision to bring a guard instead of him, but she didn't care. She was still furious that he had reprimanded her as if she had committed some grievous sin. He was supposed to be her friend and yet he was ready to sell her out to her father the second she disagreed with him.

Kinna stormed through the castle, barely noticing that Ellio was no longer following behind her, and made her way back to her room. "I am not to be disturbed," she snapped at the guards stationed outside her door.

Ten minutes later she was chin deep in a hot bath, watching her hair slowly float around her. She pulled one arm out of the water, goosebumps rising as her skin met the cool bathroom air and reached for her comb. Starting from the bottom, she slowly began brushing out the knots that her run on the beach had created. It was a soothing ritual that had always calmed her. She leaned back, resting her head on the edge of the tub and closed her eyes as she continued the slow rhythm.

———

The water had turned ice cold by the time she was woken by the sound of her own teeth chattering. After a sleepless night it wasn't surprising that she had fallen asleep in the warm bath, but the lost time still annoyed her. She still had things to do and now she was behind. Her stomach growled in protest as she began dressing and reminded her that she hadn't eaten that morning. She sighed as she slipped on a shirt that would cover the purple bruising on her left arm and ran some oil through her damp curls. At least going to the kitchens would give her an opportunity to sneak some extra food for her pack. She slung a small bag over her shoulder and left.

The kitchens were in full swing preparing lunch, and she could already feel the heat from the ovens that never seemed to turn off as she descended the stairs. Thankfully Kinna was able to walk through without being noticed and was able to tuck a loaf of bread, a block of cheese and a few apples in her bag when Maude rounded the corner, noticing her.

"You didn't come for breakfast," she said instead of a greeting.

"I went back to sleep after my run this morning," she explained quickly.

Maude eyed her suspiciously. "Ellio was here this morning looking rather pathetic," she pressed. "Didn't even finish the pastries I made."

Kinna was quiet, not quite able to meet her eyes. There was no way she was going to explain their fight to Maude. Thankfully someone yelled for Maude across the room, and she was unable to continue the interrogation. She huffed and headed towards the voice but then stopped and turned to look at Kinna. "I don't know what you two are fighting about," she whispered, her voice softer than she had ever heard it. "But forgive him, he cares for you a great deal."

Before Kinna could say another word, Maude disappeared through the kitchen and left her standing alone, more confused than ever. She knew Ellio cared about her; they had been best friends since childhood. Maude couldn't be insinuating that he felt something more for her. He certainly hadn't made any indication that he saw her as anything but a friend when they had been in the gardens. She slipped out the back door of the kitchen and headed for the courtyard, caught up in the strange drama that had filled the past few days.

Unlike the kitchens, the courtyard was mercifully empty which meant that Kinna would be able to prepare herself a spot in a wagon and stash her supply bag without being spotted. There were five wagons in total that had been lined up in an arrow formation pointing towards the outer wall of the castle and the large metal gate that stood firmly closed in front of her.

Her stomach fluttered at the thought of passing through that gate and into the world.

It had been months since she had last left the castle and even then, it had only been for a short parade through Strafford and to the temple to attend the Winter Solstice. She hadn't even been allowed outside the carriage or stop to buy a treat from one of the dozens of street vendors.

She strategized in her head but eventually chose the second wagon on the left to hide her small bag and ultimately herself. She knew that Ellio and each of the general's two captains would be placed in charge of a wagon, leaving a lower ranking guard in to lead the final two wagons. It would be her best chance at staying hidden as final checks were made and the company departed. General Resten had decided they would leave at sunset tomorrow, hoping to use the darkness of the crescent moon to his advantage.

By this evening, most of the city dwellers will have closed their stores and left the market area in favor of their homes, allowing him to lead the company through the city with fewer prying eyes. The last thing he needed was a panic to start and rumors to spread about capital soldiers being on the move. She gave the wagon door one last push to ensure it was closed before she began weaving her way back towards the castle.

———

The sun had begun to set as Kinna snuck through the castle, dodging servants as she went by hiding in the shadowed corners of the hallways. Luckily some of the lanterns hadn't been lit yet which provided some additional cover. She pulled the hood of her cloak down as she approached her sister's room, barely nodding to the guards as she passed. Her knuckles rapped against the door before it opened a crack and Suzannah's face appeared. Kinna almost didn't recognize her. Suzannah's unbound hair shone from the firelight behind her, creating a soft gold halo around her crown. Surprised flashed across her face, deepening her flushed cheeks, and she quickly pulled the door open further, dropping into a quick curtsy. "My apologies, Your Highness," she breathed, her body still blocking the gap of the door. "I was not expecting you."

Kinna smiled at her. "No need to apologize," she said. "I just had something to give Evelyn."

"She is already in bed," she responded, cracking open the door further and ushering her inside. "I will get her."

Kinna stood in the warm sitting room and edged closer to the fire, savoring its warmth. Despite her excitement about leaving the castle, she knew it would be weeks before she would enjoy these kinds of luxuries. Sleeping on the hard ground in tents wherever the company camped for the night would be a definite change of pace and despite the days growing warmer during the spring, the nights could feel as though winter had returned. She shook the thought out of her head, not wanting to ruin her excitement and listened to the muffled sounds of Evelyn and Suzannah in the other room between the pops of the fire.

Evelyn stood in the door of the sitting room wearing a pale blue silk robe wrapped tightly around a matching nightgown. She looked at her sister with confusion edged with a little alarm. "Two visits in one week," she mused. "You must be planning something really big."

Kinna flinched hoping that she hadn't been that conspicuous these last few days. "Something like that." She smirked, trying to muster her usual swagger.

"Suzannah said you had something to give me," she prompted.

Kinna played with the ring on her finger. "Yes," she said, slipping her ring off. "I need you to hold on to this for me." It was too valuable for Kinna to risk taking it with her and she wouldn't leave it in her room for someone to pilfer. Still, she hated the thought of leaving it behind and could already feel the weight of its absence on her finger, as if she was missing a part of her hand.

Evelyn took the ring from her, holding it in her cupped palm. "You never are without this," she said. They stared at each other for a long moment, Kinna not knowing how to say good-bye or if she even should. "Just be safe out there Kinna," Evelyn said, breaking the tense silence.

"I will." She nodded, leaving Evelyn standing in front of the fire.

She was almost out the door when her sister's voice stopped her. "You know I love you," she said, her voice almost a whisper.

She looked back at her sister, still standing with the ring clutched in her small fist, looking younger than her twenty-one years. "I love you, too." She smiled.

CHAPTER NINE

Kinna slept through her morning run, unwilling to face Ellio after their fight yesterday and even more unsure of what to say when she did see him. Still, she knew she should try to smooth things over between them before they left tonight. They rarely ever argued and Kinna knew she would need Ellio's help calming General Resten down once they discovered her as a stow away and the realization of her scheme set in. She would find him before dinner, she decided, and give herself the day to find the right way to apologize.

It was nearly lunch before she emerged from her rooms, having taken an extra long bath, knowing it would possibly be weeks before she had the luxury to do so. Her braided hair was still damp as she paced around her room, packing any last minute item she could think of in her pack, including her hair oil and comb. All the food she had snagged was already loaded onto the wagon with some of her other supplies, but all her personal belongings would stay in the pack and firmly on her body. One of the general's first rules of survival training was to keep everything vital attached to you.

Eventually she wandered down into the kitchens for a late lunch, stacking some cold meats onto a thick slice of fresh bread. Maude was moving through the kitchens at a frenzied pace but still managed to drop a fresh scone down beside her as she darted from place to place. She sighed as she bit into the orange scone, the tangy citrus and sweet icing drizzle was a perfect combination. Gods, she was truly going to miss Maude's cooking when they started passing out rations on the road.

As she left, she lifted a few extra pieces of bread and fruit for her bag before heading to the courtyard. She slowed her pace and walked casually out into the sunshine, hoping to look carefree while enjoying the warm spring weather. Inwardly, Kinna was taking in every detail of the waiting wagons and the two guards that were adding last minute crates into the largest one. She heard the bells of the capital's temple in the distance chime loudly, ringing three times to indicate the time of day.

As she glanced towards the city, an explosion shook the ground beneath her feet, knocking her down. She landed hard on the rough stones, head spinning from the impact and small stones pelting her back and legs. Her ears only let through muffled sounds as tried to clear the ringing from them. Her joints ached as she tried to push herself up and her vision swam.

What the hell had just happened?

She glimpsed the wagons around her through a cloud of dust where moments before guards had been standing. Some now had holes punched through them from varying sizes of debris and the two guards had disappeared, one of them leaving a trail of blood splattered against the dirt. Stones of varying sizes littered the ground, and she could smell something burning. Muffled shouting could be heard all around her and she turned to see where it was coming from. The castle stood in front of her, black smoke billowing out of the eastern wing that faced the ocean, that housed the Royal Family. It had been blown open from the inside, the exterior wall was missing, replaced with flames that were starting to peek over the edges of the exposed stone. Guards were rushing towards the castle, shouting for others to gather water to put the fire out and look for a safe entrance inside.

Reacting quickly, she pushed herself into a standing position and half jogged to the entrance that was now covered by crumbling bits of the castle. Her knees had taken most of the impact of her fall and she cringed as she pushed forward. She began hauling stone away, tossing it behind her as she fought to find a way inside. In minutes her fingers were cut open and bleeding, the jagged edges slicing through her flesh as easily as a knife through soft butter. She cursed colorfully at the shallow cuts that dotted her hands and the non-existent progress she had made. A feeling of helplessness washed over her, threatening to drown her, as she tried and failed to find the door beneath the debris.

Frustrated, she sank to the ground, her knees buckling under the weight of her body. Her eyes filled with tears as she silently stared up at the burning wreckage of the castle, her home. The home she had been so eager to leave. She was going to be sick. She tossed her braid over her shoulder just seconds before vomiting on the ground in front of her. She could feel it soaking through the knees of her leggings, but she couldn't bring herself to be embarrassed.

A harsh reality crashed into her. She had to get up and go inside. Her family was inside. *Ellio* was inside. She would tear through every piece of rubble until she found them. They had to be inside still, alive and waiting for help. She wiped the tears still flowing freely down her face, the salt water mixing with the blood from her fingertips. As she tried to stand, her stomach roiled but she clenched her teeth tightly, willing her stomach to settle, and got to her feet.

She held the layout of the castle in her mind, navigating every door and hallway, planning the best route inside that she could. General Resten had always taught her to be aware of her surroundings and prepare at least one other entrance or exit into a space. She couldn't afford to forget the lessons he had spent years instilling in her, not if she was going to be of any help to those inside. There was an entrance to the western wing that faced the stables. If it had been spared in the explosion, she could enter the castle through there and make her way through the south end towards her family's rooms. Her body was moving sluggishly as she fought to push past people and around debris, barely feeling anything as adrenaline began pumping through her blood.

She rounded a corner and immediately halted, throwing herself against the wall behind her. Four men stood in a huddle and dressed in plain black uniforms bearing no sigil. They didn't work in the castle and no guard would be on the grounds out of uniform. Another bolt of panic went through her chest. *The Rising.* Could they be responsible for the explosion? If so, the general's information had been wrong, they weren't coming to the capital, they were already here.

It was a small miracle they hadn't seen or heard her approach, so she leaned as far towards them as she dared to try to hear what they were saying. "You two go around to the supply wagons. Sift through all of it," One man instructed the group. He was plain looking and as easily forgettable as the rest of the men. "The younger princess wasn't in the castle, so she has to be on the grounds somewhere. He wants her alive."

Fear coiled in her stomach at those last four words. *He wants her alive.* These men were hunting her. She was desperate to get inside the castle, but she knew she had to run, fast and further away from the castle before they spotted her. Gods only knew what they would do if they found her. She could not be captured. It didn't matter who these men were, but it was clear they were looking for her and she knew damn well it was not to protect her.

She edged backwards before they could break out of their huddle, focusing on keeping her steps light and not making any noise. They were going to the courtyard so she would need to stay far away from there to avoid being seen. Her heart was pounding in her ears as she tried to think where to go. The stables, she decided. She didn't have time to mount a horse and she couldn't afford the conspicuousness, but she could sneak out through the small side entrance. It was only used by a few, perhaps if she was lucky, the men didn't even realize there was another way out of the castle grounds.

Once she had the stables in her sights she quickly ran inside. The horses stamped and neighed at her arrival, but she didn't have time to quiet them. Kinna crept into an empty stall and peered out the small window to make sure she hadn't been followed. The entrance was just a few hundred feet away and empty, most of the guards had likely rushed to the castle after the explosion. Kinna didn't have any time to waste, she pressed herself against the stable door and tried to slow her breath, listening for footsteps. She took one last glance and sprinted for the small gatehouse.

As soon as she was through the threshold, she slammed the door behind her, locking it into place. The room was empty, the guards stationed here had dropped everything, even leaving their food on the table. Kinna ran to the small closet that was used as a makeshift armory beside the cots. She opened the door and searched through the few items, stuffing a knife in her bag and another one in her boot. Scanning the room for anything else she could take and wishing a bow had been left behind. Kinna headed for the door that led out of the gatehouse and towards the capital.

She paused, hand on the cool metal handle that would lead her away from the castle. How many times had she wished she could leave? Well, she'd gotten her wish; she was leaving now, and she didn't know when she would get to come back. Kinna took a deep breath through her nose, forcing back the tears that were threatening to spill over again, and opened the door. She peered out, quickly checking her surroundings and then was running again.

She didn't stop until she was well within the tree line. She felt the temperature drop as she passed under the dense canopy, pausing only once to look behind her. The site of the burning castle was another blow, making it hard for her to breathe, but that wasn't the only thing that she saw. The grief turned to pure panic when she saw the man dressed in all black standing on the edge of the wall, having just watched her escape into the forest. She could swear he could still see her, partially hidden behind the trunk of an old oak tree. After a moment he disappeared down the other side of the wall, back towards the castle. He was going to find the others and they would be on her trail in minutes. She needed to get into the capital and if she was lucky maybe she could lose the men tailing her in the busy city.

———— ·

Strafford, the capital city of Ferryn, was a port city. The ocean curving alongside its edge held merchant ships, a small naval fleet and a fish market that fed many of the residents. The city had been built around the crescent beach that formed along the shoreline. It had also given the kingdom it's sigil, since the city had been built in a crescent shape around the water. Closest to the castle was the upper-class district, affectionately named the Rose Garden, where large two-story brick homes were built in long rows of immaculate greenery. Here stood the best restaurants, bakeries and tailors in the city, all ready to welcome Strafford's richest residents. Kerin often made reservations at a restaurant or tearoom in the Rose Garden to try to polish Kinna's manners. She could still remember last fall when she'd been forced to wear a beautiful but terribly itchy pink dress for their three-hour trip. Sometimes Kinna thought that Kerin only planned these little outings to force her into one of the dresses she'd commissioned. Kerin loved dressing her up like a doll and rarely got to do it unless they would be going into the capital.

The naval fleet was docked on this stretch of water, meant to protect the castle and much of the nobility that lived close to it. Kinna had ridden through the Rose Garden many times, though mainly tucked away inside a carriage. The Royal Family would ride through the city on their way to the temple during the Summer and Winter Solstice to mark the beginning of the celebrations. Kinna had spent the majority of the last Winter Solstice parade with as much of her body outside the window that she could manage while Evelyn begged her to get back inside before their mother saw her.

The middle-class district, Midtown as residents called it, was the largest, situated beyond the Rose District in the middle of the city. It shared a border with the marketplace where vendors fought over space to set up their carts and sell their goods. Midtown was built on a grid, but it was easy to get lost in the endless alleys that drew lines between buildings. The marketplace sat on the eastern edge and was always loud, crowded and smelling of fish thanks to its proximity to the docks. Beyond the market, edging towards the farmland and the Glenwood that surrounded the city, was the lower-class district, often called the Dirt District, where most residents lived in small, converted apartments.

Kinna had run through the Glenwood on a small, dirt road often used for deliveries to the castle and towards the main gate that led into the city. A long line of grey stone snaked around the edge of the capital, with two gates serving as access points. The larger of the two entered Midtown while the smaller entered the Dirt District. They normally would be staffed by a handful of guards at the gatehouse and a few others littered on either side of the wall, bows strapped across their backs and eyes focused on the forest ahead of them. However, there were only two still stationed here. She eventually realized it was because the remaining guards had rushed to the castle in the wake of the attack. She wondered how long they would look for her when her body was not discovered alongside her family. Her chest tightened but she bit her tongue, focusing on just that physical pain to stop the tears from starting again. She needed to keep moving or she would not survive the men hunting her.

She pulled her hood up and tucked her bag under her cloak before emerging from the woods onto the dirt road. A rickety wagon bumped along ahead of her guided by a pair of horses and a balding man. A short-haired brown dog trailed behind it and she quickened her pace so that she would fall in line behind it. A young woman traveling alone would perhaps cause the guards to look too long in her direction, but a woman walking with her dog behind a wagon would be much less concerning. She just needed to get within the walls and disappear in the bustling city.

The wagon stopped behind two other groups waiting to be admitted into the city. The dog noticed her behind them as they moved forward and paused to watch her. Kinna quickly dropped her hood and fished a piece of cheese from her bag and offered it to him. He accepted it happily, letting her scratch his ears before moving on. The wagon was waved through next and Kinna followed behind it, the driver still unaware that she was tailing him. She held her breath as she passed beneath the arched gate, not daring to meet the eyes of either guard until she was safely within the city walls.

Midtown was full of people, but the unusual noises of the bustling city had been replaced with an eerie quiet. It seemed that everyone had stopped their normal routines to come outside and stare up at the burning castle. Everyone had heard the blast and could see the left side of the castle where a hole gaped that had been blown apart, black smoke still billowing out.

People stood on the streets in small groups, whispering to each other about what had happened while others were beginning to close their windows and doors, preparing for a threat that had yet to present itself.

Kinna tried not to listen to the snippets of conversations as she passed but she couldn't stop hearing the same words repeated by each group she passed.

Do you think they are still alive?

I wonder who survived?

I can't imagine anyone walking away from that alive.

It was shredding the last bit of control she had over herself. She turned down an ally still not sure where she was even going but desperately needing to get away from those whispers.

The alley was narrow and dirty, trash lining both sides of the ground. Kinna needed to stop and formulate a plan, she couldn't just keep wandering aimlessly. She leaned against the wall, wishing she could slink down and sit for a moment but not trusting what she might find beneath her. Weariness was beginning to settle into her bones and the events of the past few hours weighed on her. She wanted to sleep and maybe not wake up for the next few days.

Ugh, sleep.

She needed to find a place to sleep for the night. Tomorrow she could decide what to do next and how to return to the castle without leading her tail right back there. Perhaps Ellio would find her before then and bring her home. Like a sixth sense, he always knew where to find her and when he did, she would get down on her knees and apologize. She would apologize for every hurtful thing she had said because she never wanted to be the reason for that wounded look in his eyes again.

CHAPTER TEN

Kinna stayed in Midtown, not wanting to risk being recognized if she entered the Rose Garden. She'd been to enough ladies' luncheons with Kerin, back when she had still tried to turn her into a proper lady, that someone may recognize her. Midtown was safer, a young woman on her own would draw far less attention. She walked through the capital, staying close to the shadows and using alleys whenever she could until she reached the market. Here it was easy to blend into the crowd and that was exactly what she needed. There were a few inns that dotted the perimeter of the market, mostly used by the merchants that sailed into port. She picked the most average looking one, *The Sick Fish Inn*, not truly knowing much about any of them and started weaving her way through the crowd towards it.

The exterior of the building had been painted red but years of standing by the salty spray of the sea had faded the color and rusted the small metal sign that swung over the door. Kinna took a quick breath, hand hesitating on the iron fish shaped handle and then entered. The bottom floor was a wide-open space with a bar running along the back wall and tables crowding the space closest to the fireplace. Keeping her head down and hand firmly on her bag she walked to the woman standing at the bar. Her mousy brown hair was pulled up in a loose bun with small pieces falling out around her neck. She watched her as she approached, wiping her hands on the stained apron tied tightly around her hips and grey dress.

"What can I do for you?" the woman asked.

"I need a room, just for tonight," she answered.

The woman eyed her warily, likely wondering about her age and why she was alone, but she couldn't pass up the money. "Second door on your left. Meals and laundry?" she asked.

"Just meals."

She nodded and turned to walk to the other end of the bar, pulling a small brass key from somewhere underneath. She slid the key across the bar top. "Payment is due upfront."

Kinna fished a gold piece out of her bag. She knew it was more than what one room would cost but she had a favor to ask. She placed the gold piece down next to the key and saw the woman's eyebrow raise a tiny bit. "I also have a small favor to ask," Kinna explained. "If you were to see a man dressed in a black uniform, please do let me know rather quickly."

The woman slid the gold piece towards her with one finger. "On the outs with your lover, are you?" she mused.

"Something like that," she huffed. "Can I count on your discretion?"

"For this?" she flashed the gold piece in her hand and grinned. "I'll bring your meals to your room *and* let you know if your lover makes an appearance."

Kinna didn't return the woman's smile but nodded and took the key stamped with the number *2* on it. She glanced around the room as she walked towards the stairs, no one noticed her as she went. Once up the stairs she found her room easily, grateful that no one was in the hallway to see which room she went into. The lock clicked into place behind her, and she turned to survey the room. It was small but clean, the bed smelled of fresh laundry which she was immensely thankful for. It had a small fireplace with extra logs laid to the side, a small dresser with a mirror and a window that faced the alley behind the inn. She would have rather been able to watch those that entered through the front door, but she couldn't really complain, at least she had a window.

She looked herself over in the mirror, noticing the bump in her hairline from being thrown to the ground. Her face was unharmed but as she peeled out of her clothes, she could see a patchwork of cuts and bruises beginning to form on her arms and legs. Thankfully most were shallow and wouldn't require her to attempt makeshift stitches. She grabbed a towel and dipped it into the pitcher of water and began cleaning the cuts as best she could, wincing as the soap made contact with the cuts on her fingers. Exhausted she laid down on the bed in her undergarments, planning to just rest her eyes for a few minutes.

She woke in the dark to a sharp knock at her door. Outside her window the sun had set, leaving a pink and purple sky behind. Kinna reached for her clothes in the dark, quickly pulling on her tunic and leggings before answering the door. An older woman stood on the other side with a tray in her hand. She walked past her without an invitation to come inside and sat it down on the dresser since there wasn't a proper table. Glancing around the dark room, she let out a little huff and began lighting the few candles and closing the curtains before turning silently and leaving. Kinna thought her silence was a bit rude, but she guessed it was better than a busybody who wanted to stay to ask questions or make idle conversation.

She immediately forgot about the old woman when the smell of food hit her. Pulling the tray on the bed she picked up the small loaf of bread, tearing into it as if someone were going to take it from her. The stew that came with it was steaming and smelled divine. She dunked the spoon into it, letting out a small yelp when the hot liquid burned her tongue. It was a good thing that the barkeep had agreed to bring her food to her rooms, if anyone saw the way she was eating they would have thought she was a savage, but she didn't care. She was starving and the food was delicious. Too soon the food was gone. Her stomach was warm and full and already sleep was tugging at her. She threw another log on the dying fire and pulled the comforter back and climbed in bed before dropping back into unconsciousness.

She lay dreaming of dark smoke that choked the air from her lungs and heavy stones pressing down on her, pinning her to the ground. Immobilized she lay unable to move on the ground while listening to people crying out all around her. Ellio's voice grew louder, his pleas for help were desperate and she couldn't move, couldn't get to him. Every time she opened her mouth to call out to him, smoke poured down her throat, choking her until she was gasping for air. She was powerless and every minute that passed brought another voice of someone she loved crying out for help.

The ground beneath her began to shake and she prepared for another blast to shake her. *No.* Someone was shaking *her*, pulling her from her nightmare and back to reality. She could make out a figure standing over her, the barkeep, whispering in a low voice to her. Groggily she began to sit up in bed, trying to re-orient herself with her surroundings and focus on the woman's words.

"Miss?" the barkeep took a step back, satisfied that she was awake enough to listen to her. "The man you mentioned before, he is here, and he is not alone."

Shit. Kinna was wide awake now. She moved so quickly from the bed that she startled the barkeep, rushing to shove all her belongings back into her bag. "Where?" she hissed.

"Downstairs," the barkeep answered. "They are just sitting at a table."

"How many?"

"Four."

Shit. All of them. She could take on one, maybe two but four was unlikely. Her heart was pounding in her ears while she tried to think. It was dark outside and raining hard, a storm had rolled in while she slept. It would give her enough cover to escape unnoticed if she was lucky. The group likely had no idea that she knew they were here; they were either planning to wait her out or come to her, but she wasn't going to wait around long enough to find out. She pulled a dagger from her bag on her back and strapped it to her thigh. She had almost forgotten about the barkeep standing silently against the wall until she spoke again. "Do they mean to harm you?" she asked, her voice tinged with anger.

Kinna didn't understand the woman's emotion but didn't have time to dwell on it. "Yes," she answered, sounding weary even to her own ears.

"I will help you," the barkeep grabbed her cloak from the edge of the bed and fastened it around her neck. "I will leave out the front door wearing this, and they will follow me. There are stairs at the end of this hallway that will lead you out the back of the inn."

Stunned, she nodded, accepting her plan. "Why help me?" She couldn't help the question that slipped from her lips.

The barkeep gave Kinna a sly smile. "I will not allow harm to come to our princess," she started, her smile softening. "I have a soft spot for wild things."

"I will not forget this. A life debt is now owed to you, by me or my family," Kinna vowed. She was used to the adoration that Evelyn received from their people, but it was not often that she was the target of their affections. Despite everything, the woman's protectiveness stirred something in her broken heart.

"Then live so that I may one day call in that debt," the barkeep threw the hood of Kinna's cloak over her head and pressed her ear against the door, listening for footsteps outside.

"What is your name?"

She turned to look at Kinna from underneath the hood. "Mary Nofort," she whispered before disappearing behind the door.

Kinna waited, counting ten of her erratic heartbeats before opening the door. The hallway was empty except for the few candles that burned to light the way. She raced to the end of the hallway, moving silently on the balls of her feet. The stairs were just as Mary had said and she pressed one foot down on the first step, waiting for the inevitable creaking of the wood. When they proved quiet, she took them carefully, staying low and glancing back to ensure she wasn't being followed. The stairs opened to a small hallway that led back to the entrance and a single door that led her to an alley behind the inn. The rain pelted her immediately, soaking her hair and clothes, and she wished she had been able to keep her cloak. It would have offered some shelter from the storm.

The alley ran parallel to the inn behind her, the docks to her right and Midtown on her left. She couldn't risk trying to find another inn in the middle of the night and didn't want to spend any more of the money she had packed with her. It was doubtful she would be lucky enough to run across another woman like Mary that would try to keep her safe. Perhaps she could find a secluded spot in one of the bars that were still open, at least she would be out of the rain.

She sensed movement behind her before she saw the figure slide out of the shadows. He stalked towards her; a dagger held loosely in his hand. He dropped the hood of his cloak, smiling at her. His gaze roved over her, her clothes soaked and clinging to her skin; the look made her skin crawl. He was well muscled but stood only a few inches taller than Kinna. She'd taken down men much larger than him while sparring. "Now why don't you just come with me, princess," he said, his voice nasally and laced with an implied threat. "I'd hate for something unfortunate to happen to you."

He took a step towards her, and her hand immediately found the dagger on her thigh. "I bet you would," she muttered.

Throwing a condescending look at the dagger in her hand he advanced, closing the gap between them in three easy strides, his empty hand already reaching for her. He underestimated her and she was going to let him. Kinna ducked as he swiped for her using her left hand to punch his wrist that held the dagger, causing him to drop it. It clattered to the ground, and she heard him curse as she kicked it further down the alley. She couldn't help the small smile that formed as she read the surprise and anger on his face over being disarmed in one move.

Remembering all her training, every lesson, she stood on the balls of her feet and watched his body, waiting for the moment he would give his next move away. She saw the faint tremor in his leg before he lunged at her, giving her plenty of time to whirl around him, slashing her dagger down on his outstretched arm. "You bitch!" he spat, grasping at his arm, the blood darkening his already wet clothing.

"Hasn't anyone ever taught you to keep your hands to yourself?" She taunted him, knowing his anger would make him sloppy.

He lunged at her again, this time grabbing her by her loose hair and pulling her towards him. A small gasp escaped her lips as a shooting pain broke out across her scalp and tears filled her eyes. He wasn't going to fight fair, she realized quickly. Fighting for survival was different from the more civilized sparring she was used to so she decided right then she would do anything, use any means necessary to protect herself.

His arms encircled her torso, fingers digging into her forearms painfully. He laughed as she struggled to break free of his grip. Slamming her heel down hard on his instep she shoved her head back and heard a satisfying crack as her head connected with his nose. She stumbled forward, trying to regain her footing when he charged at her, his blood running down his chin and his eyes furious. Before she could think, she stepped towards him reflexively, blade sinking into his stomach as they collided. A hot, sticky substance coated her hands as the man staggered backward, desperately trying to brace himself against the wall of the inn. He slid to the ground, and she could see the blood trickling out of his stomach and the realization in his eyes that he was going to die. She couldn't afford to stand there another moment, watching him slip away so she ran, hard and fast towards Midtown, stopping only once to try to wash the blood off her hands in a shallow puddle.

The buildings blurred as she ran through the rainy darkness and away from the body she had left in the alley. Kinna tried to ignore the stickiness she could still feel coating her hands and the guilt that danced on the edge of her mind. The city around her began to change, the little square houses blending into ramshackle apartments, and she realized that she'd been running north towards the Dirt District. Her feet began to slow but her heart still beat erratically, sweat mixing with the rain that fell down her face. She'd never been this far from the castle, and she didn't know where to go or what to do but she knew the men that were chasing her would find her soon if she didn't keep moving.

Taking a slow breath, she tried to recall anything she could from the many geography and politics lessons she had slept through, she remembered there was a secondary entrance into the capital. It was mainly used by villagers that lived in the area surrounding outside the walls of Strafford. Merchants and farmers would drive wagons through it and beeline for the marketplace hoping to find better prices in the city. Her heart wrenched at the thought of running further from the castle, but she refused to put anyone else in danger. They had left the castle grounds looking for her, following someone's orders to find her, and she wouldn't be the reason that they went back there.

Before she could change her mind, her feet were moving in towards the two orange dots in the distance that floated on either side of the gate. The rain had finally stopped but a thick mist still hung in the air and clung to her skin, making her shiver in the cool night air. Swinging the bag off her back she reached a hand inside and said a silent thank you to the gods that her clothes were still dry. Morning was a long way off and if she was going to slip through the gate unnoticed, she would need to change out of her wet clothes.

She spied a stack of crates ahead of her. It wouldn't provide much cover but at least she would be partially concealed to change her clothes. She quickly pulled on a fresh pair of leggings and a long sleeve tunic, hating every second that her skin was exposed to the night air. Once her wet clothes were packed in the bottom of her bag away from her small stash of food she crept out from behind the crates and continued weaving her way through the Dirt District. The streets here were empty, unlike Midtown and the Rose Garden where inns and bars would still be open with people stumbling out and heading home for the night. The mist limited her visibility and the rain dripped off every roof creating an eerie melody as she walked.

It took her longer than she would have liked to find her way to the gate. There had been no order when the streets had been formed here, sprouting up like weeds in any available space. Finally, she could see the outline of the wall rising above the mist. She stayed tucked behind one of the buildings, listening through the tarp that covered a gap in the wood. Two guards stood posted at the gate, their conversation carrying through the silent streets. She listened, telling herself that she was listening for any sign of the men that were following her, but she knew that was a lie. Her ears perked up at the mention of the explosion and she stood frozen, wishing that they would say anything that could comfort her.

"I'm glad we didn't get called to go deal with that mess," a raspy voice said. "Digging people out of rubble all day and night doesn't sound like anything I want to do."

"Have you heard who they think was responsible?" The other asked, his voice full of barely contained curiosity that likely belonged to a newer guard.

"It was the damned Rising I bet," he sneered. "Who else would have something to gain from killing the entire Royal Family?"

Kinna's stomach dropped, and tears rushed her eyes. She focused all her energy on taking one breath at a time, willing herself not to fall apart, not to give in to the grief eating its way through her heart. She tried to focus back on their conversation, desperate for any scrap of information she could glean from them, when she heard a new voice address the guards.

"Have you seen a dark-haired young woman tonight?" he asked, his voice the perfect mask of casual inquiry.

"Your lady run out on you?" The raspy voice laughed. "Sorry, we haven't seen anyone all night."

"Oh well," he answered, sounding bored. "Thanks

anyway."

Kinna waited until she couldn't hear his foot-steps anymore before focusing back on the two guards, their conversation having stopped for the moment. She needed to move now and not wait around to be found squatting in an alley when her tail had managed to catch up to her. Running her fingers through her hair, she shook her damp curls out, hoping to use her hair to hide some of her face, and began walking casually to-wards the gate.

She curled in on herself, hoping to give the im-pression of a timid young woman and play on the guards' willingness to help the damsel in distress. They stood a bit straighter as she approached, the raspy voice had belonged to an older man with thinning grey hair and a round belly while the other guard looked only a few years older than Kinna, his face still clinging to his boyish features. The older one stepped towards her. "I think someone is looking for you," he started, pointing off in another direction. "A man was just asking us if we'd seen a dark-haired girl walking around."

She let the fear she felt color her face hoping she could sell the story she'd concocted. "Please," she stam-mered, her voice barely a whisper. "I need to get away from him."

The guards glanced at each other, the younger clearly confused by the fear in her voice. "Has some-thing happened?" he asked.

"He gets so angry sometimes," she choked, letting the tears surface. Pushing up her sleeves she revealed the red angry marks from her fight in the alley. "Nor-mally he hits the walls but this time it was me."

The younger boy sucked in a breath and the older

man cursed. "I just need to leave. My sister doesn't live far," she sniffed. "Please don't tell him where I went."

The older man nodded to the younger guard to begin opening the metal gate. "You have our word, but get somewhere safe and do it quickly," he said. "The Glenwood is no place for a lady in the dark."

Kinna only nodded and murmured a thank you before walking under the gate, not sparing another glance back at the two guards. A tiny hint of guilt scraped against her mind for deceiving the two guards but at least she believed they wouldn't betray her if the man came back asking more questions.

Soon the lights of the city were just a dim glow in the distance as she walked to put more distance between herself and the capital. She wasn't naïve enough to believe that the men wouldn't follow her, and it was obvious that the men were already tailing her again. She had gotten lucky in the city, but it wouldn't be long before they found her again. Staying off the Glen Road and in the tree line would be her best option to stay hidden, but she could feel the exhaustion settling in with every step. She had to stop. She needed sleep and the few hours she'd gotten at the inn weren't enough for her battered body.

She spotted a low-lying branch and with all the strength she had left, took a running jump and hauled herself up, her nails digging into the bark hard enough to crack them. After settling onto the branch, she leaned her head back against the trunk and let the wave of grief and exhaustion fall over her. Tears fell freely until she had to shove her bag over her mouth to muffle her sobs.

Her throat was raw from crying and being exposed to the cold night air when she was woken by the sound of voices passing by. She rubbed her stinging eyes and tried to make out figures in the dark but only blackness stared back at her. The whispered voices grew further and further away but she sat in the dark straining to hear anything until the skies faded into blue and the sun began to rise.

CHAPTER ELEVEN

Hours had passed as she walked further north, staying hidden in the Glenwood, occasionally venturing towards the road to try to orient herself. She'd passed two small villages already but hadn't dared leave the safety of the woods despite how badly she wanted a hot meal. Instead, she nibbled at the bread and cheese she'd stored in her bag, hoping that her few provisions would last her for another day or two.

Late in the afternoon she heard the babbling of a nearby stream and was able to drink as much as she could before refilling her water skein and continuing. Her feet ached, the muscles protesting with every step she took. Finally, the sun began to fade, the sky turning a blazing orange as the sun set, and she began her search for a comfy tree to sleep in for the night.

She ate one of the apples she had packed, using her dagger to cut it into pieces to avoid the loud crunch that could give her location away. Her thoughts drifted to the castle and her family, wondering if it would be worth it to stop in the next village she passed to see if any news had reached them. Someone would have to realize she was missing. If Ellio couldn't find her among the dead or rubble she knew he would stop at nothing until he found her, she just needed to hold on a little longer. She fell asleep still clutching her dagger and thinking about what it would be like to see his face again and to be scooped up in one of his rib-crushing hugs.

The light leaking over the horizon woke her, the palest yellow sky announced a new day. Surprisingly Kinna had slept, her exhaustion having forced her into a deeper sleep than she would have thought possible. She tried to swing her legs over the side of the wide branch and immediately regretted it as her stiff legs barked in protest. Gods, she was sore. She hadn't known simply walking could affect someone like this. Taking a deep, steading breath she jumped down, hissing as her sore muscles took the impact. She spent a few minutes stretching, using the trunk of the tree to help her balance. After a few minutes her body began to loosen up and she started walking again.

She decided that she would stop in the next town she passed, needing to formulate a better plan than just walking and hopefully hear some news about the capital. By mid-morning she had ventured onto the Glen Road and found that a town was relatively close by. It would still take a couple hours to get there but at least she knew where she was headed. Glenarm was somewhere between a village and a city, named because it was split by the Glen Road. It mainly catered to those stopping for food or rest while traveling in either direction since it was situated almost halfway between Edgewood and Strafford. The past two days were a blur, and she hadn't realized how far or how quickly she had traveled.

High in the sky the sun shone brightly down on her, the long sleeve tunic quickly becoming uncomfortably warm as she walked. Once more she left the cover of the thicker woods and stood at the edge of the forest, checking that the road was clear of nosy travelers before emerging from the Glenwood and walking the rest of the way into town.

It wasn't hard to navigate the streets, unlike the endless alleys and dead ends found in the capital, this city radiated out in a circle from the small group of shops and inns that made up the town square. Kinna was able to breeze through the small groups of people milling around the town's center, finding the two inns that competed for the frequent visitors' business. A few vendors had parked their stalls in the square and the smell of hot food was too tempting for her to ignore.

She drifted towards one stall that had a small line forming, an older man with a friendly tone passing out small fried pies as quickly as he could. Joining the line, she dug the copper coins out of her bag and listened to the quiet chatter around her before ordering two fried apple pies.

"Are you heading anywhere, young lady?" the older man asked, his question surprising her.

"No, not really," she admitted, passing him two copper coins.

"Well, if you want my advice, stay away from the capital," he cautioned, handing over two warm, square pies.

"Why?"

"It's no place for a young lady right now. I heard just yesterday that the city is starting to descend into chaos over the death of the Royal Family and so many that worked in the castle," he explained, shaking his head sadly. "No one quite knows what will happen and the uncertainty is making people edgy."

She had to force herself to swallow the bite she'd taken, her mouth bone dry as she tried to force down the flaky pastry. "They are all dead?" she whispered.

He just nodded sadly. She knew her feet were moving beneath her, carrying her away from the line of people, but she couldn't feel anything except her heart beating too quickly in her chest. The last bit of hope she had been clinging to died. It was as if the breath had been knocked out of her, the grief so real it was a physical pain in her gut. She walked in a daze, out of the town square and down a small side street, desperate to get away from everyone.

Falling on her hands and knees, she vomited the small amount of food in her stomach. Gasping for breath she sat back on her heels, wiping her mouth and face on the sleeve of her tunic before rising on unsteady legs. She was so exhausted, physically, and emotionally. She wanted to just turn it off, her emotions, her thoughts, everything, so she didn't have to feel this way anymore but that was for cowards.

Kinna wouldn't let the memory of all those she loved to dwindle down to nothing, she would keep them safe in her heart, even if the pain threatened to overwhelm her.

She retraced her steps back to the square, debating if spending a night in one of the town's inns just for the chance at a hot meal and a bath when she saw a glimpse of a black figure across the square. A group of young girls passed, and she slid behind them, keeping pace with the group as she watched the man talking to one of the vendors. How had they followed her all the way here without her noticing? Could her luck really be that bad? There was no use trying to hide in Glenarm, they would find her here just easier than they had in the sprawling capital. Her sudden departure from the square was likely the only reason they hadn't already spotted her.

Without a wall surrounding the town she would be able to sneak out from any direction, making it harder for them to track her. Deciding to not waste time trying to find another way out, she headed south, constantly glancing behind her to see if any familiar faces were following her. She had the Glen Road in her sights when she spared one last glance behind her and her eyes settled on a stationary figure, dressed in black, watching her slink away. The same man that had watched her leave the castle grounds was watching her escape once again but this time he wasn't turning back for the others. Sensing his intention, she took off running, pushing past anyone that crossed in front of her and ignoring the string of curses that followed.

Adrenaline propelled her forward, allowing her to ignore her tired muscles that begged her to stop. Once she was clear of the town she turned sharply and launched herself into the woods that had protected her for the last two days. She could hear heavy footsteps behind her and realized that there were now at least two men pursuing her and they were gaining. They chased her deeper into the Glenwood, further than she had ever ventured on her own.

Footsteps pounded behind her and they sounded closer with each thud. Gods, this was bad. She shouldn't have run into the Glenwood, away from the town and other people, where they could leave her body for the birds or tie her up to cart back to the capital and no one would know. Anger bubbled up inside her, she was tired of running, tired of hiding in the woods. She was going to fight, and she would probably lose but damnit she would go down fighting.

Her anger fueled her, pushing her legs to move faster so she could make one last stand. Scanning ahead of her she found a tree that had a branch that looked like it would support her weight. She focused on it, blocking out the noise behind her, as she put one foot in front of the other. They had gained on her when her foot caught the ground and she pretended to stumble, throwing her arms out to catch herself.

Instead of falling as they had expected, she used her momentum to swing her body around the branch catching the closest one in the chin with her heel as he charged forward. He went down, unconscious before his head hit the ground. She landed next to him, swiping his dagger from his belt and then gave the two men a vicious smile as they gaped at her. Before they could react, she was running again, back in the direction of Glenarm. The expression on their faces had given her some satisfaction but she knew her strength was flagging.

If it came down to a fight, she wasn't even sure she could take one of them, let alone two. Still, she ran, knowing that it would be soon when she would hear their footsteps close behind her again.

She raced around trees looking for signs of the Glen Road but found none. Had she run in the wrong direction? She was beginning to panic as she stood at the base of a large oak, trying to remember the direction she'd come from but coming up blank. She couldn't keep running, she needed to hide quickly. She looked to the lowest limb, hoping to find a way up, but instead found a pair of turquoise eyes staring back at her and out-stretched hand.

"Up here," they whispered.

She grabbed the hand without a second thought and was hauled into the tree. Kinna found her footing on the lowest branch and began shuffling further up, concealing herself in the thick green. Crouched between the branches, one hand gripped the trunk and the other pressed over her mouth to try to hide the sounds of her ragged breathing. She watched the two dark uniformed men approach.

Swords out and eyes searching, they stalked through the trees looking for her. She saw the young woman that had pulled her into the tree close her eyes as her mouth made the tiniest *o* shape as she blew a silent breath out. In the distance Kinna heard the faintest crack, as if someone had stepped on a twig. The men below heard it as well and smiled knowingly at each other. The look made her skin crawl.

The taller one made a motion to go left, and they fanned out, stalking the noise that would lead them away from her. Kinna stared at the woman for a split second, bewildered by how she had saved her for the second time just with a small breath, before returning her attention to the forest floor. Kinna watched them until they were black dots in the distance, still not daring to move. She finally took a relieved breath when she could no longer see them.

"That was close," whispered the voice above her.

She startled, forgetting that someone had pulled her into this tree only moments ago. She looked up to find a young woman, close to her own age, with cropped white-blonde hair that stuck out in every direction and tattered clothes covered with patches of every color. Three silver hoops hung from each of her ears, the sunlight glinting dimly off their surface. She even had a tiny silver stud through her left nostril. She smiled softly at her when Kinna did not respond, a motherly expression that immediately aged her young face.

"Who are you?" Kinna whispered.

The young woman eased herself down from the branch above. "Sebrina," she said.

"How did you do that? Why did you save me?" the questions spilled out of her even as something in the back of her mind whispered the answer. *Magic*. She had magic. Even someone with just a drop of it was more than Kinna had ever encountered.

The young woman, Sebrina, smiled mischievously. "Neat trick huh?" she asked. "I thought you looked like you could use some help. I guessed they weren't friends of yours."

Kinna nodded bewildered by the sudden turn of events. "Thank you," she said earnestly. She didn't exactly care why she had done it; she was just glad she had. She'd been running for two days and was exhausted.

"Do you have somewhere to go?" Sebrina asked hesitantly.

"No, I don't," Kinna whispered back, not able to look at her.

"Then come with me. You'll be safe with us."

Sebrina didn't wait for her to respond, instead began climbing down through the branches back to the forest floor. Kinna hesitated for a moment, she didn't know who this woman was or who she meant by *us* but before she realized it, she was following her.

Sebrina waited for her to reach the ground. "Do you have anything to cover your head with?" she asked.

Kinna was immediately self-conscious. She was sure she looked horrible, not having bathed or brushed her hair in days and spending nights sleeping against rough bark. Sebrina read the hurt on her face. "I just don't want them to recognize you if we run into them again," she explained gently. "They know your face."

"Of course," she said, realizing her cloak had been lost in the capital. The price of escaping the second time. "I didn't even think of that, I only have the clothes in my bag."

"We will stay out of sight, don't worry." She nodded and silently began leading her deeper into the forest.

CHAPTER TWELVE

They had walked for what felt like hours, the sun dipping lower in the western sky, but true to her word they hadn't left the forest or seen a single person. She didn't know how Sebrina knew what direction they were walking in, but she never hesitated as she led them forward. The trees had gotten thicker the longer they walked, and she could only assume they were traveling deeper into the Glenwood. She heard Sebrina's stomach growl and dug into her bag for an apple.

She offered it to her. "We can share it," Sebrina offered, pulling a small knife from her waist band.

"Don't worry," Kinna answered, grabbing another one from her bag. "I have more. Plus, I owe you a lot more than an apple for saving me. I owe you a life debt which translates to more than a thousand apples."

Sebrina smiled, shaking her head but took the apple. Kinna now owed two life debts, both earned in a matter of days. If things continued, she would need to start keeping a written list of everyone she owed.

Kinna's eyes roved over the trees as they walked. They were packed tightly together, their branches full of vibrant new leaves that the warm spring weather had awoken. It was the perfect cover for someone wishing to remain unnoticed as they hid in the forest, which meant that she kept her eyes moving, watching for any sign that they were not alone.

She noticed him before Sebrina did, a man walking towards them, not attempting to hide his approach. She froze, eyes darting in every direction, trying to spot the others. Panic rose in her chest, and she tried unsuccessfully to slow her breathing. She wasn't going to be able to run this time, she was too lost in the Glenwood.

Slowly she slipped her hand to the small dagger at her waist, desperately wishing for her bow. How had they found them? Had they been tracking them—

Sebrina lightly touched her arm, staring at the dagger in her hand. Without thinking she had shifted in front of her, using her body as a shield. "It's okay," she said calmly. "He isn't going to hurt us."

"Do you know him?" she whispered, eyes never leaving him. He was moving quickly towards them, but his hands remained empty, unlike hers.

She rolled her eyes and bit back a smile. "Just my whole life," she whispered, walking forwards to meet him. She clearly was confident in her assessment that he was not a threat.

He stood a few feet away from them, noting the dagger still held firmly in Kinna's hand and did not approach further. He wasn't carrying a weapon, but he was definitely armed. Twin swords hung from his hips, the metal gleaming in the evening light. As if he'd need them to disarm someone.

He stood close to six and a half feet and his pants and sleeveless tunic did nothing to hide the muscle that corded every inch of his body. However, none of that was as surprising as his face. He was easily the most beautiful man she had ever seen, and she was now acutely aware of her own appearance as he watched her.

His tan skin was almost as dark as Kinna's would be during the height of summer. His brown hair was longer than most men wore it in Ferryn, but the wild look suited him. Strands floated around his high cheekbones and curled slightly around his neck.

Everything about him was warm and inviting, including his full mouth shrouded with a few days' worth of stubble, everything except his eyes. His hazel eyes were hard, assessing every inch of her. It didn't matter how beautiful she found him, one look into his eyes revealed more than his weapons ever could.

Sebrina moved towards him, giving him a swift punch in the arm. "Stop glaring at her," she demanded before motioning Kinna to follow her.

Kinna hadn't moved, still locked in a battle of wills against the beautiful man in front of her and she had no intention of losing. She scanned him, noting the additional weapons he bore, a dagger strapped against his thigh and a smaller one under his pant leg that he thought no one noticed. If it came to a fight, she would be at a disadvantage with only one dagger left. His twin swords were the length of a person's arm and looked razor sharp. Getting past them to snatch the dagger on his thigh or by his ankle would be challenging but not impossible. Men his size usually weren't very fast, she could very well be able to use her size to an advantage, moving constantly and quickly to stay out of his reach. Sebrina was obviously comfortable enough with him that she couldn't count on her help again.

Something changed in his eyes that stopped her strategizing, they had shifted from predatory focus to something else. Something like realization flashed in his eyes, like he was seeing himself reflected as he watched her. "You're debating how best to unarm me, aren't you?" his deep voice came out soft, just loud enough that she would hear him from where she still stood.

She paused, tilting her head at him. "How did you know?" she asked, honestly curious by his observation.

"The way you watched me, counting my weapons and weighing where you would strike, it's the same way that any warrior would assess their opponent," he explained, a grin tugging at the corners of his mouth. "I'm also much faster than you think."

Kinna wasn't used to having anyone notice her playing out scenarios in her head, most were content to believe she was harmless, maybe possessing some knowledge of self-defense but certainly not a skilled fighter. It filled her with a strange sense of affirmation that this man saw her for what she was, until she realized what that meant about him. Not only would he be able to physically overwhelm her, but he also knew enough about strategy that cleverness wouldn't save her either. Still, she envisioned the sparring match between the two of them and smiled for the first time in days. "Maybe we shall get to play," she purred, trying to muster the swagger that normally came so easily. "And then we'll see just how fast you are."

His smirk turned into a lethal grin, two dimples deepening on his cheeks and exposing a row of white, square teeth. "I look forward to it," he said.

Sebrina raised an eyebrow at their conversation. She laid her hand on his arm, his smile disappearing instantly. "We need to keep moving," she reminded him. He just nodded and took off in the direction that he came from, leaving the two of them to follow.

They walked for a few minutes in silence, Kinna keeping a short distance between them, before Sebrina spoke again. "Has anything interesting happened while I was gone?" she asked.

"No," he answered, glancing at them over his shoulder. "But it seems you have a story to tell. A simple scouting mission does not usually include bringing someone home with you."

"Jealous?" she teased.

His face hardened. "You were not supposed to engage with anyone," he scolded. "I won't let you go again if you are going to put yourself at risk."

"You're no fun," she said, elbowing him in the ribs.

He batted her arm away, rubbing the spot on his side. Kinna knew he had let her hit him, not doubting for one second that he couldn't have caught her arm if he'd wanted to. "Your safety is more important than having fun," he explained.

Their conversation flowed easily, familiarity and affection coloring their tones. They talked about her past few days, what she'd seen and heard, while laughing and trading insults as they walked. Kinna watched as the man constantly positioned himself around Sebrina to protect and shield her from any potential threats around them. Their banter reminded her of Ellio and the way they would tease each other in the training room while sparring and on the beach after their morning runs. It was a hot bolt of grief through her chest, remembering his laugh and their adventures. She pushed the thought away quickly, feeling her throat constrict and tears well in her eyes.

Instead, she wondered idly if perhaps the two

were together and hoped she hadn't overstepped when she taunted him earlier. Kinna knew that even though men were often possessive with their partners women could be absolutely vicious if challenged.

Soon she began to hear voices, realizing that they were taking her towards them and that she was likely to meet whoever the *us* Sebrina had mentioned before was. She wondered where they were, the trees hadn't thinned as they walked so it wasn't likely that they would be leaving the Glenwood in favor of a town.

For the second time that day, Kinna spotted a figure walking towards them. She blinked and the lone figure doubled. Two men now walked towards them and neither Sebrina nor her friend who's name she still didn't know seemed surprised by this. She was beginning to see the pattern. Whoever this group was, they weren't going to let anyone catch them unaware and their secrecy made her uneasy.

The two drew closer, their smiles faltering as they saw Kinna steps behind their two companions. Their faces were boyish and framed with auburn hair, lightly dusted with freckles and absolutely identical. The twins were gangly and couldn't be older than sixteen, but they stood there assessing her in the same calculating manner Sebrina's friend had. It was starting to get annoying.

"Who is she?" one of the twins asked, his hand drifting to a dagger at his hip.

"She is my friend." Sebrina rolled her eyes. She reached for Kinna's hand and led her past the two boys before whispering to her. "I promise they are not all this rude."

"We heard that," the twins called in unison.

The three of them fell in step behind Kinna and

Sebrina, who was still gripping her hand and half dragging her forward. The voices grew louder, followed by other noises, the crackling of wood, the clanking of metal, and the rush of water. A small camp came into view along the banks of a narrow, shallow river. A circle of a dozen or more tents had been erected around a large fire, most were smaller tents that looked large enough for only one or two people to sleep comfortably. One tent stood out as the largest, its white flaps held open to show a random assortment of tables, benches, and chairs: a makeshift cafeteria. A few people milled around but mercifully no one paid the group any attention or asked who she was.

"Bas, can you see if we have any extra tents and get the twins to set it up?" Sebrina asked. It sounded like a nickname, but Kinna wasn't sure. At least she had something to go off. He only nodded and peeled off in another direction, the twins following behind him. "If we don't have any you can share with me." Sebrina smiled reassuringly at her. They stashed Kinna's bag inside a sand-colored tent that she assumed belonged to Sebrina, but Kinna kept the dagger on her. She eyed it as Kinna kept it strapped to her waist but thankfully didn't comment.

"Thank you," Kinna said earnestly. "I don't know what would have happened to me if it weren't for you."

"Us ladies have to stick together, right?" she joked, brushing off her thanks. "I know Bastin and the twins weren't overly welcoming, but they mean well. Bas thinks because he's older he should be in charge of everything."

"You're related?" Kinna asked, surprised. The way they teased each other hadn't been flirting at all.

"Yes, Bastin is my cousin," she answered confused. "Why?"

Kinna's face flushed. "I just thought," she stammered. "You two seemed so close, that maybe you were together."

Sebrina's eyes widened, the blood draining from her face, and she whipped her head around to stare at her cousin who was silently approaching with a canvas tent in tow. His gaze hadn't left Kinna's face, and his eyes held a twinkle of amusement before he burst into laughter. It was a genuine laugh, coming from deep in his stomach and he didn't stop until he was gasping for air.

"I think I'm going to be sick," she breathed, her face still ashen.

"As if you could do better than me." Bastin chuckled.

Kinna was mortified. She did not want to offend this woman who seemed to be the only ally she had. "I'm sorry," she said quickly. "I didn't mean to offend you."

"She's just being dramatic as usual," Bastin explained. "Ignore her. I usually do."

He left still smirking and nodded for the twins to follow him to set the small faded green canvas tent up on the outer edge of the circle next to Sebrina's tent. Kinna couldn't help watching Bastin as he walked away, especially the way the muscles in his arms flexed as he carried the tent across the camp. At least she didn't have to feel guilty that she was betraying Sebrina since they were definitely not a couple. She was free to continue watching him with growing fascination and silently enjoy the view.

Sebrina interrupted her staring and motioned her to follow. "Come on, there's someone you need to meet," she said.

CHAPTER THIRTEEN

They crossed the center of the camp heading south. Kinna received a few curious glances as they passed through but said no one questioned who the stranger in their midst was, perhaps it was a common occurrence. A red, two compartment tent began to peek through the trees, situated apart from the rest of the group and nestled between a handful of Crimson King Maple trees. Their deep ruby leaves hung heavily from their branches and were so deeply colored that they reminded Kinna of blood. There were very few in the capital, one standing on the castle grounds in a rarely visited portion of the gardens and another outside the temple. It was odd that so many stood together since it was rare to see more than one in an area. She had always been told that the trees only would grow in places that had been blessed by the gods and she couldn't imagine why they would bless this random spot in the Glenwood.

Sebrina paused outside of the tent. "Stay here for just a moment," she whispered before quickly disappearing inside. Standing outside, a feeling of unease returned and settled in her stomach. Who would she be meeting and why was it so important? She listened closely but heard nothing behind the thick material. Sebrina's head suddenly popped out of the tent. "Are you ready to meet our illustrious leader?" she smiled.

"Leader?" Kinna asked.

"Yes." She grinned, grabbing her hand and pulling her through the tent. "You're about to meet the leader of the Rising."

Kinna's heart stuttered violently as she was pulled through the gap and into the tent. If this was the Rising, then who had been chasing her for days? Sebrina wouldn't have rescued her from the uniformed men if they had been working for the Rising. The general had been wrong about the threat facing Ferryn and it had cost him the lives of her family. Anger flared in her chest at the thought. How could they have been so wrong about the danger? How had everything gone so wrong?

She pushed those questions out of her head to focus on meeting the mysterious leader of the Rising. Neither the general nor anyone else had discovered the identity of the rebel leader. The highest-ranking member he'd been able to identify had been the second in command, a man named Rennick, who oversaw most of their members but even the best spies had not been able to deliver a name.

Blinking, her eyes tried to adjust to the dimness of the inside and found that the tent was sparsely decorated with one large rectangular table littered with papers and a dozen chairs strewn across the space. Through a small gap in the canvas, Kinna could see into the rear compartment where a bed sat on a wooden platform piled high with blankets and furs. A woman sat in one of the two chairs positioned at the head of the table, the other empty beside her. She was a small, willowy woman, just an inch or two taller than Sebrina's tiny frame. She did not look like the leader of a rebel group, especially since the Rising's leader had always been assumed to be a man. Her black hair was streaked with grey and had been braided back into two thick plaits. She was dressed simply except for her hands, which were adorned with a dozen rings of every color and size with most of her weathered fingers holding more than one. But the most striking of all was her eyes. Kinna felt an instant connection with the woman who, like her, often caught people staring. Her left eye was a bright blue, like the shallow waters of the ocean, but her right eye was milky white with a thick silvered scar cutting through her eyebrow and down her cheek.

Kinna's face must have betrayed her thoughts and before Kinna could say a word to her she spoke. "Aren't we two of a kind?" she asked softly, a small smile playing at the corner of her mouth. Kinna couldn't help but smile back.

"Sebrina tells me she rescued you outside of Glenarm," she said, glancing at where Sebrina stood behind Kinna.

"She did," Kinna nodded. "I owe her a life debt for what she did."

The woman mulled over her words. "A life debt," she repeated, tasting the words. "That's an old promise, one that is not given out lightly. Only in situations where one would have perished if not for the assistance of another."

"It's true. The men she helped me escape meant to harm me," she repeated.

The woman leaned back in her chair, bracing her

elbows against the arms of it. "It seems you have a story to tell," she said after a moment. "It is almost time for dinner. You will sit with me and tell me your story, then we can decide what to do next."

Sweat broke out across Kinna's neck but she nodded her agreement. She wasn't sure how to explain the events of the past few days or what information she could entrust to the leader of the Rising. Even revealing her name could put her at risk but she wasn't sure if she had any other choice.

The woman rose and exited the tent without another word. Sebrina followed behind her leaving Kinna to catch up to them both as they headed through the trees towards the large white tent where everyone had already gathered to eat. This time they all stared at Kinna as she walked behind the woman and Sebrina, mostly with curiosity and a few with slight distrust. Their distrust was now understandable as were the three escorts Kinna had encountered on her way into the camp. The Rising couldn't afford to take any chances. Sebrina must have held some sway here to have been able to bring her without anyone protesting and earn her a meeting with their leader.

The three were seated at a table at the back of the tent, facing out towards the rest of the group who had now gone back to whatever was steaming inside their bowls. A man in his late forties approached carrying a tray with four steaming bowls. His blonde hair was cut close to his head, but his handsome face and cool blue eyes revealed nothing as he quietly set down the tray and set a bowl before the woman then Sebrina then Kinna before taking an empty seat on the leader's right. Kinna noticed the silver scars peppering his forearms and wondered if this could be Rennick, her second in command. His body was slender but hard muscles still lay underneath his thin white shirt.

The four ate in silence. Kinna hungrily gulped down the hot stew, burning her tongue in the process. She was almost done with her bowl when Bastin joined them, sitting down to her left. She tried to hide her smirk at the way he dwarfed the chair and wondered if it would continue to support his weight or buckle underneath him. He didn't seem to notice, too engrossed in his own food to look up at the rest of the table.

"I assume you already met Bastin," the leader spoke up. "Otherwise, I would have to scold him for his horrendous manners."

"Yes," Kinna answered.

"The other one who did not bother to introduce himself is Rennick," she explained, giving him a pointed look which he pretended to not see. "And I am Marstella, Leader of the Rising."

Everyone at the table was paying attention now as she mentioned her name. Kinna didn't think it was something she said often or without reason. "Thank you for having me here," she said, still not able to make her lips form her own name to introduce herself.

Marstella only nodded at her thanks. "We have a few questions for you," she said. "First, do you know who the men were that pursued you and can you describe them?"

"I do not know who they are, but they wore all black uniforms. No insignia or crest marked their clothing, but it was fine material, and their weapons were well crafted," Kinna answered. "There were three that chased me into the Glenwood."

"Three? Not two?" Marstella asked, glancing at Sebrina, clearly comparing the story that she had already been told.

"I knocked one of them unconscious before Sebrina found me," Kinna explained. "Only two were chasing me when she pulled me into the tree."

"How did you render one unconscious?" Rennick cut in.

"I let them get close and used a low branch to swing back towards them," she explained. "I caught the closest one in the chin with my heel." He nodded at her explanation, either with approval or dismissal, Kinna couldn't tell.

"Did they start following you in Glenarm or before that?" Marstella continued.

"They have been following me for three days, since I left the capital," Kinna answered.

"Since the day of the attack on the Royal Family of Ferryn," Marstella said. Kinna nodded, heart racing at the mention of her family. "Where did you first see them?"

"Four of them were outside of the castle just minutes after the blast," she told them, working to keep her voice even. "They were looking for me in the aftermath."

"Why are they so focused on you?" Bastin interjected. "It seems odd that they have pursued you for so long. What's so special about you?"

Kinna bristled at his tone but immediately realized her error, it was too soon to reveal her identity. She barely knew these people and she still wasn't sure if it was safe to trust anyone with her real name.

"Bastin," Sebrina scolded.

"It's a valid question," he snipped.

Bastin looked at her expectantly, waiting for her to respond while she stood in silence debating options in her head, her heart beating wildly in her chest. Before she could find her voice to answer, another spoke for her. "It is because she is Princess Kinna Braunlin," Marstella said, her voice barely more than a whisper. "The wild second child of the late King Calvin and Queen Lena, sole survivor of the Royal Family. Now, I suppose, the uncrowned Queen of Ferryn."

Marstella bowed her head to her with genuine reverence while a single tear escaped down Kinna's stunned face. The *sole survivor*. That was the second time she had heard it aloud and been confronted with the harsh reality that she was an orphan, her family dead. And not just her parents and Evelyn but perhaps Maude, Kerin, Gavin, and her Ellio. She could barely even think his name, the grief at the mere thought left her paralyzed. She felt more tears pooling but she would not yield to them. Not in front of a group of strangers.

Bastin's head whipped towards his cousin, his attention no longer on Kinna. "You brought the fucking Princess of Ferryn, *here*?" It was more of an accusation than an actual question and it did nothing to hide the anger bubbling under his skin.

"I didn't know who she was," she answered, her eyes still locked on Kinna with confusion and the tiniest hint of fear. "There were two uniforms chasing her and she needed help."

Kinna gritted her teeth at her expression, one that others around her seemed to share. She realized that the entire tent was now listening intently to their conversation and more now looked at her with obvious mistrust. They believed her a danger and it was clearly written on many faces now watching her every breath. Where would she go if she was cast out by the Rising? What if instead of simply abandoning her, they took their need for retribution out on her? Things were spinning out of control quickly and she didn't know if she wanted to scream, cry, or both.

"Gods, she's probably going to run straight back to the capital and report us," Bastin scoffed.

"I would not do that," Kinna snapped.

"Are you trying to be funny or are you just stupid?" he asked.

Her temper flared. "I am not either of those things," she ground out.

"You must be if you expect anyone to believe that the Princess of Ferryn would willingly help the Rising," he sneered. "When your family agreed to not to interfere in a genocide in Eldridge, it left us to risk ourselves to try to save those seeking refuge. Not to mention anyone caught aiding those attempting to flee or harboring people from Eldridge are arrested by the order of your father."

Kinna had never thought of father's decision to not engage Eldridge as allowing a genocide of magic wielders. She knew it would have likely started a war that would mean the death of many of their own citizens, something she was sure her father would have avoided at all costs. The safety of his people was always his priority. Still, she couldn't help feeling a spike of shame that her father had allowed Eldridge to take and possibly murder hundreds if not thousands of their own people simply because they possessed magic.

Bastin's voice cut through her thoughts. "The look on your face makes me think it's the latter of the two."

Embarrassment charged through her, painting her cheeks a deep crimson. She felt as if there was so much that she didn't understand about her father and her kingdom. The politics of their kingdom had never been her responsibility and she definitely had not gone out of her way to understand them. Maybe that made her naive, but she was certainly not stupid.

She looked up to find Rennick watching her, but not with mistrust or anger, rather something closer to pity, and she wasn't sure which she hated more. Bastin looked at him as well. "What are we going to do?" he asked, every bit the soldier waiting for orders from his captain.

He was quiet for several seconds as Kinna's stomach knotted tighter, waiting for him to decide her fate. "We use her," he said simply. "She has invaluable knowledge."

"What if she's a spy? She could have been sent here to gather information and report back," he argued.

"Bas, that's ridiculous!" Sebrina cut in. Kinna couldn't help the tiny swell of appreciation that formed as she defended her. "They were *chasing* her. I saw it."

"That could have easily been a ruse," he countered.

Rennick put one hand up, stopping their argument. It reminded her of her father who so often stepped between Kinna and her mother to end their arguments. "She is no spy," he decided, eyeing Bastin warily. "I believe they intended to harm her just as they have done to countless others. She will stay with us, and we will protect her as we would our own."

Sebrina's shoulders sagged with relief, but Bastin stood firm, not convinced that she shouldn't be counted as a threat. "She has everything to gain from this, an entire kingdom to gain," he added.

Instead of Rennick, it was Marstella that spoke. "That is enough Bastin," she threatened. "The girl has lost her family and has been chased from her home. I would think you of all people would have more sympathy for her loss."

He looked as if she had slapped him but did not protest further. Rennick turned to her. "Would you feel comfortable telling me what you know? What happened in the capital?" he asked, and it was clear that if she refused, he would not force her.

"Yes," she agreed, keeping her voice even.

"Thank you." He nodded, then turned towards Sebrina. "Sebbie, why don't you take her to get some fresh clothes before we begin?"

Sebrina led her silently away from everyone and towards their two tents situated on the left side of the circle. Neither of them spoke as they walked but Sebrina seemed to dull slightly with every step. Guilt, cold and oily, pooled in her stomach. She had risked her own safety to help Kinna in the Glenwood and then again by bringing her to this place. There was no reason for her not to trust Sebrina, but Kinna still had not been able to even reveal her own name. The omission bothered her more than she would have thought.

"I'm sorry," she whispered before Sebrina could duck under through the opening of her tent. "I didn't mean to deceive you."

Sebrina was quiet for a moment, hand still resting on the canvas. "I know," she breathed. "I didn't ask who you were because I thought you'd tell me when you were ready. I knew you were hiding something if only to protect yourself. We've all done that, and I won't blame you for it. It's how we've all survived."

"It wasn't a reflection on my trust in you," she explained. "Or my gratitude. You put your life at risk for me and I will not forget that. You've earned my trust and my friendship if you want it."

Sebrina looked at her, the smallest glint of a tear shone in her eyes. She blinked them back as her smile returned. "Don't think I missed how you acted when Bastin first approached us. You were preparing to unleash yourself on him if you decided he was a threat," she chuckled. "I think I would very much like to have you as a friend."

Despite the cracks in her broken heart, having Sebrina accept her as a friend felt as if a few of them had been closed. She didn't know if it was because her heart felt just a bit lighter or that she desperately needed someone to hold on to, but she threw her arms around Sebrina, pulling her into a tight hug, surprising them both. Sebrina only hugged her back tighter in response.

"Kinna?" Sebrina interrupted. "As your friend I think it's my responsibility to tell you that you could probably use a bath."

Kinna couldn't help the laughter that spilled from her lips. Gods, did it feel good to laugh. "You're probably right," she agreed.

"Come on," Sebrina giggled. "There's a place not far that you can use. Trust me it's better than the river. The water is still frigid from winter.

CHAPTER FOURTEEN

They carried their spare clothes and two towels as they walked along the riverbank away from the camp. The sun was setting, leaving the sky a bright orange, and making the water's surface glow with the reflection. After a few minutes the river grew wider and Kinna began to hear rushing water. A short waterfall came into view surrounded by a dozen small pools of steaming water. Narrow mossy paths wound between each pool creating a maze. Sebrina ran towards them, navigating the strips of ground easily and stripping off clothes as she went, tossing them haphazardly on the ground. Kinna blushed at her brazenness as Sebrina tore off her undergarments and jumped into the closest pool, sinking down until the water covered the tops of her breasts.

Kinna sat her clean clothes down at the edge of the pool and peeled off her leggings and shirt, standing self-consciously in her undergarments. She tried not to think about cuts and bruises that covered her body or the fact that she was going to be naked in front of a stranger as she quickly finished undressing. Sebrina was busy scrubbing her skin with a small black bar of soap and didn't notice her quickly slip into the water. Kinna sat down low enough that the water covered her shoulders, but she immediately forgot about her nakedness when the hot water met her still sore muscles. The heat was heavenly, and she bit back a groan as she tipped her head back and went under water. When she resurfaced, Sebrina offered her the bar of soap and she started scrubbing days' worth of dirt from her skin, taking extra care to clean the dirt out from under her nails. The soap had a faint scent of vanilla and reminded her of the sweet-smelling paste Maude would add into her pastries. The two sat in the warm water for a few minutes, eyes closed, listening to the soothing sounds of running water until they heard footsteps approaching followed by a low curse.

"Bastin! What the hell are you doing?" Sebrina shrieked. Kinna scrambled to cover herself, pressing closely to the mossy edge of the pool.

"Rennick told me to come find you," he rolled his eyes before using one hand to cover them. "It's nothing I haven't seen before Sebbie, trust me."

"Gross," she whispered, reaching for her towel on the ground. "You better keep your eyes closed."

"Like I would want to look at you," he muttered, turning his back to them.

Kinna took the opportunity to hop out of the water and wrap the towel securely around her. It unfortunately barely fell past her behind, leaving her legs on full display.

"Are you two ready yet?" Bastin demanded, peeking over his shoulder. His eyes fell on Kinna, still wrapped in her towel, and lingered for just a moment before recovering and quickly turning around.

Kinna flushed a deep crimson and pulled on her grey leggings and linen shirt before folding the rest of her clothes. They walked back towards the camp with Bastin keeping a healthy distance ahead of them. Kinna attempted to dry her dripping hair with the towel, but the shoulders of her shirt were already soaked. At least it was clean, and the smell was gone.

Sebrina caught her eye. "I have a comb you can borrow," she offered.

"Thanks." She smiled.

Bastin ducked inside Marstella's tent, not bothering to wait for them. Sebrina held the flap open for her and let Kinna go in before her, giving her a reassuring smile. At least one of them had some manners, she thought. Marstella was already seated, Rennick in the chair beside her, again at her right hand. Someone had arranged the extra chairs closer to the table since there were now three empty seats waiting for them that had not been there earlier. Bastin walked straight past them and stood against the canvas wall behind the two leaders instead. She noticed the table had also been cleared, leaving only a small map of the continent unfurled on it. Sebrina took the seat to Marstella's left and Kinna the one beside her. Everyone except Sebrina seemed to be assessing her every move as if at any moment she would begin her attack and confirm Bastin's suspicion that she was truly a spy. Instead, she just sat quietly, waiting for someone to break the heavy silence.

"I imagine you have some questions for us," Rennick began. "We have some as well, but I think you are owed a few answers first."

Kinna thought for a moment, trying to be strategic about the questions she asked. It was unlikely they would answer all of them, so she needed to make them count. She started out with the most obvious thing she needed to confirm, though she thought she already knew the answer. "The men that were chasing me, that followed me from the capital, they are not connected to the Rising at all?" she asked. She had to know that she was safe here, that none of these people were going to hand her over to them, otherwise she might as well go back to wandering the damned Glenwood.

"No," Rennick confirmed. "I know there have been rumors that they were once members of the Rising, but they are as unfamiliar to us as they are to you. We know very little about who they are. We call them uniforms because they all seem to dress in black clothes that bear no sigil. They have been seen in the northern region of Ferryn but never this far south."

Kinna couldn't help but feel relieved if only because she would have a safe place to sleep tonight. A small part of her that she tried to ignore was relieved for other reasons. "Do you know what they want?" she asked.

Rennick looked to Marstella, deferring her question to their leader. "They are targeting magic wielders," she said tersely, throwing a quick glance at Sebrina. "Every one of them that they have managed to capture has ended up dead."

The full gravity of Sebrina's actions hit Kinna. She was a magic wielder. She'd seen her use her gifts in the Glenwood to save her knowing that if they had been caught, she would have likely met the same fate as the rest. Kinna couldn't understand what had made her risk so much for her. "Why did you risk yourself for me?" she whispered to Sebrina. "For a stranger?"

"I asked my daughter the same question," Marstella echoed. *Daughter*. She wasn't just a magic wielder but the daughter of the leader of the Rising, a princess in her own right. Gods, this was too much information to process at once.

Sebrina's mouth pressed into a hard line. "I would do it again," she said, her voice firm as she held her mother's stare. "It was the right thing to do, what you all would have done had you been in my position. This is my cause as much as it is the rest of yours. I am not a child anymore and I will not sit by when someone is in need because you want me out of the way."

"We understand your need to be active," Rennick cut in, his tone soothing and calm. "We just want you to be safe. You are at a higher risk than most."

"I know," Sebrina relented, leaning back into her chair. Kinna guessed that, like her, Sebrina had made this argument a thousand times. She had no idea how much Kinna empathized with her and her need to be a part of something and contribute in a meaningful way.

"That still doesn't answer why they were after me specifically," Kinna said, thinking more aloud than to anyone in particular. "I thought they just wanted me because of... of who I am."

Bastin snorted from his post against the wall, but Marstella's glare stopped him from making a rude remark. "They may have ulterior motives, but I imagine they want you for the magic you possess as well," she told her frankly.

Kinna wanted to laugh at the woman. Magic? She didn't think so. "I don't have any magic," she corrected. "My grandmother did, Queen Idalia, but no one else in our family has ever had any gifts."

Marstella just shook her head. "You have magic," she said simply. "My gift is never wrong. I can see it around you. You have a silver glow around you, the same color as your eyes."

"That's impossible," she whispered. It had to be impossible. She'd never done anything that hinted at her having any gifts. Surely if she possessed even a drop of magic something would have happened by now. Marstella had to be wrong, her gift had to be malfunctioning.

"It's not," she asserted. "I can see the glow around you the same as I can see it around Sebrina. Hers is yellow. Normally the color represents which element your gift favors, but I have never seen silver before. I do not know what kind of gift you possess but there is no doubt that you have one."

Sebrina laid a gentle hand on her arm. "We can help you learn more about it if you want," she offered. "I train nearly every day. You have to work to strengthen it just like any other muscle."

Kinna nodded absentmindedly. Sebrina seemed to take that as her accepting her invitation to train with her, but she doubted they would get very far. She would likely give up on her after a few days of her not being able to accomplish anything.

"I have a few more questions for you Kinna and then we'll be done for tonight," Rennick cut in. "We need you to tell us everything you remember from the last few days. Even small details that you think might not be important could help."

"I'll try," she agreed. The past few days had been exhausting and she wasn't sure that she could tell them anything useful, but she would try.

"When did you first see them?" he asked.

"The day of the explosion," she said. "Four of them were grouped together outside of the castle, within the walls. I heard them talk about looking for someone. They said *he wants her alive.* That's when I ran. One of them saw me leave through a side entrance and then they started following me."

"Four? Not three?" Bastin jumped in. "You said there were three that tracked you to Glenarm."

Kinna gulped, staring down at her fingers. She had been twisting her finger where her mother's ring should have sat, a nervous habit she'd always had. Could she tell them the truth, that she'd killed a man? She knew they would agree that it had been in self-defense, but she couldn't bring herself to feel guilty and that was what scared her. She had taken someone's life and she didn't even care. She took a deep breath, trying to steady herself. "Yes, there were four in the capital," she told him, looking Bastin in the eyes and willing steel into her bones. "I rented a room at an inn in the city, thinking I could sleep there for the night, but they found me. The innkeeper warned me that they were there, and I tried to sneak out the back into the alley but one of them was waiting for me. I left him bleeding out in the alley and ran."

He was quiet after that and she hated the satisfaction she felt, almost as much as she hated that she could calmly explain how she'd killed someone.

"You survived," Rennick said simply. "None of us are going to judge you for that. We have all made hard decisions and must live with the consequences, whatever they may be." Marstella nodded her agreement. "What else happened?" he asked.

"I ran north, staying off the road and in the woods," Kinna explained. "I knew the other three were following me. They came close to finding me one night. I stopped in Glenarm because I didn't have a plan and I wanted to see if anyone knew what was happening in the capital. I talked to one of the vendors there, he told me that everyone believed the Royal Family was dead. Then I saw them in the square, I tried to leave but the same man, he found me again, and the next thing I knew I was being chased through the Glenwood again."

"Do you remember anything about him?" he asked.

She shook her head no. "He just looked like a normal man," she explained. "Average height and build, short black hair, nothing special. I think he may have been the one I heard talking but I can't be sure. The only other person whose voice I heard was the one in the alley."

"Thank you for sharing this with us," Rennick said. "We may have more questions in the next few days, but we're done for tonight. Go get some rest, both of you."

Sebrina hopped up from her chair and gave her mother a quick kiss on the cheek before leaning down to press a kiss against Rennick's forehead. Could things possibly get any stranger? Rennick caught her eye and smiled at her surprise. "She is *our* daughter," he said in explanation.

Gods, he wasn't just Marstella's second in command, he was her husband. She stood to leave. She'd had enough surprises today to last a lifetime and could hardly wait to sink into unconsciousness where she wouldn't have to think for a few hours, but Bastin's voice stopped her before she could slip out.

"Who trained you?" he asked, the accusatory tone gone from his voice.

"General Resten," she said.

"How long?" he asked, something flickered in his eyes that she couldn't place.

"Since I was eight," Kinna told him. "His son is... was my best friend." A single tear escaped down her cheek, and she wiped it away quickly. She couldn't even bear to speak his name aloud. It didn't feel real, losing him. He and General Resten must be dead, or they would have found her by now, she was sure of it. Kinna didn't know what she expected but she'd always thought that if something were truly wrong with Ellio she would be able to feel it in her heart. Instead, she just felt empty.

She gave Sebrina a quick goodnight when they returned to the camp and ducked inside her tent. It wasn't nearly as large as the one she'd left but it was big enough for a cot and small side table that held a lantern. Her pack had been propped up against the foot of the cot, along with a thick blanket and pillow. She made a mental note to try to figure out who had set this up so she could thank them. Perhaps it had been the twins, but she couldn't be sure. Kicking off her shoes, she sat down in her cot and pulled the blanket up under her chin. It smelled slightly of vanilla. Her body was heavy, sleep tugging at her, so she reluctantly leaned out from under the warm blanket to blow out the lantern before giving in and falling into unconsciousness. She didn't dream and she was grateful for it.

CHAPTER FIFTEEN

Kinna slept all morning then through lunch, the events of the past few days catching up to her, her body and mind forcing her to rest. Even after she had woken from her dreamless sleep, she stayed in her tent, unable to venture out. She had spent the better part of the afternoon with silent tears streaming down her face, mourning her dead. Laying on the small cot she let their faces drift through her consciousness, replaying her most treasured memories so they would be forever etched in her mind.

Grief laid heavily on her, like stones pressing down on her chest so her breaths were labored and shallow. It felt like drowning on land. While Kinna had read about sorrow and grief in books, it was something wholly different to feel it for herself. Unlike the heroines in her stories, she did not have anyone to help shoulder her sadness. She was orphaned and completely alone, save for Sebrina, who was possibly the only friend she had but she couldn't burden her with her grief, not when she had already risked so much to save her life.

More time passed and Kinna still did not move from her cot, even as she watched the light dim outside and her stomach grumbled in protest. Her eyes were closed as she drifted on the edge of sleep when she heard a quiet voice call her name. Sebrina's blonde head poked through the tent flap. Kinna sat up quickly, causing her head to swim and black dots cloud her vision. When her eyes cleared, she saw that Sebrina was carrying a plate of steaming food.

"I thought you might be hungry," she said, offering her the plate.

Diced carrots and potatoes swam in a thick gravy poured over shredded beef. The savory smell had Kinna's mouthwatering. "Thank you," she said, her voice sounding hoarse in her ears.

Careful not to burn her tongue again, Kinna ate slowly while Sebrina made herself comfortable sitting cross-legged on the mat laid out over the ground in the tent. They sat quietly, the only sound coming from the fork clinking softly against the plate until she had finished eating.

Sebrina tilted her head, studying Kinna. "You've been crying," she whispered.

Kinna couldn't help the blush that creeped along the side of her face, fanning out across her cheeks. She only nodded in response, embarrassed that it was so obvious, or worse that someone may have heard her.

"It's okay," Sebrina said. "I would cry too. Probably for days if I had endured what you have." Kinna was silent still, not knowing what she could say. Sebrina just continued, not needing her to respond. "You can talk to me about it if you want, sometimes it can help, but you don't have to."

Kinna didn't want to, but she knew she needed to. She had promised herself that she wouldn't let their memories fade, that she would think of them often and remember their voices, their smiles, their laughs. So, she began.

"My mother was beautiful but horribly stubborn. We would argue over anything. My father was charismatic, always telling wild stories and keeping the peace. My sister, Evelyn, was kind and soft spoken, not at all like me. She never cursed or started fights, but we both loved books. We would have dinners every week by candlelight, just the four of us."

"My lady's maid was named Kerin, and she treated me like a daughter because she did not have one of her own. Maude was our temperamental Head Cook but she always let us stay in the kitchens as long as we wanted. General Resten was my father's highest ranking general and closest friend. He taught me how to use a bow, how to fight, even when no one wanted him to. His son's name was Ellio, and he was my very best friend," her voice cracked and Sebrina came to sit next to her, taking her hands in her own. She took a steadying breath before continuing.

"But the last words I said to him were angry and cruel and I will never get to take them back. I will never be able to apologize or beg for his forgiveness. I will never hear his laugh or see his smile," Kinna whispered, the words shattering every piece of her broken heart. "I will never have the chance to tell him that I think I love him and that maybe I always have. I think that's maybe the worst part, that his death made me realize that and I will have to live knowing that I will never be able to tell him."

Kinna didn't know when the tears had started falling again but fat drops were staining her shirt as she sat and listed all her loved ones. She told Sebrina about Evelyn's lady's maid, Suzannah, about the guards that were always waiting outside her door, even about Gavin and his sultry smile and rumbling laugh. She talked until her voice was nothing more than a rasp. All the while, Sebrina sat listening, rubbing soothing circles on her back, letting Kinna lean against her tiny frame. The more she confided in Sebrina, the more she felt the bond between them grow. With each passing story the rope that once bound them turned to steel, fortified and un-breakable. When she was done the two sat silently on the cot. "Thank you," Kinna whispered.

Sebrina weaved an arm around her, squeezing her tightly against her side. Despite being several inches taller than her five-foot frame, Kinna felt remarkably small as she tucked herself into Sebrina. "I think you are the strongest person I have ever met," Sebrina told her.

Kinna did not feel strong.

She felt like asking if she could stay nestled in the safety of Sebrina's arms forever, but she didn't. Instead, she took a deep breath, the first she had been able to take all day and realized that Sebrina had been right. She needed to talk. It had been painful but necessary to heal, like resetting a broken bone. Already she could feel the slightest weight removed from her chest, as if a few of the stones had been pushed off.

———

Her eyes cracked open the next morning and she stared at the tent above her letting the memories of the past day replay in her mind. It was still dark outside, and she couldn't hear any sounds outside her tent that would point to anyone else being awake. Rolling on her stomach she pressed her face into the pillow, trying to force herself to fall back asleep but the years of being up at dawn to run on the beach with Ellio had trained her body to be awake. Sighing she tossed the blanket off her and sat up, shivering for a moment in the cold morning air. Maybe she would go for a run, just a quick one alongside the river. It would be good for her stiff muscles and maybe it would soothe her aching heart just a bit to keep their traditions alive.

Just as she suspected no one was outside their tents yet, the large fire in the center of the camp reduced to coals. The sky was starting to turn a pale blue as she walked to the water's edge, the sunrise was not far off, so she didn't have much time if she wanted to remain unnoticed. She didn't want to explain why she was up before the others running alongside the river, she doubted it would make sense anyway. It made her long for home, where no one would question her coming back from the beach, drenched in sweat before breakfast.

She stretched her limbs before taking a deep breath and taking off in a dead sprint downstream. Racing towards the rising sun she felt the pain in her chest ease ever so slightly as she fell into their morning ritual. Her heart was thundering in her chest as the trees whizzed past her and even with her breath coming in big gulps, she could feel a smile break out across her face. Ellio would have loved running through the Glenwood, the hard ground pushing her faster than the soft sand would allow. He would have insisted they run through the thick woods, dodging trees and roots, arguing that it would make an excellent training exercise.

She could swear she could hear his footsteps pounding along the ground behind her as she ran. Except she did hear footsteps. The next thing she knew strong arms were wrapped around her waist and she was on the cold ground, wincing as her knees took the impact of the fall. She threw her elbow back, colliding with a hard, muscled chest and flipped on her back, cursing herself for not bringing her dagger with her. She was ready to use her legs to kick her attacker off but stopped when she looked up to find two amber eyes glaring at her.

"Are you insane?" she seethed. Bastin didn't respond, his arms still planted firmly on either side of her shoulders, his body caging her in. "You can get off me now."

"Where were you going?" he ordered, his voice an icy calm.

Realization hit her. He probably thought she was running away, back to some unknown enemy to spill the secrets of the Rising just as he had thought last night. Gods, this was just great. "I was going anywhere," she rolled her eyes. "I was just going for a run. I do this every morning so for future reference you don't need to tackle me to the ground."

He only stared at her, trying to decide if she was telling the truth, still holding his body over hers. She tried not to stare at his sculpted chest, but his loose shirt hung down exposing tanned skin dusted with dark curls and the start of a tattoo inked over his heart. Bastin grunted and stood, leaving Kinna blushing on the ground. He didn't bother to help her up before asking another question. "Why?" he asked. "You've spent days avoiding the uniforms, why would you risk leaving the safety of the camp?"

Her heart sank. This was the very question she'd been trying to avoid. "Why does it matter?" she retorted.

"Just answer the question."

She sighed; he wasn't going to budge. Bastin stood with his arms crossed over his chest, waiting on her to respond. He was the absolute last person she wanted to explain this to, but gods he sounded just like Ellio had when he'd found her running on the beach alone. The memory of her hateful words to him burned like a hot knife in her chest. She pushed the feeling down and focused on the man in front of her, not wanting to make the same mistake again. She hated to admit it, but Bastin did sort of have a point. She hadn't thought about how dangerous it could be to run so far from the camp.

"Every morning I would get up and run on the beach next to the castle with Ellio," she explained, her voice reverent as she said his name. "It was like a ritual. Every day began the same, always with the two of us on the beach. I couldn't go back to sleep this morning, so I started to run. For a moment it was like I could feel him with me. He would have loved running here, treating the forest like his own personal obstacle course."

"You loved him." Three words had never rang truer in her ears.

"I still do," she breathed, staring into the rushing water.

"Were you going to marry him?" he asked.

Her head whipped up in surprise. "Marry him?" She coughed. "Gods, no, it wasn't like that. He was my best friend, but it was never more than that."

"If you say so." He shrugged. Her temper flared. He didn't know the first thing about Ellio. How dare he stand there as if he knew his thoughts or hers. She ignored the small voice in her head that reminded her that not long ago she had thought about exactly what it would be like to marry Ellio Resten and live her life freely with him. That voice be damned, Bastin was still an arrogant bastard. She opened her mouth to tell him as much, but he just turned and started walking back towards the camp, leaving her fuming and jogging to catch up to him.

They spent the long walk back to the camp in silence. She hadn't realized how far she'd run and was secretly glad that someone had noticed her leaving, even if it had been Bastin. If she had been attacked that far away it would have been unlikely that anyone would have heard her scream for help. Everyone was awake as they neared the camp, and most were dragging their still sleepy selves into the cafeteria tent for breakfast. Kinna could see Sebrina's white-blonde head at a table with two steaming mugs of tea and she passed Bastin to join her.

He grabbed her arm before she could get more than two steps away. His large hands were warm as they encircled her slim arm easily. "Instead of running through the woods like a lunatic," he said. "Just join us for training so I don't have to track you down." She wiggled out of his grip and her hands curled into fists. He glanced down at them, and his mouth turned into a smirk, exposing his dimples. "No brawling outside of training." He tsked. "Camp rules."

"Whatever," she said, pushing past him. Maybe she would show up in the morning just for the chance to wipe the grin off his face.

Sebrina watched her approach and plop into the chair opposite her. "Where were you this morning with my most annoying cousin?" she asked, waggling an eyebrow at her.

"He tackled me by the river," she said.

"Is that some kind of euphemism that I'm not familiar with?" she laughed.

"Gods no," she cringed. "I went for a run this morning. He thought I was trying to escape, so he tackled and then interrogated me."

Sebrina almost fell out of her chair laughing. Kinna just rolled her eyes and grabbed the extra mug of tea, warming her hands on the sides. "I'm sorry," she laughed. "But that is hilarious."

"Yeah, it was exactly how I wanted to start my day," she scoffed.

Sebrina looked past Kinna. "Good morning boys," she called out. "Did you bring my breakfast?"

The twins appeared, setting plates overflowing with eggs and bacon down on the table before dragging chairs to join them. "Yes, we got your breakfast, Your Highness," one of them joked. He glanced at Kinna, and his face fell slightly. "No offense."

Kinna only smiled reassuringly. "No one called me that, if I could help it," she said. "I'm just Kinna."

"Well just Kinna," he said, his smile returning. "I'm Ronan and that's Rory. We are twins, obviously, but I am the older and much more charming of the two."

Rory kicked him under the table, and he grunted. "He also is the one with the worst manners," Rory explained, sliding a plate in front of Kinna. "It's nice to meet you."

"You too," she said, liking the pair already. "Were you two the ones that set up my tent? I wanted to thank whoever did."

"Anything for a damsel in distress." Ronan

winked. Rory only blushed, keeping his face fixed on his plate.

"What's on the agenda for today, boys?" Sebrina asked, stealing a piece of bacon off Ronan's plate.

"Bastin has us training this morning and then on watch all afternoon," Ronan whined. "Nothing exciting ever happens and we end up spending hours staring at trees. Well except yesterday when you two showed up, that was interesting."

"Maybe we'll come watch you train," Sebrina suggested, nodding to Kinna. "Us ladies are free until this afternoon."

"What's this afternoon?" Kinna asked.

"You and I will be training." Sebrina smiled.

"Ah yes." Ronan leaned back, tapping his fork to his brow. "You are going to try to teach the new girl with magic, who doesn't believe she has magic, how to use it."

Sebrina giggled. News moved fast around here. If the twins knew about her so-called gifts, Kinna was sure that everyone else did too. "I don't have magic," she assured them.

"Boss is never wrong," Ronan shrugged. "If she says you have it then you do." They weren't going to believe her no matter how many times she said it. Until then she would just have to listen to their musings.

"You better get going boys," Sebrina said, rising to collect plates. "Bas will be pissed if you are late." They groaned in unison before stacking their chairs upside down on the table and saying goodbye. Sebrina looked at Kinna. "I'm going to help with cleanup and lunch prep first, want to come?"

"Sure," she agreed, taking her plate and following

Sebrina. They walked to the back of the kitchen tent and through a small opening into a second, smaller tent. It was lined on all sides with worn tables, bowls of rising bread, produce, and knives. The backside was left open to access a large rectangle fire pit with metal grates laid over one side and a large cauldron on the other.

Sebrina dropped the dishes in a bucket of soapy water and began scrubbing. "You can rinse and dry if you want," she said. Kinna sat down next to her and fell into an easy rhythm of rising and drying while watching people run back and forth from the tent. Sebrina would point out some and tell her their name, a few even came to introduce themselves. By the time they were finished she had met a dozen people and hoped she could remember their names when she saw them again. They stacked the clean dishes on a clear spot on one of the tables while a short man with a deeply wrinkled face called out his thanks as he hustled past them. He slowed and stared when he noticed Kinna standing with Sebrina.

"I don't think we've met," he said, propping the basket of produce he carried on the table's edge. "I'm Ira."

She shook his extended hand. "I'm Kinna," she said.

"It's nice to meet you," he said. She noticed that he didn't seem to know her name like everyone else had, instead let her introduce herself. Maybe he truly didn't know, but she doubted it. No one knew or saw more than the cook. "Are you staying to help prepare for lunch?"

"If you'll have me," she offered.

"Do you have any experience in a kitchen?" His

eyes flashed with discernment, searching her for some sign of culinary skill. Thank the gods she'd spent so much time in the kitchens with Maude. At least she had some skills besides being able to rinse and dry dishes.

"I do well with breads and pastries, plus I'm excellent with a knife." She grinned, smiling at her own private joke.

He gave a curt nod. "Vegetable prep then," he decided, passing the produce basket to Sebrina. "Let me know when you are done."

Kinna glanced over the knives and picked a large one with a sturdy wooden handle and got to work peeling and dicing potatoes. She couldn't help her thoughts that drifted to the early days of working in the kitchen with Maude.

Her addiction to sweets had started early and one day she'd grown bold enough to try to steal a few pastries off the counter when she thought no one was looking but nothing got past the Head Cook. Maude had caught her, scaring her enough that she was willing to sell her soul to get away from her. Instead, she demanded that Kinna show up to help with breakfast prep for the next two weeks. Kerin of course heard about the incident within minutes and was determined that Kinna serve out her punishment, working early in the kitchens long before the sun would rise.

Of course, the first few days were terrible. Kinna, groggy and inexperienced, barely escaped cutting vegetables without losing a finger. Then Maude had moved her to the bread station where she would knead until her arms were numb. Eventually Maude had warmed up to her, teaching her how to craft the pastries she was so famous for and not objecting when she would lick icing off a spoon. Even after she had served her two weeks of punishment, she kept visiting the kitchens every morning, sometimes just staying long enough to eat breakfast and other days staying for hours while Maude taught her yet another of her dishes.

"How are you doing that so fast?" Sebrina's voice pulled her out of her memories.

"Huh?" She looked down at the small mountain of potatoes.

"You weren't kidding about the knives," she muttered. "Ira! Potatoes are done, where do you want them?"

The old man appeared behind them, glancing over Kinna's shoulder, appraising her work. "Who taught you?" He asked.

"Her name was Maude," she explained. "She was the Head Cook at the castle. I spent almost every day in the kitchens with her."

His brows raised. "I've never heard of Maude taking an apprentice," he said.

"I wasn't really an apprentice," she mumbled, not quite sure how to explain. He really must not know who she was. "Wait, did you know her?"

"Not well. We trained in some of the same places when we were very young, long before she found her place with the Royal Family," he explained, sweeping the potatoes into a deep pot, shaking his head. "Only Maude would dare put a princess to work in the kitchens."

So, he did know who she was. He just didn't care. "I deserved it," she told him, immediately defensive of Maude. "She caught me stealing pastries."

"How old were you?" he asked.

"Seven," she admitted.

His laugh echoed around them. "Who gives a knife to a seven-year-old." He chuckled under his breath. "You two are free to go. I'll see you for lunch." Kinna watched him walk off with the pot still laughing to himself.

Kinna turned to find Sebrina studying her. "You really spent your time in the kitchens, didn't you?" she asked.

"If I wasn't in the kitchens then I was in the training room. Or sometimes the beach," Kinna added.

Sebrina just grinned. "You are the weirdest princess I've ever met," she told her. "Not that I've met very many, but I imagine you're still the strangest."

It felt like a compliment, so she took it. Kinna knew she wasn't what others expected a princess to be like and she was fine with that. "So, what do we do now?" she asked.

"Let's go torment the guys at the training ring," she said cheerily, clapping her hands together.

CHAPTER SIXTEEN

The two made their way through the camp, walking along the river's edge until it narrowed slightly. Kinna realized just beneath the water's surface there was a line of strategically placed stones that made a path across but wouldn't be obvious to someone passing by. They crossed easily and entered the edge of the woods, following a slightly worn path in the grass until they could hear a voice barking orders through the trees. Kinna recognized it instantly as Bastin. She didn't want to think about the fact that she had already memorized a man's voice that she'd known for all of three days.

"Keep your feet moving Ronan!" Bastin shouted.

A small training space had been erected in the woods. A dirt sparring ring stood in the middle, currently occupied by Ronan and Rory with Bastin leaning over the wooden fence bordering it. Three targets sat to the left, hanging from the branches above them, where two men stood practicing under the watchful eye of Rennick. They passed between two tan tents that stood guard at the entrance of the space. Kinna couldn't help her gaze from drifting back to the targets and wishing for her bow. The furthest target didn't look more than thirty yards back, an easy shot. She was accurate at three times that distance.

Sebrina had stopped at the sparring ring, climbing onto the fence to watch the twins spar with dulled blades. Kinna joined her, keeping her distance from Bastin even though it seemed he hadn't noticed their arrival as he continued correcting Ronan's form. Rory was beating him.

Kinna watched him advance over and over, almost disarming him twice as he whirled around his brother faster than a snake. Ronan was slower but stronger and each time he landed a blow she could see it reverberate through Rory's body, but Ronan had a temper and it made him sloppy. Their swords clashed, Ronan forcing his brother's blade down and stopping, giving Rory the opportunity he needed. Quick as an asp he pulled his sword back and swiped his leg out, knocking Ronan off his feet. When he opened his eyes his brother's sword was at his throat. Kinna couldn't help but laugh at the string of curses that poured from his mouth. She was used to the colorful language she'd heard the guards use in the training rooms and had been known to be just as bad when she had sparred with Ellio or Gavin.

"That's what happens when you stop moving," Bastin chided as the boys joined them at the fence. "Don't give your opponent the chance to catch you. Go rack your swords. We're done for now." Ronan just nodded, glaring sideways at his twin who wore a smug smile but didn't taunt him. Bastin turned to the two women. "What are you two doing?"

"Ira let us off early," Sebrina told him. "I thought maybe Kinna would like to see the training space and you could show her around."

Kinna glared at her, she most definitely did not

want to be left with Bastin to show her around. She wouldn't mind being left alone with the bows for a while though. Sebrina just winked at her. "I need to prepare for our training this afternoon," she told him, already walking away. "Thanks Bas! I'll see you two at lunch."

Kinna just gaped after her as she flitted away. The little witch was more conniving than she had given her credit for. Bastin sighed and muttered something that sounded like babysitting duty that only stoked her outrage. "Come on," he said, motioning her to follow.

She stood firm. "You don't have to," she argued. "I'll be fine by myself."

"If I don't, she'll just make my life hell." He shrugged. "Come on."

They walked towards the other side of the training ring where a man even taller and more heavily muscled than Bastin had appeared. His ebony skin was flawless, a deep rich brown that meant he must have some lineage in Zotia, the southernmost kingdom on the continent. His head was shaved except for a thick braid that ran down the middle of his scalp and down his back with small gold rings woven into it. They matched the gold rings that adorned his ears, nose, and the center of his bottom lip. In total she counted ten piercings, but Kinna swore she could see two small circles pressed against his tight shirt as well. His obsidian eyes watched Kinna with a tiny hint of amusement as she surveyed him and mentally counted his piercings.

"This is Emhyr," Bastin introduced.

"Hello," his deep baritone echoed across the ring as he walked towards them.

"I'm Kinna," she introduced herself.

"No need to introduce yourself." He chuckled, exposing a gold stud bolted through his tongue, her count now rising to eleven. "Everyone here already knows who you are."

"I can't tell if that is a good thing or a bad thing." She nodded. He just shrugged.

"Rennick asked me to make you stop piercing Sebbie," Bastin interjected, filling the silence.

Emhyr just laughed at him. "I will not anger the tiny pale one," he told him. "I prefer to keep my balls attached to my body. You tell Rennick to take it up with her."

"He almost had a stroke when he saw her nose." Bastin smirked.

Emhyr turned to Kinna. "I'm quite good with a needle and the first one is always free." He winked. "If you ever want one just let me know. My tent is just over there."

Kinna was starting to like Emhyr and his easy laugh. It didn't hurt that he was quite nice to look at either. "Do they hurt much?" she asked.

"Ears are the easiest and don't hurt for more than a few seconds. Nose, lips and eyebrows are going to hurt a little more and take longer to heal." He smiled at his potential customer and stuck out his tongue. "Not going to lie, tongues can be a bitch so I wouldn't recommend starting there."

"Maybe I'll take you up on your offer." She smiled. Kinna's ears had been pierced only once when she was a child. She wasn't even sure if she could still get an earring through them, but she thought Sebrina's and Emhyr's piercings were beautiful and could imagine herself with colorful studs adorning her ears.

"I think you and I are going to be fast friends." He grinned.

"For her sake I hope not," Bastin muttered and steered her away from Emhyr who waggled his fingers at their retreating figures.

They passed Rennick and the two men she'd seen earlier as they made their way towards the other side of the clearing. Bastin introduced the younger dark-haired man with bright emerald eyes as Thane and the other with straw colored hair and dark eyes as Jax. The two gave her a quick welcome before jogging to catch up with Rennick who was busy discussing something with Emhyr. Kinna found herself gazing at the targets long enough for Bastin to notice.

"Do you know how to use a bow?" he asked, picking one up.

She snorted. "Of course," she said. "It was the first weapon I was taught to use."

He arched one eyebrow and tossed her the bow. She caught it easily, her body almost singing just having it one in her hands again. "Show me," he commanded. "Hit the first target."

The first target? No way. She was going to wipe that smirk right off his face. Pulling an arrow from the quiver beside him she stalked to the last target hanging thirty feet ahead of her. Drawing her arrow back, she held the string taut against her cheek. She eyed Bastin, his blank face unreadable, and gave him a quick wink before letting her arrow fly. The familiar snap of the string against her arm and the quiet thud as the arrow landed was the most beautiful noise she had ever heard. She broke the stare down with Bastin to see that her arrow had landed perfectly, in the dead center of the black bullseye. A smug smile broke out across her face, and she didn't even pretend to hide it.

Bastin walked unhurriedly to the target and jerked her arrow out. "Lucky shot," he said, dropping the arrow back in the quiver.

Lucky? Oh, he was absolutely infuriating. Before she could stop herself, she had grabbed three more arrows from the quiver, nocking them in place and then firing them in rapid succession. Each landed within the bullseye with only a hair's length separating them. She dropped her bow and turned, a sarcastic retort already on her lips, but she fell silent when four new sets of eyes stared at her from behind Bastin. Great, she'd drawn a crowd.

Emhyr broke out into a slow clap, grinning like a fiend. Thane and Jax stared at her with a mix of shock and admiration, even Rennick looked somewhat impressed. Bastin only glared at her with barely concealed anger. At least she had managed to piss Bastin off.

"Can you show me how to do that?" Thane asked. "I can barely hit the bullseye on the first target."

"I can try," she offered. "I've never taught anyone before."

He eagerly nodded his agreement. Rennick eyed her. She could see the thoughts swirling behind his eyes, the plans forming. It was a look she'd often seen on the general's face as he monitored the guards during evaluations. "I think we could use someone with your talents," he admitted. "How far are you still accurate?"

"Nearly a hundred yards," she preened.

Emhyr let out a low whistle and Bastin frowned. She couldn't understand what his problem was. Wasn't she supposed to be proving to him that she wasn't a spy? Wouldn't being able to help the Rising do that? It didn't matter, she decided. Him and his opinions didn't matter. She was going to help however she could whether he wanted her there or not.

"We could use you on a little transport mission in a few days," he pondered.

She didn't know what exactly a transport mission entailed but she didn't waste time asking questions. "I'm at your disposal," she said and dared a quick glance at Bastin. His eyes were practically simmering as he stared at Rennick.

Rennick thanked her, promising they would talk in more detail soon, and the group dispersed. She racked her bow and headed for the river. The sun shone high in the sky above her, meaning the camp would start gathering for lunch soon. As she moved through the clearing, she passed the twin tents that marked the entrance and could hear hushed arguing coming from a painfully familiar voice. Instead of staying to listen, she forced her feet to keep moving, stomping unnecessarily hard across the stones as she crossed the river.

Kinna found Sebrina at the same table they'd eaten at this morning, already half finished with a helping of chicken and fried potatoes. Sebrina pushed the plate across the table. "How was your morning?" she asked, smirking.

"Just great," Kinna told her, stuffing potatoes in her mouth. Sebrina had definitely left Kinna with Bastin on purpose, she just wasn't sure which one of them she was trying to punish.

"Are you ready for this afternoon?" She asked. "Ready to get your magic mojo flowing?"

Kinna rolled her eyes. Magic mojo her ass. "What

makes you all so sure I have magic?" She countered.

"Mom said so," Sebrina shrugged. Hearing someone call Marstella, the mysterious leader of the Rising, *mom* just seemed wrong.

"But she didn't even know what my gift was," she reminded Sebrina. "She didn't know what my silver aura meant, remember?"

"I guess we'll find out." She grinned. "Let's meet at the hot springs in ten minutes."

CHAPTER SEVENTEEN

Kinna arrived at the hot springs to find Sebrina sitting with her pant legs rolled up and her feet dangling in the water. Marstella stood across from her daughter, an unexpected addition to their session. Noticing her arrival, Sebrina hopped up from her perch and unfolded her pant legs, giving Kinna a reassuring smile. Marstella motioned for the two girls to follow her and began weaving her way through the hot springs until they reached the largest pool in the center. It's water so blue it almost glowed in the sunlight. "Sit," she ordered, and they obeyed, sitting cross-legged at the edge of the water. "Since we aren't sure what gift you possess, I thought we'd start with the water element since it was the element your grandmother was gifted with."

Kinna nodded. The logic made sense; too bad this would turn out to be a waste of time. She'd spent her life around water, living in a castle on the coast meant that she'd had countless days sitting on the beach and in the water. Never once had she been able to manipulate water in any way and gods had she tried. Like all magic, the element someone had an affinity for could manifest in different ways. Some controlled the element out-right, like her grandmother who could direct the tides or send waves crashing on the coast. Other gifts were more subtle, like those that could coax plants to grow from earth and use them to heal everything from a cold to severe illnesses. Each ability was different like the person who possessed it and she wondered idly what else Sebrina could do with her wind.

"I want you to create a ripple in the water," Mars-tella said simply. "Focus your energy on the water, make it an extension of yourself and you will control it."

"It helps in the beginning if you focus on your breathing," Sebrina added. "Draw your energy as you in-hale and push it out over the water as you exhale."

Again, the logic made sense, but she knew there was a greater chance of an earthquake shaking the water than her. She kept those thoughts to herself and closed her eyes, resigned to at least try for Sebrina's sake. Drawing in a deep breath through her nose she imagined a silver ember rising up through her body, settling in her core. As she exhaled, she tried pushing it out, extending her palms for good measure. Over and over, she tried it, but the water's surface remained un-disturbed. She huffed an irritated breath. This was obvi-ously not working.

"You're doing fine," Sebrina whispered encour-agingly.

Kinna risked a glance at Marstella hoping she wouldn't find anger or disappointment but her back was turned. "What do you know about the origins of magic Kinna?" She asked.

Not much. Kinna had gone to the temples for winter and summer solstice and the spring and fall equinoxes, but nothing said during the hours-long cere-monies had ever captured her attention. Her grand-mother had been a pious woman, spending time fre-quently in the temple dedicated to Narelle near the coast but it was not a sentiment her parents shared. She had been taught that the five gods guarded their world and had blessed the continent with magic but not much else. "I don't know very much," she admitted.

Marstella turned and sat across from them. "Then I will tell you," she said. "When the world was young and the first people made their home on the continent the gods were sent to guard them, meant to be their pro-tectors. We do not know who sent them, but their mis-sion remained the same. Some were content to watch over us, aiding those who called out for their help, but others were not. The most discontent of them all was Alev. Known for his gift of fire and his short temper, he grew bored of watching mortals. He cared little for their lives and wanted to no longer be responsible for our world."

"So, he began sowing discord among the five, gaining support from Jela, goddess of the land, who had grown tired of watching mortals cut down her beloved forests and pollute the earth. However, the other three were not so easily convinced, Narelle, goddess of water and the sea, and Era, god of the wind and air, argued that it was their duty to protect this world and those dwelling in it. They cared for the mortals and did not want to see them suffer without their aid. Orella, god-dess of sight, seeing that a war between the gods would lead to destruction of the very world they were meant to protect, offered a compromise. Orella wanted to gift the mortals with magic of their own, so they did not rely as heavily on the gods. Knowing that Orella would have seen the solution with the best outcome they agreed."

"However, when the gods gifted the continent with magic, it wasn't just given to the mortals, but also to the land itself. The moment the gods stepped foot on the continent, their magic began seeping into all manner of things, but the people were too enthralled by their new power to notice other things were changing alongside them. Even the Glenwood was changed that day, given an extra drop of magic by Jela who had always loved cultivating the crimson maple trees that grew here. The magic transformed ordinary things into objects of power. Stones became gems, plants were given medicinal properties, water took on healing abilities, even the forests seem to have a mind of their own," Marstella explained. "It's believed that over the years Jela continued to visit her beloved Glenwood, causing the unusual number of crimson maples that grow here."

Kinna sat enthralled listening to Marstella weave the story of the beginning of magic. It made sense that so many believed that the gods had abandoned them, if it hadn't been for Narelle and Era, they may have. "So, why is magic fading then?" she asked.

Marstella sighed. "That is something I cannot explain," she told her. "Some believe it is because our mortal bloodlines have weakened the original gift given so long ago but I do not think so. Magic does not age, and it cannot be diluted. It is too pure and powerful."

Kinna mulled over her words. Something had to be causing the magic to leech from their world, but she had to agree with Marstella, she didn't think it would just fade away on its own.

"The gods also left this world with one other

thing, a prophecy. Spoken by Orella and passed down from generation to generation. The prophecy was a promise that even though the gods would no longer intervene in mortal affairs, they would bless a champion with the power to do so in times of great need."

"I've never heard of such a thing," Kinna said.

Marstella looked to Sebrina who shifted, straightening her back before beginning to speak in a soft voice.

"For the gods were not cruel or without mercy
So, when a great darkness comes
They will send a champion
With power greater than all
And they will protect their people
And rescue those that call"

Kinna sat motionless while Sebrina recited the prophecy a second time. She pondered how she had lived for nineteen years and never once heard of a prophecy given by Orella, much less the actual words. Then again, she had spent most of her time in the temple asleep or staring through the colored glass into the city around it.

"I think it's time for us to retire from our practice for the night," she decided. "Ira will be upset with us if we don't show up for dinner."

The three headed back to camp, Kinna infinitely glad to be up and walking. Her legs had gotten stiff from sitting cross-legged on the ground for so long. They quickly joined everyone for dinner and Kinna studied the tables, trying to match names to faces of those she'd been introduced to earlier. She spied Thane sitting with Jax and watched as he pulled a pretty girl that had introduced herself this morning as Lalie into his lap while she giggled and half-heartedly tried to get back up. They finished eating and Kinna noticed a few people beginning to gather around the large fire in the center of the settlement, some dragging chairs and others laying out on blankets.

"What are they doing?" she asked Sebrina.

"Most nights we all gather around the fire after dinner. Sometimes my parents will address everyone and fill us in on all the Rising news, but we usually just relax," she explained.

Ronan waved them over and they joined the twins on a worn quilt close to the fire. The warmth was delicious against the cool night air, and she found herself stretching her legs closer to the blaze. Kinna watched as little groups began to form, laughter and a hum of voices filled the air forming a strange sense of peace in her heart. She was starting to believe that all the things she'd heard about the Rising were a lie because what sat before her was nothing more than a family, one she could so easily see herself belonging to.

The flames danced in the fire, casting an orange glow on the faces around her. All too quickly the peace that had cultivated vanished. The orange glow was too familiar and the last time she had seen it, it had been coming from within the castle walls after the explosion. Guilt ate at her, souring her mood. She should be working to get back to the capital, to rebuild her home and her kingdom, not frolicking around and trying to make new friends. As much as she wanted to stay here and belong, she had a duty to her people and if what the merchant in Glenarm had said was true, her kingdom was going to need her. Gods knew what would happen if Ferryn were left too long without a ruler protecting its people. It was just the kind of opportunity Eldridge would use to launch an attack on Edgewood or worse take the entire kingdom. She was going to have to leave, she decided, but telling Sebrina was going to hurt, and she hoped it wouldn't cost her the only friend she had. The thought of losing someone else was misery.

Emhyr's roaring laughter startled her as he crashed into the quilt in the middle of them clinging to a glass bottle sloshing with amber liquid. All his golden hoops gleamed in the firelight as he gave them a conspirator's grin. "Anyone care for a drink?" he offered, throwing an arm around her and Sebrina and swinging the bottle between them.

Ronan agreed quickly, grabbing the bottle and taking a quick drink that ended in him coughing into his fist. Rory declined politely and grinned at his brother who was still recovering from the strong liquor. Sebrina agreed, taking a small sip, her face screwing up as she exhaled. She turned to offer the bottle to Kinna. She normally didn't drink and found most liquor to burn rather than be pleasant, but she knew what lay ahead of her and tonight she just wanted to pretend she was a normal nineteen-year-old. As she expected it burned as it slid down her throat but settled in her stomach as a warm feeling flowed through her body.

Emhyr smiled as she passed the bottle back to him. "So, are you going to join us in the morning to train?" He asked. "I promise I'll hang another target for you, one much further away."

His offer was tempting, and her body was so warm thanks to the liquor. Just a few more days wouldn't hurt. Plus, she had agreed to help Rennick with his transport mission and she wouldn't break her word. She could leave for the capital after that. "It's a deal." She grinned, grabbing the bottle from him, and taking a long drink.

The rest of the night consisted of Emhyr regaling them of Kinna's abilities with the bow, exaggerating the story from this morning beyond belief, and then all coming down with a serious case of the giggles. Everything was hilarious and even quiet Rory seemed to have caught their infectious laughter. They were the last ones to leave after the fire had burned so low that they were all stumbling in the dark. She watched Rory try to support his brother and Emhyr as he led them away from the fire, smiling and shaking his head as they protested his help.

"I think you're going to have to help me up." Sebrina giggled, falling backwards after her second attempt at standing.

Kinna had made it into a crouch but couldn't keep her balance long enough to stand as she laughed at Sebrina's efforts. They might as well throw another log to reignite the fire and sleep here because there was no way they would make it back to their tents. Suddenly firm hands gripped under her arms and began pulling her to her feet. Thank the gods, Rory must have come back for them.

"Can you stand on your own?" a brusque voice asked. *Shit.* That was definitely not Rory's voice.

Bastin stood behind her, broad hands resting on her shoulders. His perfect face was unmistakable even in the dim light. His mouth formed a hard line as he waited for a response, but it did nothing to distract her from his full lips. Gods, she wanted to touch them. She felt her hand rising without her consent, fingertips reaching to brush his bottom lip. It felt like the finest satin. When she looked back at his eyes, they were like living fire. He grasped her hand gently, pulling it away from his mouth and turned wordlessly to help Sebrina into a standing position.

He was silent as he shuffled them across the clearing and into their tents. Sebrina was tucked in first before squealing something that sounded like goodnight as Bastin left her tent. Once inside, Kinna snuggled down into her warm cot, understanding exactly why people drank the burning liquor. It made her feel like sunshine was living inside her body. Her heavy eyes closed, and she immediately began drifting towards sleep when she thought she heard a soft goodnight and the rustle of a tent. One eye cracked open but no one was there and as soon as her eyes closed again, she was asleep.

CHAPTER EIGHTEEN

Bastin

He was heading back to his tent after making his nightly rounds on the perimeter of the camp when he heard the familiar shrill laugh of his cousin. His bed was calling but it was late and Sebrina didn't need to be out wandering around doing gods knew what. Sighing he changed directions, heading for the sounds of feminine laughter. Unsurprisingly he found Sebrina on a blanket with the princess. They'd become attached at the hip since Sebbie had brought her home just days ago.

Princess Kinna Braunlin. When he'd spotted her in the Glenwood, all wild curls and a wicked tongue, he'd been entranced. The second their eyes had met it was like his very essence recognized hers. The voice in his mind began a soft chant in response: *worthy, equal, mine.* Over and over the last word rang through him, igniting a fire fueled by her face. *Mine, mine, mine.* He had spent the next few painful hours watching her with Sebrina, mesmerized by those eyes. That is, until he'd heard his aunt say her name and the light inside him that had been growing steadily started to dim. The gods had a cruel sense of humor. It didn't matter how *much he wanted her, how much his very soul was drawn to her like a fire to kindling, there was no fucking way he was going anywhere near the Princess of Ferryn. He was already dreading the transport mission that Rennick had conveniently invited her on after her little stunt with the bow. She'd been good and he'd hated how much he enjoyed watching her, especially when she'd winked at him and sunk three consecutive arrows into the target. It was going to be a test of his self-control to spend more than a week with her without Sebrina there to be a buffer.*

Even though it was likely to find the two together, he was surprised to find them both drunk and giggling in front of the dying fire, trying and failing to stand up. He had a sneaking suspicion he knew who'd gotten them drunk. Emhyr was quite possibly the worst influence he could imagine, and he was going to throttle him tomorrow for leaving the two helpless in the dark. Neither of them noticed his approach, which only annoyed him further. They had no sense of self preservation. His annoyance turned to anger as he stood behind Kinna and slid his hands under her slim shoulders and lifted her easily onto her feet. She wasn't as small as Sebrina, more muscle clung to her body, but he still towered over her.

Her smile faded instantly when she saw him, her full lips parting slightly as she stared at him. Gods, she was always staring at him like she could see right through to his soul. "Can you stand on your own?" he asked, watching Sebrina still struggle to get up.

Instead of answering her eyes locked on his mouth and her hand reached up to brush her soft fingertips across his lips. Her touch sent a bolt of heat through his spine that he tried to ignore. He told himself that she'd taken him by surprise, but he knew the truth, if he had wanted to stop her, he could have. Taking her hand gently from his face he stepped out of reach before he could do something very stupid.

He hauled Sebrina off the ground as she let out another round of giggles and tucked them both under an arm, herding them back to their tents. Thankfully they were situated right next to each other. He sat Sebrina down in her bed, rolling her onto her side and sliding her blanket up to her chin, hoping Kinna was still standing outside without his arm supporting her. Mercifully she was exactly where he'd left her, a sleepy grin plastered on her face as he pulled her toward her own tent and got her in bed. Her eyes were closed before he could grab her blanket, a faint smile still tugging at her lips. He pulled the blanket up around her, tucking the edges in around her knees, then hips, then shoulders, letting his hands graze over the curve of her body. Still, his eyes stayed fixed on her face and the mess of curly hair that spilled out around her like a dark halo. He let himself study her for just a moment, inexplicably drawn to her, before he whispered a goodnight and ducked out of her tent. Staying away from her was going to be harder than he thought and the reasons to do so had already started to seem much less important.

CHAPTER NINETEEN

A sharp jab on her shoulder woke her up. Her head was pounding, and she didn't bother to open her eyes, nothing good was going to happen if she tried to get out of her cot. Another jab landed on her shoulder, and she swatted the hand away. "Go away," she moaned.

"Sorry but I can't," the voice said, stifling a laugh. "You need some food if you're going to be able to train this morning."

Training? Absolutely not. She would be lucky if she was able to walk without puking. "No way," she muttered.

"Come on. Everyone's already at breakfast and I saved you some bacon," the voice tempted. Bacon did sound good. She cracked open one eye to see Rory standing over her. "See, this is why I don't drink with Emhyr."

Well, she never was going to again. Him and his liquor were evil. She told Rory as much and he just laughed and left her tent, convinced that she wasn't going to go back to sleep. Groaning, she sat up, trying to stop her head from spinning from the movement and stumbled her way out of the tent. She tried to tame her hair into a braid as she walked but eventually gave up, twisting the top layer into a bun and leaving the other half down since the curls were mostly intact. Luckily Sebrina and Ronan also looked as bad as she felt. Rory dropped a steaming mug of tea in front of her and slid the plate of bacon and biscuits her way.

"The tea and food will help," he offered.

The tea had a minty, herbal taste that immediately soothed her dry mouth and stomach. She sat and nursed her drink before attempting to eat. "That is amazing. Thanks, Rory." She sighed, taking another drink, and crunching a piece of bacon. "By the way, how did you manage to get both Ronan and Emhyr back to their tents last night?"

He flashed a proud smile before explaining that after dropping Ronan in their tent, the real challenge had been trying to get Emhyr across the river without them both falling in. "My pants were soaked by the time I got back across, and Ro was already snoring when I got in bed, so I got to listen to that all night." He grinned. Ronan threw a biscuit at his brother's head, but he caught it easily and took a large bite out of it.

Rory had been right, after finishing her tea and having a few biscuits Kinna felt infinitely better. Good enough to train and ensure Emhyr hung her extra target like he'd promised. Sebrina however was still looking like she might be sick at any moment. They left her still nursing a cup of tea as she weakly waved them off.

They found everyone in the clearing, training already in full swing. Thane and Jax sparred in the center ring and Kinna spied Emhyr straddling a branch and hanging a target. He gave her a wink as she approached the base of the tree. "How are you feeling this morning," he snickered, climbing down. Clearly the liquor hadn't affected him the same way.

"Like shit," she admitted.

He laughed and nudged her shoulder as he passed. "I'll cut you off earlier next time," he promised and joined Ronan and Rory at the edge of the sparring ring. She rolled her eyes at his retreating figure and turned to examine the target he'd hung for her. It was probably no more than sixty feet, but it would be a better challenge. She turned to look for a bow and found Bastin staring at her. Shit. All the memories from the night before that she'd conveniently forgotten in the wake of her hangover rushed her. She'd been so drunk he had needed to put her to bed but not before she'd decided that it would be a good idea to touch the lips she couldn't stop staring at. A blush broke out across her entire body, moving from her face down her neck and across her chest. She wanted to run and hide from him for the next week.

"I'm surprised you are standing up right," he said without humor.

So, it was going to be like that with him. No jokes like Emhyr or helpful mugs of tea like Rory had offered, just straight up asshole-ness. "Look I'm sorry you had to help me get up and to my tent." She sighed. "Trust me I have no intentions of drinking with Emhyr any time soon."

"What about your wandering hands," he asked coolly, no hint of the fire she'd glimpsed in his eyes last night. "Are you going to apologize for that too or have you been wanting to do that since we met?"

He might as well have slapped her; she would have been less stunned if he had. Apparently, all the times she'd been staring at him hadn't gone unnoticed and she hoped it hadn't been so obvious to everyone else. "I have no idea what you are talking about," she insisted, feigning ignorance and attempting to stalk past him.

Too easily his hands grabbed her, pulling her face close enough that she could smell the rich mint and citrus scent of his skin. A day's worth of stubble flecked his tanned face and before she could stop herself, she was staring at his mouth again, wondering if it would taste as good as he smelled. "You're staring again, princess" he breathed, the warm air caressing her face.

Kinna focused on his eyes and tried to ignore how painfully aware she was of every spot where his body pressed against hers. Heat radiated off him and she couldn't help leaning closer to him. His broad chest stood at eye level, and she vaguely wondered what his tattoo on his chest was and if he had more. His finger and thumb lifted her chin, raising her head to meet his gaze again and her heart pounded in her ears as he smoothed his thumb over skin. "Hopefully next time you touch me you won't be drunk, and I won't have to stop you," he whispered before turning on his heel and leaving her suddenly chilled without his warmth.

She stood, rooted to the ground, while she tried to process what had just happened. Slowly her senses returned, and she could hear the sound of voices and clashing swords. Dazed, she found her way to the edge of the sparring ring, bracing herself against the fence because honestly, she needed some tangible to hold onto at the moment.

Bastin had joined Ronan and Rory in the ring, and it was clear he meant to spar with them both. That pulled her thoughts back to reality because she was about to see if he was as good as he thought or if he just spent his time barking orders from the sidelines.

The twins advanced, trying to catch him between them so he would have to focus on only one of them at a time, but Bastin wouldn't allow it. He struck over and over on their weak side, forcing them together in the center of the ring. For his size, he was surprisingly fast and had yet to break a sweat while toying with the boys.

The twins however were losing steam, tired from blocking blows from a man twice their size. She watched as they made one last ditch effort to advance on him, moving in synchrony so Bastin would have to choose only one blow to block. Instead, he ducked, blocking the stronger blow from Ronan and swinging one leg out to catch Rory in the stomach, sending him staggering back. He whirled behind Ronan, his fore-arm clamped around his throat, and sword pointing at Rory's chest, a triumphant look plastered across his face. The two yielded and were dismissed from the ring.

While Kinna had been watching him, she debated on whether she would engage with him after his be-havior earlier. She decided yes, if to do nothing more than get under his skin. She stalked towards him with all the feline grace she could muster, entering the ring as surprise flashed across the faces of the men gathered to watch. Bastin watched her approach, sizing her up before giving her a taunting smirk that set her teeth on edge. Her anger was quickly rising to the surface, and she needed a release before it started to boil over. A feral grin spilled across her face as she picked up a sword and weighed it in her hands. She was finally going to have some fun.

Kinna didn't waste any time before launching

herself at him, swinging down hard against his sword, throwing all her anger and rage from the past week into her movements. Before he could force her off, she moved again, ducking as his sword swung upwards without her weight bearing down on it. Bastin stepped back, regaining his footing, and putting a few feet of distance between them. She charged him again, swords singing as they collided. Bastin used his weight to his advantage, throwing her back. She hit the ground hard but used the momentum to somersault backwards. Dust rained down from her hair as she stood in time to catch his next blow.

Glancing down at his wide stance an idea formed in her mind as she remembered what he kept hidden under his pant leg. She retreated a few paces before charging again, but instead of meeting his sword she tossed hers aside and slid between his legs, ripping the dagger free from the leather strap at his ankle. Distracted by her deviation Bastin hesitated and she sprang up behind him, pressing the dagger against the soft flesh of his neck. "I win," she whispered in his ear before letting go and stepping back to bow to the stunned crowd as they offered a small round of applause before dispersing.

Bastin had moved quietly to stand behind Kinna. "You're clever," he conceded, leaning down so his lips almost grazed her ear. "But you got lucky with that little stunt. Next time you won't be."

He glided away grinning leaving her confused and shaken for the second time that day. She started walking out of the ring before anyone noticed and joined Thane for target practice. They spent the next hour talking through form while Kinna showed him how to aim and corrected his stance. By lunch he had improved, hitting the bullseye on the first target twice. Thane was thrilled and Kinna was thankful for the distraction that kept her thoughts from focusing on Bastin and everything he'd said that morning.

When she joined Sebrina for lunch her friend still looked like she hadn't recovered from last night but was adamant that they continue their lessons this afternoon. Kinna left her at their table with her head pressed against the wood and searched the back of the tent to find the herbal tea that Rory had brought them this morning. She poured it into a large mug and took it to Sebrina. She lifted her head and took it gratefully, gulping down the hot liquid and sighing at the warmth that settled inside her.

"Thank you," she murmured. "I don't know how you are functioning right now. Ira tossed me out this morning since I couldn't look at any of the food without gagging."

She thought it might have something to do with Sebrina's tiny body not being able to metabolize the alcohol as quickly, but she kept that to herself. "I must be lucky," she guessed. "Do you want something to eat?"

Sebrina nodded and Kinna went to grab a plate from Ira who was passing out meat pies as he made his way through the tent. She thanked him before returning to Sebrina who had some color returning to her face now that she'd finished her tea. "How was training this morning?" Sebrina asked after devouring two pies.

"Good," she lied. She desperately wanted to tell her about what had happened with Bastin, but she couldn't make her mouth form the words. He was her cousin, there was no way Sebrina wanted to hear about how close she'd come to kissing him or how the slightest touch sent her heart into overdrive. Besides, nothing was going to happen between them. Sexy or not, he was still an arrogant bastard that had been less than welcoming. She was leaving for the capital as soon as the transport mission was over, and she did not need anything distracting her.

"I heard you sparred with Bas." She smirked. "And you won."

Gods, was there anything these people did besides gossip? She'd left training less than an hour ago and Sebrina had already been filled in on the morning's events. Maybe she'd come to spy on them since she hadn't helped with lunch prep. "I did," she said carefully, hoping Sebrina couldn't read her as easily as her cousin seemed to.

"That's impressive," she hedged. "Even more impressive is that I heard he was smiling afterwards."

Kinna ignored her implication. "Bastin is good, and I didn't exactly fight fair," she admitted.

Sebrina snorted. "No one fights fair outside the sparring ring anyway," she argued.

"You have no idea," she murmured, the night in the alley behind the Sick Fish Inn floated up in her mind. The terror as the man had used her hair to drag her backward and laughed in her ear still made her stomach roil. She knew she'd never forget how dirty she'd felt that night, like he had stained her, body and soul.

"Hey," Sebrina whispered, a worried look on her face. "You okay?"

Kinna realized she'd gone silent at the table. "Of course," she said, trying to sound reassuring. "I just get lost in my head sometimes."

"If you need to talk about it, I'm a pretty good listener," she reminded her.

Kinna's heart tightened. "Thank you." She smiled. Sebrina was already a better friend than she deserved, and despite the circumstances surrounding it, she was grateful to have met her.

CHAPTER TWENTY

They made their way back to the hot springs and sat with their feet in the water while they waited on Marstella to arrive. Kinna wondered if she would have to try to control the water element again today or if they would move on to another. Marstella arrived on silent feet, causing both girls to jump when she appeared seemingly out of thin air before them. Their startled faces brought a rare smile to her lips.

"Kinna, I think you should try controlling the air element today," she said. "It is the most similar to the water element and Sebrina can help by demonstrating. It might help you to see someone wield their gift."

Sebrina pulled her feet from the water, settling into the same cross-legged position as they had sat in yesterday, and closed her eyes. Her slim hands rested lightly on her knees, and she took a deep breath in and as she exhaled Kinna felt a gentle wind blow through, lifting strands of her hair.

"I can channel the wind as gently or sharply as I want," she explained, eyes still closed. "I've also learned how to bounce it off objects. That's how I distracted the uniforms in the woods. I bounced it off a tree in the other direction so they would think you had gone that way." Sebrina grinned as she demonstrated it, making Kinna jump at the sharp crack that sounded on the water, like a whip coming down over the surface.

They spent the next few hours the same as they had the day before, Kinna trying and failing to channel the energy inside her into something tangible. Sebrina was relentlessly encouraging, offering to show her again and again how she controlled the air around her, but Kinna couldn't so much as create a breeze. A small part of her was secretly disappointed. Sebrina's gifts really were incredible. Despite not being able to do anything, she'd enjoyed watching Sebrina create little funnels of wind that spiraled out across the water or swayed the branches overhead.

Sebrina's stomach growled, and her mother decided they were finished for the day. Even though Sebrina hadn't used huge amounts of magic, Kinna learned that it tired her as if she'd been training all afternoon. Each time she directed the wind it drained her energy just a bit more. "It's kind of like a muscle," she explained. "The more you work it the stronger it'll be and the more stamina you'll have but eventually you'll run out of energy just like you would if you were running. You can feel it start to strain the longer you wield or the more you try to control."

"What happens when you run out?" Kinna asked.

"You'll drop." Sebrina smirked. "Your body won't let you cause serious damage to yourself so if you push too far or too fast, you'll take a nice, forced nap."

"So, you just pass out?"

"Yep." Sebrina nodded. "Not something you want to happen. You feel like shit when you wake up, worse than any hangover."

Kinna mulled that over as they ate dinner. They were joined by Ronan and Rory which was quickly becoming her new normal. There was so much about magic that she didn't know. If she was being honest, there was so much she didn't know in general, about magic, about the Rising, and even about her own kingdom. She'd been living in a bubble at the castle, wrapped up in her own selfish life, not particularly caring to learn about what was happening around her.

Well, she was over that. There was an entire world out there and she wanted to learn and see everything she could.

Kinna volunteered to clear the table while Sebrina and the twins saved them a spot by the fire before they all filled up. As she left the tent, she spied where the three were, sitting on the same wide quilt they'd used last night. She started to make her way towards them when Bastin slid in front of her, arms crossed and blocking her path. Irritated that he always seemed to appear out of nowhere, she glared at him, if only to keep herself from drooling. It had been an unusually warm day and he had traded his normal attire for a sleeveless shirt which put his well-defined arms on display.

"Can I help you?" she asked when he didn't speak.

"No drinking tonight," he ordered.

"I don't recall needing your permission." She rolled her eyes at him.

His brows raised, brushing the chestnut strands that fell over his brow, and she swore she could see a smile tugging at his lips, like he was enjoying pissing her off. "If you're planning to go on the transport mission, I suggest you don't," he said. "Rennick wants to meet with us tomorrow before breakfast to go over the details."

She just nodded, stepping around him to go join

the others. His arm stretched out, catching her across the stomach and stopping her. "One more thing," he whispered, glancing down at her. His eyes settled on her lips, and he grinned, enjoying his own personal joke. "Try to keep your hands to yourself. I'm the jealous type."

She just stared at him, not quite believing the words she'd heard come out of his mouth. He had been playing with her head all day, his words trying to eat through her self-control. Well, two could play that game, she thought.

Kinna let her hand wander up his arm, finger trailing lightly over the taut muscles as she pressed herself into his side. Her chin rested on his chest, and she felt him stiffen under her touch, going utterly still. Glancing up through her lashes she saw his amber eyes simmering and she knew she'd won this round. "Don't worry," she assured him, her voice husky. "I don't like sharing either."

With her chin resting on his chest, she knew he hadn't taken a single breath until she pulled away, pushing past him like he was no more substantial than a feather. She didn't turn as she walked away but she knew he was still standing there, watching her move towards the fire, so she put a little extra sway in her steps as she went.

"What was that about?" Sebrina asked as she sat down.

"Showing your cousin that he's not the only one that can play games," Kinna explained, risking a glance behind her only to find him gone.

———

It was cold when she woke up for the early morning meeting with Rennick, a thick fog hanging over the water and weaving through the camp. Digging the blue sweater out of her bag, she gave it a small smile before tugging it over her head. She couldn't help pressing her face against the thick material. She swore it still smelled like Ellio even though he hadn't worn it in years.

The red tent came into view as she passed through the grove of crimson maples that surrounded it. A small group had assembled inside, crowded around the same wooden table she'd sat at when she'd first been brought to the camp. It felt like a lifetime ago instead of a few days.

Marstella was seated, sipping on a steaming mug of strong coffee, while Rennick, Jax, Emhyr and Bastin stood around her looking like guards surrounding their queen. She supposed she was a queen in a way. Queen of the Rising, she mused. That would make Sebrina laugh, especially since that would make her a princess too.

She joined them, taking a spot next to Emhyr while she tried to ignore Bastin's stare. He'd been staring at her since she walked in, and she prayed that he would just keep his mouth shut for a few minutes. Thankfully Rennick started their meeting before any snide remarks could slip out.

"In a few days, the four of you will be traveling north, through Edgewood to connect with our sister group that maintains a camp on the outskirts of the city," Rennick explained. "There is a family of three that will need to be transported across the border of Eldridge and Ferryn. Normally we wouldn't try to move that many at a time but it's a father and two children. We didn't want to risk separating them."

The three men nodded around her. This was

nothing new to them and Kinna wondered how many of these missions they'd been on. It wasn't easy to move across the border and a group this large was going to be hard to hide, especially with children involved. Eldridge border guards were notoriously brutal. Kinna had heard stories of what happened to those they caught trying to escape into Ferryn, especially those with magic, and wondered if maybe this hadn't been her best idea. No, she reprimanded herself, there were children involved. She would do this; she would help keep them safe because no child deserved to grow up in fear.

"Kinna will be joining you to provide additional coverage. She's skilled with a bow, as I'm sure you've all seen, but is not to engage directly with the guards or any uniforms you encounter." His gaze fell on her. "I will not risk your life. If Bastin thinks your safety is in danger, he is to extract you. Your safety will be the top priority while you are away."

"Respectfully, I can handle myself," she argued, working to keep the resentment hidden in her voice. She knew Bastin was behind this decision despite proving that she was more than capable of defending herself. "There are two children that should be the focus, not me."

"This isn't up for debate," Bastin interjected. "You either agree to the terms or don't go."

Kinna opened her mouth to remind Bastin how their last sparring match ended but Marstella stopped her. "It is admirable that your concern remains for the children, but you are the uncrowned Queen of Ferryn. Someone that has the power to not only protect those two but entire generations. We cannot afford to jeopardize you any further than we already are."

Shit. Marstella was right and now she sounded like a brat. Their decision wasn't based on her talent but because of who she was and what she could do once she returned to the capital. It was disturbing how easily Kinna was able to forget what awaited her when she left the Rising, a future she never could have imagined. She couldn't help wishing she could trade it for the comfortable safety she had found here. "I understand," she agreed.

"Good," Rennick added and unfurled a map across the table in front of them. It was littered with little red *x*'s snaking down from the border towards Glenarm. She counted nine. Something about the pattern was familiar, like she'd seen them before but couldn't quite place it.

Rennick began mapping out the path they would take, avoiding the larger villages where they may encounter a heavier guard presence, or worse the men that had been following Kinna that they called uniforms. They only had three days to meet their contact in the north so their pace would be fast, and they couldn't afford to waste time trying to lose a tail.

"Everyone needs to memorize this map," Rennick said. "We can't send it with you so get familiar with it."

"I have a map," Kinna offered. "I had it with me when I left the capital."

"That would be very helpful," Rennick nodded.

"I'll go grab it," she said, already heading for the entrance to the tent.

She jogged across the camp towards her tent and dug through her bag until she found the folded slip of paper. Unfolding it, she tried to smooth out the paper as best she could as she admired her handiwork. She was not an artist by any means, but her little map was well done if she did say so herself. Still, something about the map was sending off little warning bells in her mind. She was still staring at it, trying to figure out what she was missing when she entered the tent again and re-joined the group. Her stomach dropped as her eyes flew back and forth between the map on the table and the one in her hand. Every single red *x* marked on their map coinciding with the ley lines on her map intersecting.

"What does the red *x* stand for?" She asked quietly.

They were all quiet, glancing back and forth between each other. It hardly mattered what they told her; she already knew. In her gut she knew this had to be connected to the reason the general was planning to leave the capital.

"A body," Bastin answered. "It marks every place we've found a body. Every month a day or two after the full moon."

"A body that looks as if it has been burned, al-most unrecognizable," she whispered, remembering El-lio's words in her room.

"How do you know that?" he asked seriously.

"General Resten was leaving to investigate them before they got any closer to the capital. Ellio told me about the bodies, how they'd been found. That's what I was doing when the castle exploded, trying to sneak out with the company so I could go with them," she ex-plained, her heart aching as she repeated the events that had led her here. "I made this map because I thought it would help us."

The yellowed paper fluttered onto the table, an almost identical rendering of the larger one beside it.

"Why did you draw all these lines?" Rennick asked. "These aren't latitude or longitude lines."

She shook her head. "They are called ley lines. I just copied this out of a book in the castle."

"What are ley lines?" Bastin asked.

"They crisscross the continent," Marstella explained, picking up Kinna's map to study it. "They are said to carry energy across the land and magic is stronger in areas where they converge. I've never seen a map of them though, not like this."

"They line up perfectly with where the bodies were found," Rennick murmured. "That cannot be a mere coincidence."

"No, I don't think it is," Marstella agreed and turned to Kinna. "Can we keep this? I'd like to learn all I can about these."

"Of course," she agreed.

Rennick dismissed them for breakfast, he and Marstella stayed behind to further study the map of ley lines Kinna had drawn. She couldn't escape the feeling that there was still something she was missing, that this was just a small piece of a larger puzzle that anyone had yet to figure out. It kept her distracted through breakfast and while she ran drills with the bow through the morning. The feeling gnawed at her until she was distracted enough to miss the target she was aiming for. Frustrated and glad her error had gone unnoticed she left the clearing, hoping to find something to keep her mind busy.

Luckily, she ran into Ira and quickly offered herself up to help prepare for the camp's next meal. He quizzed her on which recipes she knew as they walked back towards the kitchen area and mess tent, his eyes lighting up when she listed Maude's cinnamon bread. His excitement grew as he gathered supplies and formed a station to work on after Kinna agreed to teach him how to make it. The pair stood kneading bread and discussing which desserts they preferred while they formed loaf after loaf. Her hands and wrists were coated in flour as Kinna explained how Maude had taught her to form the loaf so the cinnamon filling would maintain its perfect swirl and Ira watched her, completely absorbed, until his technique was perfect.

"There you are!" Sebrina greeted. "You didn't show up for lunch."

Kinna glanced outside the tent, looking for small shadows on the ground but the cloudy sky had hidden the sun. She must have been here longer than she had thought but working with Ira had been exactly the distraction she had needed. "I didn't realize what time it was," she said, dusting her floured hands off and unrolling her sleeves. "Am I late for our training session?"

"That's why I was looking for you," Sebrina explained. "It's just going to be the two of us today."

"I can finish up here," Ira interjected, taking the loaf Kinna hadn't finished forming. "You two go."

"Thank you," Kinna said.

"Don't be late for dinner," Ira warned. "These loaves will go quickly."

The two smiled and promised to be back for dinner early before heading towards the pools to begin another afternoon of training. Kinna was secretly glad that she would get a break from training while on the transport mission, they could be remarkably boring since she had yet to produce even a tiny wisp of magic.

Sebrina dropped the bag she'd been carrying on

her shoulder at the edge of the soft grass. "I want to try something different today," she announced. "I think you need to relax if you are going to access whatever magic you have. Your emotions and feelings are tied closely to your ability to control it so I think we should try something new."

Kinna nodded. "What exactly did you have in mind?"

Sebrina dumped the contents of her bag out revealing two towels, black soap, a nail file, and a brush. "Baths," she said proudly. "I think we should pamper ourselves and relax then see if you can access something when you aren't feeling pressured to."

Kinna thought it was an excellent plan, especially since she would get to spend the afternoon spending some much-needed time on her hair. The tangles were quickly becoming matted, something she couldn't stand. "I love it." She smiled.

Sebrina clapped her hands and stripped down before grabbing the bar of soap and sauntering towards the deep, innermost pool. One foot hovered over the water before she launched herself in, her body disappearing beneath the clear blue water. Kinna undressed quickly, leaving her clothes in a pile on the grass before taking the comb and following Sebrina's lead, slipping into the warm water.

After scrubbing her skin until it was pink, Kinna went to work on her hair. With unending patience, she brushed through each strand until the knots were gone, leaving behind gentle waves that floated on the water's surface. Sebrina traded the nail file for the comb and Kinna cleaned and shaped her nails, something she rarely did since long nails weren't practical for handling arrows. She set the file on the small strip of earth that separated the pools and let herself float towards the middle, enjoying the sensation of being weightless.

In the quiet, Kinna searched for the spark inside her, finding it easier to identify than before. She focused on her breathing and tried to push the energy out with each exhale. Her hands glided over the surface of the water, pushing through it as she exhaled, trying to control the element as her grandmother had.

With her eyes still closed, Kinna's mind was blank as she felt for the energy living inside her, but it was like reaching for someone in the fog. She knew it was there waiting, but she couldn't quite find exactly how to grasp it. She kept trying until her skin pruned from being in the water and she heard Sebrina rising noisily from her spot.

She opened her eyes to a cloudless blue sky above her head, still floating on her back, but instead of feeling discouraged or frustrated she just felt relaxed. Maybe Sebrina had been right, and this was the best way for her to figure out if she had any magic.

"How do you feel?" Sebrina asked her.

"Relaxed." She smiled and Sebrina giggled. "We should try this again. I think you were right. It's like I can feel something, but I just can't hold onto it."

"We can try again my approach when you get back if you want," Sebrina agreed. "It may take time. Control doesn't happen overnight."

Kinna agreed but was left feeling guilty for doing so. She had promised herself that after the transport mission was over, she would go back to the capital, back to the castle. The responsibility of her kingdom now weighed on her shoulders and even though it was easy to forget while she was here, the reality of it was never far from her mind. Kinna thought about the night she had walked the gardens with Evelyn and the resignation she had seen on her face, knowing she would have to trade her happiness for her kingdom's prosperity. It was ironic that she now knew exactly how she had felt in that moment and wished her sister was there to rest her head on her shoulder, to provide that small comfort to her.

The clouds had returned by the time they arrived for dinner, everyone pulling tables and chairs beneath the large canopy in case the clouds turned to rain. Sebrina and Kinna joined the twins and Emhyr as food was passed around, including thick slices of the cinnamon bread she and Ira had spent the day making. The sweet and spicy smell of the cinnamon was mouthwatering, but the taste was even better, the soft, creamy filling paired perfectly with the crunch of the bread's crust. Even Maude would have approved, and the thought brought a small smile to her face.

CHAPTER TWENTY-ONE

After dinner their group disbanded, the twins had been roped into helping Emhyr prepare for their trip north, leaving Kinna and Sebrina on their own. Kinna started to make her way to their usual spot in front of the fire, but Sebrina's arm caught her. Her mischievous smile indicated she had different plans for them tonight. "Let's go to the clearing," she whispered, half dragging Kinna without waiting to hear her response.

"Why?" she whispered back.

"I want you to teach me how to shoot a bow." She grinned.

They skipped across the stones hovering under the river's surface, Sebrina's steps slowing as they neared the twin tents that sat at the entrance. She stopped beside a tree and craned her neck to listen.

"What are you—" Kinna started to ask before she was promptly shushed. She stood with her arms crossed, waiting for an explanation.

Finally, Sebrina relaxed and motioned for her to follow. "I think it's clear."

"Clear of what?" Kinna asked.

"People. Bas will only teach me basic self-defense, nothing that would help in a fight."

"Who exactly are you planning on fighting?" Kinna smirked. The thought of Sebrina in an actual fight was amusing. She couldn't imagine her tiny fists would leave a mark on Kinna, much less someone like Bastin.

"Gods, you sound exactly like him," she grumbled. "I can't stay tucked away here forever. I could do something meaningful for the Rising if they would let me. I have actual magic, remember?"

Sebrina did have a point and Kinna knew her frustration better than anyone. She knew exactly what it was like to not be taken seriously, to not be allowed to do the one thing your heart was screaming at you to do. At least she'd had General Resten, who had taught her to fight and let her train, Sebrina didn't even have that. Gods, she had gotten so tired of being told to stay home and sit out the action that she had planned her own escape. "I know how you feel," she admitted. "My whole life all I wanted to do was leave the castle and do something, anything important. It chipped away at me each time I was told no until I was desperate enough to try to escape on my own."

Sebrina's eyes gleamed at the recognition and acceptance. "I knew you understood," she said, squeezing her hand.

Together they walked towards the row of targets, stopping at the first and closest one. Kinna grabbed a bow, testing the string and bringing it to where Sebrina stood with a quiver of arrows in her hands. There wasn't an armguard anywhere, so Kinna shrugged off her thick sweater and offered it to her.

"Put this on," she explained. "The string is going to slap against your arm, and it will leave a nasty bruise. This won't stop it, but it might help."

Sebrina nodded eagerly, pulling it over her head and cuffing the sleeves around her wrists. Kinna passed her a bow, seeing the excitement bubble under Sebrina's skin and Kinna couldn't help but smile. It reminded her so much of herself when the general had first handed her a bow.

Kinna took her stance, explaining how to position her arms and feet, keeping her back straight and eye on the target before her. Once she finished, she dropped her bow, letting Sebrina take her place in front of the target.

She copied her, letting Kinna adjust her elbow or tweak her aim before she announced she was ready to fire. Sebrina hesitated for half a second before focusing on the black bullseye and released her hold on the arrow. The arrow flew straight but fell before reaching the target.

Sebrina huffed in disappointment. "It's fine," Kinna assured her. "It's going to take some time before you can pull the string back far enough to hit targets at a distance. Right now, we are focusing on your form."

"I want to try again," Sebrina said.

Kinna nodded encouragingly. "Take a few steps forward and show me your stance."

After a quick adjustment, Kinna shook her head, ready for Sebrina to shoot again. This time the arrow made it to the target, sinking into the outer blue ring.

"I hit it!" Sebrina squealed.

"Your aim is pretty good." Kinna smiled. "Someday you may even be able to use your magic when you shoot."

"What do you mean?"

"Well, the wind always affects your aim," Kinna explained. "But if you were controlling it, you could use it to push your arrow faster in the direction you're aiming."

Sebrina's eyes grew wide with wonder. "I want to try it," she breathed. "Can I try on an arrow you shoot?"

"We can try," Kinna agreed, grabbing an arrow out of the quiver on the ground. "Just please do not push it towards me. These are dull but they will still hurt."

"I won't, I promise," she said quickly.

Kinna stood, pulling the arrow back into position, while Sebrina positioned herself behind her. "On three," Kinna said. "One, two, three."

Kinna released the arrow. The sound of the string snapping overpowered by the narrow bolt of wind whooshing in her ear, propelling her arrow forward. She dropped the bow and looked at the target.

"Wow," Sebrina breathed. "It worked."

The two walked towards the target, Kinna not quite believing what they had done. It had passed almost completely through it, the dull arrowhead just barely visible through the wooden back. If Sebrina could do this with an arrow shot from a bow, perhaps one day she may be able to forgo the bow entirely and use only her magic to fire arrows.

"You're scheming," Sebrina accused, breaking her train of thought.

"I wasn't scheming, I was thinking," she argued.

"Same thing." Sebrina laughed. "What were you *thinking*?"

Kinna gave the arrow a tug, but it held firm in the

wood. "I think you could shoot arrows without a bow by using your magic."

"Really?" she breathed.

"It might take a lot of practice, and I can still teach you to use the bow, but yes. I think you might be able to use just your magic," Kinna said, wiggling the arrow again. "Look at what you can do when you just guide an arrow someone else shot. This thing is stuck."

Panic flashed across Sebrina's face. "It can't be stuck," she grunted, grabbing the arrow herself. "Bas can't know we were out here."

"Calm down," Kinna soothed. "Let me hold onto the target while you pull."

After a few minutes of straining and a few splinters they managed to wiggle the arrow free. Although there wasn't anything they could do about the rather large split it left in the target. They returned the bow and quiver before making their way across the river and back to camp. Sebrina tugged off the sweater and passed it back to Kinna as they reached their tents.

"Thanks." She smiled. "I really had fun."

"I did, too," Kinna agreed, pressing the still warm sweater to her chest. "I'll see you at breakfast."

Sebrina pulled back the flap of her tent and said goodnight through a yawn then disappeared beneath the tan fabric. Kinna saw her lantern flicker to life before she ducked inside her own tent, her feet skidding to a stop before she ran into a solid figure standing in the dark.

Her heart was thundering in her chest as she glanced down towards her bag still propped up at the foot of her cot where her only dagger lay tucked inside. Cursing herself for not keeping it on her she lunged for the bag, pulling it close to her chest while she fumbled for the dagger inside. She had it out and was on her feet, aiming towards the unknown assailant when the tent was suddenly lit from the inside with soft yellow light. Bastin stood before her, her lantern sitting lit in his hands.

"What the fuck is wrong with you?" Kinna hissed, dropping the dagger she still had aimed in his direction and grabbed the sweater off the ground. "I could have stabbed you."

"Considering how long it took you to dig the dagger out, I think I was safe," he said humorlessly.

His dismissal only fueled her anger. He seriously had some nerve waiting for her in the dark like some kind of stalker then criticizing her for being unprepared. She doubted anyone was ever prepared to be attacked in a tent surrounded by a dozen people. "Sorry, I wasn't expecting visitors," she said acidly. "Would you like to explain why you're waiting in my tent or am I supposed to guess?"

Bastin set the lantern down on the small side table, moving to the center of the tent where he could stand up straight without his head grazing the ceiling. Even with his back to the light and his face cast in shadow, his amber eyes kept their unearthly glow. She started folding the sweater in her hands so she wouldn't stare.

"Whose sweater is that?" he asked.

"Mine," she answered, confused by his question.

"That is a man's sweater. Last I checked you were not a man."

Kinna felt the heat rise and settle across her face. "Is this why you are here? To learn the origins of my sweater?"

He sighed heavily through his nose. "No, it is not. Still, I would like to know who it belongs to."

"It belongs to me," she reiterated, rubbing her fingers across the soft material. "But before that it belonged to my friend."

"Ellio," he said, a hard edge in his voice. She was surprised that he remembered his name, that he remembered anything about the rambling story she'd told after he had tackled her on the river's edge. "The one you were going to marry."

So much for remembering the entire story. "I was not going to marry him," she corrected. "He was my best friend. That's it."

"If you say so," he shrugged.

Kinna tossed the sweater on her cot. "Well, if that is all, I would like to go to bed."

"No," he said, crossing his arms. "That is not why I am here."

"Then what do you want?"

"I want you to stop teaching Sebrina how to use a bow, or any other weapon," he said, glaring at her. "Make up some excuse, I don't care, but no more."

"Excuse me?" Kinna seethed.

"Do I need to repeat myself?" he asked.

Her blood had gone from boiling to being a living fire beneath her skin. She had thought Sebrina was exaggerating about Bastin, but this was taking being overprotective to a whole new level. The voice in the back of her mind wondered how he even knew what they had been doing for the past few hours, but it wasn't able to break through the string of curses she was hurling at him in her head.

"Let's get a few things straight," she fumed. "I do not take orders from you, and I certainly will not stop teaching someone how to protect themselves and others."

"She knows how to defend herself, I made sure of that," he challenged. "But she won't need to know anything beyond that. I won't let her put herself in a situation where she must fight her way out. She is all the family I have left, and I will not put her in danger."

For half a second her rage quieted. Yes, he was definitely being overprotective, but she couldn't help but wonder if his need for control was coming from a place of loss. She knew very little about him or his past, aside from what Marstella had said when she first arrived, that he had lost his family.

Perhaps there was a better way to approach this. "Listen," she said, working to keep her voice calm. "I get that you want to protect her but treating her like she is made of glass isn't going to work. I promise you she will put herself in more danger trying to prove to you and everyone else that she is capable. No one knows that better than I do."

"My answer is no," he snapped.

So much for the sympathetic approach. "Gods, you are insufferable," she muttered. "I'm not going to stop. If she wants to learn, I'm going to teach her whatever I can."

A muscle flexed in his jaw, and he looked like he was using all his self-control to keep from shaking her. "If something happens to her, I am going to hold you personally responsible. I don't care if you are a princess, I'll stuff you in a cell myself," he added before storming out, leaving Kinna a little bruised.

She undressed and climbed into her cot, replaying their conversation over in her head. Every time she got stuck on the way he had said princess, like it was a dirty word. There had been many times in her life when she had wished she didn't have her title and the responsibilities that came with it, but no one had ever used it as an insult the way Bastin had. Hearing it said aloud had never hurt the way it did when he said it.

Her mood only worsened when she thought of spending days with him traveling to the border. The close quarters and long days would already have her on edge but adding him to the mix was a recipe for disaster. Maybe it would result in a fight. She had to admit, the thought of punching him right in his perfect mouth did improve her mood. Kinna fell asleep with a small smirk on her face, imagining pummeling Bastin and rubbing his face in the dirt.

———

Bright sunshine woke her up, the light breaking through the thick canvas of the tent. The morning was unusually warm and Kinna was sweating underneath the quilt. She threw it off quickly and sat up, raising the hair off her neck, underneath damp with sweat, as she tried to cool off. Her sleeveless tunic was somewhere in the tent, likely crumbled somewhere on the ground after she had dumped her bag out last night looking for her dagger. Gods, it was too early in the morning to think about Bastin. She did not want to start her day in the same mood she had been in last night.

Finally, she found her tunic in a ball under her cot. She lifted it to her face and sniffed at the wrinkled fabric. It, along with the rest of her clothes, had smelled better. She laid all the clothes from her bag out on her cot and decided to ask Sebrina if there was any soap for her to wash her clothes with at breakfast. She really needed to wash everything before she left, and it definitely was not an excuse to avoid training this morning.

Breakfast was in full swing when she arrived, the warm air and sunshine seemed to have brightened everyone's mood and pulled them from their beds earlier than normal. Kinna grabbed a steaming mug of tea and found Sebrina sitting alone, slathering a piece of bread in butter. She smiled sheepishly as she approached, an unusual greeting compared to Sebrina's usual enthusiasm.

"Good morning," she said softly.

Kinna slid into the chair across from her, watching her avoid eye contact. "Good morning," she answered. The two sat in silence, Sebrina staying focused on buttering her toast until Kinna grew tired of waiting. "Is something wrong?"

Sebrina bit her lip. "I may have overheard you and Bas last night."

Shit. Kinna probably hadn't been very quiet last night. She had been so angry that she hadn't thought about much besides wanting to stab Bastin and she especially hadn't been thinking about Sebrina's tent sitting just a few feet away. "I'm sorry," she said.

"Sorry?" Sebrina blurted. "What do you have to be sorry for? I should be the one apologizing."

"Why would you be apologizing?" Kinna countered.

Sebrina laid her toast down, sighing. "I knew Bastin would find out you were teaching me how to shoot and get pissed," she said. "I didn't think it would happen so quickly, but I shouldn't have put you in the middle of this."

"Sebrina, I could care less what Bastin thinks. If you want to learn, I will teach you."

"I know." She smiled. "I heard what you said last night. I know you used to feel the same way I do now. You understand why this is so important to me and I love you for it."

Her words spread out over Kinna's heart like warm honey, filling the cracks and making it whole and she realized she loved Sebrina too. Not only had she saved her life, but she had also brought her to this place and offered her more. She had offered her a home when she had been homeless, a friend when she had been friendless, and even a family when she had been orphaned. It had happened so fast, the Rising tucking her into their fold and accepting her as one of their own. The realization of how deeply she had needed everything they offered her brought tears to her eyes.

"I love you, too," she whispered, eyes gleaming.

Sebrina saw the raw emotion in her eyes, somehow understanding everything that had just hit her without Kinna saying a word. "I'm going to miss you while you're gone," she said. "I know it's only a few days, but things are about to get infinitely more boring without you here."

Kinna giggled but thankfully remembered her impending laundry before she got too distracted. "Speaking of that," she said. "I really need to wash my clothes. Do you have any laundry soap?"

Sebrina raised an eyebrow. "I thought I smelled something."

"Very funny."

"Ira keeps some in the back." Sebrina laughed. "I'll

show you where it is if you help me with the dishes."

"Deal," Kinna agreed.

After finishing the dishes, Kinna stopped in her tent to gather her clothes and a towel before heading to the pools. She soaked her clothes in the warm water before working the soap into a lather, using the rocky edge to scrub it into her clothes and spending extra time on her socks that smelled especially ripe.

The lavender scent of the soap wafted up as she washed. The sweet floral scent already replaced the mix of sweat and dirt that had been clinging to the material. She repeated the process for all her tunics and leggings before slipping off her clothes and washing them as well. Once they were rinsed, she laid them flat on the grass, letting the sun dry them while she sank back down in the warm water.

An hour passed and she emerged from the water to check her clothing, everything had dried except for her sweater that was still slightly damp. She dropped her towel and pulled on her tunic and leggings before folding the remaining clothes. After depositing them all back in her tent, Kinna laid the sweater on the grass behind her tent to let it continue to dry in the sun.

She wasn't sure when they would be leaving in the morning, but she assumed it would be early, so she took advantage of the free time to pack her bag. After her clothing was folded into small, tight bundles and stowed in her bag she retrieved the sweater from its spot in the sun and added it on top. When there was nothing left for Kinna to do she laid down on her cot, staring up at the peaked ceiling of the tent and without something to occupy her, her mind drifted to the very person she had been trying to avoid all day.

Her feelings had been a tangled mess since she had first met Bastin. She wouldn't deny she was attracted to him. He was the picture of masculinity, all hard muscles and tanned skin. Not to mention his face looked as if the gods themselves had formed it. No one with such a terrible demeanor should be allowed to have the face of an angel.

Kinna closed her eyes, letting herself unashamedly remember his features. His square jaw and high cheekbones would have been a gift themselves, but nothing captivated her more than those amber eyes and perfectly full lips. Just the thought set her skin on fire.

She sighed because despite all that, his temper and acidic words had burned her more times that she would like to admit. He had made it obvious that he thought she was naïve and careless but then he would toy with her, whispering words that washed away all her anger and sent her thoughts in a very different direction. It was madness trying to understand his every cryptic remark, but she had reveled in it. She had let it distract her from reality, but she couldn't anymore.

Her kingdom should be her focus, she reminded herself harshly. It needed to be her only priority. She would engage with Bastin only when necessary and once the transport mission was over, she would leave the safety of the Rising and go back to the capital, no matter how much the thought broke her.

Kerin's favorite words whispered in the back of her mind. *Remember who you are.* Kinna was determined to let that mantra guide her, because this was her duty, her burden to bear and she would not run from it.

CHAPTER TWENTY-TWO

Kinna left her tent when she heard the noise of the camp gathering for lunch. Sitting with Sebrina, Ronan, Rory, and Emhyr at their table she soaked in everything around her. The smell of herb roasted chicken and the taste of buttery potatoes floated around her. It was a staple meal served in the camp and one she still had not tired of. She watched the conversation bounce between her new friends, listening to the hum of people talking and the frequent bubbles of laughter. Kinna knew that this may be one of the last times she would sit under the wide tent and share a meal with her friends, so she etched it all in her mind and stored it deep in her heart.

Ronan's voice carried her name, bringing Kinna out of her thoughts. "I can't believe I am going to miss another trip north," he griped. "If Kinna can go I don't see why Rory and I can't."

"Can you shoot an arrow at a hundred yards?" Emhyr teased, shoving Ronan's shoulder with his. When he didn't reply Emhyr only grinned. "I thought so."

"If you both went, who would run patrols?" Sebrina offered. "Even Rennick is staying behind to make sure the camp stays protected."

That seemed to lift Ronan's spirits a bit. He leaned his chair back, balancing on the back two legs and rested his hands behind his head. "I guess you're right," he admitted, his smile returning. "Someone has to stay behind and protect all the ladies."

Rory rolled his eyes and used his foot to tip Ronan's chair backward. He lost his balance and fell noisily on the ground, cursing his twin as two younger girls giggled. Kinna recognized the dark-haired one as Lyla, the young sister of Thane's girlfriend Lalie, who Kinna had determined was Ira's right-hand woman in the kitchen. The other girl had a darker complexion with deep brown eyes that Sebrina had once pointed out as Cleo. Ronan's face burned crimson as he picked up his chair and returned to his seat. Emhyr bit his knuckles to hold back his laughter.

With their plates licked clean the group dispersed, the twins and Emhyr leaving for their afternoon patrol duty. Sebrina discarded their dishes before circling back to retrieve Kinna from their table. "We aren't going to train today," she announced.

"We aren't?" Kinna asked.

"No, I'm supposed to help you get ready for your trip. You'll leave before sunrise with the others."

Kinna followed Sebrina through the camp, towards a tiny grey tent that sat on the edge of the circle closest to the forest. It stood only a few feet tall, making them both duck to get inside. Trunks of varying sizes filled the space with blankets and canvas bags stacked on top of them. Sebrina cleared a stack of quilts off a brown trunk before grabbing the scratched metal handle and dragging in towards the middle of the tent.

"What is all this?" Kinna asked, grabbing the opposite handle to help.

"It's a closet of sorts," she answered. "We keep extra clothes in here, along with more blankets and tents. Most of our winter clothes are stored here too."

Sebrina began pulling out the neatly folded stacks and placing them on the floor. One by one she would unfold a piece and hold it up to Kinna, judging whether or not it would make it into the keep pile. She wasn't sure what exactly the criteria was that earned a piece a spot outside the trunk but after half an hour of searching Sebrina had amassed a small wardrobe for her.

Two thick wool sweaters, one a deep purple and the other a emerald green, were joined with a thick pair of grey pants and a wrap skirt that she could layer over her knit leggings. Sebrina found another pair of thick socks that would reach almost to her knees in a stiff canvas bag and added them to the growing pile. Finally, a midnight blue cloak was draped around her shoulders, fanning out around her, the edges brushing against her ankles. The thick material was surprisingly soft and the silver clasp that sat at the base of her collarbone still shined. Sebrina gave a satisfied smile.

"I think that will work," she said, her fingers quickly unfastening the cloak.

The two gathered everything and brought it back to Kinna's tent. She laid out her traveling clothes for the next day, her knit leggings and deep burgundy cap sleeve tunic, and left the cloak out since it wouldn't fit in her small bag. They decided to leave her other tunics behind to save space and then worked the additional clothes into her bag. After a fair amount of stuffing, they were able to close the bag but waited a moment to ensure it wouldn't burst open. Once they were satisfied the contents would remain inside the bag, it was propped against the cot, ready for the morning.

———

Dinner consisted of a hearty vegetable stew, complete with large chunks of potatoes floating in a fragrant broth with diced carrots, celery, and little round peas. Circular loaves were placed in the center of the table, the crusty bread soaking up the leftover liquid. Kinna sat with her bowl in hand, savoring the warmth on her fingers, watching Ronan and Emhyr fight over the last slice of bread. Sebrina snatched it off the plate while they argued, tearing it in two and tossing the halves in their bowls.

Kinna spied Rennick and Marstella approaching, making an appearance at the end of a meal that seemed to signify something to the rest of the group. One by one each table quieted as bodies turned to face the two standing in the entrance of the tent.

"We have some news," Rennick's voice rang out. "Once everyone has eaten and is gathered outside, we will share it."

The pair turned to leave, positioning themselves in front of the large fire while the tent erupted in a flurry of activity. People began rising from their seats, rushing to return their dishes and take their place on the blankets outside. "I'll get these," Emhyr said, collecting the bowls littering their table. "Save me a seat."

They all nodded in agreement and quickly found an empty space big enough for the five of them towards the left of the wide crescent shape that had formed in front of Rennick and Marstella. Emhyr joined them moments later, his large frame settling behind Kinna. Finally, the sounds of hurried footsteps and fidgeting ceased and Rennick stepped up to speak, Marstella standing behind him with her chin held high, a serene look fixed upon her face. The sun was setting behind them, casting a yellow glow along the edge of their figures, their hair shining as if two golden crowns adorned their heads.

"Tomorrow morning, we will be sending a group to rendezvous with our northern faction and complete a transport mission," he began. "A man and his two children will be brought over the border and into the protection of the Rising."

The group thundered around her, fists smacking the ground in unison, showing their support for their leader. Kinna was reminded that despite her viewing the Rising as a makeshift family, they were also a rebel group with a cause.

"As you already know, we have a newcomer in our midst," he continued. "Kinna has agreed to accompany three of our finest Risers on this mission and lend her exceptional archery skills to protect and ensure their success."

The thundering grew louder, fists hitting the ground in rapid succession while a few hoots rang out around her. One of the loudest coming from behind her. This time their support was for her, and the three that would travel with her. The chorus of pounding hands did not stop, finding a rhythm until they were one heartbeat.

"Their task is not one without risks, this we know," Rennick warned. "We remember the many that have fallen for our cause, fallen to protect the vulnerable and in need."

The faces around her turned solemn but the pounding continued. Kinna wondered how many sitting here had lost someone they cared about, how many had fallen to save those in both Ferryn and Eldridge from meeting a terrible fate.

"Instead of mourning, we honor our dead. We honor their sacrifice by continuing to give hope to those who need it most," Rennick said. "Because like smoke in the wind, hope is rising."

The pounding reached a crescendo as Rennick uttered those last three words. The air sparked with energy, goosebumps rising on her skin. Rennick's hand raised and all at once the pounding stopped.

"Enjoy your night." He smiled softly then took Marstella by the hand and departed.

Chatter broke out as soon as their figures disappeared into the fading light. Emhyr nudged her shoulder with something hard, before dropping down next to her, his large shoulder brushing hers. She turned to find him grinning, a bottle swaying from his hands. "Anyone care for a celebratory drink?" he mused.

Ronan grinned and agreed immediately. "Do I need to remind you how it turned out last time?" Rory teased.

"Don't worry, little brother," Ronan said, taking a quick drink. "I won't overdo it this time."

Rory rolled his eyes but didn't push further. Ronan passed the bottle to Sebrina who quickly declined. "Not a chance," she said. "I'm with Rory on this one."

Ronan shrugged and offered the bottle to Kinna. She took it, weighing the pros and cons when she caught movement by the river. Bastin was standing away from the groups, his eyes full of warning. He shook his head pointedly as she held the bottle, a clear order to pass the bottle back.

Her anger surfaced. Once again, he was attempting to control her. She smiled at him as she uncorked the bottle and took a long drink, not caring about the burn that rushed down her throat. A muscle flexed in his jaw and despite his expressionless face, Kinna could tell he was furious. She broke his stare to pass the bottle back to Emhyr and found that her friends had gone quiet, watching the exchange between the two.

Bastin had moved on silent feet and was now standing over them. He reached down and took the bottle, giving Emhyr a glare that would wither most. "I think that is enough for tonight," he said, his voice deathly calm. "Emhyr, you're needed elsewhere."

Turning on his heel, Bastin stalked off in the opposite direction, heading for the river. Kinna mouthed an apology as Emhyr stood but he waved it off. "I'm used to his sour moods," he whispered before jogging to catch up with him.

CHAPTER TWENTY-THREE

Bastin

She was absolutely infuriating. Bastin uncorked the bottle and tossed back some of the cheap liquor that he'd just confiscated. It did nothing to quell the anger rising up. He could hear Emhyr's heaving footsteps padding after him. Maybe knocking him around the sparring ring would help him work off his temper.

Emhyr joined his side, and he pushed the bottle back into his hands. "I thought I made myself clear," he snapped.

"It was one drink," he countered, taking another swig.

"The last time you drank with them, I found them both alone in the dark, so drunk they couldn't stand up," he reminded him, the memory bringing forth a fresh wave of anger.

"I apologized for that."

"Either of them could have been seriously hurt."

"But they weren't," Emhyr said. "She only did that because you told her not to. She probably would have passed if you hadn't given her a death stare."

The two crossed the river, heading for the two tents that sat situated within the tree line. Emhyr was probably right, if Bastin had just continued on his way Kinna probably would have handed the bottle back, but he hadn't been able to stop himself. The memory of finding her and Sebrina struggling to stand in front of a dying fire was still too fresh in his mind. It had been a long time since he'd felt the cold spike of fear but that night it had wormed its way under his skin.

He thought he had been subtle tonight, just a quick shake of his head, but apparently that had been a challenge and damn it if she couldn't resist a challenge from anyone, especially him. She had taken one look at him and tipped the bottle back, making it clear to everyone what she thought of him and his opinions. It didn't matter that they would be up in a few hours to leave the camp, she would have drunk herself into oblivion just to prove to him that he couldn't control her. He wished that Sebrina had never brought her home, never dropped this frustrating, stubborn woman into his lap.

Liar, a voice in his mind whispered and he knew it spoke the truth. His life had revolved around her from the moment she opened her mouth. He just wasn't ready to admit that, especially to himself.

He stalked into the sparring ring and Emhyr followed him, grabbing a dulled sword from the rack at the edge of the wooden fence. Just like every night since she had arrived, Bastin readied himself, planting his feet in the dirt and preparing for Emhyr to make the first move. For the next few hours, they would spar, again and again until Bastin was fighting for breath. When they finally stopped, he would be exhausted, barely able to make it to his tent. It was the only thing he knew to do to stop himself from walking back across the river and into the faded green tent where he wanted to be.

CHAPTER TWENTY-FOUR

Kinna lingered by the fire, savoring her last night sitting peacefully in front of its warmth. The nearly full moon shone overhead, it's white light overshadowed by the orange glow before her. It had been almost two weeks since she had run from her burning home in the capital and somehow, she had managed to find another one, here hidden in the Glenwood.

The twins had already turned in for the night, leaving Sebrina and Kinna lying together across the blanket. They sat quietly, the dying fire crackling beside them. Sebrina reached out, her hand finding Kinna's as they stared up at the night sky full of blinking stars. She wondered if perhaps the gods were staring back down on them, if they had cared enough about an orphaned princess to lead her to this place. As if in response, a single star flashed across the sky leaving a thin silver trail in its wake.

Sebrina squeezed her hand quickly. "Make a wish."

Kinna pressed her eyes closed and wished for one simple thing, that someday she would get to see this place again because tomorrow she would leave, and she didn't know when she would feel this peace again.

Sebrina held onto her as they walked back to their tents, like she knew that after tonight things would change and if she just held on tightly enough, she could stop it. Kinna just held on tighter in response. They whispered their goodnights before Kinna pushed through the canvas and collapsed on her cot, snuggling down beneath the thick quilt. Sleep found her quickly, pulling her into a dream of a dark-haired woman dressed in white with aqua eyes that shined like Kinna's favorite ring that lay somewhere lost inside the castle.

———

Morning came quickly and before the sun peeked over the horizon Kinna was dressed, her cloak clasped around her throat and bag slung over her shoulder. Her hair was braided in a thick plait that hung down her back, with a few curls escaping and floating around her face. The single dagger was strapped to her side, concealed beneath the deep blue fabric of her cloak.

She spent an extra moment carefully folding the quilt and placing it neatly in the center of the cot. She wasn't sure if she would ever spend another night in the green tent. She ran her hands across the rough material as she stepped outside in the quiet camp, saying a silent goodbye to her little home.

Kinna walked through the still sleeping camp, her boots leaving prints in the dewy grass. The crimson maples appeared, their leaves almost black in the dark of the early morning. The sound of voices trickled through the trees and soon she saw the small group that had gathered outside the red tent, surrounding three horses.

Rennick and Marstella were standing with the

horses, helping Bastin, Emhyr, and Jax load their saddle-bags with provisions for their trip. Sebrina and the twins stood to the side, their tired faces brightening when they saw Kinna appear. She was rushed by them, three sets of arms encircled her in a warm embrace; Sebrina finding her way under Kinna's chin while the twins laid their copper-colored heads on top of hers. She choked back the tears while she stood wrapped in the safety of her friends, each of them unwilling to be the first to let go. Kinna heard someone clear their throat and the group reluctantly unfolded. She already missed the warmth of their bodies surrounding her as she approached the three men already seated atop the horses.

Rennick stood with his arm wrapped around Marstella's slim waist, an unusually public display of affection. "Remember, do not put yourself at risk," he reminded her and Kinna nodded her agreement.

Marstella slipped out of her husband's grip, coming to stand before her. Even standing inches shorter, Kinna still seemed to have to look up to the woman. "Safe travels, Princess," she said, gripping Kinna's hands in her own.

"Thank you," Kinna whispered softly. "Thank you for taking me in, for accepting me. I will not forget your kindness."

"You are a part of this family now," she said. "Always."

She held her tears back even as they stole her voice, but Marstella did not miss the heavy gleam in her eyes as she released her hands to step back into Rennick's waiting arms. Kinna turned back to face her friends, Ronan and Rory stepping forward to press a chaste kiss on either side of her face. "Come back quick,"

Ronan teased. "Don't leave us with Sebrina for too long."

She snorted a laugh that was quickly silenced as Sebrina wrapped her arms around her middle. Kinna let a few tears slide loose as she held her, her cheek resting on her soft blonde head. "Please be careful," Sebrina whispered into her chest, her tears leaving damp spots on her cloak.

"I will be," she promised.

Sebrina let her go, stepping back and smoothing the sides of her cloak. She gave her hand one last squeeze and turned to face the group waiting for her, Sebrina stepping back between the twins and clinging to Rory's arm.

"I'm ready when you are," she announced, passing her bag to Rennick who quickly tied it on the back of the saddle.

Bastin reached a hand down from where he sat on a dark brown stallion. She realized then that with only three horses she was meant to ride with one of the men. Of course, Bastin would decide she would ride with him, especially since he'd been tasked with her protection.

Gritting her teeth she took his hand, ignoring the way her face heated as she felt his warm, calloused skin, and let him pull her up. Once she was situated in front of him, scooting as far forward as possible so she wouldn't be pressed against him, they said one last goodbye and entered the woods.

Bastin quickly took the lead, Emhyr and his chestnut mare trotting behind them while Jax and his spotted mare rounded out their group in the back. They traveled in silence, their horses' hooves thumping against the dirt in unison. Kinna watched the sun rise through the gaps in the trees, her position in the front giving her a clear view. The sun had fully risen, giving way to a clear morning when she noticed the trees begin to thin and Emhyr urged his horse forward to pass Bastin and take the lead.

"Put your hood up," Bastin murmured. "We are going to be on the Glen Road for a while."

She nodded and slid the hood over her head, adjusting her braid so that it would hang over her shoulder. Minutes later they emerged from the tree line onto the empty road and continued to head north. When they didn't pass through Glenarm Kinna assumed they had avoided the town and joined the road once they had traveled far enough north.

Hours went by with little conversation between them, stopping only once to let their horses drink from a small stream and eat a quick lunch of dried meat and crusty bread. Kinna stretched her stiff legs while they ate. She wasn't used to riding long distances and already she was feeling the effects of spending hours on horseback. Too soon they mounted their horses again, Kinna letting Bastin lift her up before he slid in behind her.

They resumed their pace, kicking the horses into a trot down the empty road. Kinna could feel her eyes growing heavy, a product of their early morning. She tried forcing them open, pinching the soft skin under her arm to try to keep herself awake but it was a losing battle.

"Wake up," a deep voice whispered, a warm breath tickling her neck.

Kinna's eyes fluttered open. She had fallen asleep, and worse, she had fallen asleep on Bastin. Her body was pressed against his chest, her head resting on his shoulder. His arms had tightened around the reins and slid around her, keeping her from falling off one side. She cleared her throat and scooted forward, her cheeks aflame with embarrassment.

"Sorry," she said.

"We'll be sleeping together while we travel so I might as well get used to your snoring." He smirked.

Kinna's head whipped around quickly, her braid smacking into Bastin. He blinked back his surprise at being hit with her hair. "What did you just say?" she breathed.

"About the sleeping arrangements or the snoring?"

"Firstly, I don't snore," she retorted. "Secondly, we most definitely are not sleeping together."

"You do snore and it's either me, Emhyr, or Jax. There are only three tents."

"Why can't you sleep with Emhyr or Jax?"

He gave her a dimpled grin. "The tents are small. We wouldn't fit. Plus, it's part of your protective measures. You don't go anywhere without one of us, even to sleep."

Kinna rolled her eyes and turned to face forward again. "I am capable of protecting myself," she muttered.

"You agreed to our terms," he reminded her. "There's no use arguing now."

Annoyed, Kinna turned back around, taking care to ensure she was far enough forward that she was no longer touching him. She kept her eyes focused ahead of her, watching Emhyr lead the group further north until the sun started to slide beneath the trees casting long shadows across the Glen Road. The horse began drifting to the right and Emhyr turned, giving the group a slight nod before leading them into the woods.

The road quickly disappeared behind them, the thick trees swallowing them up as they continued. Kinna hoped that Emhyr was sure of the direction they were heading because she was already lost in the endless forest. The horses began to slow, gathering in a small clearing where a small soot-stained circle ringed with stones was the only indication that this was where they were meant to stop for the night.

Emhyr slid from his horse, passing the reins to Jax who had already dismounted. Kinna felt Bastin shift behind her before he appeared next to her. She threw her leg over and let his hands fit around her waist to pull her out of the saddle, her hood flying back to expose her face. He quickly unloaded their saddlebags, passing her bag to her before allowing Jax to take the stallion's reins and disappear.

"Where is he going?" she wondered aloud.

"There is a stream close by," Emhyr answered, dumping his bags in a pile. "He'll be back once the horses have been watered."

Kinna nodded in response and watched as the two men began unfolding their tents, setting them up parallel to each other. She couldn't deny that they were small and the thought of spending the next few nights squished into one with Bastin made her blood pulse in her ears. She took a steadying breath and looked around for something to keep herself busy. Finding nothing she turned around. "Is there anything I should be doing?" she asked.

"You can grab some firewood if you want," Emhyr offered.

"Absolutely not," Bastin answered for her.

She rolled her eyes, too tired to argue further. "Fine," she said. "I'll just sit here then."

Emhyr chuckled. "I'll gather the firewood if you want to unpack the bedrolls."

Kinna agreed, tossing off her cloak and grabbing one from the pile. She worked on untying the knot that secured the tight spiral and then carried the thick pad into Emhyr's tent. The low ceiling forced her to duck while inside and she struggled to imagine how any of the men would get inside without crawling. After spreading out the bedroll on the ground, she backed out, careful not to let her boots dirty the material.

Bastin had set up the third tent and was already stuffing a bedroll into the one they would share so Kinna repeated the process, adding a bedroll to the tent that Jax would occupy. Emhyr had returned by the time she was finished in Jax's tent, his arms full of neatly cut branches and a small axe dangling from his hip. He laid the stack down on the edge of the stone circle before crouching down to begin forming a thick triangle, leaning each piece at an angle to support the weight of the others. When he was satisfied, he added some dry bark and moss underneath the structure along with a few smaller sticks to use as kindling. Then, using his thumb and middle finger, he flicked the edge of the bark and a spark appeared.

Kinna gasped as she watched the kindling light, igniting faster than should be possible. The fire quickly ate its way up the logs and the warmth from the flames grew, reaching to where she was standing next to him. Emhyr glanced at her over his shoulder, his dark eyes dancing with laughter as he saw the shock etched across her face.

He bit his lip to keep from laughing aloud. "Surprise," he said innocently.

Kinna just stared, eyes wide and lips parted as she tried to process what she had just witnessed. After all the time she had spent around him, he had never once hinted that he possessed any magic, especially the kind that could start literal fires.

"She's so cute when she's confused," Emhyr grinned, giving Bastin a wink.

That comment broke through her confusion and awe. She swung her arm, her fist connecting with Emhyr's shoulder while his head was still turned towards Bastin. Kinna ignored the cracking sound her knuckles made as they connected with hard muscle.

Unable to prepare himself, he tumbled sideways as he lost his balance. "Hey!" he yelled. "What was that for?"

"You..." she started, anger and curiosity mingling, fogging her brain. "Gods, I don't know if I want to yell at you or ask about a thousand questions."

Emhyr stood, rubbing the spot on his massive shoulder where she'd hit him. Kinna wasn't fooled, she knew she had likely hurt her hand more than she had hurt him. "Why don't you start with the questions and decide later if you need to yell at me," he offered.

She watched him for a long moment. "You have magic?" Kinna asked.

"Wasn't that obvious?" Bastin snorted. "Who do you think builds the big bonfire and keeps it burning all day?"

Kinna glared at him, an insult already poised on her lips, but Emhyr spoke first. "Yes, I have magic. More specifically, I have a fair amount of control over fire."

It was the least common and often those who possessed it had only had a small amount of control over it. Alev, the god who had gifted it, was stingy. He chose the fewest mortals to wield the element, offering it to the hardened desert people living at the southern point of the continent. They were used to the heat and its dangers, and he had believed them best suited to use his gift.

Emhyr was likely being modest, downplaying his power, and Kinna knew that it was to protect himself. It still stung. He had kept this part of himself, this huge part, a secret because he hadn't trusted her. At least not until now.

"Why now?" Kinna asked, hoping they couldn't see the hurt on her face.

"Because you came with us," he answered simply. "Until now, I didn't know if you were going to leave. I couldn't risk it."

Emhyr had waited for her to prove herself and she couldn't blame him. She had done the same thing; she had kept her identity hidden as long as she could. "I understand," she said.

The corner of his mouth raised, turning into a crooked grin. He rushed her, scooping her up easily in his arms and bringing her face close. She could feel her feet dangling high off the ground. "I knew you would." He grinned. "Am I forgiven?"

Kinna laughed and rolled her eyes. "Yes, now put me down."

Emhyr planted a quick kiss on her forehead before placing her gently back on the ground. Her smile faltered when she glanced at Bastin. His arms were folded tightly across his chest, and he was glaring at Emhyr as if he could bore holes in his back with just his eyes. Kinna couldn't understand his response until the voice in her head reminded her of his words a few days ago; he didn't like to share. She ignored the voice because there was no chance he had said that for any reason other than to annoy and embarrass her, two things he excelled at.

Jax returned with the horses, securing them on the trees surrounding their little campsite. He pulled water skeins from the horses' saddles, offering one to each of them. "Anyone hungry?" he asked.

They murmured their agreement and he nodded. Pulling out a block of cheese, he speared it with a stick and held it over the fire, letting the heat melt the side. Before any could drip into the flames he pulled it back, using slices of bread to mop up the melted cheese and adding a few strips of dried meat to make a sandwich. He passed the first one to Kinna. "It's not much but it's warm and will keep you full," he said, sounding like a concerned father.

"Thank you." She smiled.

The melted cheese was delicious and thanks to a full day of travelling she found she was starving. Her sandwich was gone before Jax had managed to construct a second one, but a tiny smile tugged at his lips at the way she had demolished her dinner. More sandwiches were passed out and one by one they all devoured the cheesy goodness.

They sat quietly, Emhyr adding more wood to his fire eliciting loud pops as the wood cracked beneath the weight of the additional logs. Jax yawned loudly. "I'm going to try to get some sleep before my shift," he announced, pointing at them. "No fighting while I'm asleep."

Kinna smirked. He definitely sounded like a father now. The two men grinned but nodded their heads in agreement. Jax then turned to her, waiting for a response.

"Me?" she gasped. "Those two are the ones you should be worried about."

Jax let out a gravely laugh. "I worry about them plenty, but I think you could cause more trouble than both of them put together."

Emhyr howled, holding his sides while he tried to quiet his laughter. Bastin let out a low chuckle and pinned Kinna with a stare that whispered, *See? We all know you're trouble.* Jax patted her shoulder as he passed then disappeared into his tent.

"You all are infuriating," she muttered.

The three sat in the fading sunlight, the air cooling as the sun dropped lower behind them. Kinna found herself scooting closer to the fire and wondering how much colder it would get as they continued traveling north. She had never seen the northern part of Ferryn, or the city of Edgewood and she couldn't help the excitement that built at the idea.

Emhyr added another log and it immediately caught fire, the bark turning black under the flames instead of suffocating them. "How are you doing that?" Kinna asked.

He shrugged. "Creating it comes easy and spreading it is even easier," he said. "Stopping it is the hard part. Fire has a will of its own."

"It's so similar to water though," she mused. "Just like the ocean, it's easy to swim with the waves towards shore but swimming against them is almost impossible."

"I wouldn't know, I've never been on a beach."

"Really?"

He nodded. "There is a stretch of beach that runs the eastern border of the castle. It's one of my favorite places," she told him.

"Maybe I'll get to see your beach someday."

"You can build the biggest beach bonfire you want."

His eyes lit up at the mention of a massive bonfire. "Deal."

CHAPTER TWENTY-FIVE

Night had finally come. Tiny stars began to glimmer in the purple sky overhead, surrounding the growing moon. The full moon wasn't far away and once they reached Edgewood, they would have to wait for the cycle to begin again, using the darkness of the new moon to sneak their way across the border and back again.

Emhyr had said goodnight, wanting to get a few hours of sleep in before he took over watch for Bastin, who was taking the first shift. Watching him worm his way inside his small tent made Kinna even more curious how Bastin expected them both to fit into one.

"We will fit," Bastin snorted as if he could read her thoughts.

"How do you do that?" Kinna asked.

"Do what?"

"Always seem to know what I'm thinking."

He smirked. "Every thought you have is instantly written across your face. It's not hard to figure out."

Kinna doubted that. No one else seemed to answer questions without her asking or make snide comments about whatever was going through her head. No one but him. She was about to play a very dangerous game, but she didn't care. "No," she cocked her head. "I don't think that is what it is."

"Then what do you think it is, princess?" Bastin taunted, leaning closer to where she sat across the fire. "Enlighten me."

She stiffened as he called her princess, as if it was the ultimate insult. His taunts just made her bolder, caring less about the consequences of her words with every passing second. "I think it's because you can't stop watching me," she said, his jaw tightening as the words left her mouth. Oh, he did not like being called out. She could see she had hit a sore spot and she was going to keep poking at it until it was raw.

"I think you watch me every second of every day, unable to draw up the slightest bit of self-control to stop. You can't help but make rude little remarks because you watch me, playing scenarios out in your head of how you would respond and every once in a while, one slips out. You think my thoughts are obvious to everyone else, but they aren't. They are only obvious to you because you've spent the last few weeks memorizing my every expression and watching my every move."

He was silently gritting his teeth and she couldn't help the smug smile that played at her lips because she had won. He thought she was oblivious to him, that he was hiding it so well, but she had seen it. From the very beginning she had watched him just as closely as he watched her, she was just better at hiding it.

He didn't speak so she just continued her monologue, happy that he seemed near speechless. "Do you want to know why I think this? Because I've been watching you too. I watch you skirt around the bonfire, avoiding everyone, keeping up your reputation for being a big, moody brute. I watch you drag Emhyr into the sparring ring at night, fighting him until you collapse so you can't do something you would regret."

"And what do you think I would regret?" he whispered, cutting her off. The light of the fire turned his amber eyes into a glowing gold.

"Me," she whispered. "You fight so hard to keep from wanting me."

She stared at him, the minutes stretching out endlessly as she waited for him to argue, to refute her statement.

"I'm losing," he admitted softly.

Kinna was silent, because of all the things she expected him to say, she had not expected that. She had not expected the truth.

"I've been losing that battle since the first day I met you," he said with a sigh. "But what does it matter? It doesn't change who you are, what you are, and where you're going as soon as we return."

"I've never said anything about that."

He gave her a knowing smirk, one dimple appearing on his cheek. "You didn't deny it either."

Unfortunately, Bastin was right, that had been her plan and her promise, to go back to the capital and ensure her kingdom was secure. "I don't have a choice," she whispered. "I have to go back."

"Everyone has choices, Kinna," Bastin said seriously. "Some are harder to make than others but, in the end, you always have a choice."

She thought about his words while she stared into the fire. Did she really have a choice? Could she choose him, choose the Rising and decide to stay, to be selfish and let the world believe she was gone so she didn't have to assume the responsibility of a kingdom she had never wanted. The idea was tempting and for a moment she let her mind run wild, imagining the life she could have if she chose to stay.

Too bad it was only her imagination.

"You should get some sleep," Bastin interrupted. "I have the first watch so I will be up for a while."

"All right," she agreed, getting up to gather her cloak and her bag.

The muscles in her thighs had grown stiff and spending the night sleeping on the ground was not ideal but her early morning was evident in the tiredness behind her eyes. She tossed everything into the tent before ducking inside, careful to step around the bedroll.

Once seated she quickly discarded her boots in the corner and folded her cloak, placing it on top. Pulling her braid free she ran her fingers through the plaits to loosen them before finding the comb Sebrina had lent to her and started to remove the tangles. After adding a drop of oil to the ends of her hair and putting on a fresh pair of socks she tucked all her belongings back into the bag and added it to the stack in the corner.

Two thick maroon woven blankets sat folded on the bedroll so Kinna took the top one and spread it out over her, tucking the edges underneath her so none of the warmth would escape. Surprisingly the bedroll was relatively comfortable, and she fell asleep quickly.

Kinna woke hours later to a light pressure on her stomach. Sitting still on her side, her eyes as they darted around the tent and upon seeing that it was still empty and dark, her frantic heart calmed. A soft snore sounded in her ear, and she quickly realized the pressure she felt around her midsection was coming from a large arm that held her in a firm grip. She gave the smallest tilt of her head and saw Bastin was behind her, his eyes closed and face relaxed.

In the darkness she could still make out his full lips, slightly parted as he slept. The dark fringe of eyelashes fluttered over his cheekbones, and she quickly turned, not wanting to be caught staring again.

After a moment she was convinced he was still sleeping, his slow breaths moving his chest behind her, so Kinna tried not to move and wake him. His left arm was wrapped around her waist, his hand splayed out across her stomach as he held her to him. There wasn't an inch of her that wasn't pressed against him, and she was finding it very hard to stay still. She let a slow breath out her nose and closed her eyes, hoping she could force herself to go back to sleep. Just like she had done as a child, Kinna began counting, letting the rhythm slow her heart rate and help her drift back to sleep. She had almost made it to one hundred before she fell back to sleep.

CHAPTER
TWENTY-SIX

Bastin

Something was itching his face. He was trying to ignore it but whatever it was wouldn't stop moving beneath his nose. Reluctantly he cracked one eye open and was immediately met with a tangle of dark hair. It took him a moment to realize that the thing itching his face was a rouge curl and the reason it was so close was because he was clutching Kinna to his chest, like a child holding tightly to its favorite toy.

He distinctly remembered coming into the tent earlier that night, after Emhyr had relieved him of his watch duty with an annoying grin and positioning himself as far away from Kinna as he could on the small bedroll. He had left half a foot between them and fallen asleep facing away from her so that he couldn't gawk at her sleeping figure like he had done when he had first entered the tent. He hadn't been able to stop himself from staring.

Even in the dark he had been able to make out her figure beneath the quilt, eyes catching on how tightly she had tucked the fabric beneath her. Her hands rested gently beneath her cheek as she lay with her hair thrown out be-

hind her, curling wildly in every direction. It took all his self-control not to touch it, not to run his fingers through the spirals that looked as if they had been spun from silk. Then the scent of her had hit him. The small warm tent had circulated it through the very air he breathed, the sweetest mix of amber and vanilla always floated around her as if the perfume lived beneath her skin.

Banishing those thoughts from his head he shifted his focus on untangling himself from her, hopefully without waking her. She had exposed him last night, speaking so plainly everything he had been trying to hide. The thought of it still put his teeth on edge because for all her observations, it was clear that who she was and what she planned to do had not changed.

He slowly lifted his arm until he could draw it backwards, then inched backwards, checking to see if he had woken her every few seconds. Finally, he put enough distance between them that he could roll onto his back and push himself into a seated position. He carefully inched out from underneath the quilt, stepping into his boots before ducking out of the tent. The sun had barely begun to rise, casting an orange glow to the east. He stood in the early morning light, rubbing his eyes as if he could erase how it felt to hold her sleeping body from his mind. He stopped and noticed Jax, crouched in front of the fire, wearing the faintest hint of a smile.

"What are you smiling about?" he glared at him.

Jax's gaze never left the fire he was tending. "Why do you deny what even the blind could see?" he mused.

"You and your riddles," he muttered and stomped between the tents, heading for the small stream close by.

The cold water splashed his face, rinsing the sleep from his eyes and mind, but even after scrubbing his face *he still could feel the phantom itch. Sighing he began stripping out of his shirt and pants. The water would be frigid against his skin but if he was going to spend another day with Kinna pressed between his thighs he would need the cold water to squash the thoughts already invading his mind. Before he could talk himself out of it, he walked into the stream and plunged himself under, letting the gentle current wash him clean.*

CHAPTER TWENTY-SEVEN

Kinna woke up alone. She craned her neck to check over her shoulder and found Bastin was already gone. Her fingers reached out and brushed his pillow. It was still warm, and the smell of citrus and mint still clung to the air around her so he couldn't have been gone long.

Leaving the warmth of the quilt was the last thing she wanted to do but she knew they would likely be leaving their temporary camp as soon as they could. Steeling herself, she quickly flung the quilt back, letting the cool morning air creep its way towards her and began dressing. After adding one of the thick sweaters Sebrina had packed for her, she clasped the cloak around her neck. Surprisingly her curls had survived the night, so she kept her hair down, braiding two small strands before securing them to keep the hair out of her face. She quickly rinsed her face, wiping the sleep from her eyes before ducking out of the tent.

She found Jax tending the dying fire outside but there was no sign of Bastin or Emhyr. "Morning." He nodded.

"Good morning," she said, scooting closer to the

fire and stretching her hands out to warm her cold fingertips over the last of the glowing embers.

"We will be leaving soon. Can you help me take down the tents?"

"Of course."

The two worked in silence, Jax showing her how to dismantle his tent and then letting Kinna take down her and Bastin's tent. After everything was taken down and packed away, they gathered it all in a pile, ready to be strapped back to the horses. Bastin and Emhyr were still nowhere to be seen and Kinna was beginning to get curious. "Where are the other two?"

Jax crooked a grin. "Bas went to the stream to wash off and Emhyr is still asleep. You can go wake him up so we can get moving. He's less likely to take a swing at you than he is me."

Kinna huffed a laugh but agreed. She leaned her ear against the tent, listening for signs of movement but heard none. "Emhyr?" she called out. "Are you awake?"

The silence continued. "Emhyr?" she called a bit louder. Still nothing.

Shaking her head, she pulled back the tent flap and poked her head inside. Emhyr was laying on his back still asleep, his broad chest uncovered. Twin gold hoops pierced his nipples, confirming what she had observed through his shirt when she had first met him. Swirling tattoos were also drawn across his chest and abdomen, the ink only slightly darker than his rich brown skin. She couldn't tell what they were in the dark, so she focused on why she was here, which was not to ogle a half-dressed Emhyr.

She slipped inside, keeping her distance in case

Jax's earlier suspicion was correct. Toeing his leg with her foot she tried waking him again. "Emhyr, wake up," she said. She nudged him harder, but he continued sleeping, his even breaths never faltering.

Sighing, she stepped closer and tried again. When she still did not receive an answer, she leaned down and started shaking his shoulder. "Emhyr, I am serious, you have to wake up," she half yelled.

Suddenly his eyes popped open and before she could move away, his hands gripped her wrists and flipped her beneath him. She landed hard on the bed- roll with a yelp, the breath whooshing out of her as she landed. Gasping for air and in a daze, she laid still for a moment, not quite able to move yet.

"Oh shit, sorry, Kinna," she heard Emhyr mutter. Hands reached beneath her shoulders and pulled her up into a seated position. "Are you okay?"

"I'm fine," she said a bit breathlessly.

Emhyr was sitting on his knees, watching her with an amused look on his face. "I promise. I'm fine," she reassured him.

Before she could stand, Bastin's head peered into the tent. "I heard you scream," he said, his eyes catching on Emhyr's shirtless chest and hardening. "What are you doing?"

"Kinna tried to wake me up," he explained. "She scared me."

"I scared you?" Kinna accused. "You flipped me when I tried to wake you up."

"I was startled, therefore I reacted." Emhyr shrugged, a grin forming on his lips. "I cannot be blamed for that."

Kinna opened her mouth to argue but Bastin

stopped her. "Come on," he said, extending his hand to help her up. "Em, get dressed. We need to get moving."

Emhyr gave him a mock salute that Bastin ignored. Kinna took his hand, allowing him to pull her off the ground and shuffle her out of the tent. Once outside he turned to her. "Are you okay?" he asked quietly.

"Yes, I'm fine," she repeated. "It just surprised me. Jax asked me to wake him up and said something about not wanting to be hit by Emhyr, but I thought he was joking."

Bastin's mouth formed a hard line as he glared at Jax who was busy saddling the horses. "He shouldn't have asked you to do that," he said. "Emhyr doesn't like to be woken up. You're lucky he didn't swing at you."

"I feel really lucky," she muttered sarcastically, thinking about her bruised backside.

Bastin's face softened, and a smile tugged at the corner of his mouth. "Next time just come find me and I'll wake him up," he offered. "I'm used to dodging his fists."

"You don't have to tell me twice," she agreed.

After a quick breakfast of dried fruit and bread they began loading the horses. Kinna stood in front of the brown stallion rubbing his nose and snuck him a slice of her apple she had been saving. He snatched the apple up quickly, nosing her hand to search for more but found none. She laughed at his greed and promised him she would bring him another treat. As she turned, she found Bastin watching her.

"His name is Alder," he told her.

She smiled at the horse, glad to know his name. "I used to visit the stables often when I was a child," she said. "I loved feeding the horses."

"Did you have a horse?"

"No, but Ellio did. A grey stallion named Ash. He was always my favorite."

Silence fell between them. Kinna was surprised that they had made it through not one but two conversations today without arguing. It was almost normal, like two friends speaking. Still, she wouldn't hold her breath that it would continue.

"Are you ready to go?" Bastin asked.

Kinna nodded and let him boost her up and into the saddle before he joined her. Her chafed legs were already protesting being in a saddle again, but she tried to ignore them, focusing instead on Alder and patting his soft neck. Emhyr and Jax had already mounted their mares who were stamping their feet, ready to be on the move instead of standing idle.

Bastin nodded and Emhyr began leading them through the woods and away from their camp, towards the Glen Road once again. The party slowed as they approached the road. Kinna could see the road ahead of her through the trees, the dirt path empty of any other travelers.

Emhyr stopped, letting Bastin lead his horse to stand on his right with Jax to his left. "I'll go ahead," he said to Bastin. "Give me a few hundred yards before you follow."

Bastin agreed and Emhyr ambled out of the tree line and onto the road, allowing his horse to trot faster than she had while weaving through the trees. Kinna watched as his figure bobbed along until she could barely see his dark figure in the distance. Bastin then kicked Alder into motion and he trotted them out onto the road, picking up his pace to match the one Emhyr's mare had set.

"Why are we traveling so far apart?" Kinna asked, glancing back to see Jax still waiting in the shade of the Glenwood. "Isn't that more dangerous?"

"The further north we go, the less we want to be noticed," he explained. "Guards in the northern cities deal with the Rising more often and are more suspicious of groups of travelers than they are of individuals."

"Is that why the camp is so far away?"

"Partially. Obviously, we need to keep Marstella and Rennick as safe as possible," he said. "But our camp also has the highest population of young people and magic wielders, two groups we want to keep far away from Eldridge."

Kinna hadn't thought about the average age of people at the camp, but he was right, most were around her age or younger. As far as magic wielders went, there were at least three, now including Emhyr. She wondered if there were more. "Are there more magic wielders that I don't know about?" Kinna asked, glancing sideways at him.

He huffed a laugh. "Yes, there are."

"Will you tell me who they are or am I still not trustworthy enough?"

"I will tell you as long as you don't make it obvious that you know. It's normally something that someone should tell you themselves."

Her curiosity was growing, bringing an excited smile to her face. "I promise," she agreed quickly.

"Ira and Lalie both have earth magic. They help tend a garden that feeds the camp and keeps fresh produce year-round. Lalie is also decent at mixing herbal remedies but her younger sister, Lyla, is better."

"Wow, that is amazing. Sebrina was the first magic wielder I had ever met. I didn't think there were that many left."

"There are more than you think. Most of them keep their gifts a secret though, fearing the worst because they have seen the worst done to others like them."

Kinna was quiet for a few moments as they trotted on. Once again she was confronted with the harsh reality of how naive and sheltered she had been growing up inside the castle. She had heard stories of what happened to magic wielders north of the capital, but she couldn't imagine seeing it for herself, much less watching it happen to someone she cared about. Her thoughts drifted to Sebrina and the danger she had put herself in to rescue her and her throat clogged with emotion. Kinna understood perfectly why the Rising risked so much to do what they did. She would do the same, she would risk herself without hesitation to protect Sebrina from meeting that fate.

They rode in silence and Kinna was grateful for the sunshine overhead and Bastin's warm body behind her to keep her warm. The further north they traveled the cooler the air became, the warm spring weather disappearing with every passing hour.

When Bastin began leading his horse towards the edge of the road he informed her they would be stopping for lunch, meeting up with Emhyr and Jax. Alder navigated them through the roots and rocks as they descended a small hill, disappearing into the woods once again. Kinna noticed that the trees here had fewer leaves, tight buds still sat unopened on their branches allowing them to see through the forest more easily. They quickly spotted Emhyr, already dismounted and standing by his mare that was drinking loudly from the small stream and rode to meet him. Jax followed behind them after a few moments completing the group and bringing their food stash with him.

Lunch was a quiet affair while they listened to the horses noisily drinking behind them and filled their own water skeins. Once they had finished eating Jax and Emhyr began to re-pack the few items they had used but Bastin motioned for Kinna to walk with him.

"There is something I want to show you," he said quietly.

She followed him, walking behind his large frame as he led her along the edge of the stream. Noticing her behind him he shortened his long strides, letting her catch up and walk beside him. "When we travel, we take the same routes," he began. "Stopping and sleeping in the same locations that we've scouted previously, that was how we stumbled upon this a few months ago."

"Stumbled upon wh—"

Kinna stopped as she saw it. A large circle almost two feet in diameter rested on the ground that wasn't the same as the newly sprouted grass around it. It was grey and dead, its edges clean as if someone had burned the shape into the ground intentionally. She stepped closer, sliding onto her knees to inspect the ground further and found that it wasn't burned. The grass that had once been there remained but instead of a soft jade it had dulled to a deep charcoal, as if the life had been sucked out of it, leeching the color from the blades. She had never seen anything like this. She could feel the wrongness of it as she reached out to brush her fingertips across the surface. The texture bristled beneath her touch, disintegrating into ash at the slightest pressure. Something very wrong had happened here.

"What did this?" Kinna asked.

"We don't know," Bastin answered somberly. "This is where we found the first body months ago, just a few days after the full moon. It was a woman, but we couldn't determine age or much else. Whatever happened to her also happened to the earth beneath her. Her face was gaunt, her skin grey and paper thin, even her chest looked deflated, like she had been drained of her very life. We couldn't even move her without her body crumbling. We burned her because we couldn't move her enough to bury her."

Kinna was having a hard time processing what he was saying, along with what she was seeing before her. What could have possibly done this? "Could it have been caused by a normal fire?" she asked.

"No, I don't think so. Her skin wasn't blistered, and her hair and clothes weren't singed. There weren't any remnants of wood or coals, just her crumpled in this circle on the ground." They were quiet for a moment, Bastin letting Kinna take in everything she was seeing and hearing. "We check it every time a group passes close, the ground hasn't changed, as if the earth has been tainted and nothing can grow here now."

"Are there more of these?" Kinna asked.

Bastin nodded. "Each body we have found has looked the same and the earth beneath them is marked in the same manner. Whatever is happening, it must be the same person doing it. We just don't know who or why."

Kinna couldn't help the shiver that escaped her,

and it had nothing to do with the cooler temperatures. Even as she stood, she couldn't tear her eyes away from the eerie circle marring the earth.

A hand gently gripped her chin, drawing her gaze away from the ground and towards a pair of hazel eyes that were secretly becoming her favorite. They watched her seriously and she swore the tiniest hint of worry clouded them. "I didn't show you this to scare you," he murmured, thumb skimming her face causing goosebumps to rise on her skin. Kinna was grateful her cloak covered them because she doubted it would have escaped his notice otherwise.

"I know," she said. This hadn't been a scare tactic. It had been a show of trust, letting her in on yet another secret that the Rising had been keeping.

Kinna didn't pull her face from his feather light grip and put some distance between them like she knew she should, like she might have a few days ago. Instead, she held his gaze and let him stroke her cheek with his thumb. Just that small touch stirred something inside her. Heat quickly filled his eyes and she stilled under his gaze while all intelligent thought left her head and the intense urge to touch him overtook her. Her hand twitched, breaking his focus and he regained some semblance of control, dropping his hand from her face.

He cleared his throat loudly, drawing her out of the haze. "We should get back," he said gruffly.

"Of course," she agreed, not able to keep the disappointment out of her voice.

They had taken all of three steps before Bastin stopped suddenly in front of her. "Fuck it," he growled and spun, catching her around the waist and flattening her against his muscled chest.

Her sharp breath was cut short as he crushed his mouth against hers, one arm staying securely around her waist while his right hand snaked its way up her body and into her hair. His kiss was vicious, fueled by pent up desire. When a loan moan escaped her, he took full advantage, slipping his tongue past her lips to take full possession of her mouth. He nipped at her bottom lip hard, and she yelped, earning her a deep chuckle before he reclaimed her mouth.

The hand that had been toying with her hair now gripped a fistful at the nape of her neck. His kiss turned slower, exploring her mouth slowly while his other hand stroked the inside of her hip. Kinna could feel the heat building in her core as she dug her fingers into his shoulders. Gods, she was ready to strip her clothes off right here and now. Before she could stop herself, she started to reach for the clasp on her cloak, but Bastin missed nothing. His hand still gripped her hair and he used it to pull her face back so he could look her in the eyes.

They were both breathing hard, their breaths warming the air between them. Kinna could feel how swollen her lips were and brushed her tongue across them, tasting the sharp tang of blood. "You bit me," she gasped.

His eyes gleamed with amusement. "You liked it," he whispered. She had, but she certainly wasn't going to admit that. "Plus, I think you broke the skin when you were clawing at me."

"I did not," she muttered.

Bastin tugged open his shirt with one hand to reveal several half-moon shaped impressions in his skin as if to prove his point. "No blood," Kinna challenged, running her finger lightly over the crescents until Bastin shivered in response.

He grunted but didn't argue further. He still held her waist and Kinna swore she could feel his arousal against her stomach. "I thought we needed to go," she reminded him, giving him a gentle poke in the chest.

"We do," he agreed but made no move to release her. She wiggled in his grip and immediately stopped when she realized what exactly she was rubbing against. He gave her a sinful smile. "Why'd you stop?"

"That is not happening," she blushed.

His unrestrained laugh startled her as it bounced across the empty forest. He leaned in, resting his forehead on hers. "You keep telling yourself that, princess," he whispered. "We can just pretend you weren't about to take your clothes off for me."

Her jaw dropped the same moment he let her go but the sudden lack of warmth on her skin wasn't the reason she stood there stunned. She watched his retreating figure knowing a smug smile was plastered to his face. It took a few seconds before she came to her senses and followed him. Taking a deep breath through her nose she knew everything she was doing would lead to nothing but trouble, but gods if that didn't just excite her more.

They rejoined the group silently, Emhyr casting them a tentative glance from where he sat on his mare. Kinna was confused by his expression but quickly realized that he was likely checking her response to being shown the lifeless circle in the woods. She gave him a curt nod, hoping to convey that she was okay so that he would stop studying her face. Her lips still felt puffy and the last thing she needed was someone to point it out.

Bastin lifted her onto his horse without a word, not bothering to wait for her permission, and then situated himself behind her. Both Jax and Emhyr turned their horses to begin walking them out of the cover of the woods, leaving in silence. Kinna felt a kernel of guilt at their somber behavior. They obviously felt the weight of the secret Bastin had just shared, the lives lost to an unknown evil on the forest floor. Too bad Kinna could barely think about anything except replaying her kiss with Bastin in her mind. The voice inside her head sneered a bit at the selfishness of it all but Kinna silenced it quickly.

The Glen Road appeared in minutes, and they exited the forest separately, keeping the same order as before. As soon as they were out of Jax's direct line of sight, Bastin's arm wrapped around her middle, quickly sliding her back towards him and closing the appropriate space she had left between them. Warmth was seeping through her cloak while she sat pressed against his front while his arm stayed firmly wrapped around her stomach.

Slowly his hand wove its way under her thick sweater, making her whole body still in anticipation. Bastin palmed her waist, letting his thumb gently stroke her side in a lazy rhythm that made it hard for Kinna to breathe.

Over and over his calloused fingers trailed across her skin while she hung on to every last shred of her self-control, trying desperately not to alert him to how much his touch was affecting her. Every muscle strained against her as her body fought for control. On the next brush of his fingers his hand slipped lower, brushing the waistband of her pants and causing her hips to roll into his touch. He noticed her reaction, his fingers now toying with the material while she shouted curses at him in her head.

Bastin leaned down, his cheek hovered by her temple. "Everything all right, princess?" he asked innocently. "You seem a little tense."

Kinna could hear the taunt in his voice and an idea sparked in her head. If Bastin wanted to play games with her she was going to remind him just how well it had gone the last time. She arched her back and pushed herself backwards until her ass was pressed firmly against him then she let the motion of the horse do the rest. With every step the horse took, she jostled against him, and it took only a few seconds to have the desired effect.

Bastin's hand stilled and Kinna felt him harden behind her. She let her hand rest on his thigh and gave him a little squeeze. "That's better," she purred, wiggling slightly for emphasis. "I'm much more comfortable now."

After a moment of silence, she heard Bastin release a long breath. "This is going to be a long day," he muttered.

Kinna couldn't help feeling a little smug knowing that she had won this round of the dangerous little game they were playing, and it pleased her to know that she seemed to be affecting him every bit as much as he affected her.

CHAPTER TWENTY-EIGHT

Bastin

The next few hours passed in agonizing slowness and not once did Kinna shift or falter in her decision to punish him. She could be cruel when she wanted to be, there was no doubt about that. Part of him could hardly wait until the moment they would rejoin their group and she would be forced to move, ending her slow torture. The other part was already dreading it, knowing that once they were reunited with the others her mask of cool detachment would slip back on and their game would be over.

The sun was beginning to slip below the top of the tree line and Bastin knew that they weren't far from their stopping point for the night. Tonight, would be the last night they would sleep in the cover of the Glenwood before making the final leg of their journey into Edgewood where they would meet Leo.

First in command at the northern sect, Leo would help coordinate their mission and house them until they were ready to return home. Bastin wondered how his old friend would respond to the Princess of Ferryn joining their ranks. While Rennick had given the order that she would be coming, there was no way to tell if Kinna would find acceptance so quickly in the northern sect. A swift wave of defensiveness washed over him at the thought and his grip on her hip tightened reflexively.

Kinna noticed and turned to watch him over her shoulder, the dimming sun lighting her face and turning her silver eyes molten. Her bright eyes only were contrasted further by the dark halo of hair that floated around her tanned face. Even her lips formed a perfect bow shape, something he found amusing considering her weapon of choice. He hadn't been able to stop staring at her strikingly beautiful face since he met her and now had every curve memorized.

A smile played at her lips and Bastin realized how long he had been staring. Clearing his throat, he refocused. "We will be camping soon," he informed her.

"Why so early?" Kinna asked, a small crease forming between her eyes.

"We will leave the Glenwood and reach Edgewood tomorrow, but we will stop early tonight so we can stay camped in the forest," he explained. "Better to stay in the protective cover of the woods than out in the open."

She nodded at his explanation and turned back to face the road ahead of them. Soon a forked tree appeared on the road's edge, marking their stopping place. He quickly surveyed their surroundings, but the road was empty as it had been for most of the day, so Bastin led Alder towards the forest. He felt Kinna shift herself forward after they slipped between the trees, but he waited to see if she would physically remove his hand from where it still sat against her smooth skin.

He couldn't help the smile that formed as Emhyr appeared ahead, his back turned while he unloaded his *saddlebags, and she hastily jerked his hand from beneath her sweater and mumbled a curse under her breath. He couldn't remember the last time he had smiled so much. Every taunt and quip kept him on his toes, and he could admit he was thoroughly enjoying their back and forth. Still, the thought of her leaving them, leaving him, loomed in the distance, wiping the smile from his face.*

Bastin slid easily off his horse, hands already wrapped around Kinna's narrow waist as he gently lifted her down. She scrutinized his face, sensing his change in mood like she had heard the direction his thoughts had taken. Nothing seemed to escape her notice, especially when it came to him. He could sense her concern, but he stopped her from asking any questions with a shake of his head. Instead, he focused on unpacking the saddlebags in silence.

CHAPTER TWENTY-NINE

Kinna was quiet for the rest of the evening, half-heartedly making conversation with Emhyr after dinner while they sat close to the fire. She had momentarily been distracted when she watched fire erupt from his fingertips to light the kindling underneath the small pyre he had built, but her thoughts quickly circled back to Bastin and the strained look on his face as they entered camp. He had actually been smiling as they entered the woods, but his smile faltered after she had pushed his hand off her and it had not returned since. He'd turned silent and broody, barely saying a word to anyone.

The sky turned dark and Kinna watched through the trees as stars began to blink into existence against the midnight blue expanse. Without the sun to warm her, a chill swiftly crept up her skin and within a few minutes she was stuffing her fingers under her arms to keep them warm. Kinna stifled a yawn against her shoulder but not before someone caught it.

"We should go ahead and get some rest. We are leaving before sunrise," Jax told her, not able to stop himself from mothering them. "Bastin has the first watch."

Emhyr threw Kinna a knowing grin and they both smiled at his nudge to go to bed. "You got it, Pops." Emhyr grinned, rocking himself up into a standing position before offering his hand to pull Kinna up.

Jax rolled his eyes before slipping into his tent, not bothering to respond to Emhyr's jab. Emhyr said a loud goodnight, clapping Bastin on the shoulder before disappearing into his own tent. Kinna stood between the tent flaps for a moment, watching Bastin's stiff form from behind until giving up and flopping down on the bedroll. Huffing, she sat up and quickly dressed for bed, not wanting any of the night air to touch her exposed skin, and then snuggled down under the thick blanket.

Bastin had the first watch, but Kinna could wait a few hours because they needed to talk. Unfortunately, it was proving harder to stay awake than she had anticipated. Before she could talk herself out of it, she flung the blanket off her, letting the cold shock her awake, and sat up.

Needing something to occupy her hands, she pulled her comb out and began detangling her hair. She took extra time to work her hair into two complex braids that fell down her back. She had just finished when she heard the rustling of fabric and Bastin appeared, a disapproving look plastered on his face when he saw her awake.

"Why aren't you sleeping?" he asked brusquely.

Kinna pulled her legs up and wrapped her arms around her shins, resting her chin on her knees. "I needed to talk to you," she said.

"It couldn't wait until the morning?" he countered, as he landed heavily on the bedroll next to her, his arms stretched out behind his head. Kinna couldn't help but appreciate the way his muscles flexed at the motion.

"No, it couldn't."

"Well, make it quick, princess, before I fall asleep."

She ignored the nickname. It had lost the sting it had held and now felt more endearing than anything. "I didn't mean to upset you earlier."

"What?" He sat up to face her. Even in the dark, she could make out the confusion etched on his face. "Why do you think you upset me?"

She bit the inside of her cheek. "I pushed you off when I saw Emhyr, and I shouldn't have. I'm not embarrassed. I like you and I don't care if he or Jax sees that."

Bastin was silent, not even a breath escaped his lips while he listened to her admission. He listened as she admitted liking him and he let those three stupid words wrap around his heart. She waited for him to respond and watched as his face softened slightly.

"Kinna, that didn't upset me," he whispered, his voice soft.

She huffed. "Well, something did. One minute you were smiling, genuinely smiling, and I got to see the real you for just a second and then he was gone. If it wasn't because of me then what was it?"

The corner of his mouth kicked up. "I didn't say it wasn't because of you. I just said that you pulling my hand out of your shirt didn't bother me."

"Then what was it? What did I do?"

He sighed, rubbing his hand over his face in a gesture that instantly reminded her of Ellio and sent a pang of sadness through her chest. "You did *do* anything, princess, but I remembered that someday, possibly very soon, you will go back to being a princess and whatever it is that we are doing will end."

Once again Bastin said the unexpected, sending her mind whirling. She knew that what he said was true, but it didn't stop her heart from aching at the thought of leaving not just him, but everyone she had grown to care about in the past few weeks. Kinna was so tired of losing people and the heartache that followed. She felt her throat constricting as tears built behind her eyes.

"Please don't cry," Bastin whispered, taking her hands in his and rubbing circles with his thumb.

"I'm not," she mumbled, but she sounded unconvincing in her own ears. "I am just tired of losing the people I care about."

Bastin's hands slid up her arms, pulling her towards him until he had her situated between his muscled thighs, his arms circling around her. "You aren't losing anyone," he said, leaning his forehead against hers. "We can protect you, I can protect you, if you choose to stay here with us."

"I want to. I want to so badly," Kinna whispered back.

He ran his nose up the side of her cheek before pressing a swift kiss on it. He tucked her into him, her cheek resting on his shoulder. She felt him press another kiss on her head. "I know," he said. "Just remember you have choices, Kinna. I won't stop you if you choose to go back but you will always have a home here with us."

Kinna couldn't stop the few tears that escaped while he held her because she knew that she would have to leave and when she did it would shatter her barely healed heart once more.

———

Breakfast had been eaten on the road after the group had silently packed their bags and left under the cover of darkness. They wanted to arrive in Edgewood sometime in the afternoon, so their pace had been set faster than before and Kinna's tired body was already feeling the effects thanks to the late night before.

As they rode, the trees around them began to thin, the landscape gradually changing from thick forest into farmland. Kinna watched in fascination as they passed a number of small cottages surrounded by rows of crops. The smell of freshly tilled soil hung in the air; the earthy smell so different from the salty sea air she had grown up with.

It was a few hours before Kinna finally caught a glimpse of the sea again and the sprawling city that was their destination. The rich blue expanse gleamed in the sunlight, reminding her of the home she had left behind. Her eyes turned towards the city as she shoved her memories to the side. Edgewood hadn't been built around the ocean; it wasn't the lifeblood of the city from which all things emanated. Instead, it had been designed to exist alongside the water, separating itself with a thin strip of land that was bordered by a sea wall. A few boats dotted the coast, rocking lightly against the small docks by the wall, but it was nothing compared to the sprawling marina in the capital.

The city itself was ringed by a large stone wall and as they drew closer, Kinna could see that the streets followed the same pattern, forming circles around the city. There were only two straight lines that intersect the city streets, one running north to south and the other running east to west.

Kinna knew from her schooling that the center of the city is where Lord Duran's estate sat, and she wondered what had become of him and his daughter in the capital. Her brows furrowed and she shook that thought from her head too. Being this close to Edgewood had broken the protective bubble she'd formed too quickly, allowing too many wayward thoughts to enter her mind. She didn't spend any more time staring at the city as they approached, instead she kept her eyes trained on Emhyr's back as he led their trio of horses along the dusty road.

The countryside slowly melted away as they drew closer to Edgewood, replaced by tightly packed buildings and crowded streets. The horses slowed as they navigated between other travelers, people pushing vendor carts, and children darting across the cobblestone path. They stayed on the main road, avoiding the side streets and alleyways until the city wall came into view, the afternoon sun casted a long, dark shadow over the surrounding buildings.

Finally, she saw Emhyr veer left onto a side street that ran parallel with the city wall, the only indication she'd had so far that they wouldn't actually be staying in the city. Bastin urged the stallion to move closer to Emhyr's mare, tightening their ranks now that they had left the busy streets. They passed into a quiet, residential area lined with two story buildings that were split into apartments. Small balconies and windows were thrown open and full of laundry that had been hung to dry in the sun. It looked nothing like the camp they had come from and Kinna wondered where they would be staying tonight.

Kinna leaned back and glanced up at Bastin.

"Where are we going?"

"We are going to meet up with Leo and then head back to the Nest." Bastin informed her, his eyes never meeting hers. Instead, he continued scanning every person or building they passed, waiting for an unknown danger to present itself. She could see the rigidness in his body, tense and ready to throw himself into action to protect her.

She considered trying to distract him so he would relax but she doubted he would appreciate that, so she continued questioning him about their mysterious destination. "Who is Leo and what is the Nest?"

A ghost of a smile crossed his face. "Leo is the leader of the northern sect of the Rising," he whispered, leaning down closer to her face. "The Nest is their home base. They maintain a semi-permanent residence like we do."

"Does ours have a name too?"

"Ours?" Bastin teased, breaking into a genuine smile.

Kinna rolled her eyes and chewed on her lip nervously while she waited for him to respond. For once she didn't have a smart response ready.

After a moment his arm wrapped around her middle and tugged her closer to him. "Yes, princess, *ours* has a name too," he whispered close to her cheek. "Want to guess what it is?"

"The circus?" Kinna guessed, earning a soft chuckle from him.

"No, although that isn't bad. Ours is called the Hearth."

"Why?"

"Long ago a hearth used to be the center of

the home. From the hearth everything was provided for those living inside, food, warmth, light; everything they needed would rise from that spot. Marstella named ours the Hearth because that is what most have found in the Rising, a hearth to call our own."

"I guess that is why the others named theirs the Nest, because it's another type of home?"

Bastin nodded as his face turned serious. "I need you to promise me something."

Her brow furrowed at his sudden change. "What?"

"Promise me that while we are here you will stay close to me or Emhyr. Don't go anywhere without one of us."

"If I promise, will you tell me why?"

"Yes."

"Then I promise. Now why do I need a chaperone everywhere?"

"The members here won't know you or trust you. They may be less than welcoming because of who you are," he trailed off and unease settled in her stomach at his insinuation.

"Do you think they would try to hurt me?" Kinna whispered.

"I don't think anyone would directly disobey Marstella; they respect her too much. However, anger and hate can make people irrational so I can't rule it out," he said, gently nudging her with his shoulder. "If someone tries, you don't hold back. Take them down and if they survive you, then they will have me to deal with."

Heat pooled in her stomach, quickly replacing the unease. His protective nature was becoming more bearable when it wasn't aimed at controlling her every move. She had to admit that his willingness to defend her while acknowledging she could handle herself was incredibly attractive.

They continued along until the street was almost empty. Kinna noticed the buildings around them had thinned and become more dilapidated, with the windows boarded up and roofs leaning as if they would collapse under a strong wind. A thin layer of dirt seemed to cover every surface of the buildings casting an empty, haunted look over everything.

Emhyr led them down a narrow alley where a figure stood leaning against a wall, their face concealed beneath a gray hood. This must be Leo, Kinna thought. The group slowed, Emhyr stopping first and sliding off his mare easily, jogging towards them and clapping a large hand on a shoulder. Bastin had dismounted, letting Kinna slide off the horse and into his open hands before he set her firmly on the ground. She heard Emhyr's rumbling laugh as he spoke and Jax appeared behind her, effectively sandwiching her between them.

Bastin leaned down to whisper in her ear. "Remember your promise. Stay close to us and play nicely."

She snorted a laugh but nodded in agreement.

Emhyr was leading the still hooded Leo towards them and Kinna tensed in preparation of meeting the leader of the northern sect. Bastin took a heavy step in front of her, half concealing her behind his large frame and Emhyr rejoined them, taking up her right flank with Jax still on her left. Gods, it was like they were preparing for battle, a thought that did not sit well with Kinna.

"Good to see you Leo," Bastin nodded.

"You too," a deceptively light voice answered then tugged their hood down to reveal a woman who looked to be in her mid-twenties. Her olive skin and bright green eyes were a stunning combination but her cropped hair that had been shaved on one side added a no-nonsense aura to her. Her angular face and tall stature made her even more imposing as she stood a few inches taller than Kinna's five-foot six frame.

"I see you brought Grandpa as well," she said, her eyes shifting to Jax.

"So nice to see you again Leona," Jax echoed. Emhyr laughed, trying and failing to disguise it as a cough. Leo's grin faded into an annoyed frown. She obviously did not appreciate anyone using her full name.

Her gaze then landed on Kinna, and her frown deepened. "I assume you are the princess," she accused, lacing obvious distaste into her words.

Bastin bristled at her tone and Emhyr took a hesitant step closer. "My name is Kinna," she said, keeping her eyes fixed on Leo and offering her hand. "Thank you for having me."

Leo noticed the subtle shift in the men's behavior, but her face did not betray her thoughts. She cocked her head sideways, seeming to debate whether or not she would take it. After a moment of tense silence, she clasped her hand into Kinna's, giving it an almost painful squeeze as she shook it. When Kinna returned it with equal force, Leo's eyebrow arched slightly in surprise before she quickly recovered her mask of detachment.

"Well, we better get moving," Leo said, turning on her heel. "Better not to be out here once it gets dark."

Everyone nodded their agreement and began

leading their horses along the alleyway behind her. Bastin's hand found hers as they walked and gave it a small squeeze. "You did good," he whispered.

"Did you doubt me?" Kinna asked in mock outrage.

"Never," he answered, keeping her hand in his as they walked.

CHAPTER THIRTY

They arrived in front of a rundown two story building that had every available window and door tightly boarded up. It was connected to a series of buildings, leaving no space between them, and Kinna guessed that this used to be a row of townhomes before neglect had overtaken them. Jax and Emhyr volunteered to take their horses, although Kinna wasn't sure where, leaving her and Bastin with Leo and their luggage.

Without a word, Leo climbed the two stairs leading to the front door and rapped her knuckles against it three times, leaving a short pause before the third tap. It must have been a signal because in seconds the door swung open to reveal a middle-aged man with a dark beard and a scowl permanently etched into his face. "Took ye long enough, girl," he muttered.

Leo rolled her eyes but continued past him without another word. The man must have been someone of importance if she allowed him to speak to her that way. Kinna didn't get the impression that Leo would tolerate that attitude from just anyone. After she had disappeared behind the door, the man turned his sharp eyes on Bastin and Kinna swore she saw his scowl soften.

Bastin marched up the stairs to meet him, dragging Kinna along by her hand. He used his free hand to grip the man's forearm and pull him forwards in a familiar gesture. "It's good to see you Saul," he said. "It's been too long."

"Wouldn't be so long if ye would come an' visit," Saul said, releasing his hand to clap him on the shoulder. Glancing down, he noticed their hands still intertwined. "Who's ye pretty lass?"

Bastin grinned over his shoulder at Kinna. "This is Kinna," he said, a touch of pride radiating through his voice.

Saul's eyes widened in surprise, releasing the scowl and revealing a rather handsome face. Kinna took his momentary silence as an opportunity to untangle herself from Bastin and extend her hand to him. "It's nice to meet you, Saul." Kinna smiled politely.

He took her hand gently, dipping his head to press a light kiss to her knuckles instead. "Your Highness," he said. "It is a pleasure."

He released her hand and Kinna felt her face warm beneath his gaze. "Please, call me Kinna," she said. "I never liked titles."

"Of course," he agreed without further argument, then turned back to Bastin. "Boy, ye are going to be in one heap o' trouble with this one."

He huffed a laugh. "I already am," he agreed quietly.

Saul grinned before waving them through the door. "Dinner shouldn't be too far off," he told them. "I'll get ye settled in the meantime."

Once inside Kinna understood instantly why this location had been named the Nest. The townhomes had their interior walls and ceilings partially knocked out, allowing people to pass through the exposed brick archways and into other buildings. Peering to her left, she could see that it had created one continuous hallway while still separating the space.

The first room looked like a small armory, bows, swords and an array of weaponry hung from the cream-colored walls, likely strategically placed so it could be easily grabbed as someone left. Beyond that sat a meeting room of sorts that held a large round table and an assortment of mismatched chairs stuffed around it. Kinna thought she could see a kitchen towards the end, but her attention was quickly drawn elsewhere as footsteps sounded above her. A ladder sat in front of her, reaching through a wide square hole in the ceiling to a room with hammocks strung in every direction on the second floor.

Without any further instruction, Saul began to climb the worn wooden ladder. Bastin nodded for her to follow and then gave her ass a hard pat as she climbed the first rung, earning him an evil glare. Saul's outstretched hand helped her off the ladder, something she was grateful for since there was no railing around the opening.

The second story was much like the first, lacking most of its interior walls, and consisted of living spaces and sleeping quarters. The first two rooms were a jumble of hammocks, cots, and bunks lining the walls while still leaving some space to walk amongst them. Blankets hung from every surface turning the room into a kaleidoscope of colors and patterns. Kinna smiled at the whimsy of it as Saul led them deeper into the Nest, the spaces growing more defined and private as they walked.

They passed through a gap that was just barely

wide enough for the two men to fit through without having to sidestep inside and into a thin strip of hallway. Two doors sat on either side, presumably leading into small bedrooms and Saul stopped them in front of a blue door with chipping paint.

"Ye can take that'n—" He motioned to the door. "The other two can have the one next to ye. There's two baths at the end of the hall, lads on the left and lasses on yer right."

Without another word he ambled back down the hall and back towards his post keeping watch at the door. The mention of a bath had Kinna almost sighing in relief. She doubted it would be anything like the steaming baths she had loved taking at the castle, but she hardly cared as long as the water was warm, and she could scrub the dirt of days of traveling off her body.

"I'll put our things away if you want to go ahead to the baths," Bastin offered.

Kinna wondered again if maybe he could read her thoughts, or at least sense her emotions but decided she had probably just been staring longing in that direction for too long. "Was it that obvious?" she teased.

"That and you sort of smell." Bastin smirked then disappeared behind the door, closing it firmly behind him while she stood there gaping.

"Asshole," she muttered under her breath.

Her annoyance faded with ever step closer to the bathroom, the prospect of restoring her limp curls was too enticing. She found them easily enough, the doors were left open to reveal a small circular tub, toilet, and sink. There was even a little square mirror hung above the sink, a perk she hadn't been expecting. Kinna shut the door behind her, sliding the lock across, then dropped her bag and started the water over the tub. To her surprise, steam billowed out over the water almost instantly and she scrambled to undress before sliding down in the hot water while the tub filled. The hot water was a balm to her tired body, and she couldn't stop the low moan that escaped her lips. Gods, she loved a bath.

She cut the water off as soon as the tub was halfway full, not wanting to be selfish with the luxury, she leaned back and massaged water into her hair before scrubbing her scalp and skin clean of the dirt and oil that had built up over the last few days. She wrapped herself tightly in a towel once she was finished and began the slow process of detangling her hair, adding drops of oil as she went. Twirling her hair between her fingers she coaxed each of her curls into a spiral until they were all perfect and shining. Rooting around her bag for her cleanest pair of clothes she quickly dressed in a dark pair of leggings and a deep green tunic before stuffing her dirty clothes back inside. She was running out of clean clothes fast so she made a mental note to see if she could wash them while she was here.

Shrugging her bag over her shoulder she unlocked the door and made her way back to the room she would share with Bastin, marveling at how she had just accepted that without even a moment's hesitation. It was obvious things had changed between them in the last few days, but it caught her by surprise sometimes. Their attraction had been instant from the beginning, but the last few days had solidified something between them. It had happened so quickly, but it was as if something in her had recognized him from the start and now a bond had formed that she wasn't sure if she could break.

Yawning, she pushed through the door of their room, wondering if she would have time to take a nap before they were needed elsewhere but froze when she realized Bastin was half naked, dressed only in a pair of low hanging pants. Kinna couldn't have stopped her eyes from roving over every inch of his exposed chest and arms if she had wanted to, and she really did not want to stop.

Bastin was pure muscle and it showed in every powerful line and curve of his body. His broad chest and stomach were perfectly sculpted and dusted with a light smattering of hair that traveled all the way down to the perfect V-shape beneath his navel before disappearing beneath his waistband. Subtle veins snaked their way up his forearms and over biceps and Kinna couldn't help but want to trace them with her fingers, or maybe her tongue; she wasn't opposed to either option.

Once again, her eyes locked on the tattoo that rested just above his heart but unlike the last time she glimpsed it, it was now on full display. It was an intricate design, a knot of braided strands inked in blue, twisting and curving in a never-ending circle. Again, she wondered what it meant and who had drawn it on his skin. He shifted under her intense study and her eyes snapped back to his face. Bastin was watching her with a smug, satisfied smile that made her realize exactly how long she'd been ogling him.

"See something you like, princess?" he asked, his voice like velvet.

Kinna could feel the heat staining her face, but it was nothing compared to the inferno raging beneath her skin. She had never felt more out of control and spent the next minute slowly counting in her head until she was sure her words could be trusted.

"Nothing to say?" he taunted, taking a step towards her, and not bothering with a shirt. "I've never known you to be so speechless. If this was all it would take to stop you from arguing with me, I would have done so much sooner."

She knew he was trying to undo the tenuous hold she had over herself, so she resumed counting, averting her eyes to stare at the ceiling and trying to think of anything except him.

"I don't think so," he scolded, grabbing her chin, and holding her face hostage so she would have to meet his eyes. He stood just inches from her, heat radiating off his skin and the smell of mint and citrus invading her senses. His thumb traced lightly over her skin. "You didn't answer my question."

His hazel eyes gleamed wickedly. He was enjoying teasing her, testing her limits, and it was clear she was losing this battle. She tried to rally. "What question?" Kinna asked, her voice a breathy whisper instead of the nonchalance she was aiming for.

His smirked deepened at her voice and half-hearted reply, exposing his shallow dimples. He smelled an easy victory, so he pushed forwards and Kinna quickly found herself pressed between hard muscle and the door.

"Don't play coy, princess," he hummed, his left hand finding the hem of her shirt. "We both know you took your time leering at me when you barged in here. I'm just curious if you found anything to your liking in the process?"

His hand toyed with the edge of her tunic, his

knuckles casually brushing over her stomach in the process. Fire erupted under her skin in every place he touched, stoking the growing need while he stood there casually. It was clear he wasn't going to stop teasing her until he heard what he wanted.

He wanted her to admit that she was burning alive with want for him.

Bastin leaned his head down, until his lips were flush with her cheek. "I'll only ask one more time," he whispered against her overly sensitive skin. "Did you see something you like?"

"Yes," she breathed.

"And what was that?" he pushed, using the side of his nail to scrape across her bottom lip.

"Everything," she whispered, releasing an unsteady breath.

Instantly his hand left her face, sweeping down to lift her into his arms and slam her against him. He caught her surprised gasp in his mouth while her legs wrapped around him, and his other hand gripped the base of her neck. His tongue pushed past her lips while his hand slid up her shirt to palm her breast. Kinna's fingers dug into the smooth skin of his shoulders, and she relinquished control, giving in to the sensation of him. She was lost in the feel of his silky lips as they left her mouth and traveled down her neck, pressing light kisses against her skin just as he started rolling her nipple between his fingers and another gasp fell from her lips.

She wove her hands through his hair, needing to hold on to something as his onslaught to her senses continued. He nipped at the sensitive skin between her neck and shoulders and her hips rolled in response, finding him hard between her legs. He bit her again, slightly harder and she pushed firmly against him again, making him groan. Bringing his head back up to meet her eyes she could read the desire in them clearly, but a sliver of hesitation caught her.

"There isn't a lot of privacy here," he cautioned.

Just as Kinna was about to explain to him how little she cared about *privacy* at that moment, a swift knock came on their door, the same one her back was still firmly pressed against.

Bastin heaved a sigh and turned, still carrying her, to where his shirt sat on the small bed. She hadn't even noticed the room's furnishings when she had arrived, too entranced by the man she found inside to care. When she didn't make any move to untangle her legs, he simply sat down with her in his lap and wrestled his shirt over his head. The knock came again, this time more insistent.

"I am going to have to get that," he whispered. "I can either do it while still holding you or not."

Kinna hesitated to answer, a small frown forming on her lips, and he chuckled. Bastin stood back up, firmly supporting her weight with one hand splayed out across her ass before she spoke. "You can put me down," she whispered.

He sat her back on the floor with unsteady legs and took two steps before turning back around and grabbing her chin. "Don't misunderstand me," he whispered. "We are not done here. Not in the slightest."

Kinna couldn't stop the shiver that ran down her spine at his words and she gripped the metal bed frame for support. He noticed and smirked, placing a swift kiss on her nose before releasing her and going to answer the door to an unusually annoyed Jax.

Jax had informed them that dinner was already being served on the first floor and Leo wanted to talk strategy while they ate. While he spoke to Bastin, he kept his eyes firmly fixed on him, not daring a glance at Kinna who could feel the flush still lingering on her skin. No doubt her lips were swollen and red from the rough three-day stubble Bastin was sporting.

Bastin had closed the door on him as soon as he finished talking and Kinna could hear him grumbling on the other side of the door but eventually heard his footsteps disappearing down the hallway. In seconds of him leaving, Bastin was seated on the bed and pulling her into his lap. Kinna rested her head on his shoulder, enjoying the warmth that radiated from his skin and breathing in his delicious scent. Her hair hung loose around her shoulders, and she felt Bastin's fingers start twirling the freshly washed curls.

"I love your hair," he murmured, giving the strand a gentle tug.

Kinna smiled. "I like yours too," she whispered. "Maybe I'll try to braid it sometime."

He chuckled. "I'm tempted to say no just to see you try to persuade me."

"I can be very persuasive," she purred, sitting up and shifting so she was straddling him.

Bastin bit back a groan as she wrapped her arms around his neck and pressed herself closer. She leaned in and placed a soft kiss on his neck, before taking the tip of her tongue and running it up a sensitive patch of skin behind his ear. She felt his hands wrap around her waist but instead pulling her closer she found herself being tossed forwards on the bed and Bastin escaping across the room. Her face met the blanket that covered the mattress as she fell forward, the rough material scratchy beneath her cheek. She quickly returned to a sitting position to glare daggers at Bastin who was wearing a cheeky grin.

"That wasn't very nice," she snapped.

"That wasn't very graceful," he laughed. "We need to go downstairs and meet with Leo before someone comes looking for us again."

"Fine," she answered, grabbing her boots from where she'd dropped them on the floor and tugging them on.

"Come on, princess," he said, taking her hand in his and opening the door. "Dinner is waiting."

CHAPTER THIRTY-ONE

Bastin

They had joined Emhyr, Jax, and Leo at a round meeting table situated away from the others that sat full of listening ears. Leo wanted to talk strategy for their transport mission, so the fewer people involved and less details known the better. Two bowls of some kind of stew were waiting for them though he knew from experience it wouldn't be anything as tasty as the food Ira prepared for them at the Hearth. He had an unmatched gift and no one's cooking had ever compared in his mind. Kinna slid into the seat next to Emhyr, letting him take the spot at her right. Everyone ate in silence, but Bastin didn't miss the curious glances being cast in their direction, especially those that lingered too long on the woman at his side. Instead, he met every stare with a warning displayed clearly on his face.

Leo had finished her food and begun to make light small talk, asking about our journey and people she knew at the Hearth. She continued until the dining hall was almost empty, everyone having left after finishing their meal and learning nothing about why we were here from listening to our empty conversation.

"Finally," Leo huffed, standing to retrieve a map that had been tucked into her waistband. She unrolled it on the table, using two bowls to hold down the edges and pointed to our target location. "Here is where we are heading tomorrow night."

Her finger indicated a sliver of land just beyond the Ferryn-Eldridge border that ran along the base of the Warchill Mountains. The mountain range had always provided a natural protection for Eldridge, keeping large armies from crossing since they were capped in ice and snow regardless of the season. The terrain at their base would be rocky, something they may be able to use to their advantage if scouted properly.

"Warren knows where to meet you," she continued. "He will have two children with him, his daughter, Noelle, and his son, Mac. Noelle is gifted with the earth element which puts me on edge."

"Why?" Kinna asked, her brow furrowing.

"She's young and lacks control," Emhyr answered. "If she gets upset or scared her magic could respond and likely not in a controlled manner. She could hurt anyone, even her own father, without meaning to. Her magic's only goal will be to protect her; everyone else would be viewed as a threat."

"Exactly," Leo finished. "Emhyr, I think you should keep the two children close to you. Bastin will take the lead and Jax will take the rear as usual. Kinna, I think you should join Jax in the rear of the group, keep a wider angle for your bow."

"Absolutely not," Bastin argued, his words clipped. "She can stay with the kids in the middle and Emhyr can take the rear."

"That isn't the best position for an archer," Leo re-

minded him. "She serves us best being in the rear."

"Bas, I'll be fine with Jax," Kinna assured him, placing her hand on his forearm.

His eyes flicked to her. "You already agreed to your orders," Bastin reminded her, then turned his attention back to Leo. "She will stay in the middle of the group, that's final."

Bastin could see that Kinna was turning over another argument in her head, so he quickly nodded to Jax, a signal that the three men had worked out days ago before leaving the Hearth to find a reason to distract Kinna. It was perhaps a bit manipulative, but he didn't care as long as it kept her safe.

Jax slowly pushed away from the table, bracing his hands against the edge. "You all can stay here all night and argue," he rumbled. "There is much to prepare for. Kinna, would you mind helping me?"

She flashed Bastin an angry glare, seeing through their distraction easily but mercifully not arguing. "Of course," she said, rising from her seat, looking very much like the princess she was, and following Jax to do gods knew what.

Once they were out of earshot, Bastin turned his attention back to Leo. "I outrank you and I have decided where she will stay in the convoy," he emphasized. "We are under direct orders to limit the risk to her safety and end her participation in this mission if it is jeopardized."

"I know that," Leo placated. "I am just trying to ensure the success of this mission and bring everyone back safely, including two small children whose lives are at stake."

"Understood," he said, his tension easing slightly at her agreement. "Let's run through the rest of the plan."

Leo nodded before launching into the detailed version of the itinerary for the next day. Emhyr kept the conversation going, asking the right questions, and staying engaged but Bastin's mind had drifted. His thoughts bounced between every possible threat to Kinna and how he could anticipate and outmaneuver it. Over and over different scenarios replayed in his mind until a heavy weight had settled in his stomach. Once again, he felt fear and dread, two emotions he thought he had mastered, find their way back. Whether the other two noticed he wasn't sure, but he at least kept his eyes focused on them and the map in front of him until they stopped talking and Leo left.

Emhyr leveled him with a disapproving stare. He had obviously noticed how far Bastin's mind had drifted, and he cursed his friend's ability to read him. "Where is your head at?" he asked.

"Everywhere," Bastin responded quietly.

"Well get it together," he told him, standing up. "No distractions. Get focused so we can keep our girl safe."

Emhyr gave his shoulder a squeeze before leaving him sitting at the table alone. Bastin let his words repeat in his mind, letting them strengthen his resolve. When he stood up from the table, his mind was calm, the tension leached from his body. He was going to do exactly what Emhyr suggested; tomorrow he would be solely focused on two things, a successful mission and keeping his girl safe.

Those last two words kept ringing in his ears as he trudged up the ladder, the wood creaking softly beneath his weight. With each step the words chanted in his head, his girl, his girl, his girl. They kept pace like the sound of a war drum, hammering into him and crushing any remaining resistance he had been clinging to.

He turned the knob that led to their small bedroom

softly, *careful not to wake her if she had already fallen asleep. Slipping silently into the room his eyes adjusted to the darkness and he quickly found her sleeping form, a thick blanket tucked under her chin. She was sleeping in the center of the bed, something that should have annoyed him but only made him smile as he crept closer to her.*

Slowly sinking down onto the bed beside her, he let himself study her. While asleep, there was no creasing of her brow or smirk to her lips, just a serene peace etched into her features. Her long eyelashes fanned out, nearly brushing against her cheekbones with every breath she took. A tiny snore escaped her and Bastin had to bite down on his lip to stop his chuckle. He would enjoy telling her about that tomorrow.

He reached down to tug his boots off and toss his shirt on the floor, content just to slide into the sliver of bed that remained when he sensed her watching him. Her gaze was like a brand on his back, and he could always feel when she turned it on him. He glanced over her shoulder to see her watching him with one eye cracked open, a sleepy smile on her face. Her eyes fluttered closed, and she shifted slightly to give him more space.

"In," she murmured, lifting one edge of the blanket out to him.

He smiled, thinking about how she'd gone from pissed when he had first informed her they would be sharing a tent to ordering him into bed. Tucking that thought away to tease her with tomorrow he settled down next to her, the sheets already warm and smelling of her and her amber scent. He looped an arm around her waist and dragged her to his side, wanting to feel her warmth pressed against his skin. She had already fallen back into a light sleep but at his closeness snuggled her face into the crook of his arm. Something bloomed in his chest at the sight of her cradled against him, safe in his arms, but sleep found him too quickly before he could think on what exactly that feeling was.

CHAPTER THIRTY-TWO

Kinna woke to the bed moving beneath her. Her hands reached out to steady herself but instead of sheets and mattress, she found hard muscle beneath her fingers. She opened her eyes to find Bastin beneath her, her body resting comfortably atop his.

"Good morning, princess." He smirked. "I was trying not to wake you but as you can see you made yourself quite comfortable last night."

A vague memory wormed its way into her mind of her opening the blankets for Bastin and him pulling her close, letting her snuggle into his chest. How she made it on top of him, clinging to him like moss on a tree, was a mystery she didn't care to investigate further, not at this hour. Jax had kept her busy loading their horses with supplies and after three long days of travel, all Kinna wanted to do was stay in this very comfortable bed for a few more hours.

"The sun isn't even up yet," she moaned, sliding off him and onto her back where she wrestled the blankets back up under her chin.

Bastin climbed out of bed now that she'd freed him. Kinna couldn't stop herself from watching the muscles move across his back as he hunted for his shirt in the dark room. "I know," he said with a bit of softness. "You can sleep for a few more minutes. I'll be back soon."

Her curiosity overpowered her exhaustion and she sat up on her elbows. "Where are you going?"

"To shower. Want to join me?" Bastin quipped, giving her a smug smile.

She swallowed back a yes, her body already burning beneath his stare. "I think I'll stay right here," she answered, settling back into the warm bed.

"I'll be quick." He chuckled and ducked out of the room, closing the door quietly behind him.

She closed her eyes, hoping to snag a few more minutes of sleep but nervous energy was already seeping into her bones. Sighing, she reluctantly rose and started dressing in her black leggings and a tightly fitted long sleeve tunic. After working a brush through her tangled hair, she braided it back in two tight plaits that fell past her shoulders.

Despite a firm hand with her hair, a few stray curls escaped and hovered over her ears. By the time Bastin returned, Kinna was dressed and waiting, eager to find some breakfast and question him about what had happened last night after she left. In her sleepy state she had forgotten to pester him with questions and scold him for having her kicked out of the meeting under the guise of needing to help Jax.

All her questions disappeared once Bastin walked in with a towel loosely wrapped around his waist, flaunting every one of his perfectly sculpted muscles. Beads of water still dripped off his freshly washed hair and onto the broad expanse of his chest. He watched her admire him with a self-satisfied smirk as he reached past her to grab a neatly folded pile of his clothes.

Realization hit her, bringing her back to reality and she quickly shuffled towards the door. "I'll let you get changed," she mumbled, pulling the door closed behind her before he could respond.

Gods, he really was trying to destroy all her self-control. With her back still against the closed door she took a steadying breath before opening her eyes. She found Emhyr watching her from the wall he stood perched against, laughter glinting in his eyes as if he knew exactly why she had bolted from her shared room. With a wink he disappeared into his own room, leaving her to steady her breathing alone.

Luckily, she found the bathroom at the hall empty and after rinsing her face in some icy cold water she left with a clear head. All three men were waiting in the hallway, talking in hushed voices when she emerged from the bathroom, straining to pick up a few snippets of their conversation as she approached them. Jax was the first to notice her, Emhyr and Bastin had their backs turned in her direction but went quiet when Jax nodded a greeting to her.

"Good," Bastin said. "Now that you're here we can eat and get ready to depart."

Single file they walked down the narrow hallway and into the less private sleeping quarters. There were plenty of bodies still curled up in cots and hammocks as they quietly shuffled through the dark room and down the ladder, trying not to wake anyone up as they went. The lower level of the Nest was surprisingly well lit for the early hour. Lanterns hung along the walls and were sprinkled across tables casting a soft yellow light across each room.

Kinna noticed Leo was situated at the same round meeting table that they had used last night; a plate of biscuits and sausage lay steaming in front of her, but her focus remained on the small map. She heard them approach, each of them sliding into the seat they had occupied previously with Kinna sandwiched between Bastin and Emhyr and slid the plates of food towards them.

Kinna split her biscuit open, adding a sausage patty, thankful to have something to quell her growling stomach. She spotted Saul walking towards them with a tray of mugs balanced precariously on a too-small tray. He sat them at the center of the table, not caring as the liquid inside splashed over the edges and took one for himself before joining them.

"Mornin'," Saul mumbled.

"I see you're still not a morning person." Emhyr grinned, passing the mugs out to everyone before taking one himself.

Saul grunted in response before tearing into a biscuit and Kinna watched Bastin and Emhyr's lips tilt into a smile. They were obviously in on some private joke about Saul and his dislike for mornings and weren't going to share it.

"Now that we are all here," Leo started, her attention finally fixed on the people before her instead of her map. "I'd like to go over everything one more time before you leave."

Kinna sat sipping on her tea, the brew a little stronger than she was used to and listened to Bastin go through their plan once again. Saul would be their guide out of the city and beyond. They would travel across the border to the small sliver of land that sat at the base of the Warchill Mountains where the family they would be smuggling back should be waiting for them. Saul would be traveling ahead of them, serving as their scout and backup, should they need it. Apparently Bastin had gotten his way because Leo hadn't argued with him when he mentioned their formation which had Kinna firmly in the middle of the group.

It would be a full day's ride to the section of border where they could cross. They wouldn't risk doing so this close to Edgewood so they would travel east into the more rural parts of the border where they were less likely to encounter any guards.

According to the fat red *x*'s on Leo's map, the Rising had a few spots along the border that they used to cross, each with a number listed beneath it that Kinna assumed corresponded to the number of guards they should expect patrolling the area. A small red *3* had been written under the *x* they would be using. Between the five of them, three guards should be no problem.

They planned to cross at dusk, using the shadows to hide them. They would then cross back near midnight when the sky would be at its darkest thanks to the new moon, which would provide them the most coverage possible to travel with such a large group. Once back in Ferryn, they would ride through the night, reaching the Nest again by dawn the next morning.

Everyone was in agreement and Kinna could see the thought and planning that had gone into this mission. It was obvious that the Rising had carefully weighed the risks and used everything in their arsenal to ensure they were successful, including sending two of their best men into the fray. Kinna was reminded how flippantly she used to think about the Rising, as if they were nothing but a rag-tag operation hell bent on causing chaos.

Gods, how wrong she had been. They were so much more than she had ever given them credit for. Perhaps, she thought, that was what they wanted though, to be overlooked and underestimated. Maybe it was easier for them to let everyone believe that and use it to surprise people at every turn. They had certainly surprised her.

With their meeting adjourned, Leo wished them luck before disappearing towards the kitchen area. Saul clapped his hands loudly and ushered them towards the makeshift armory where they would each load themselves down with weapons.

Naturally, Kinna found herself in front of the bows and quivers, her hands running gently over the three hanging from the wall before choosing one and testing the string. It fit easily on her back, the familiar weight resting against her comfortably. Bastin approached her with twin daggers, and she let him strap them against the outside of each of her thighs. He added one smaller knife to her right ankle, his warm fingers skimming softly over her skin, then situated her pant leg back over it with a wink. The memory of her snatching his knife from the very same place the first time they sparred brought a small smile to her face.

Twin swords now hung from Bastin's hips, along with gods knew how many other daggers and knives strapped to him. Emhyr stood waiting, a vicious looking curved sword tied across his back and his long locks pulled up in a tight bun.

Jax waited, a slight frown on his face. Kinna

fought the urge to make a joke about him being an overprotective parent because she knew the gravity of this situation. Two young children's lives were at stake, along with her friends. He had every right to worry over everyone in the room.

Once they were all satisfied with their choice of weapon, Jax led them all through the back of the Nest, into the small garden they had spent the previous night in. It had been a surprise to see all the greenery and the small stable surrounded by high brick walls covered in deep green ivy. Kinna would bet that someone here had a touch of earth magic since the raised wooden beds were overflowing with ripe vegetables and fruits despite it still being early spring. It was a peaceful spot despite being tucked between abandoned buildings and hidden from sight. Their horses had joined three other mares in the now crowded stables. The three men went to retrieve their mounts, Bastin slipping something to Alder as he ruffled his ears affectionately.

Saul stood to the side with Kinna; she could feel him watching her from the corner of her eye. "Ye look so much like your mother," Saul whispered, so soft she wasn't sure if she was meant to hear it.

"Did you know her?" Kinna asked, surprised.

"No, not really," he gruffed. "I worked in the capit'l when I was a youngling. Made deliveries to the castle. I was there the day she arrived, being sold to someone like chattel."

Kinna's brow tensed at his words. She knew her mother had not wanted to marry when she sailed across the ocean and arrived on the shores of Ferryn. She had just turned eighteen at the time and had never left her home in the capital city of Vanna. Sailing to

Ferryn had been her grandfather's idea, one that he had hoped would secure a lucrative alliance for himself and his kingdom.

"Apologies," he added. "I'm sure it 'twas never said like that."

"Actually," she chuckled. "It kind of was."

He gave her a confused stare. "My father's favorite story to tell was how my mother snubbed him at their first meeting. How she didn't care about him or his castle, just walked right past him," she explained. A sad smile graced her lips as she remembered the last time she heard her father tell it.

Saul chuckled. "Aye. I remember. I watched the whole thing and knew I liked her moxy." He grinned, striding forward to gather the reins of his own horse now that the other three were out of the small space.

Emhyr and Jax were already mounted, leading their mares towards the narrow gap in the brick where a heavy iron gate stood, an intricate floral pattern blocking anyone from being able to glimpse inside. Bastin led Alder to where she stood, his muzzle reaching to search her empty hands before he huffed in frustration. She laughed at his reaction then let Bastin hoist her into the saddle before he slid in behind her.

Saul joined them, pushing his ebony mare to the front of the group. A reed thin boy appeared near the gate, his auburn hair glinting in the morning light as he pushed open the door for the four horses to pass through. His freckled face and hair reminded Kinna of the twins, an intense longing to see them and Sebrina shot through her. Her gaze lingered on the boy as they trotted past him, and she returned his hesitant smile.

"We will be home soon," Bastin whispered, assuring her as his thumb rubbed her thigh gently.

He seemed to always be able to read her thoughts as if she had spoken them aloud. Seeing the boy, his thoughts had likely drifted to their friends waiting for them to return too. Still, his words had knocked all the remaining air from her lungs. *Home.* The Rising and the Hearth had truly become her home. Despite all her resolutions to leave, she desperately wanted to stay. Every painful reminder that she couldn't had started to feel like a knife twisting in her chest.

Kinna took a few steading breaths, pushing all her feelings down and held them in an iron grip. She couldn't afford to be unfocused now that they had left the safety of the Nest and she vowed not to put any of the men here in danger because she couldn't keep a handle on her own emotions. No, she would shut herself off from everything until they were back safely with three new additions to their group. Then perhaps she could give herself the space to grieve the decision she'd made.

Saul led them through alley after alley, the streets slowly becoming less populated, the buildings grew increasingly farther apart until they shifted to farmland completely. Just like when they had entered Edgewood, cottages began dotting the tilled ground around them, most with their occupants trudging around outside to complete morning chores. None of them bothered to look up or speak as they passed by, too immersed in their own daily lives to care about the strangers riding past.

The morning air was crisp, but the sun shone steadily in the cloudless sky, its rays warming her face as they rode further into the countryside. They traveled in silence, Emhyr and Jax keeping them tucked safely between them as they rode. Kinna periodically would spot Saul ahead of them, his mounted form reduced to a small dot on the road ahead. They stopped only once when Saul indicated a small stream where they could let their horses rest and drink for a few moments, offering them an opportunity to stretch their legs before departing again.

The sun was beginning to dip in the west when Kinna noticed the terrain beginning to change from bright green grasslands to rockier ground with sparse vegetation and scraggly trees. The colors of spring disappeared with every step of their horses and were replaced with a myriad of browns and greys, even the air seemed to cool and retain an acrid smell.

Bastin motioned up ahead of them where a grouping of grey mountains had appeared, standing sharply against the blue sky. Low peaks continued past the initial incline, each stretching wider than the last. Kinna could make out a white dusting of snow on a few tops that loomed in the distance, situated firmly in Eldridge. "That is the beginning of the Warchill Mountain range," he said. "They call the stretch of land before the mountains the Chasm."

The wind had picked up speed, its icy tendrils working their way beneath her thick cloak and stinging her exposed face and hands. The weather had grown steadily worse as they neared the mountains and now Kinna could see a growing darkness just beyond the peaks. It was as if the sky itself was issuing a warning.

Fat rain clouds were looming in the distance, the wind pushing them closer and eliminating their remaining daylight faster. They would need to cross the border quickly and get into position before the storm broke or they would be wasting precious time and energy fighting the elements while they trekked towards the Chasm.

Everyone seemed to sense the growing unease and Saul urged his horse faster, leading the group towards a huddle of reedy trees. The dark clouds moved in faster blocking the last of the setting sun's rays. Saul pulled on the reins of his mare, turning to face them. "We need to cross now," Saul said, the men nodding in agreement. "Ev'ryone stick to yer path and move fast."

Without another word he kicked his horse into a sprint, bolting to the left and disappearing into the distance as Emhyr and Jax both took the center route.

"Why are we splitting up?" Kinna asked nervously. She didn't like being separated from both Emhyr and Jax, not knowing whether they were safe or not left a queasy feeling in her stomach.

"It's easier to cross in smaller groups," Bastin explained, his voice soothing the tension in her shoulders. "If there are any guards, there are likely only a few. Splitting up means they won't be able to pursue all of us and the rest can get past them."

"Is that why we are going last? So we have the best chance of getting across the border?"

"Yes," he said, giving Alder a gentle nudge before he began sprinting right, away from the other two groups.

Kinna leaned forward, the speed of the stallion beneath her forcing her to cling tightly to him. She watched his powerful legs eat up the ground beneath them while they charged towards the mountains that grew with every passing second. Finally, their pace slowed as they approached a massive rock outcrop the color of ash. Its sharp points crisscrossed past each other, and a small gap formed at the base of it, just tall enough that a normal person could sit beneath it. Of course, it was too small for Emhyr to fit his large frame inside, but she finally breathed a sigh of relief as she saw him and the other two men waiting in the shadows.

Saul had already begun passing out their meager dinner as they dismounted and Kinna's stomach rumbled appreciatively at the promise of something to eat. She ate her cold sandwich while everyone settled into a spot, content for now that everyone was safe and accounted for.

"What now?" Kinna asked, wiping a crumb from the corner of her mouth.

"Now we wait," Emhyr chuckled. "We gave ourselves extra time in case a border guard spotted us but since we were so stealthy, we just stay here until it's time to meet the others."

After all the food was eaten, they fell into silence, each of them busying their hands with something while the minutes drug by. Kinna took to testing the string of her bow, going over every inch until she was satisfied and then began inspecting each arrow in the quiver she'd taken.

Luckily the task kept her mind distracted enough that she barely noticed the darkness overtake the sky, the only light coming from the small lantern that Saul lit beneath the rock that shielded them. They wouldn't risk a fire and potentially drawing any attention to them, but the lantern was safely hidden in the small gap in the rock, only illuminating a crescent of ground around them.

CHAPTER THIRTY-THREE

Finally, it was time to begin the final leg of their trek to the meeting spot located deeper into Eldridge and closer to the base of the first mountain that was now barely distinguishable against the night sky. Their horses had been secured to a clutch of nearby trees that looked as if one good tug from Alder could rip any of them from the ground. Saul was the first to disappear into the darkness, slinking between shadows as he scouted their path ahead. Kinna hoped that the storm clouds she'd seen earlier would pass them by so as to not spook the horses.

A few moments later a soft chirp echoed back to them. If Kinna didn't already know the sound of their signal she would have sworn it was just the noise of a bird chirping into the spring night. Bastin gave Emhyr a swift nod and then pressed a kiss onto Kinna's forehead before following Saul's trail. The second he was out of sight, unease spread through her body, making her tighten her grip on the bow in her hands.

Emhyr laid a heavy hand on her shoulder. "He'll be fine," he assured her. "We have done this a hundred times and he always comes back."

"I know," she agreed and then stepped forward with Emhyr once another quiet chirp floated towards them.

They crept along two sets of footprints in the dirt letting them lead them in the direction of their waiting companions. Kinna kept her bow out, an arrow ready and nocked into place while she walked behind Emhyr who's curved sword was poised in his left hand. He raised his hand slightly, indicating for them to pause so he could send the last signal to Jax who was still waiting behind, acting as the rear of their line. Once again, they began moving, slowly and quietly, listening for any sign of trouble.

Each second seemed to last longer than the one before. Her eyes strained in the darkness, cautiously watching their surroundings, and listening to the quiet pad of their footsteps. The hoot of an owl rang through the air, the sound causing both Kinna and Emhyr to pause, their weapons rising simultaneously in their hands. Her heart kicked into overdrive, the sound of blood pulsing in her ears drowned everything out while they waited for any movement. The rush of blood had heated her skin, erasing the cold that had settled over her. When nothing came, they began walking again, their weapons still drawn, and the tension clear in their every movement.

Even in the dark, Kinna started to make out a form looming in the distance, its shape standing just shades darker than the midnight sky. Soon the form sharpened, long crooked arms branched out in every direction from a thick middle that rose two stories high. The massive tree was at odds with everything Kinna had seen so far in Eldridge and the sheer size of it was all the more impressive considering the scrawny brush they had been traveling through.

A circular meadow had formed around it, the roots sprawled outward from the base claiming all the land around it for itself and preventing anything else from occupying its space. Unfortunately, it created dangerously uneven terrain, forcing them to step carefully over each root that protruded from the earth to not lose their footing.

As they drew closer, Saul stood leaning against its trunk and Bastin paced nervously in front of him. He quickly stopped when he spotted them, meeting her in a few long strides.

"You're late," he muttered, glaring at Emhyr.

"We heard something," he explained. "It sounded like an owl, and it probably was one, but we stopped for a moment to make sure."

Bastin's brow furrowed at that. Saul pushed himself off the tree to nudge Bastin. "Calm down," he grunted. "It was probably a wee birdie. Em did exactly as I taught him."

Bastin nodded at him absentmindedly and tugged Kinna towards him, tucking her underneath his arm and steering them back towards the tree. She relaxed into his touch, leaning her head against his shoulder as they walked.

"You're staying with me from now on," he whispered.

"That wasn't the plan," she challenged, poking his side. "I'm supposed to be in the middle with Emhyr."

"I don't care. I can't focus when I can't see you."

She ignored the flutter in her chest. "Is it smart to change the plan at the last minute?"

"No." He sighed and rubbed his face roughly. "Fine, we'll stick with the plan, but you need to stay alert. I can't get rid of this uneasy feeling."

"You're just being paranoid because I'm here," she teased, trying to lighten his mood. "Everything has gone perfectly so far, there's no reason to be worried."

He nodded but didn't loosen his grip on her.

Jax appeared moments later to complete their group and then the waiting began again. The five of them stayed close to the trunk of the giant oak, each watching a different edge of the circle for the arrival of Warren and his two children. Time dragged on and Kinna decided that this may turn out to be the longest night of her life. Each minute sound reverberated through the clearing, capturing the attention of everyone for a few seconds before their watch resumed.

Eventually the quiet shuffle of feet could be heard, and all eyes turned to the western edge where a grim-faced man appeared followed by two children. Warren nodded curtly at the group as he motioned for the children ahead of him. The eldest was gripping her younger brother's hand tightly as she walked towards them, shifting to keep him behind her small body. Kinna instantly liked Noelle as she watched her maintain her protective stance in front of her brother, striding forward with her head high despite the group of strangers waiting for her. Kinna caught her eye and gave her a small smile.

Warren stayed steps behind his children, waiting until Noelle stopped in front of Kinna before placing a hand on each of their shoulders and gently tugging them towards him. "Thank you for doing this," he said earnestly, his eyes roving over each of them and catching on Bastin and Emhyr.

Despite Noelle's brave face, her brother Mac clung tightly to her arm, his eyes downcast. Kinna stepped forward and knelt down in front of the two while Warren watched her cautiously. "I'm Kinna," she said softly. "Would you two like to walk with me?"

Mac peeked up at her through his eyelashes then looked to his sister for an answer. Noelle studied her for a moment. Kinna watched her sharp eyes peer over her shoulder to the bow strapped across her back and then back to her face. "Are you good with that?" she asked.

Kinna's smile grew. She definitely liked this girl.

"She's the best I've seen," Bastin answered for her.

Noelle glanced at him and then back to her before nodding, Bastin's words convincing her that she could be trusted. Kinna held her hand out and she took it without hesitation, pulling her brother along with her.

"Warren, you'll be in the rear with Jax," Bastin said.

Jax waved a hand and Warren walked to join him. Kinna led the two children towards Emhyr who gave them a friendly wink. Saul and Bastin were leading the group and with everyone in position, gave the signal for them to draw their weapons. Kinna slid her bow off her back and fished an arrow out of her quiver, nocking it into place but not drawing it back.

They got in position at the southern edge of the clearing, Kinna and Emhyr keeping the two children tucked closely between them. Bastin kissed her forehead quickly then walked to the front of the group, nodding for Saul to begin leading them back towards the border. Saul stepped forward, Bastin following close behind him with his twin swords ready in his hands.

Emhyr was next, followed by their two wards then Kinna, Warren and Jax taking up the rear.

Tracing the route that had led them in, they silently walked back along their previous tracks. Moving quietly with a large group was challenging so their progress was slow. They had almost made it to the halfway point when the hoot of an owl was heard, and the group froze. The sound was almost exactly what Kinna had heard earlier that night. Before she could voice her suspicions that it was not truly an owl and warn her companions, something shot through the air.

She had heard the unmistakable whiz of an arrow behind her, a sound so familiar that she would recognize it anywhere. On instinct she turned to face it but before she could shout to the others a white-hot pain struck her shoulder. She fell to her knees as a scream escaped her and the fire began spreading down her arm and across her back.

Barely registering what was happening around her, she stared at the arrow that had pierced clean through her shoulder, the bloody point visible behind her. She reached her hand out to touch it, needing to feel it to prove that it wasn't a figment of her imagination. Even the slightest touch to the shaft or shift of her body sent a fresh wave of pain through her arm along with a fresh rush of blood.

Bastin's face suddenly invaded her vision, the fear in his eyes bringing her back to reality. His hands gripped her face. "Can you walk?" he asked again.

Kinna could barely stay focused on him, blackness was starting to creep into the edges of her vision, but she managed to nod. Panic was beginning to set in, but she braced her right arm on his shoulder and used him to help push herself up. It took all her self-control to not scream as the movement shifted the arrow still lodged in her shoulder. Her teeth were clenched so tightly that she thought they may crack, but no sound escaped her lips.

She looked around through the rain and noticed that no one remained aside from Bastin and a worried looking Emhyr. Kinna sent a silent prayer to the gods that no one else seemed to be injured, that Bastin was standing beside her whole and unharmed. His arm looped around her middle and he hurried her along. She let him half guide half drag her forward, leaning into him more heavily with each step. Her shirt beneath her cloak was soaked, her cooling blood sticking to her and beginning to seep into the waistband of her pants.

Her vision was fading quickly, and she knew that it wouldn't be long before she no longer could walk on her own. She was losing too much blood far too quickly and she realized this night could end very badly for her. She couldn't bring herself to care about the fire burning in her shoulder or her fuzzy vision though, all she cared about was Bastin. Her head was so heavy but used every last drop of strength to lift her head to look at his grim face. She focused on his face, the sound of his breathing as she put one foot in front of the other. The words were on the tip of her tongue, but she couldn't make a sound, her strength failing with every step.

Bastin sensed her distress like a hound and stopped. "I'm sorry but this is going to hurt," he whispered, briefly kissing her forehead before scooping her up so he could carry her.

She gasped at the pain as her feet left the

ground. He clutched her close to his chest, trying not to jostle her, and took off running. Emhyr kept pace beside him as they raced towards the border. The movement shifted the arrow and more blood trickled from the wound faster than before, staining Bastin's chest red.

After a moment of running, she lost the battle to stay conscious, her vision faded completely, and her head slumped against him as she faded in unconsciousness.

CHAPTER THIRTY-FOUR

Bastin

Her scream was the first indication that the owl's hoot was more than just a bird calling into the night. He had seen her turn in the periphery of his vision just before the arrow sliced clean through her. It was a small miracle that it hadn't pierced her chest as the archer had intended, her familiarity with the bow and the sound of an arrow firing was perhaps the only thing that saved her. A crack of lightning shot through the sky, illuminating the scene before him and the arrow that he could see protruding from her back. The sight sent him into a murderous rage, made worse when he saw her kneeling on the ground, blood already running down her chest.

A man dropped from a tree behind them, a bow still in his hands and his aim focused on Kinna. Jax was the closest since Warren was already running for his two children, their faces etched with horror as they watched the bleeding woman in front of them. Bastin blinked and the unknown archer had a small knife embedded in his right eye, courtesy of Jax.

Another man appeared, not sparing a glance at his

fallen comrade and advanced on Jax with his sword drawn. The sound of swords clashing and rain pouring rang in his ears while he rushed to Kinna, falling before her, and watching her stare in fascination at the arrow in her shoulder.

"We need to run," he said as he felt the trickle of raindrops down his forehead. She didn't hear him, instead she lifted her fingers to touch the wound. "Kinna, baby, come on, we need to go."

Still no response. She was going into shock. He looked around at Saul already pushing Warren and his children away from the scene and Jax following behind them, his sword dripping, and his shirt covered in a spray of blood. "Go," he told them. "Get the children to safety."

Emhyr stood next to him. The rain poured faster, splattering them with large fat drops. "What do we do?" he asked, wiping the water from his face. "There could be more coming.'

"Fuck." Bastin shook his head confused. "Did you recognize anything on them?"

"No, they didn't have a sigil, but they didn't look like any Eldridge soldier we've encountered," Emhyr answered.

"Kinna," Bastin said, turning his attention back to her. She was still staring at the arrow piercing her shoulder, so he gently grabbed her face, pulling her gaze away from the wound. "Can you walk?"

He finally saw some recognition in her eyes, and she nodded. He let her use him to stand, noticing the tension in her jaw as she tried not to cry out in pain. His stomach roiled at the sight and how much pain she was in. He carefully held on to her waist, trying to keep her upright as they started moving, heading away from the now bloody patch of dirt.

Her pace was growing slower as they walked, the rain during the dry dirt into mud that clung to their shoes. "She's losing too much blood, Bas," Emhyr yelled over the wind that had turned the rain into a full-fledged storm.

He surveyed the blood still oozing from her shoulder with barely concealed despair. Bastin sucked in a breath and nodded, he knew what he needed to do. "Fuck," Bastin muttered, stopping her. "I'm sorry but this is going to hurt," he whispered, kissing her cold, clammy forehead.

He looped his other arm under her knees and pulled her to his chest. Her gasp was like a physical blow, but he pushed aside his feelings, focusing only on Emhyr ahead of him and started to run. Kinna lost consciousness after a moment, so Bastin ran faster, pushing his body to its limit. They finally caught up to the others where they had left their horses, everyone soaked from the unexpected storm that was now a light drizzle. Saul cursed when he saw Kinna lying limp in his arms.

"We need to stop the bleeding," Emhyr cautioned.

"How?" Bastin asked.

"I can remove the arrow and try to cauterize the wound," he offered. "It may buy us enough time to get back to the Nest."

Bastin weighed their options quickly, formulating a plan while the woman he loved lay bleeding in his arms. "Saul, Warren, you two take the children and ride back now," he ordered. "Jax and Emhyr will stabilize Kinna and be right behind you."

"Aye," Saul agreed, mounting his horse, and sitting Mac in front of him. Warren loaded Noelle onto his horse and then joined her atop the mare. "Be careful."

Bastin nodded as they rode off then turned to Emhyr. "What do you need me to do?"

"Lay her on her side and remove her cloak," he instructed. "Bas, hold her arms. Jax, hold her feet. This will probably wake her up."

He did as directed, locking her slim wrists in his grip. He watched Emhyr use a small knife to sever the arrow shaft and form a small flame at his pointer finger. "Ready?" Emhyr asked.

"Do it," he said.

Emhyr quickly pulled the arrow through the back of her shoulder then brought the flame to the dark hole that was left behind. The moment the flame touched her skin another feral scream sounded in the night. Her back arched off the ground as the flame burned her skin and she fought for control of her limbs. In her weakened state it was disgustingly easy to keep her hands restrained but fighting against the instinct that roared at him to stop Emhyr, stop her suffering, was brutal. After a moment the smell of singed flesh assaulted his nose. Emhyr removed his hand and used the edge of his shirt to gently wipe the area.

He nodded grimly. "It's not bleeding anymore," he announced.

Bastin pulled her into his lap, her eyes dazed in the wake of the pain. She reached a shaky hand up to his face and he felt the unfamiliar rush of liquid in his eyes. "You stay with me baby," he whispered. "We are going to take care of you."

He took her bloody hand in his and kissed her knuckles. Cradling her in his arms he stood up. "Let's go," he said. "Jax tie Alder to you. Emhyr, I'll ride with you."

He carefully transferred Kinna to Emhyr while he mounted his mare. He took a blanket from the saddlebag and created a makeshift cocoon for Emhyr to place her in, wrapping her body to try to preserve her warmth while they traveled. Once Emhyr was seated they let Jax take the lead and Bastin held her, silently begging the gods that he'd never prayed to or cared about to help him keep her safe.

CHAPTER THIRTY-FIVE

Kinna woke up in the bedroom she had shared with Bastin in the Nest, weighed down by thick quilts and with a dull ache radiating from her shoulder. She had a few groggy memories of riding in Bastin's arms and then arriving at the Nest, her body laid on a hard surface while they cleaned and dressed her wound. Not only did her body ache but her head was a fuzzy mess and the hours of time unaccounted for left her feeling disoriented. She wasn't even sure how long she'd been in this bed or what time of day it was thanks to the heavy curtains that blocked out any light from escaping through the small window. Sighing she used her right arm to try to prop herself up in bed and hissed at the fresh pain that her movement caused.

Finally, she managed to sit up, breathing deeply at the effort. Her left arm had been bandaged tightly across her chest underneath the large shirt she was wearing, making it almost impossible for her to move it. Glancing around the room her eyes immediately found Bastin sleeping in a chair propped against the door, his arms crossed over his chest. He still wore the same clothes, her blood dried and smeared across his shirt.

She might have laughed at his stubbornness, his unwillingness to leave her side to bathe and change, if she didn't vividly remember the pain of the arrow ripping through her and the feeling of losing consciousness in his arms.

She watched him for a moment, noting the deep shadows visible under his eyes and debating letting him sleep. Not willing to risk his wrath when he found her sitting alone and awake in bed while he slept, she looked around for something to throw at him. A stack of gauze sat on the small table beside the bed, she reached for it, balling it up in her fist before tossing it at his head. She immediately regretted it as the ache in her arm roared to life but could stop the giggle from escaping as it bounced off his forehead and he jolted awake.

His hands immediately fell to his waist, searching for a sword that wasn't there before he realized the projectile had been soft gauze. His confusion gave way to panic as his eyes flew from the crumpled ball on the ground to the woman stifling laughter in the bed. Rising quickly, he knocked the chair into the door loudly as he rushed to kneel at the edge of the bed. "You're awake," he whispered, his fingers reached for her reflexively, but he jerked them back quickly. "How do you feel? What do you need? Are you thirsty?"

"Calm down," she snorted, her voice gravelly from disuse. "I'm okay. Some water would be great though."

His eyes narrowed. "I will not calm down. You almost fucking died," he argued, shaking his head and getting to his feet.

"Well, I didn't and now I'm telling you I am fine."

He rolled his eyes, scoffing at her reassurance.

"I'm going to get you some water. Do not move."

She gave him a mock salute with her good arm as he slipped out of the room, closing the door quietly behind him. Sighing she tried to sit up straighter in the bed and slowly began stretching her sore muscles the best she could without using her left arm. She heard the click of the door handle and looked up to find Emhyr and Jax peeking their heads inside. Relief was evident on their faces when they saw her awake and sitting in the bed.

"Hi." She smiled as Emhyr pushed past Jax and half ran to her side.

"You're finally awake," he exclaimed, plopping down at the foot of the bed. "I didn't think you were ever going to wake up and Bas was going to remain unshowered for the rest of his life."

"How long have I been asleep?" Kinna asked cautiously. She was known to sleep well into midday and cringed at the thought of Bastin not showering since they had returned yesterday.

He hesitated a moment. "You've been asleep for five days," Emhyr said quietly as Jax stepped closer to stand behind him.

Kinna's mouth fell open. It wasn't possible that she had been unconscious for that long. Her arm was definitely sore, and she wouldn't be using a bow for a while, but she truly felt fine. "That's not possible," she whispered. "Five whole days?"

Emhyr nodded. "They gave you a sedative so you would sleep," Jax explained. "You were in bad shape when we got back. Emhyr cauterized your wound, but your body was in shock. Leo called for Pearl, she's an earth elemental that lives here and has an affinity for healing and herbal remedies. She cleaned you up, made some kind of poultice for your shoulder and then said you needed to sleep, that your body would do the rest if we gave it time."

"Pearl's been coming up twice a day to change your bandages and check on you," Emhyr told her. "She's the only one Bas would let in. We've been worried sick. No one told us that it would take this long for you to wake back up."

"Gods, what a mess," Kinna murmured. "Well, now that I'm awake we can go home. I'm sure you both are tired of waiting around here."

They both chuckled. "Bastin won't be letting you go anywhere until you've been cleared by Pearl," Jax confessed. "I'm surprised he even left this room."

"I told him I was thirsty, and he practically went running." She smiled.

Emhyr patted her cheek. "Get used to it, love." He grinned. "You have no idea how bad he can be."

"Do you remember when Sebrina broke her arm when she was ten?" Jax mused.

Emhyr started laughing. "He spoon fed her for weeks," he teased. "This is going to be so much worse."

Kinna sighed and covered her face. "Great," she told them. "That is just great."

The door handle jiggled and Bastin appeared carrying a pitcher of water along with a steaming bowl. His face hardened when he saw the two men laughing at the end of the bed. "Who let you in here?" he scolded, kicking the door shut. "She needs to rest."

Emhyr threw Kinna a smug look and Jax shook his head in sympathy. Bastin had shifted from protective to suffocating and she'd only been awake for ten minutes. "I think I've rested enough," she told him. "Five days is a long time."

"Pearl is on her way to see you," he quipped, dropping the tray onto the side table. "You're not leaving that bed until she says so."

She groaned while Emhyr tried to disguise his laughter with a cough. Bastin poured some water into a glass and handed it to her. "If you're sick you need to leave," he told Emhyr sternly. "She doesn't need a cold on top of everything else."

Taking a long drink of water, she let the cool liquid wash away the stale taste in her mouth and the dryness accompanying it. "Stop fussing," Kinna warned.

"Not a chance," he said, taking her empty glass and refilling it. "Despite what these two idiots may have said, your injuries almost killed you. They may be joking now but we were going through hell wondering if you were going to make it, if we would ever see your eyes open again. That is not something I wish to relive."

Her head started to droop at his reprimand, but he caught her chin between his fingers. "I almost lost you," he whispered. "I could not bear it if something happened, and you were taken from me."

Before she could respond to his sudden declaration a sharp knock sounded at the door. Bastin kissed her cheek tenderly and then opened it to reveal a middle-aged woman with silvery blonde hair piled into a neat bun on top of her head. She was dressed in a plain grey dress with a crisp white apron tied tightly around her waist, in her arms she carried a large wicker basket overflowing with supplies. She breezed past Bastin, her eyes focused on Kinna and shooed the men away from the bed.

"You must be Miss Kinna, nice to finally meet you," she said, setting her basket on the bed and unpacking her supplies. "I'm Pearl. How are you feeling?"

"It's nice to meet you too. Thank you for taking care of me," Kinna replied. Pearl waved off her thanks and continued unpacking. "I feel fine, just a bit sore."

Pearl nodded. "That's to be expected."

"She's had some water but nothing else," Bastin interjected. "I brought up some broth, is she okay to eat?"

"Yes, of course," Pearl answered. "She needs to regain some strength and food is as good a way as any."

Pearl began unrolling a thick cylinder of gauze, taking a pair of scissors to make cuts periodically and create long strips. "We are going to need to change your bandage," she told her.

"You two," Bastin pointed. "Out."

Emhyr snuck a quick kiss onto her head before he and Jax slipped out, promising they would be back to check on her in a little while. She waved them on with her good arm and then began to slip it out of the shirt. Bastin was instantly at her side, helping her slide the shirt over her head and pulling her blanket to cover herself as best she could.

Her cheeks flamed at her body being bared to a complete stranger but those thoughts vanished quickly as Pearl began unwinding the bandages that wrapped across her arm and then around her shoulder, exposing her wound for the first time. Her nimble fingers moving quickly without touching her skin, a practiced movement that she had done all her life. Once her arm was free, she straightened her elbow, wincing at the stiffness in her joint.

Bastin noticed immediately. "Are you okay?" he whispered.

"Yes," she said. "Just a little stiff."

"I kept your arm tied so you wouldn't jostle it in your sleep," Pearl explained as she unraveled the white bandages. "Now that you're awake you can wear a sling instead. You'll need to work on stretching it too until you regain your full range of motion."

Kinna nodded at her instructions, slowly extending her arm, and rotating it. The stretch of her muscles was unpleasant but not unbearable. Pearl watched her intently as she did so, touching a few places on her shoulder while she moved. "The joint feels fine," she announced and Kinna rested her arm by her side. "There doesn't seem to be any infection in the skin, but I still want this covered for a few more days."

Kinna looked down to inspect her shoulder for the first time. A dark red circle lay on her skin, the skin around it puckered where Emhyr had cauterized it to stop the bleeding. Just shy of an inch in diameter it looked so innocent when in reality it had almost killed her. She touched it with the tip of her finger, feeling the roughness of the scab that had formed. Pearl laid a small pad of gauze on the spot where the arrow entered her shoulder, adding a small dab of a white paste, then began to wrap the strips she cut around it, holding the poultice in place.

"That should do it," she announced when she had finished tying the bandages in a tiny knot and slid her arm into the sling. Bastin looked to her for instructions, ever the waiting soldier. "I'll be back in the morning. Make sure she eats and has plenty of water. It wouldn't hurt to get her up and walking around either. Try not to get the bandages wet either."

He nodded, hanging on her every word. "Thank you, Pearl," he said.

She nodded and patted his shoulder before grabbing her basket off the bed. "I'll see you tomorrow, Miss Kinna," she chuckled, throwing her a wave. "Good luck with your three mother hens."

Kinna smiled. "Thank you."

Once Pearl had left, Bastin helped Kinna into a fresh shirt, holding the loose sleeve so she could ease her good arm into the opening. She caught a whiff of citrus and mint as she pulled it over her head, and she knew instantly who had donated her new wardrobe. "Is this your shirt?" Kinna asked.

The corner of his mouth tilted up into a smile. "Yes," he said.

"I think you may need it more than I do," she pointed to his still ruined clothes. "Why don't you go change and have a bath? I'll be fine for a little while."

He shook his head. "You need to eat something," he argued, picking the tray up and pulling his chair to sit next to her. He stirred the clear liquid carefully. "I brought you some chicken broth since I wasn't sure what you could have."

"Thank you," she said, holding her hand out for the bowl. He shook his head again, lifting the spoon to her mouth. She rolled her eyes. "I can feed myself."

"If you keep rolling your eyes they are going to fall out of your head," he muttered. The spoon still hovered in the air. "Eat."

Emhyr and Jax had been right, there was no use arguing with him because he wasn't giving up. She took a bite, then another, letting him spoon feed her until she had finished the entire bowl and the broth warmed her belly. Kinna would never admit it, but she liked his mothering.

Bastin loaded the tray with the empty dishes but left a full glass of water on the table beside her. "I'll be back in half an hour," he said, stopping to pull her quilt up further. "Get some rest and shout if you need anything, Emhyr is in the room across the hall."

"I will," she said. "Go bathe, you're starting to smell."

"Very funny," he grumbled, shutting the door behind him.

———

Kinna didn't remember falling asleep but when she woke Bastin had returned in fresh clothes and resumed his vigil in the chair beside her bed. He sat reading a small leather-bound book next to the lantern on the side table. She watched him for a few moments, the soft light casting shadows across his tanned face, sharpening the angle of his jaw. His hair had gotten longer since they'd met, the ends curling softly around his nape. A few strands hung down across his forehead where he had run his fingers through it. She smiled; he was still the most beautiful man she had ever seen.

He glanced up to check on her and found her awake and smiling at him. Closing his book, he got up to sit next to her on the bed. "What are you smiling at?" he asked.

"Nothing," she said, pushing herself into a sitting position. "What time is it?"

"Just after sunset," he answered, offering her some water. "Do you want something to eat?"

"Maybe in a bit. I need to go to the bathroom and maybe take a bath."

"You aren't supposed to get your bandage wet."

She sighed. "I forgot."

"I have an idea." He grinned.

"What?" Kinna eyed him suspiciously.

"Just trust me," he replied, tugging her blankets off.

She let him help her up and clung to him until the wave of dizziness passed. Gods, lying in bed for five days after almost dying did weird things to the body. She felt like a newborn colt standing on shaky legs and as much as she hated to admit it, she was in no condition to travel days on horseback yet. He walked her slowly to the bathroom at the end of the hall, letting her shuffle along on her own and letting her brace herself against his forearm.

When they finally made it Kinna was trying and failing to disguise how out of breath she was. Her grip on Bastin had tightened but she made it to the toilet on her own while Bastin filled the tub with hot water. Her good arm stayed on the wall as she walked the few steps to rinse her hands in the small sink. Steam had started to swirl in the air, leaving dots of moisture clinging to the mirror in front of her.

Kinna did not recognize the face that stared back at her. The woman in the mirror was too pale, deep circles sat beneath her dull silver eyes, her full lips were dry and chapped. Her hair was the worst of all, knotted and greasy tied in a loose knot on her head. It would take her hours to return her curls to their former glory.

Kinna looked nothing like the woman she was used to seeing in the mirror. She sighed and rinsed her face, hoping she could wash away the haggard look with the warm water. It brought a little color back to her face and while it wasn't much it still made her feel slightly better.

Bastin's face appeared behind her. "Come on," he coaxed. "Stop glaring at your reflection."

"Would it have killed one of you to run a brush through my hair?" she grumbled.

"We had bigger concerns," he said, leading her to the edge of the tub. Steam rose off the water's surface, the sweet smell of vanilla rising with it. Kinna savored the familiar scent, letting it relax the tension from her body.

She slid her good arm out of the shirt and pushed it over the sling then shimmied out of her leggings, letting them drop onto the floor in a pile. Kinna tried not to focus on the fact that she was standing naked, so she watched the tiny bubbles spin in circles, obscuring the water below. She knew it wasn't the first time he had seen her; it was obvious he hadn't let anyone else in the room while Pearl worked on her, but this felt different. They were crossing a line that they had been toeing for weeks and she couldn't help the nerves that knotted in her stomach.

Bastin had only filled the tub half full to keep any water from reaching her fresh bandages. He stood behind her, silently untying the sling to release her arm, his fingers gently tugging open the knot. His lips brushed over her shoulder to kiss the small bit of exposed skin close to her neck.

"Let me help you in," he whispered against her skin.

"I can do it myself," she huffed, feeling a rush of

embarrassment heat her body.

He kissed her neck, days of stubble rough against her neck. His arm snaked around her waist, blazing a trail of fire everywhere he touched. Kinna closed her eyes against the myriad of sensations while he trailed kisses down her back, his other hand caressed her thigh. Suddenly her feet were no longer touching the floor and she was held tightly against a familiar chest. Bastin leaned out over the steaming water and deposited her safely beneath the bubbles.

"Sneaky," she scolded.

He grinned, dragging a stool towards the tub where a stack of washcloths, hairbrush and an assortment of soaps were balanced precariously. "You are much more agreeable when you're distracted," he said.

She flicked water at him, splashing him across the cheek and neck. "I'll take a washcloth," she said, holding her hand out to him.

"Nope," he said, his grin turning smug. "Pearl said not to get your bandages wet so I will be doing the washing."

Kinna actually laughed aloud. "So, this is why you were so willing to let me out of bed and have a bath?"

"Absolutely." He chuckled, dunking the washcloth beneath the surface, and then drizzling the honey-colored soap over it.

He reached for her ankle, lifting her leg out from beneath the water and then gently began scrubbing her skin until the layer of grime she felt was washed away. He worked meticulously, walking circles around the tub so Kinna barely had to move and true to his word her bandages remained dry. While he washed, he also spoke to her softly, catching her up on the days she missed while she had been asleep. She closed her eyes and rested her head against the tub while he talked, enjoying being pampered.

"Do you think you could lean forward?" Bastin asked.

"Yes, why?" Kinna asked, opening one eye to peer up at him.

"We can try to wash your hair, but I'll need your help."

"Gods, yes. I'll do anything to fix this mess."

Bastin snorted and grabbed a small mug from the sink. Kinna shifted forward into a sitting position and tore the tie out of her messy bun, cringing as matted strands fell against her back. Leaning her head towards the right, Bastin laid a towel over her left shoulder and then began wetting her hair.

Once her hair was thoroughly soaked, he scrubbed her hair with the same honey colored soap, massaging it into her scalp and the small matts. Kinna couldn't stop the blush from staining her cheeks. This felt more intimate than anything she had ever done before but instead of the normal feeling of nervousness; she was completely relaxed. She realized how much she liked feeling cared for, how much she liked being cared for by him.

After rinsing all the soap, he took the brush and gently began untangling it, section by section, until it was hanging in loose waves. The smell of her amber oil began filling the room while Bastin applied small amounts to the ends of her hair. Kinna started grabbing individual pieces and twirling them around her finger, helping shape them into curls again. "How do you know how to do this?" she asked sleepily.

"How to do what?"

Kinna's eyes kept fluttering closed, her body already growing tired again. "My hair," she whispered.

"Come on," Bastin ignored her. "Let's get you out before you fall asleep in here."

His arms slid beneath her, and he lifted her out of the tub. "You're getting wet," she whined.

"At least this time it's with water and not blood." He chuckled.

He wrapped her in a thick towel and then scooped her back into his arms before carrying her swiftly down the hall and back into their bedroom. Setting her gently on the bed and he disappeared back to the bathroom to gather her clothes and sling. Kinna was losing the battle against her exhaustion when he returned. He helped her back into her sling and his oversized shirt before tucking her beneath the quilt.

"You didn't answer my question," she prodded.

"What question?"

"How did you know how to do my hair?"

He brushed her damp hair back, tucking a strand behind her ear. "Because I haven't stopped watching you since the day I met you," he whispered. "Every little thing you do fascinates me, it puts me into a trance that I can't seem to break."

Kinna couldn't form a response, his declaration had her fighting for control of her hammering heart. She blinked back the rouge tears and tried to swallow the emotion that clogged her throat. She wanted to thank him for saving her, bring his face into her hands and tell him how every beat of her heart screamed at her to say the words she had been thinking since that arrow sliced through her flesh. She wanted to tell him how in those brief moments she grieved over the thought of never having the chance to tell him how she felt.

Before she could regain control of her voice, Bastin was climbing onto the other side of the bed. He slipped an arm around her neck, careful to avoid her shoulder and she nestled into his side. Warmth and exhaustion swept over her, and she quickly began to give in to the siren's call of sleep.

"Get some sleep, baby," he whispered before she drifted off.

CHAPTER THIRTY-SIX

Kinna woke up alone, her shoulder was still tender, but she felt stronger and more like herself. Peeling back the blankets, she slipped out from beneath them and onto the smooth wood floor. She worked her arm into the sling but then stared down at her bare legs, Bastin's shirt hanging down to her mid-thigh, and began hunting for her leggings. After a quick search yielded nothing, she cracked the door and peered outside, finding it empty, and she dashed to the bathroom.

After relieving herself and giving her face a quick scrub, she finger-combed through her hair in an attempt to tame it. She cursed herself for sleeping with it damp without braiding it first. Since she couldn't manage any styling with one hand, she frowned at her reflection and then stormed out of the bathroom frustrated.

She made it a few feet before she heard a door close and Bastin appeared in the hallway, frantically searching for her. His eyes landed on her, and his panic transformed into disapproval as he realized she was standing in the hallway in only his shirt.

Kinna bit her lip, preparing for reprimand that

she knew he was already preparing in his head, and continued to stroll down the hallway. Deciding to play dumb, she stopped in front of him and grinned. "Good morning, Bas," she said brightly.

"Where are your clothes?" Bastin asked, clearly not amused by her cheerful attitude.

"I couldn't find them."

"I had them laundered. You could have waited; I was bringing them up with your breakfast."

She smiled at his thoughtfulness. He was taking her rehabilitation and turning it into a full-time job. "I needed to use the bathroom, but I'm glad you brought breakfast. I'm starving," she kissed his cheek and then pushed past him into the bedroom.

A large tray sat on the side table, the bowls hanging over the sides and filled with an array of eggs, biscuits, and oatmeal. Steam rose off each bowl and the smell of warm bread filled the room, making Kinna's stomach growl in response. A stack of clean folded laundry also sat on the unmade bed, and she spied a pair of her own leggings on top. She slipped her arm out of the sling and then started stripping Bastin's shirt off, ready to trade it for her own clothes.

"Whoa!" Bastin yelled, rushing to her side. "Let me help you, you'll injure your shoulder."

She waved him off. "I can dress myself, thank you."

He snagged her clothes off the bed and held them high over his head. "Nope," he argued. "I won't give them to you unless you let me help you."

"You're being childish," she complained. He shrugged but kept a tight grip on the clean clothes. After a moment of staring, Kinna sighed. "You're a tyrant," she muttered, conceding to let him help.

Despite her protesting, Kinna quickly realized putting on anything besides a loose shirt required more effort than she had previously thought. Putting on leggings with only one hand would have been a serious challenge. Once she was dressed, Bastin picked up a stray lock of hair and twirled it around his finger. "Do you want help with your hair?"

She arched a brow at him. "You can do hair?"

"No," he said with a smile. "But I can do a basic braid. Sebbie taught me when we were kids."

The thought of a tiny, blonde Sebrina teaching Bastin to braid while playing with dolls made her smile. Gods, she missed her friend. "Wait, does Sebrina know what happened to us? Why we aren't home yet?"

Bastin ran his hand through his hair. "Gods, no. She would have demanded to come straight here. I sent a raven to the Hearth and said we were delayed and would be back two weeks late."

"She is going to kill you," Kinna said with a snicker. The image of the fuming blonde woman chasing Bastin through the camp when they returned, and she learned the truth was hilarious.

"I know." He sighed, moving to stand behind her as he began combing her hair to split into three plaits. "She might try but she will forget all about it when she sees you. She and the twins will be too busy with you to remember to kill me."

"I miss them," Kinna confessed, letting Bastin finish her hair and then grabbing a biscuit.

"I do too," he agreed, motioning for her to sit while she ate. "We are hoping to leave in a few days. As long as Pearl says you are healed well enough to travel."

"I really feel fine," she said between bites. "We could leave tomorrow."

Bastin just shook his head at her while spooning some eggs onto a biscuit to make a sandwich. "You aren't going anywhere until Pearl says you can. She will be here sometime this morning to check on you."

"Great." She smiled smugly, taking the last biscuit. "I am sure she will agree with me."

Almost an hour later, Kinna heard a knock on the door and a familiar face popped her head through the door. Pearl's hair was again tied into a bun on her head that bounced as she walked in with her trusty basket of supplies propped on her hip. She raised an eyebrow at Kinna as she noticed her sitting on the made bed, flipping through the book she'd seen Bastin reading earlier. He had left with their tray of dishes just moments ago and Kinna was surprised he wasn't returning on Pearl's heels.

"You seem to be feeling well," Pearl observed. "Especially for someone who has just recently returned to the conscious world."

Kinna smiled and set the book aside, scooting to the edge of the bed so Pearl could reach her more easily. "I do feel better," Kinna agreed. "It's amazing what a bath and a good night's sleep can do."

"I hope you didn't wet your bandages while bathing," Pearl fretted.

Bastin pushed through the cracked door. "She didn't," he answered for her.

"Ah, Mr. Bastin," Pearl smirked. "I was wondering where her nurse had gone."

He blushed as if he'd been scolded. "I had to take our breakfast dishes down."

Pearl laughed, patting his chest. "I'm sure you have taken excellent care of our patient, dear."

She carefully slid Kinna's arm out of the sling and helped her remove it from the shirt before unwinding the bandages that she had placed the day before. After peeling back the gauze and wiping the salve remnants away her brow furrows.

Bastin quickly advances. "What's wrong?"

"Nothing," she said. "She is healing remarkably well."

"Isn't that good?" Kinna asked.

Pearl's mouth picked up in a small smile. "Yes, dear, it's excellent," she assured. "You are just healing much faster than I anticipated. Nothing to be concerned about, just surprising to an old woman who is not often surprised anymore."

"I told you I was fine Bas," Kinna muttered.

He ignored her teasing. "What does that mean that she's healing faster than normal?"

"If I were guessing," she said, applying fresh bandages. "I would think she has a touch of earth magic. Perhaps enhancing the salve that I have been placing on her wound to allow her to heal faster."

"That isn't possible," Kinna disagreed.

"Uncommon but not impossible," Pearl said. "There are not many of us left but a few earth elementals have been able to heal themselves and others by imbuing their remedies with their magic to help heal."

"No, it's impossible because I don't have any magic," she clarified.

"Just because you believe that does not make it so," Pearl said.

"How long do you think it will be until she can

travel?" Bastin interjected.

Pearl thought for a moment while she finished repacking her basket. "She could travel tomorrow if she feels up to it. The wound is healing and there is no risk of it reopening at this point."

"Are you sure?" Bastin pressed.

She gave him a withering stare and huffed. "Yes, I am sure. I wouldn't jeopardize my patient, especially not our uncrowned queen."

Bastin winced and looked at Kinna, but she wasn't seeing him. She felt as if a cold bucket of water had been dumped on her. Hearing Pearl call her a queen, albeit one without a crown, was a long overdue shock to her system. She had completely forgotten about her promise to return to the capital, to a life of duty to her kingdom, since she had been shot on the border. It was too easy for her to forget, to push aside the weight of her duty, and be herself while surrounded with her found family.

Spending the last few weeks living without reservation, wholly authentic, had given her a taste of true freedom and she was heartbroken knowing how soon it would be ripped from her. Still, she had made the decision to return and assume the role she had never wanted.

For her sister, her parents, and their legacy, she would do this.

Pearl and Bastin both watched her, searching her face for any response to the reminder of who exactly she was. Kinna took a deep breath and schooled her face back into neutrality.

"Thank you for everything you have done Pearl," Kinna said, standing and taking her wrinkled hand in hers. "I will always remember your kindness. If you ever need anything, please do not hesitate to ask."

Pearl squeezed her hand and gave a small curtsy. "I hope to see you again," she said. "Perhaps I will visit the capital soon. I hear it is lovely in summer."

Kinna grinned. "It is. Just stay far from the docks, the fish market smells horrific in the summer."

She chuckled and opened the door to leave. "Good to know," she said. Pausing in the doorway, she turned once more to wink at Kinna. "Remember who you are, Kinna, and rule well."

Kinna nodded, the familiar phrase stealing her voice as tears clung to her lashes. Pearl's face disappeared, leaving her wondering how she knew the four words that had been spoken over her since childhood. It could simply be a coincidence, but Kinna didn't believe that Pearl was unaware of the power those words held over her. The question was how.

"Why are you crying?" Bastin whispered, wrapping his arms around her waist and pulling her against his chest.

"My lady's maid, Kerin, used to say that to me. I heard it at least once a week." She sighed, wiping the moisture from her eyes. "It caught me off guard when she said it."

"Were you close to her?"

"She basically raised me. Kerin helped me with my lessons, taught me how to do my hair, she noticed every time I didn't wear my arm guard and bruised myself. We ate dinner together most nights and discussed the novels we had read. There was hardly anything I did, or even thought about doing, that she didn't know."

"She sounds like she loves you very much."

Kinna blinked back fresh tears as the memories resurfaced. "She does and I love her too. Kerin didn't have any children and she always treated me as if I was her own." She roughly wiped away more tears. "Gods, I don't even know if she is alive. She may have died with the rest of my family, and I don't even know."

Bastin spun her around to face him, holding her shoulders in his hands. "You cannot blame yourself for that," he said firmly. "You were not responsible for what happened there."

"I know that, but I am responsible for running away," she argued. "I left them all there and have been hiding ever since. I can't stay away any longer."

Kinna could see the worry and fear creep into his eyes and wished more than anything that she could soothe him. She wished she could tell him that none of it mattered, that she would stay with him, with the Rising, and forget her old life, but she couldn't. Instead, she just laid her cheek against his chest and listened to his heartbeat in a steady rhythm that had become her favorite song.

"Tell me more about you," Bastin whispered.

"What do you want to know?"

"Everything. Anything. Whatever you will tell me."

She smiled and began.

Hours passed as Kinna told story after story. They ignored the rest of the world for those few precious hours as she entertained him with stories from her childhood. Kinna told him about her many tutors, all of whom she tortured mercilessly by pulling a variety of stunts, from loosening the legs on their chair to replacing their books with an array of erotic romance novels. She recounted all her failed attempts in the kitchen with Maude and how she had learned to bake to satisfy her sweet tooth. She told him about the long days she would spend in the training room and the summers she spent on the private stretch of beach. They laughed until their sides ached and only left as the sun was setting when they both could hear their stomachs growling.

They walked hand in hand down to the main level of the Nest in search of dinner. Instead, they found Emhyr and Jax sitting at an empty table passing a familiar bottle back and forth as they refilled their short glasses with liquor. Both men were lounging across the table, red-faced and laughing as they threw back their drinks.

"Kinna!" Emhyr exclaimed upon seeing them. He stood abruptly, shoving the table aside and making Jax scramble to keep the bottle and glasses from rolling off the table. "Look who has returned to the land of the living."

His arms surrounded her and swept her into a crushing hug as he gave her a sloppy kiss on the cheek. "Watch her arm!" Bastin chastised.

"Oops," Emhyr winced and set her down carefully.

"I'm fine," Kinna laughed, wiping the wetness from her cheek. "Pearl said I was healing well, and I was ready to travel again."

"That is excellent news," Jax agreed, patting her cheek affectionately. "But there is no rush, we will stay until you are ready."

Once again, Kinna was touched by how thoughtful Jax was. "I appreciate that, but I am ready." She smiled, squeezing his arm.

"Another day wouldn't hurt," Bastin added. "Judging by how little is left in that bottle, I can't imagine these two will be up to traveling tomorrow."

"Are you suggesting we wouldn't be up to the task?" Emhyr teased, throwing his arm around his friend.

"That is exactly what I am suggesting," Bastin huffed, slipping out of Emhyr's grasp.

"We can be ready," Emhyr scoffed. "We will meet you right here at sunrise."

Bastin raised a brow. "Fine," Bastin agreed. "We will leave in the morning and no amount of begging will stop it."

"Ha! Me? Beg? Never," Emhyr bellowed.

Jax grinned and shook his head before he took Emhyr's arm to lead him back to their shared room, leaving Bastin and Kinna in the empty mess hall.

Kinna slid into one of the empty chairs and grabbed the bottle to pour them both a drink. Bastin took the chair opposite her and finished his glass in one drink before pouring another.

"No snarky comments about drinking tonight?" Kinna teased, taking a small sip.

"I think we've both earned a few drinks after the past week," he answered.

"I think you're right," she agreed, clinking her glass against his before he finished his second glass.

"I'll find us some food," he said. "You shouldn't be drinking on an empty stomach."

Kinna giggled and rolled her eyes. "There he is. I was afraid you were turning into someone fun for a minute there."

He shook his head and disappeared, returning moments later with a plate of roasted chicken, a loaf of bread and a small bowl of soft butter. Kinna immediately reached for the bread, tearing off the heel of the loaf and smothering it with butter. Bastin instead reached for the chicken and poured himself a third glass of liquor.

They ate in comfortable silence for a few minutes while Kinna tried to soak up every moment with Bastin that she could, knowing it was likely that they only had days left together. She had spent the day trying to be present, not dwelling on her eventual departure, but she couldn't help the sadness that would slither in during the quiet.

"I wonder how Jax got Emhyr up the ladder," Bastin mused, finishing his drink.

"I bet we find them both asleep at the bottom." Kinna laughed.

When they were finished, Bastin stacked their empty plates and glasses to carry off before coming back. He held his hand out to help her out of her seat, tucking her under his arm as they walked back through the Nest and towards their room. Thankfully they did not step over an unconscious Emhyr and Jax, so they assumed the two made it back to their own room. Bastin helped Kinna change into one of his oversized shirts before climbing into bed where she settled against his side just like the night before.

"Goodnight, baby," he whispered into the darkness.

Kinna nuzzled in closer before whispering it back.

CHAPTER THIRTY-SEVEN

Morning came quickly but with a new day Kinna felt herself grow stronger, her mobility slowly returning to her. She checked her bandaging and found she no longer needed her sling or much assistance dressing. Pearl's assertion that she possessed some magic replayed in her mind and Kinna quietly considered the possibility of her possessing some healing abilities.

It would have explained Marstella's earlier assumption and since she had never been seriously injured, could have remained unnoticed by her until now. Kinna certainly wasn't complaining about the speedy recovery, especially since the memory of losing consciousness in Bastin's arms, and her subsequent fear, was still fresh in her mind.

Bastin had woken hours earlier than Kinna, allowing her to sleep as long as possible, and packed all their belongings for their departure. He must have also paid a visit to their friends' room since they both had their bags packed and waiting outside the stable. Despite being present, Emhyr and Jax were pale and bleary eyed as they stood beside the stable, looking as if they may fall asleep atop their horses.

Saul and Leo were also waiting with them, Saul frequently glancing over at the two almost gleefully, snickering each time one of them swayed on their feet. Upon seeing Kinna, Saul gave her a wide smile.

"Aye, it is very good to see you walking about," he said, waving her down.

"It's good to be up and walking," Kinna agreed. "I assume you didn't have any trouble on your way back? You look as handsome as ever."

Saul blushed at her compliment. "No, no trouble at all. Got those two youngins and their da' tucked away, safe and sound."

"Good, I'm glad they are safe," Kinna said, relieved.

"Care to give me a hand?" Bastin called out to Saul from inside the stable. "These two aren't much help."

"Aye, they're a right sorry bunch." Saul laughed, leaving Kinna standing with Leo.

The two stood quietly and Kinna could see Leo watching her in her peripheral vision. "You healed remarkably well," Leo said quietly. "I really wasn't sure if you were going to survive."

"I got lucky," Kinna snorted. "If Emhyr hadn't stopped the bleeding I probably wouldn't have made it here."

"I don't think it was luck," Leo mused. "I think the gods are watching you, whether it's because they like you or have a purpose for you, I am not sure, but they have definitely noticed you."

"What would they want with me?"

"I do not know, but you, the next Queen of Ferryn, stumbles upon the Rising after your home was destroyed and finds favor with their leader, befriends half their ranking members, and then miraculously heals from near fatal wounds; that cannot be a coincidence. Something is changing and you are the catalyst, of that I have no doubt."

"It sounds unbelievable when you say it like that." Leo shrugged. "I wouldn't have believed it if I hadn't seen it for myself."

Kinna watched Bastin and Saul lead out their horses so Jax and Emhyr could clumsily climb on, both looking a little green as their mares walked ahead.

"I better go." Kinna smiled. "Maybe the gods will let our paths cross again under better circumstances."

"Oh, I have no doubt that we will meet again, Kinna Braunlin," Leo nodded. "Rule well."

Kinna gave the stoic leader a small wave as she crossed the lawn towards her companions. Bastin was waiting with Saul who surprised her by giving her a quick, tight hug before releasing her when the former began scolding him for touching her injured arm. She kissed Saul's stubbly cheek while ignoring Bastin's scolding and thanked him for his role in bringing her back to the Nest safely. He muttered his goodbye, blushing heavily, and promised that this would not be the last time they would meet. Bastin quickly loaded her onto Alder while Saul opened the iron gate, and their journey home began.

———

Jax and Emhyr remained sickly pale for most of the morning, passing on the breakfast offered in favor of copious amounts of water. Kinna couldn't help but snicker every time one of them swayed on their horse and had to grip the reins firmly in order to remain seated. Bastin decided this experience would be good for them. He thought it had been too long since they had faced any consequences of their late-night drinking and took pleasure in mocking them relentlessly when they stopped for lunch that neither man could stomach.

When the group finally departed from the Glen Road around sunset, they made camp in an unfamiliar spot. The Glenwood had grown thicker over the days since they had left the Hearth. The trees were full of fresh, vibrant green leaves and thick grass had sprouted over the forest floor that squished softly under their feet.

"Why aren't we staying in the same place?" Kinna asked as they worked to set up their tents for the night.

"We have different stopping places when we travel back in case anyone is using the ones leading towards Edgewood. Too many people at one time would be conspicuous," Bastin explained.

"The Rising is nothing if not careful," she mused.

"It beats the alternative of getting captured and jailed," Bastin pointed out.

"Fair point."

They finished raising their tent before joining Jax and Emhyr by the small fire. Kinna was glad to see the two with some color in their faces and picking at some of the bread that they had packed with their supplies. The further away from the safety of the Nest they rode, the less entertaining she found their diminished state. After the attack in Eldridge, she wanted everyone alert and aware of their surroundings. She knew how quickly a seemingly safe situation could turn deadly.

After eating their conversation livened up, as everyone seemed to return to their normal selves. Emhyr's face grew mischievous as he leaned back, supporting his large frame with his arms. "What do you think will happen when Sebbie realizes Bas lied to her, Jax?"

Jax grinned and rubbed his hands together. "Oh, I'm going to bet that she goes for his face. He won't be so pretty with a broken nose, will he?"

Emhyr howled. "I think she's going to go for the groin, really hit him where it hurts," he argued. "What do you think, Kinna?"

"Hmm," she thought. "I think she will enlist the twins. Rory and Ronan will hold him down while she goes for the face."

Emhyr howled with laughter. "I think she's right," Jax agreed. "The twins will be just as angry. It would be easy for her to use them in her attack."

"As funny as your predictions are," Bastin interjected sourly. "May I remind you all why we lied about Kinna's injuries? So that no one would come rushing here and make themselves or the Nest an even bigger target?"

Despite his point, the snickering continued. Kinna patted Bastin's arm sympathetically. "I understand your logic. You did what you thought would best protect the people you care about," she soothed, kissing his cheek. "However, lying to protect people is still lying. Sebrina is going to be very upset and you're just going to have to face the consequences."

He sighed, kissing the hand he held. "I know," he muttered. "But don't you three encourage her."

Emhyr raised his hands in surrender. "Promise. I'll be on my best behavior."

"You don't have a best behavior," Bastin muttered, pushing himself off the ground and extending his hand to help Kinna up. "We leave before sunrise. Get some sleep."

They echoed their goodnights as Kinna and Bastin slipped inside their tent. Within moments of laying down on their thick bedroll, a wave of exhaustion crashed over Kinna. She had forgotten how easily traveling sapped her energy. Kinna fought to keep her eyes open as Bastin situated her beneath one of the thinner quilts, not wanting to reveal her exhaustion and receive a lecture about traveling before she was completely healed. Bastin laid beside her on top of the quilt, gently stroking her hair and cheek.

"I have the first watch tonight but then I'll be back," he whispered. "Stop fighting it, sleep and get some rest."

"I'm not," she muttered as her eyes fluttered closed again.

"You're a terrible actress." He chuckled, leaning over to press a long kiss on her lips. "Go to sleep."

"Fine," she agreed. "Come back soon."

"I will," he promised before ducking out of the tent.

Morning came too quickly, and it took a few tries for Bastin to wake Kinna before her eyes fully opened. She had slept so deeply, not even moving when he re-entered the tent hours later that he had checked to make sure she was still breathing a few times during the night. Despite his accusation that she was a terrible actress, he was no better at hiding the worry lines that creased his face. She smoothed them away with a kiss when she sat up, holding his face in her small hands so she could kiss him until she cast all the worry from his mind.

She lost herself in him, letting him slide her into

his lap so he could wrap his arms around her waist. Their bodies pressed against each other, and his touch quickly turned aggressive, his mouth assaulting hers with hard, firm kisses. Gone was the gentle tenderness he had been treating her with since she woke up injured in the Nest. She returned his fervor, clinging tightly to him while she slipped her tongue past his lips. His rough hands dipped beneath the oversized shirt she had worn to bed, running along her bare back and side. He gently grazed the underside of her breasts, sending a shiver down her spine as he teased her.

They were suddenly interrupted by a loud coughing outside the tent. "What is taking you two so long?" Emhyr's voice asked through the canvas.

Bastin sighed and leaned his forehead against hers. "Can we just ignore him?" he rasped.

"It was your idea to leave before sunrise," she reminded him, kissing him again.

"An idea I am seriously regretting right now." He sighed.

"I can hear you two talking in there," Emhyr called out, clearly annoyed he was being ignored. "If you don't come out, I'll just come in there."

"You absolutely will not," Bastin called back. "We are coming."

Bastin stood abruptly, causing Kinna to have to cling to him to avoid falling out of his lap. He grinned as he swung her into his arms, kissed her once more, and then sat her on her feet to get dressed. The weather was warming steadily, and the cooler morning air would be gone quickly so she chose a short sleeve tunic and leggings. Tugging her hair out of the messy braid she ran one hand through the plaits.

"Do you want me to braid it again?" Bastin asked, already dressed and looking far too handsome for someone who only slept for a few hours.

"Please," Kinna said, moving to stand in front of him. He effortlessly worked her hair back into a single plaited braid then pulled out a few loose pieces to frame her face. "You really are quite good at this."

"I'm good at everything." He smirked, patting her backside. "Let's go before Emhyr barges in here."

Kinna rinsed her face with a small amount of water before finishing stuffing her things in her bag and then exiting the tent. Emhyr and Jax had already packed away their tents and were smothering the fire in preparation for their departure. Kinna noticed they were both shoveling food into their mouths while deconstructing the campsite, their bodies protesting the lack of subsistence from the day before.

"Finally, you're awake," Emhyr crowed. "The sun has already risen, Bas!"

Indeed, the sun had crested the hills in the east, shining golden rays through the forest and waking the land. Birds sang through the air, their chirps echoing all around in a harmony unique to springtime.

"Kinna needed to sleep," Bastin scolded. "We traveled for hours yesterday and, in case you forgot, she was very recently injured."

Emhyr's face fell, eyes darting to Kinna to gauge her reaction. "I'm sorry love, I wasn't thinking," he said. "We can take more breaks today. There isn't a rush."

"He is just trying to make you feel guilty," Kinna clarified. "I don't need any more mothering from the three of you."

"Prick," Emhyr muttered to Bastin.

"Serves you right." He laughed.

"Enough arguing boys," Jax started. "Let's get moving."

Bastin and Emhyr quickly finished breaking down their tent, both still muttering insults at the other. Jax placed a deep crimson apple into Kinna's empty hand as they waited near the horses. She thanked him and bit into its sweet flesh, happy to have something in her empty stomach. He moved towards his spotted mare, gently rubbing her nose while subtly slipping her an apple slice he had saved. His mare was the oldest of the three horses, and like himself, was a steady and calm presence among Bastin's standoffish stallion and Emhyr's wild-hearted mare.

"What's her name?" Kinna asked between bites.

"Chesna," Jax replied. "It means a calm place. Emhyr's mare is named Basa, which means wild."

"What does Alder's name mean?"

"It means revered one." Jax smiled. "We chose their names carefully, but Alder's seems a bit pretentious if you ask me."

Kinna giggled. "It sounds like you spent actual time researching this."

"We did. Names can hold great meaning and should be chosen carefully."

"I suppose."

"Do you know what your name means, Kinna?"

"No, do you?"

"Yes." He smiled. "Your name means greatest champion. Do you think it is a coincidence you were given that name?"

Kinna was quiet. She thought it was unlikely that there was some deeper meaning to her parents' choice of her name. They probably had just liked the name. Still, she couldn't stop the tiny voice in her head that asked how many coincidences she was willing to overlook, how many glaring signs she was willing to ignore in order to preserve the illusion of normalcy.

"I don't know," Kinna admitted finally.

Bastin and Emhyr joined them and soon the group had returned to the Glen Road as they traveled home. Kinna spent much of the day's ride in silence, rolling Jax's words around in her head and trying to make sense of what, if any, significance there could be in her name and the events of the past few weeks.

———

Again, they stopped in a new place for the night, preparing a quick dinner before breaking off into their respective tents to sleep. Kinna was thankful that their current spot had a small stream a few yards away where she was able to scrub the two days' worth of dirt from her skin. She inspected her left shoulder and the coin sized scar that had already formed over her skin. The water was barely warm enough to bathe in, but she still waded in far enough to scrub her scalp and rinse her hair with the small bar of vanilla soap she had brought from the Nest.

Once out of the water and dressed, she sat cross legged on the soft moss that covered most of the ground along the edge of the stream. The sun was setting behind her, casting long shadows across the water and turning the water's surface golden.

Combing her damp hair out, she twirled the curls in her fingers absentmindedly, her thoughts on the now healed wound on her shoulder and Pearl's certainty that she had somehow healed herself. The meaning of her name and Jax's belief that it was no mere coincidence joined them in her head, adding to the tangle that was her thoughts.

There were so many things she wished she could ask, but the only people that could possibly give her the answers she so desperately wanted were dead. She toyed with her finger, missing her ring that used to sit there and the woman who had given it to her. For all their arguing, Kinna knew that her mother would have had answers even if she wasn't ready to share them. She could picture her mother's face so clearly, how her full lips would press into a thin line when Kinna would annoy her and how they both had a tendency to roll their eyes. Her father had always said that was when they looked most alike, when they were irritated and rolling their eyes at him.

The thought of her father and his easy laugh made her throat constrict. Their last dinner as a family was still so fresh in her mind, but it had been weeks since that day. She wished more than anything she had known that it would be the last time she would see them, just so she could squeeze in one last hug, one last I love you. Kinna wiped the stray tear that had escaped down her cheek, taking a deep breath to clear her senses.

Hopping up from the ground, she shook out her half-dried hair, letting the curls fall down her back and headed back towards their camp. She couldn't change the past; she couldn't go back and say all the things she wished she could to her parents, but she could avoid making that mistake again. For whatever reason, she had been given another family, one that loved and protected her, and she wouldn't let the chance to tell them how she felt pass again.

Kinna found Bastin alone in front of the fire. The glow from the flames had turned his hazel eyes golden and highlighted his high cheekbones. Even strands of his hair seemed to shimmer like spun gold in the soft yellow light. Judging from the snoring coming from the farthest tent, she assumed the others had already turned in for the night.

She watched his lips turn up into a half smile as she approached, the faintest outline of a dimple appearing. "Feel better?"

"I always feel better after a bath," she answered, sitting down beside him. "Even one in a cold stream."

He slipped his arm around her waist, pulling her closer to him, then rested it around her shoulders. Between him and the heat from the small fire she started warming instantly as she snuggled into his side, threading her fingers through his. His thumb stroked lazy lines down the inside of her palm, the motion tickled her skin while still being pleasant.

She peeked at him through her peripheral vision and found him watching her intently. "You have something to say. I can see it on your face, in the way your brow is furrowed," he said, touching his finger to the small line that had formed between her brows.

"I do," she admitted.

She took a steadying breath trying to ignore how easily he seemed to read her every emotion but was quickly interrupted. "You're killing me," he whispered, shifting her smoothly into his lap so they were facing each other. "Just tell me and put me out of my misery."

"Well, I was about to, but I was rudely interrupted."

He grinned, tightening his grip on her waist. "Apologies, princess. I promise not to interrupt again."

The mention of her title sent a wave of flutters through her stomach. What had once been wielded as an insult was now a snarky form of endearment. It was incredible how a few weeks could change things. Hearing Bastin use it no longer made her see red, but instead made her smile.

"I wanted to thank you," she said quietly.

Bastin opened his mouth to ask why but she silenced him with a stern look. He pressed his lips closed and nodded for her to continue.

Kinna watched him for a moment, the intensity of his stare ripping through any hesitation she held onto. "You saved me. You carried me, bleeding and broken, out of Eldridge and then sat by my side for days until I woke. You kept me tethered to this world, to consciousness, while we crossed the border. You are the reason I am sitting here right now."

Her hands had found their way to his face, resting on either side as she held onto him while his hands wrapped around her wrists. "I would do it a thousand times over," he told her, the sincerity dripping from each word. "There is nothing that could keep me from you, nothing that would be able to stop me. I would tear anyone apart who stood to harm you, no matter the cost."

Her heart ballooned to the point of pain. Every word he spoke was a balm to the still healing parts of her and the words she had been desperate to speak rose to her lips. Just as her lips parted, Bastin swept her close into a crushing kiss. Her fingers slid into his hair, and she put every feeling, every word she wanted to say into their kiss.

His left hand slid up her back and gripped her hair at the base of her neck, allowing him to hold her mouth hostage while his right hand palmed her backside. She was pinned against his body and his arousal was becoming increasingly obvious as she felt his hardness beneath her hips. Heat pooled low in her stomach as a flush broke out across her skin. As his kiss intensified, she rocked her hips against him, seeking any friction she could find. Bastin pulled away, nipping her lower lip with his teeth.

"Sit up on your knees," he whispered roughly.

Confused, she lifted slightly off him and onto her knees. His hand quickly found the waistband of her leggings, the loose band offering no resistance as he slipped his hand in. He reclaimed her mouth, silencing the moan that escaped her as he trailed his index finger along the wetness between her thighs. He teased her, continuing to stroke her slowly as her blood heated and her breaths came faster.

His lips started to stray from her mouth, and he began trailing kisses down her jaw and neck. Just as he scraped his teeth against the soft spot behind her ear, he slid a finger deep inside her. Without him to stifle it, she let out a sharp gasp.

She heard a low chuckle, and her eyes found his. "You look so perfect right now," he whispered against her skin.

Kinna felt the flush spread up her throat and across her cheeks. Bastin only grinned and returned his attention to her lips while he pumped his finger in and out in a slow rhythm, letting her build. He smoothed his thumb over her swollen center and groaned when she convulsed under his touch. In seconds she found her climax, her nails digging into his shoulders as her head fell back in ecstasy.

He quickly clamped a hand over her mouth to muffle the cry that escaped her lips. "Quiet baby," he whispered. "I don't want anyone hearing you except me."

She rode his hand until she collapsed in a sated exhaustion against his chest. He gently slid his hand from beneath her, wrapping it around her waist to support her weight. Fingers brushed her hair from her damp forehead, pushing it back so the cool night air could sweep over her skin. "So perfect," he whispered as her eyes fluttered closed.

CHAPTER THIRTY-EIGHT

Bastin

He felt her limbs go slack within minutes, but he didn't stop the slow stroke of his hand down her silken hair, mostly because he worried she would wake up and want to go to bed. Instead, he soaked up every moment as she slept in his arms, studying her. Her skin had turned golden in the firelight, highlighting the darkness of her long eyelashes that fanned out over her cheeks. Her still damp curls fell down her back and shined in the soft light. Gods, he couldn't keep his hands out of her hair.

She still straddled him, her long, toned legs tucked beneath her. Bastin slowly pulled her legs across his waist so her hips wouldn't grow stiff while she slept. He cradled her in his arms, wrapping one arm across her legs and holding onto her hip, while the other continued stroking her hair.

His mind drifted to his parents; their absence was something he tried not to think too long about but he'd thought about them often in the past few weeks. He wished he could have introduced them to Kinna. His father would have loved her and likely conspired with her against him. His mother would have spent hours telling her stories of *him as a child and all the trouble he'd gotten in, something he thought Kinna would love. He would pretend to hate it but would have enjoyed every moment watching them interact, watching them grow to love her the way that he did, and he did. He loved her.*

He had spent years watching Stella and Ren, listening to Sebbie ask them to tell the story of how they met over and over. Ren would describe the first time he had seen her and felt like he'd been struck, how the attraction had been instant, and he'd spent the next week following her around hoping he would have the chance to speak to her. Sebbie had loved the story, especially the part where Stella had eventually confronted him about following her by waiting for him in an alley, daggers out.

Bastin had always thought they had romanticized the story for their daughter; he'd always thought love was a choice, not something that just happened to you. He had believed that right up until he'd come face to face with a dark-haired woman with silver eyes, holding a dagger and waiting to strike. From the moment he'd laid eyes on her, he knew he would love her.

He smiled at the similarities between Ren and Stella's story and his own. Before he could stop himself, he had begun to hum an old lullaby that his mother used to sing to him. It had been years since he had thought of it but holding Kinna asleep in his arms, it felt right to hum it once again.

Hours passed and Kinna slept soundly in his arms, the only movement came from the subtle rise and fall of her chest as she breathed. The moon sat high in the sky, a sign that his shift would soon be over, and he would be able to slip into bed with her. Emhyr stumbled out of his tent moments later, yawning heavily as he made his way towards them. He arched a brow at Kinna asleep in his lap and ambled over to them.

He reached down and brushed his hand over her hair.

"How's our girl?" Emhyr asked.

"Exhausted, I think," Bastin replied. "She hasn't moved in hours."

"Has she slept out here your whole shift?"

"Yes."

Emhyr grinned. "You've gone soft. If I had tried that, you would have lectured me about how dangerous that was and how being distracted on watch jeopardized the entire group."

"Shit," Bastin's face fell.

A laugh rumbled through Emhyr's chest. "Good thing I am not you, brother." He chuckled. "You won't get a lecture from me."

Emhyr added a few logs to the fire. It had grown dim in the hours Bastin had sat with Kinna, not willing to wake her to add more to it. He joined them on the ground, sitting beside Kinna's head as he watched her sleep. They sat in silence for a moment, the fire cracking with the added wood while fresh heat washed over his skin.

"I've never seen you like this," Emhyr murmured.

"It's never felt like this," Bastin admitted.

A touch of worry crossed Emhyr's face but disappeared so quickly that Bastin almost missed it. "I worry for you, for you both," he said quietly.

"Why?"

"She is a queen. Our queen. Her life will not be an easy one."

"Kinna does not have to take her title if she doesn't want it."

Emhyr shook his head. "You know her better than

that. She will return to the capital; she will not run from her destiny."

"She hasn't mentioned it."

"That is why I worry. I know you want her to stay, I do too, but I think we both know eventually she will have to leave, and you will have to choose whether or not you will follow."

"I can't leave the Rising."

Emhyr grinned. "As a wise man once said, you always have choices."

"What would I do in the capital? I'm no diplomat."

"No truer words have ever been spoken." Emhyr laughed as Bastin grimaced. "You could do or be whatever you wanted, Bas. If you were near her, you would be happy."

Bastin stared into the fire, letting Emhyr's words roll around in his head. A picture began forming, Kinna in gowns and crowns, leading her people, making her kingdom into something great. He could even picture himself by her side, watching in awe as she commanded the attention and respect of councils and foreign diplomats. He would support her every decision, standing by her side to protect her, maybe even make himself useful by overseeing the Royal Guards.

The life he was imagining was something he'd never remotely considered, balls and castles had never been interesting, but a life with Kinna, that was all he wanted now, no matter where or how.

"Go get some sleep, Bas," Emhyr said, his voice pulling him out of his fantasy. He leaned over and kissed Kinna's head quickly. "I'm sure you both would be more comfortable in a tent.

Bastin smiled at his friend's display of affection and tightened his grip on Kinna as he rose with her still in his arms. "Goodnight, Em."

CHAPTER THIRTY-NINE

She had only meant to rest for a moment, but the next thing she knew she could feel the familiar sway of being carried. Blinking awake, she could see the moon shining brightly overhead as Bastin carried her into their tent. He settled her onto their bedroll and then sat down beside her before he pulled her head onto his chest.

"Go back to sleep," he said.

"Don't you have to watch the camp?" Kinna asked sleepily, the familiar weight of his body around hers made staying awake a challenge.

"My shift is over," he told her. "I couldn't bring myself to wake you up so I just let you sleep in my lap until I could bring you to bed."

"Oh," she mumbled, his sweet admission tugging at her heart.

"Sleep," he ordered, kissing the top of her head.

She didn't argue and let her mind drop back into unconsciousness.

The next morning, they packed their camp quickly, eager to start on their last day of riding and return home. Leaving the woods and returning to the

Glen Road, the sun began to crest over the horizon, illuminating the dark road ahead. Moisture clung to the ground as they trotted along the road, glimmering like diamond against the emerald-colored grass. As they rode on moving south, the air warmed quickly, summer was nearing, and the temperatures rose the farther they traveled south, away from Edgewood.

After a short stop for lunch and to water their horses, they waited by the small stream as Alder took his time drinking and splashing in the water. Kinna giggled as she watched him play and Bastin tried to convince him to leave the stream.

Eventually Bastin was able to bribe him away from the water with one of their extra apples and he munched happily on his snack while Bastin lifted Kinna into the saddle. He muttered curses at the horse as they joined Emhyr and Jax who were waiting ahead of them at the edge of the woods. The two grinned but didn't tease Bastin further as they popped out of the Glenwood one by one.

They rode for a couple of hours before Kinna began to recognize their surroundings. Glenarm wasn't far off but they hadn't dipped off the main road yet to head for the Hearth.

"Where are we going?" Kinna asked, turning in the saddle to look at Bastin.

"We are stopping in Glenarm to pick up a few supplies for home," he answered. "Since we were passing through it seemed easier than having Rennick and the twins come. It won't take long. You'll be safe with us."

"I'm not worried; I can handle myself. Just merely curious."

They rode on, their ranks slowly closing as they

neared the town until they were traveling in a tight group. Dark tiled roofs began appearing in the distance spreading out in a familiar circle with a road splitting the town down the center. Kinna couldn't help but think about the last time she had been here, the portly vendor that confirmed her worst fears and then the men that chased her straight into the arms of the Rising. So many small, seemingly inconspicuous coincidences had led her to this point that she wondered if maybe the gods had been guiding her after all.

Passing under a faded stone archway, they entered into the city and dismounted their horses, securing them at a small stable after passing the young boy who stood watch over them a silver coin. Kinna slid her pack out of the saddle bag and slid it around her shoulders. She still had a few coins inside in case anything caught her eye, like a pastry or some other sugar filled confection.

Bastin led them over to a trough of fresh hay and water while they followed the road towards the city's square. Bastin led the group with his twin swords swaying at his hips. He walked ahead of Kinna, while Emhyr and Jax flanked her on either side. They fell into this formation instantly, guarding each side of her as they walked. Kinna couldn't help but smile at her three mother hens turned guards.

"What are you grinning at?" Emhyr asked.

"You three." Kinna smiled. "You all look so serious."

Bastin's head turned back a fraction so he could side eye her. "We are serious. Your safety is not something we are going to risk."

The other two murmured their agreements. "Yes,

I am aware," Kinna said. "It's just funny to me. A few nights ago, Emhyr and Jax were so drunk we weren't sure if they would make it to bed. Now they are storming down the streets as seriously as any Royal Guard."

"I would like to see any of your guards spar with me," Emhyr said proudly. "They would be crawling from the ring."

Kinna patted his arm. "Of course, they would."

The smell of fried food and spices floated through the air as they reached the city's square and the small market that gathered there. A dozen vendor stalls formed a circle through the square and people milled between them, stopping to make purchases or haggle over the price of their goods. Jax split off from the group and entered into one of the small shops in the square to pick up whatever supplies they would be bringing home with them.

Kinna was about to suggest that they take advantage of being in Glenarm and find a vendor that was selling desserts when she caught a flash of someone across the square. She spotted a familiar profile of a man with sandy colored curls and stepped forward to get a better look. Bastin started to speak but Kinna could no longer hear anything except the pounding of her own heart as a pair of ocean blue eyes met hers and she bolted forward.

Tears blurred her vision as she sprinted forward, running harder and faster than she ever had on the sandy beaches by the castle.

His arms spread wide, and she threw herself into them. He caught her easily, lifting her from the ground so she could wrap her legs around his torso. Fat tears rolled down her cheeks uncontrollably as she buried her face in his neck. She breathed in his scent, praying that this wasn't a dream. Finally, she leaned back so she could see his face. His eyes swam with unshed tears as he leaned his forehead to rest against hers.

"Ellio," she whispered.

"Hi, Kin," he whispered back, pressing a kiss to her nose. "I've been looking for you."

She took a deep breath, unwrapping her legs so she could stand but refusing to let go of him. Her hands fisted in his shirt as she slid under his arm. Kinna couldn't stop staring at him, her Ellio, her best friend, alive and in her arms. It was almost too much to believe. A pointed cough sounded from somewhere, drawing her attention away from Ellio.

"I assume you're Ellio," Bastin ventured, his tone clipped, and face strained. Emhyr stood beside him, his eyes wide and full of concern as he watched Kinna cling to the stranger.

"I am," Ellio replied. "Who exactly are you?"

"Bastin," Kinna answered. "Bastin and Emhyr. Jax is somewhere around here too."

Ellio looked down at her quickly, leaning close to her face. "Have they been keeping you against your will?" he whispered quietly.

"Of course not," Kinna defended, stepping back from him. "Why would you think that?"

"You just disappeared without a trace. I've been a mess for weeks trying to find you. I never gave up once, not even when everyone told me to."

Kinna's face softened, reaching for his hand again. "I'm sorry. It's a long story."

Jax joined Bastin and Emhyr, his arms full of packages wrapped in brown paper and his face tight with worry. "Is everything okay?"

"Yes." Kinna smiled. "Jax, this is Ellio."

"Nice to meet you." Jax nodded.

Ellio's mouth was pressed into a firm line as he nodded back but quickly returned his attention to Kinna. "We need to find the guards that I came with, they can take us back home. You can tell me the whole story on the way back."

Kinna's face faltered, glancing at Bastin and then back to Ellio. She was supposed to have more time. Time to prepare herself to say goodbye to Bastin, to Sebrina, to all of them. Hesitation rippled through her, Ellio noticing her too long pause. "I don't know," she whispered.

"What do you mean you don't know? We need to get you home; everyone believes you are dead. My father, the council, everyone needs to know you are alive."

"You don't have to go with him," Bastin said firmly. "You can come home with us, come back to the Hearth."

"She has a home," Ellio interjected angrily. "It's in the capital, not wherever the hell you three came from."

"Stop it, Ellio," Kinna chided. "He only wants what is best for me."

Ellio eyed Bastin suspiciously, but Bastin's eyes never left Kinna's face. "You have the choice, Kinna," he urged, stepping forward to stand in front of her. "We will protect you if you choose to stay with us."

Kinna reached out, clasping his hands. "He's right though. If they all believe I am dead, the only way to show them the truth is to go. It isn't fair to make them grieve someone who is alive."

"I don't give a fuck about them. I only care about you. Stay. Please."

Hearing him plead with her broke something in her chest, something irreparable. For a moment she questioned her decision, making the right choice shouldn't feel like walking towards a slow death. Fresh tears welled in her eyes as her resolve overshadowed her feelings and she reached a hand to his cheek. "This has been my duty since my family died. I am the only Braunlin left. I have to go. I cannot forsake my kingdom, no matter how much it hurts."

The devastation in his eyes was visible despite his attempt to hide it. It was so at odds with his words and nodding head as he resigned himself to her decision. Just for a moment Kinna swore she saw a tear gleam in his eye before he cleared his throat and nodded. "Just say the word," he told her gruffly, his voice thick with hurt. "We will come. No matter the cost."

She threw herself into his embrace, the tears coming faster as his mint and citrus scent surrounded her, and she tried to commit it to memory. He smoothed her hair as he held her and kissed her one last time, long and sweet. She turned to Emhyr with tears still in her eyes and he opened his arms to let Bastin pass her to him.

He pulled her into a crushing hug, leaning down to rest his head on hers. "Bastin is right, we will come if you change your mind."

She nodded, unable to form words. Emhyr passed her to Jax as she stepped around packages to his gentle hug. She felt him slip a piece of paper into the neck of her tunic. "In case you need us," he whispered.

"Thank you," she choked out. "All of you."

She gave Bastin's hand one last squeeze as she passed him. Ellio watched her with equal measures of confusion and hurt, as if he was envious of the bond she now shared with them that she had once had with him. He led her towards the southern gate of the city and Kinna couldn't help but glance back at her friends, at Bastin, who remained rooted to the ground, unmoving, in case she changed her mind. She watched them until they had walked too far away, and the three men disappeared from view. A small carriage waited at the city's outskirts, a driver she didn't recognize sitting atop with a book in hand as they approached.

Ellio held the door open for her and she climbed inside, choosing to sit on the cushioned bench across from him. The shock of seeing him alive had not yet worn off and she couldn't help staring at him in an awed wonder.

"Why do you keep looking at me like that?" Ellio asked, a hint of a smug smile on his lips.

She smiled weakly, that was the Ellio she knew, her Ellio. "I didn't think I would ever get to see you again."

"I knew I would," he said, reaching to hold her hands across the small aisle. "Not for one second did I think that I wouldn't find you."

She didn't tell him how she had clung to that thought in the days following her escape from the capital, or how quickly she had forgotten it once she'd found the Rising. There were many things she wasn't sure if she would ever share with Ellio. While he looked and acted like the same man she'd left behind in the capital, she was not the same woman who had left months ago. "Tell me about the capital, about the castle," she said instead. "What has happened since I've been gone?"

As they rode, Ellio recounted the days following the explosion, how they had spent hours each day digging through rubble. They had been able to save a few but many who had been in the western wing of the castle at the time had died instantly, including her parents and sister. General Resten had organized a funeral for all of them except Kinna since her body had never been recovered.

The funeral had been a short affair, but it hadn't stopped the masses from descending on the castle to pay tribute to their king, queen, and princess who had been killed. More funerals followed in the next few days for members of the castle staff, including over half of the Royal Guards. In total, almost fifty people had died that day.

Despite the heavy sadness that settled over her at the news, Kinna was overjoyed to know that Maude had escaped death thanks to a produce delivery that she had been in the courtyard inspecting. Her obsessive behavior regarding produce had likely saved her life that day. Kerin and Suzannah had also survived with minor injuries, having been walking through the gardens during the explosion.

Knowing happy reunions awaited her in the capital helped to take the edge off the grief that was slowly building each mile she traveled away from Bastin and the rest of her friends. Kinna knew that when they returned to the Hearth without her it would break Sebrina's heart. She hated knowing she would cause the heartbreak of the one person who helped her heal and brought her slowly back to life.

Their carriage bumped along the uneven road

and constant bouncing made her stomach roil. That, in addition to her unease about what she would find when they returned to the capital, made it impossible to eat anything Ellio offered as the sun set. Instead, she laid back on the small bench, hoping to get some sleep as they rode. Ellio had said it would likely be the early morning before they would reach the capital, so she had plenty of time to rest.

Sleep proved difficult, her mind racing from one topic to the next, trying to process everything that had happened in the past twelve hours. Once again, she was reminded how quickly things could change. She finally fell into a light sleep, but nightmares tormented her.

Images of the burning castle assaulted her mind, the smell of the smoke so real in her dream. The black uniformed men appeared and the next thing she knew, she was running through the capital streets, away from the man she'd left bleeding in the alley behind the inn. When she looked down, blood coated her hands but no matter how much she wiped them against her clothes the red stain remained.

As she ran, someone pursued her, a man hidden in shadow so she could not make out his face. He ran faster than a normal man should have been able to, catching up to her quickly. She stood to fight but he clamped chains around her wrists and began dragging her through the street. Struggling against him she heard herself shouting, demanding that he let her go, but then she felt something tugging at her shoulder and a familiar voice called her name softly.

"Wake up, Kin," Ellio whispered.

Her eyes fluttered open as she took in the small carriage walls, their windows foggy as rain dripped down the glass. A crack of thunder sounded, and she jolted upright, startled by the sound.

"It's okay," Ellio soothed, rubbing her arm. "You were having a bad dream, probably because of the storm."

Kinna nodded absently, pushing her hair back from her face where a thin layer of sweat had formed. She reached for her bag on the floor and pulled out a small skein of water to rinse her dry mouth. The temperature had dropped significantly, likely caused by the storm, so she also retrieved her faded blue sweater and slid it over her exposed arms.

Ellio noticed the sweater and smiled. "I always wondered where that went." He grinned. "I should have known you would have it."

A blush rose to her face. "I've had it for years," she admitted. "I couldn't get rid of it."

"It looks better on you anyways." He winked.

Kinna rolled her eyes affectionately and leaned back into the wall. Her stomach rumbled loudly, and she instinctively sat a hand on her stomach. "Did you leave me any food, or did you eat it all?"

He chuckled and handed her the small basket of food. She pulled out a bright green apple and bit into it, the tart juices filling her mouth. Inside, she also found a small heel of bread that she claimed. The food quieted her rumbling stomach and Kinna turned to watch the rain continue to pelt the small window. "Do you know where we are?"

"I think we are an hour or two from Strafford," he answered. "The storm kicked up a little bit ago so it's harder to tell without being able to see the sky."

In a couple of hours, she would be riding through

the capital streets once again. The last time she had been there, she had been chased by strangers and killed someone. Kinna wondered what Ellio would say if he knew. She decided not to mention it. What if he didn't understand? Ellio had never killed anyone. What if he was horrified at her indifference to what she'd done? Gods knew it still weighed on her every time she thought about it, but she couldn't bring herself to feel guilty. She thought about Rennick and his quiet understanding as she had laid herself bare, admitting to her actions that led to the death of a person. He and Marstella had understood and offered no judgement, she wasn't sure she would receive the same treatment from everyone.

"You okay?" Ellio cut in, bringing her back to the present.

She nodded slowly. "Honestly, I'm nervous to be back," she admitted.

"Do you want to talk about it? About where you were?"

She wrung her hands, toying with her finger and an imaginary ring. "No... not right now."

"I understand," Ellio answered. "You don't have to until you are ready, but everyone will have a lot of questions."

"I know."

"I won't let them bombard you." He smiled, trying to lighten the mood. "We can hide in the kitchens or on the beach like we used to if you need a break."

Kinna couldn't help the smile that rose to her lips. Memories flooded her of the two of them in the kitchens, fighting over pastries, afternoons sparring with each other in the training room, and mornings on the beach, sprinting through the sand. That used to be all that she wanted, a lifetime of moments with Ellio. Unfortunately, the small voice in her head whispered the same question her heart refused to answer, is that still what she wanted? Her smile quickly faded as she realized the answer.

CHAPTER FORTY

Kinna dozed on and off, not letting herself fall into a deep enough sleep where the nightmares could return. Finally, the rain had ceased, and a faint blue started to spread across the sky, the sun soon to follow. She kept her eyes on the road ahead of them until a sliver of ocean could be seen on the horizon. In minutes the city began sprawling out in front of her, tiny lights dotted the winding streets, and the docs were completely illuminated, many already setting sail for the day.

Before they reached the high wall that surrounded the city, the driver veered off the road and onto a small, even bumpier, dirt path that wound further into the thick woods. Without the city ahead of her to serve as a guide, it was harder to judge their direction. "Where are we going?" Kinna asked.

"We're taking a back entrance into the castle," Ellio replied. "I've been using this the past few weeks because it was quicker, and I didn't have to travel through the city."

After a few minutes, the castle wall came into view along with the second gate that led into the eastern courtyard. A strange sense of deja vu settled over Kinna as they rode closer to the very gate that she had escaped through weeks ago. Perhaps it was fitting that she would return to this very spot.

The gate that had before only ever been staffed with one or two guards, now had six men patrolling it, none of them guards that Kinna recognized. They still patrolled dressed in the traditional cobalt uniforms with the crescent moon stitched over the chest, but they seemed off. It was probably just the dim morning light, but they seemed duller than she remembered.

She peered through the glass at their stony faces. If they recognized her, they didn't show it as they waved them through. The increased security was likely a measure that General Resten had insisted upon, but she wished he had picked more friendly looking guards, or at least ones that looked as if they could feel emotion.

"Who are these guards?" Kinna asked.

"My father recruited them from all over the kingdom. He's doubled the number of guards at the castle. About half of the previous guards remained after the explosion and the subsequent investigation. He filled the ranks back in with the new recruits."

"Investigation? Into what?"

Ellio looked at her surprised by her question. "An investigation into who planted a bomb in the castle. How they got in, who helped them, and who could still be trusted."

"Did you find out who did this?"

"The Rising of course. Apparently, there is a sect of them relatively close to the castle. They are the only ones that make sense. A few of the guards must have turned on us and decided to join their ranks."

Kinna opened her mouth to defend them but quickly closed it. She knew exactly where the Rising was and that there was no godsdamn way they had been behind it. Unfortunately, she couldn't explain how she knew that without exposing the Rising and she was not about to put them at risk. She would have to continue to let Ellio believe whatever lies he'd been fed. Once she was crowned and could share her story, she would set the record straight.

Their carriage had stilled, parked in the courtyard as the first of the sun's rays began to shine on the tallest spires of the castle. She threw her bag over her shoulder and reached for the door handle, but Ellio caught her hand. "Listen, Kin. Things are different now. It isn't the same as when you left. The guards, the security around the castle, things aren't going to be exactly like before."

"I know that."

"Will you promise me something?"

"What?"

"Don't go anywhere by yourself. I will ask my father to let me personally oversee your guard detail. These men are different, harder; they aren't like Eron or Macklin or any of the others that we grew up with."

His warning made her stomach uneasy, but she agreed. These men would be strangers to her, and she wouldn't put herself in any unnecessary danger. "I promise."

Ellio's face relaxed and he turned the handle, pushing the carriage door open and holding his hand out to help her out. Standing in the courtyard, staring up at her home, she could still see the remnants of the damage the explosion had caused but for the most part, the castle had been restored. Large patches of new stone had been feathered in alongside the darker, worn stone. No longer did it resemble the smoke filled, rubble strewn ruins that had haunted her dreams.

Four guards moved from the shadow of the castle; their expressions just as blank as the ones that she'd see at the gate. They stopped in front of them, the middle guard nodding to Ellio in recognition before turning his attention on Kinna. He stood a few inches taller than Kinna but with a stocky build. His muted brown hair and grey eyes were a handsome combination but the frown that seemed to be a permanent fixture on his face ruined his appeal.

"Princess." He bowed quickly. "This way."

"I will get her settled in Brycen," Ellio countered. "We are both tired from our travels."

"General Resten asked us to escort you to the throne room upon your arrival."

Ellio's jaw twitched as he took in the four men that had been brought to escort them, as if they expected resistance from him and came prepared. Reluctantly he nodded and they turned to lead them into the castle. Ellio hovered closely to Kinna as they walked, his hand resting on the dagger he wore at his hip.

It took a moment for Kinna's eyes to adjust to the dark hallway as they walked. Only a few of the sconces on the walls were lit, casting long shadows and small pools of yellow light that were few and far between. Still, she'd grown up running through these halls and the darkness did little to erase the familiarity of the floors she stood on. She breathed in the scent of the castle, still carrying the same hint of the salty air beyond the walls. After she met with the general, she would make sure the very next thing she laid eyes on was the sea.

They followed their escorts, led by the man Ellio had called Brycen, as the sound of their steps bounced off the walls, echoing through the hallway. Finally, they stopped in front of a large wooden door, adorned with a large engraving of the crest of Ferryn. Two guards pushed the door open as they approached and once again Kinna stepped into the throne room.

Instead of a sunshine filled room, she entered into a dim, candlelit space. All the thick velvet curtains had been drawn, blocking the sun from seeping through the wall of windows that faced the sea. More guards stood around the perimeter of the checkered tiled floor, standing at attention and not sparing a glance as they arrived.

On the dais, where her parents had once stood, sat a single throne occupied by General Resten. A guard stood before him at the bottom of the few steps, reading off a long piece of parchment while he sat with his eyes closed, listening to him read its contents. Kinna noticed a bit more grey peppered his temples and dark circles under his eyes as if he was suffering from sleepless nights and felt a pang of guilt. He had been bearing the weight of the kingdom on his shoulders for months while she hid and healed. She wondered if he'd even allowed himself time to grieve for her father, his closest friend.

Ellio cleared his throat as they approached, alerting his father to their arrival. His eyes snapped open and immediately landed on Kinna. He rose slowly, as if he couldn't trust what his eyes were showing him. "Kinna?" he whispered. "It's truly you."

"I told you I would bring her home," Ellio said softly, pride shining through his voice.

The general shuffled down the steps quickly and crossed the few feet between them in seconds before placing his hands on her shoulders. He looked slightly awed as his hands touched a solid body and didn't pass through an apparition. "Welcome home."

"Thank you," she said, a soft smile rising to her lips.

"We have much to discuss," the general confirmed, schooling his face back into neutrality.

"We've traveled all night," Ellio interjected. "This can wait until she has had a chance to eat and rest for a few hours."

"It cannot," he argued. "War is at our doorstep, and we cannot afford any more delays."

"War?" Kinna rasped. "With whom?"

"Eldridge and the Rising," General Resten said solemnly. "We believe the attack against you and the Royal family was executed by the Rising who have been working in tandem with Eldridge."

"That's impossible," she whispered. It wasn't possible that the Rising could be responsible for the attack on her family or the castle.

The general gave her a sorrowful look and confirmed it with a nod. He rested a hand on her shoulder in a comforting gesture. "Guards, please give us some privacy."

All the guards that had been positioned along the perimeter quietly exited the room, leaving only the four that had escorted them here standing by the door.

Kinna's head was whirling. She knew that the Rising would never orchestrate an attack in Eldridge's name, nor would they risk the lives of so many innocents. Marstella and Rennick would never allow it. "That isn't possible," Kinna reiterated, her voice stronger.

"I know it's hard to believe your friends would take part in this, but you cannot let your feelings cloud your judgement," the general argued. "Who else could have done this?"

"Friends? What do you mean friends?" Ellio asked.

"Ah, I see you have not told him," General Resten winced, climbing the stairs to take a seat again on the single throne. "Well, I guess there is no time like the present."

"What is he talking about, Kinna?" Ellio asked, confusion and hurt welling in his eyes.

She blew out a deep breath, steeling herself. "I didn't know who they were. I had been running for days and Sebrina found me. She brought me back to their camp and I didn't plan to stay, it just happened. They aren't what we've been told, they aren't like that at all."

The words tumbled out and she knew she wasn't explaining it well enough. She had to make Ellio understand that they had saved her, that they had been her family when she'd had none, but she didn't know how to say it. She didn't have the words to tell him what they meant to her, not without hurting him in the process. "They are a family; they are *my* family now too. They would never do what you are saying they did."

"What the hell are you talking about Kinna!" Ellio shouted. "You've been with the Rising this entire time? With that man that I saw you with in Glenarm? How could you do this? We are your family. We've always been your family."

His anger didn't shock her, but his words still stung as if he'd run blades across her skin. She'd only been back in the capital for mere moments, and everything was already unraveling. She glanced up at the general, looking for anyone who would help reason with Ellio and found him with a hint of a grin on his face. Realization hit her seconds later.

"How did you know where I was?" she questioned, turning her attention away from a still fuming Ellio. "You said I was with my friends, how did you know that? Have you known where I was this whole time?"

"Of course." He nodded. "As if I would let the heir to the throne just run away."

"What?!" Ellio exploded, but his father ignored him.

"My men found you shortly after you arrived, but instead of bringing you back, I thought it might be useful to let you stay there. I wanted to see how much control over your magic that old witch could teach you before I brought you home. I didn't expect them to send you away. That complicated things," he chided. "Luckily you saved me the hard work of tracking you down again and came back on all on your own."

Ellio whirled on his father, charging up the steps and gripping his shirt with both hands. "You knew where she was this entire time?" he seethed.

A moment of surprise flickered across the general's face before it was replaced with fury and he shoved his son off, causing him to stumble down the steps. Before he could race back up them and continue his interrogation, the guards caught his arms and pulled him back into their grip. Ellio struggled against them but four against one were bad odds and he quickly stopped. The general smoothed his shirt, ignoring his son, and then turned back to Kinna. "I'm sorry where were we?"

"You were saying you've been watching her and letting someone try to teach her magic," Ellio laughed, still attempting to wrestle his arms free. "Ridiculous. Kinna doesn't have any magic."

"Ellio, stop interrupting or I'll have Brycen gag you." The general sighed like a frustrated parent when their toddler was throwing a tantrum. "For your information, the princess most definitely possesses magic, a great deal of it I believe, she just doesn't know how to call on it yet."

"I don't," Kinna denied. "I was never able to do anything during my lessons. I don't have any magic."

"You weren't able to do anything during your lessons but what about other times?" he questioned. "Didn't you notice what seemed to coincide with the feeling of intense emotion? The volatile way in which the world responded to your anger or sadness? My spies certainly did."

Kinna tried to grasp onto her memories, shuffling through them until she found the times she had felt the most out of control. The night she'd stayed in the inn, an arrow sailing clean through her shoulder, the carriage ride back to the capital; each time, a storm had surfaced. Each time she could remember the whip of the wind and sting of the rain as her emotions had raged inside her. Could it be a coincidence? Did she even still believe in those?

General Resten was watching her float through her memories, grinning as the realization of his story washed over her. He knew he was right. This wasn't a story that he was spinning to entertain her. He knew the truth, but her mind kept snagging over the question of how. How long had he known? Why tell her now? Too many questions formed in her mind, building until they overflowed and spilled out her mouth.

"How did you know?" Kinna asked, mystified. "When no one else did, when I didn't, how did you know?"

"I'm so glad you asked," he purred, the sound raising goosebumps on her skin. "When you were a child, my late wife shared something with me, something your mother had confided in her. Our late queen had begun to notice the storms that would rock the city's shoreline and that they would often coincide with you and your moods. I also began tracking them and was quickly convinced her suspicion was correct. Do you remember when you broke your arm?"

"I was nine and a rack of weapons fell on me in the training room."

"Do you also remember the storm that followed? One that pulled a dozen ships out to sea, never to be seen again."

A vague memory surfaced of Kerin, and her mother stationed in her room, ensuring she wouldn't leave and reading to her when she grew restless. They had nestled her so deep into a mountain of pillows and fluffy comforters, movement had been impossible. She remembered a lot about the days following but didn't remember a storm washing away ships. But why would anyone have told her? She had been a child. Adults didn't burden children with those kinds of things. "No, I had to stay in bed for a week."

"Because your mother insisted on it. She knew you had been the one to cause that storm. She was afraid if you injured yourself further, which was highly possible considering you loved taking risks. She couldn't afford you triggering another storm. I even once approached her about it, trying to hint that I had also noticed the strange storms that frequented our coastline aligned with you, but she dismissed me quickly. I must admit, her dismissal only further convinced me that I was correct."

The general was spending so much time trying to convince her that his words were true, but Kinna couldn't figure out why. His motivations were elusive, but the excitement she could see shining in his eyes was what disturbed her. Something had changed in him in the weeks she had been gone. Or maybe he had always hidden it behind a mask that was now fading.

"After that," he continued when Kinna didn't respond. "Your mother unfortunately managed to quell the magic growing inside you. In the months following, she kept you close, and the erratic nature of the weather calmed. I have never been able to figure out how, but around the time of your tenth birthday, your power seemed to vanish and my hopes for you were squashed."

Kinna remembered the weeks leading up to her tenth birthday and her mother's constant hovering. She had attributed most of it to the ball being held in her honor and her mother's desire to ensure everything went perfectly but now she saw everything in a new light. Reflexively she gripped her hand where a gifted ring should have sat but quickly dropped her hands. "Let's say I do believe you," she began, pretending to pace to put more distance between them. "Why are you telling me now?"

"Because your gifts have returned! Now you can control it and *we* can use it," he explained excitedly, as if his intentions should be obvious.

"Use it for what? I just told you that the attack on the capital could not have been carried out by the Rising."

He waved her off. "The Rising will soon be the least of my concerns. They were simply a convenient scapegoat that the people accepted easily. My sights are turned to the north. Eldridge is a large kingdom and our borders have remained unchanged for far too long."

"Even if I learned to control whatever it is that I have, I'm not going to become some kind of conqueror. My father would have never wanted that."

A cold laugh escaped his throat. "Ah, yes, your father never did share my interests in conquest. Calvin was much too soft. He didn't understand that sacrifices had to be made in the name of progress."

"I'm not interested in that kind of progress."

He pinched the bridge of his nose, sighing deeply. "I had hoped you wouldn't respond this way. Why don't you just think on this-"

"I don't need time to think on anything," she interrupted, her anger growing. She would not be coerced. Something dark had taken root in him and she wouldn't let it poison her or her kingdom. "I will not be starting a war. I am the heir, and my decision is final."

"That is unfortunate," he tutted, sounding as if someone had told him that the kitchen was out of his favorite dessert. "However, considering that the kingdom believes that you are either missing or dead, I am the de facto ruler. The decision is currently mine. I, of course, would have liked your support but as you've clearly stated I won't have it."

"I came back to assume my duty as the heir, to be

crowned queen and rule. The people will never accept you as long as I live."

"Perhaps, but they don't know you live, and I have no desire to relinquish my control."

Two of the guards had begun the slow creep behind Kinna and as he spoke, their hands clamped down over her arms, locking her in an iron grip. She looked over to where Ellio struggled against the two remaining guards that still held him, but his hands remained firmly bound behind his back. A white strip of fabric had been tied around his mouth, muffling his words beyond recognition. Panic beat wildly in her chest.

"What are you doing?" Kinna demanded. "Let me go."

"They won't be doing that," the general shrugged. "They do not answer to you."

"So, what now? Your plan is to hold me prisoner until I comply?"

A cruel smile spread across his face and Kinna saw nothing of the man she had once known staring back at her. "Not exactly. I'm simply going to give you some time to reconsider. I would hate for another accident to befall the castle and take another life."

"You..." she whispered stunned. "You caused the explosion. You murdered dozens of innocents, including my family, so you could assume the throne."

"I knew you would figure it out quickly. You always were a strategist at heart," he murmured, giving her shoulder a squeeze before she could shake his hand off. "Think about my offer. Before you say no again, let me offer you a gift as a sign of my goodwill."

"I don't care about gifts."

"You don't even know what it is. I promise you

will care about this one."

He nodded sharply and the guards that still gripped her arms began tugging her away. She didn't struggle against them, not while they still held Ellio gagged. General Resten was too unpredictable, and she would not risk his safety by continuing to argue. She would let them lead her to whatever room she would be locked inside of and accept whatever gift he offered. Then she would start planning, a way to escape, a way to rescue Ellio, and then she would come for the crown.

CHAPTER FORTY-ONE

They walked silently, weaving through the hallways and down two flights of stairs. Kinna knew every inch of the castle, having spent her childhood exploring it as if it had been built so she could forge adventures within the walls. She knew they were leading her towards the cells that sat unused underground, a small prison that rarely was ever occupied. Whatever gift the general had promised her, it was definitely not going to be a luxury suite to stay in.

Underneath the castle, the walls were made of thick stone with years of dirt and moss growing on it. Her eyes worked to adjust to the darkness, and she wondered how good her unwanted companions' eyesight had to be in order to lead her around in the dark. A pair of torches hung at the end of the hallway, glowing like the bright angry eyes of a beast that was waiting to swallow her whole.

They passed another set of guards stationed just outside of the ring of light given off by the torches, concealing themselves in the shadows. The heavy metal door that led to the row of cells was unlocked but squealed loudly as the hinges moved, making Kinna wince against the sound. A few rays of light shone through the rectangular windows that sat high on the walls. Despite being mostly underground, the cells faced the exterior of the castle and were dug just deep enough that the ceilings were almost level with the ground outside.

Passing a few empty cells, they finally stopped in front of the cell at the end of the hallway. This door was wooden and had a small slit at the bottom where she assumed they would shove food through. The guard to her left pulled out a small key ring from his pocket and thumbed through a number of dirty brass keys. The lock made a dull click as he unlocked the door and thrust her inside.

The door shut quickly behind her as she tried to keep her footing and not fall after being pushed. Kinna stood unmoving, staring at the door until she could no longer hear their footsteps echoing down the hallway. A rustling behind her made her flinch and she spun around expecting to find a rat or some other vermin sharing the cell with her. Instead, she saw a figure move on the makeshift bed in the corner as her eyes began adjusting to the soft light shining through the single window.

A pale, dirty hand gripped the edge of the cot and carefully sat up. It was a girl, or what was left of one. She was a wraith, thin and grimy, as if she had been trapped in this cell her entire life. Her hair was greasy and matted in an attempted braid and she wore remnants of a dress that may have once been blue but was now grey with dirt. Kinna thought to ask the girl her name but before she could speak the girl stood.

"Kinna?" the girl whispered in an all too familiar

voice that broke her world apart.

She fell to her knees, barely registering the pain as they hit the stone floor. *Evelyn.* Her sister was the wraith standing in front of her. Not dead but alive.

Evelyn took the few steps across the room faster than she would have thought possible in her emaciated state. Kinna had barely opened her arms before Evelyn collapsed next to her on the floor, locking her in a tight hug and sobbing into her hair.

"You're alive," Kinna breathed.

"*You're* alive," Evelyn laughed through her tears.

ACKNOWLEDGEMENT

Firstly, thank you reader for being here and making it to the end of *The Uncrowned Queen*! Writing and publishing this hasn't been without challenges, but it has been so rewarding to see it finally come to life.

Secondly, there are numerous people I need to thank but the first must be my partner, best friend, and biggest supporter - Juelz I wouldn't have made it without you. A huge thank you to Belle Manuel, my wonderful editor, and Franziska Stern for designed the beautiful cover of this book. To my mom and Susie, thank you for supporting me enthusiastically and always believing that I could do this, it meant the world to me.

More special thanks to the numerous friends and co-workers that cheered me on while I wrote - you kept me going when I was ready to quit.

ABOUT THE AUTHOR

Lucy Steele

Lucy was born and raised in Central Kentucky. She has always been an avid reader and story writer, attributing much of her love of books to her aunts. When she isn't reading and writing, she can be found outdoors and enjoying the many hiking opportunities in Appalachia.

Printed in Dunstable, United Kingdom